ACCLAIM FOR ABBY JIMENEZ AND
THE FRIEND ZONE

O, The Oprah Magazine **Best Romance Novels of the Year**
Bookish Best Books of the Year
Women's Health **Best Romance Novels of the Year**
Good Housekeeping **Best New Books for Summer**
PopSugar Best Books of Summer
SheReads Best Romances of the Year

"Your next rom-com to obsess and cry over."   —*Cosmopolitan*

"Your next favorite romantic comedy... *The Friend Zone* is that rare beach read with tons of heart that will make you laugh and cry in equal parts."   —PopSugar

"Jimenez's dazzling debut is a brilliantly written romantic comedy that seamlessly toggles back and forth between scenes of laugh-out-loud, snarky wit and serious emotional issues without missing a beat."   —*Booklist*, starred review

"Jimenez manages to fulfill all expectations for a romantic comedy while refusing to sacrifice nuance. Biting wit and laugh-out-loud moments take priority, but the novel remains subtle in its sentimentality and sneaks up on the reader with unanticipated depth.... Deeply relatable."   —*Publishers Weekly*, starred review

"An excellent debut that combines wit, humor, and emotional intensity." —*Kirkus*

"A deliciously hot, sweet debut full of banter I couldn't get enough of. This book is an absolute treat."
—L. J. Shen, *USA Today* bestselling author

"*The Friend Zone* gave me belly laughs, shook me up, and made me feel hopeful about love and the human strength of spirit. A romance for the ages!" —Tessa Bailey, *New York Times* bestselling author of *Fix Her Up*

"Heartbreaking, gut-wrenching, and emotional. Abby Jimenez wrote a difficult story line with sensitivity, heat, humor, banter, and unwavering friendship." —*Harlequin Junkie*, Top Pick

"A beautiful tale of learning to accept the love you deserve and finding a path to self-acceptance along the way...a zippy, instantly recognizable voice and fresh, funny characters."
—*Entertainment Weekly*

"A laugh-out-loud, wickedly clever book that sneaks up on you with a cathartic emotional payoff."
—Jenny Holiday, author of *Mermaid Inn*

"This novel doesn't shy away from anything—it's fiercely loving all the way to the HEA." —NPR

THE HAPPY EVER AFTER PLAYLIST

ALSO BY ABBY JIMENEZ

The Friend Zone

THE HAPPY EVER AFTER PLAYLIST

ABBY JIMENEZ

FOREVER

New York Boston

Copyright © 2020 by Abby Jimenez

Cover design by Elizabeth Turner Stokes
Cover illustration by Jenny Carrow
Cover copyright © 2020 by Hachette Book Group, Inc.

Forever
Hachette Book Group
1290 Avenue of the Americas, New York, NY 10104
read-forever.com
twitter.com/readforeverpub

First Edition: April 2020

Forever is an imprint of Grand Central Publishing. The Forever name and logo are trademarks of Hachette Book Group, Inc.

The publisher is not responsible for websites (or their content) that are not owned by the publisher.

The Hachette Speakers Bureau provides a wide range of authors for speaking events. To find out more, go to www.hachettespeakersbureau.com or call (866) 376-6591.

Library of Congress Cataloging-in-Publication Data
Names: Jimenez, Abby, author.
Title: The happy ever after playlist / Abby Jimenez.
Identifiers: LCCN 2019026595 | ISBN 9781538715642 (trade paperback) | ISBN 9781538715635 (ebook)
Subjects: GSAFD: Love stories.
Classification: LCC PS3610.I47 H37 2020 | DDC 813/.6—dc23
LC record available at https://lccn.loc.gov/2019026595

ISBN: 978-1-5387-1564-2 (trade paperback), 978-1-5387-1563-5 (ebook)

Printed in the United States of America

LSC-C

Printing 4, 2022

This book is dedicated to my husband and kids.
Thank you for being my happy ever after.

THE
HAPPY
EVER
AFTER
PLAYLIST

CHAPTER 1

SLOAN

PLAYLIST: ♪ IN THE MOURNING | PARAMORE

Do you want me to meet you at the cemetery, Sloan?"
Kristen was worried about me.

I shook my head at my car's center console, where my phone sat on speaker. "I'm fine. I'm going to the farmers' market afterward," I said, hoping that would placate her.

My car idled at the red light next to a sidewalk lined with worn-out businesses and thirsty, drought-resistant oaks that looked like the lack of rain had finally broken their spirit. I baked in the blazing sun. My open sunroof had broken over Easter weekend a few weeks ago and I'd never fixed it, part of my time-honored tradition of not repairing things in my crappy car.

"The farmers' market? Are you going to cook?" Kristen's voice lit up with hope.

"No. A salad maybe," I said as the light turned green. I didn't cook anymore. Everyone knew that.

I didn't do a lot of things anymore.

"Oh. Well, do you want me to come over later?" she asked. "I'll bring cookie dough and liquor."

"No. I'll be— *Oh my God!*" A furry, copper-colored blur darted into the road, and I slammed on the brakes. My phone became a projectile into the dash and my purse dumped over the passenger seat, spilling tampons and single-serve flavored creamers.

"Sloan! What happened?"

I clutched the wheel, my heart pounding. "Kristen, I gotta go. I...I think I just killed a dog." I hit the End Call button and unbuckled myself, threw the car in park, and put a trembling hand on the door to wait for a break in traffic to get out.

Please let it have been quick and painless. *Please.*

This would destroy me. This was just what it would take. The limp body of somebody's poor pet under the tires of my shitty car on this particular cursed day, and what little joy I had left would just pop out and float off.

I hate my life.

My throat tightened. I promised myself I wouldn't cry today. I *promised...*

Barking.

A floppy-eared dog head popped up over my bumper, sniffing the air. I barely had time to process that this animal was still alive before it leapt up onto the hood. He yapped at me through the glass and then grabbed my windshield wiper and started tugging on it.

"What the..." I tilted my head, actually laughing a little. The muscles involved felt weak from disuse, and for a heartbeat, just a flicker of a moment, I forgot what today was.

I forgot I was on my way to visit a grave.

My cell phone pinged with a quick succession of texts. Probably Kristen, losing her shit.

This was why I never got up this early. Nothing but mayhem.

Was this what went on in Canoga Park at 9:00 a.m. on a Friday? Dogs running all willy-nilly in the streets?

A horn blared and a middle finger shot up from a passing convertible. My car sat parked in the road with a dog on the hood.

I leapt into action to stage a mid-street rescue. I didn't want him to bolt and get hit in the road. I waited again for a pause in the cars while the dog crouched on his haunches and barked at me through the glass. I was shaking my head at him when he backed up, gave me one more smiling head cock, scaled my windshield, and *dove through my sunroof.*

He landed on top of me in a wallop of flying fur and legs. The air was pushed from my lungs in an *oomph* as a foot slid right down my tank top into my cleavage, sticking the landing and scratching me from collarbone to belly button. Then he was on me, paws on my shoulders, licking my face and whining like we'd grown up together and I'd just gotten home from college.

I screamed like I was being eaten alive.

I wrestled him off me into the passenger seat, gasping and disheveled, dog drool on my face, and when my cell phone rang I grabbed for it reflexively.

"Sloan, are you okay?" Kristen asked before I even got the phone to my ear.

"A dog just jumped through my sunroof!"

"What?"

"Yeah." I wiped my cheek with the bottom of my tank top. "It's...it's in my front seat."

The dog *smiled* at me. He actually grinned as his tail whacked back and forth. Then he lowered his head and made a single *cack*ing noise. I watched in horror as he hacked up a slimy ball of grass right into my drink holder over my untouched latte.

Aaaaand police lights fired up in my rearview.

"You have got to be kidding me," I breathed, looking back and forth between the barf, the dog, and the lights in my mirror.

I started to giggle. It was my stress response. That and a twitching eyelid. Both of which made me look insane.

This cop was in for a show.

"Kristen, I need to call you back. I'm getting pulled over." I laughed.

"Wait, what?"

"Yeah. I know. I'm parked in the middle of the street and now the cops are here."

I hung up and the police car made an impatient siren whoop behind me. I crawled along until I could pull into a mini mall. I looked down, fixing my tank top and shaking my head, alternating between grumbling to myself about irresponsible dog owners and giggling like a lunatic.

I considered whether I looked cute enough to get out of a ticket.

All evidence pointed to *no*.

There was a time, in another universe, when this face had won beauty pageants. Now I looked like I'd been in a fight with a raccoon over a pizza crust—and lost.

Scratches streaked my arms from the dog's nails, and I was covered in enough orange fur to make a puppy. My blond hair was pulled up in a messy bun that had been half yanked loose in the melee, and my yoga pants and paint-stained tank top weren't doing me any favors. My bare face looked pale and tired.

I'd looked tired for two years.

"We'll have to ride this one out on personality alone," I mumbled to the dog. He smiled with that lolled-out tongue, and I gave him a reproachful look. "Your parents have a lot of explaining to do."

I rolled my window down and handed over my license and registration to the cop before he asked for it.

"That was quite the scene back there, Miss"—the officer glanced down at my information—"Sloan Monroe. It's illegal to obstruct traffic," he said, his tone bored.

"Officer, this wasn't my fault. This dog bolted into the street and then he just jumped through my sunroof."

I could see my reflection in his aviator sunglasses. My eyelid twitched and I squeezed it shut, squinting up at him with one eye. God, I looked nuts.

"This isn't my first rodeo, young lady. Find something that doesn't require you to block traffic for your next YouTube video and just be glad you're only getting an obstruction ticket and not one for letting an unleashed animal run around."

"Wait. You think he's *mine*?" I plucked a long piece of fur from my mouth. "I get that nothing says dog ownership more than one diving through the top of your car, but I've never seen this guy before in my life." Then I looked down and started to giggle. The dog had his head on my lap doing an Oscar-worthy performance of being-my-dog. He looked up at me with "Hi, Mommy" eyes.

I snorted and descended into manic laughter again, putting a finger to my twitching eyelid.

Today. Of all days, this happens today.

The cop stared at me for a solid half a minute, soaking in all my crazy. I'm sure the dog barf in the cup holder didn't help. Not that it did much to take away from the original ambiance of my dilapidated car. I hadn't washed it in two years. Still, he must have seen something he believed on my face because he entertained my story for a moment.

"Okay. Well, I'll just put a call in to animal control." He leaned toward the radio mic on his shoulder. "Get this dangerous stray off your hands."

I sobered in a second, dropping my finger from my eye. "No! You can't send him to the shelter!"

His hand froze on the mic, and he arched an eyebrow. "Because this is your dog?"

"No, because he'd be terrified. Haven't you seen those ASPCA commercials? With the sad dogs in cages? And the Sarah McLachlan song?"

The cop laughed the whole way back to his squad car to write me a ticket.

When the dog and I got home, I stuck my ticket to the fridge with the flip-flop magnet Brandon and I had picked up in Maui. Both the ticket and the magnet made the lump rise in my throat, but the dog pushed his head under my hand and I somehow muscled down the urge to sob. It was 10:00 a.m. on The Day, and I'd so far kept my vow not to ugly-cry.

Yay me.

I called Kristen, who was probably freaking out and gathering a search party since I hadn't answered her last five calls. She picked up on the first ring. "What the hell happened? Are you okay?"

"Yes, I'm okay. I have the dog. He's at my house. I got a ticket for stopping in the middle of the street."

"Are you fucking serious?"

"Unfortunately, I am," I said tiredly.

She made a *tsk*ing noise. "You didn't push your boobs up, did you? Next time use your boobs."

I pulled my tank top out and rolled my eyes at the scratches between my breasts. "I think I'd rather have the ticket and what's left of my dignity, thank you very much."

I grabbed a blue plastic bowl from the cabinet, filled it from the tap, and watched as the dog drank like he hadn't had water in days. He pushed the bowl across the tile of my dated kitchen, sloshing as he went, and I pinched my temples.

Ugh, today sucks.

This was way too much excitement for me. Most days I didn't even leave the house. This was *why* I didn't leave the house. Too many people and *things.* I wanted to hiss at the sun and go back to sleep.

"I'm gonna call the number on his collar. Let me call you back."

I hung up and looked at his tag. Weird area code. *Tucker, A Good Boy.*

"A good boy, huh? That's debatable. Well, Tucker, let's see what excuse your people have for letting you run around in traffic," I muttered as I punched the number into my cell phone.

The call went right to voicemail and a deep male voice said, "Jason. Leave a message."

I left my contact information, hung up, and shook my head at the dog sloshing water all over my kitchen floor. "You're probably hungry too. Well, I don't have any dog food, so we need to go to PetSmart."

I might have a half-eaten Starbucks lemon loaf in the car, but it was probably petrified.

I didn't have a leash, so I made one from the belt of my black Victoria's Secret robe, the one Brandon had given me the Christmas before his accident. Tucker immediately began to gnaw through it.

Just perfect.

When we got to PetSmart, I took him to the store vet to see if he was microchipped. He was, but the number on file was the same as the one on his tag. No address.

This was seriously so inconvenient. I kept checking my cell phone to make sure the volume was up.

No calls or texts.

I was contemplating my limited options when, like the cherry on top of the sundae, Tucker peed on the floor of the vet's office.

The vet looked unfazed. She pulled paper towels from a dispenser without looking up from her chart and handed them to me. Tucker retreated under a chair and looked on with sorry puppy dog eyes.

"He was eating grass too." I crouched and dropped towels on the mess. "I think he has a stomachache."

"He might have a bladder infection. We should test the urine."

I whirled on her from my pee puddle. "Wait, *me*? You want *me* to pay for this test? Seriously? This isn't even my dog."

She shrugged over her clipboard. "Well, just be aware that if he has an infection he won't be able to hold his urine. Tomorrow's the weekend, so it'll cost more to bring him in then if he doesn't get picked up. Plus he's likely in pain. If you can't afford it, you could always take him to the Humane Society. They might treat him there."

The shelter was out. And the pain thing bugged me. With my luck I *would* end up with him until tomorrow and I'd be back here paying double, begging them to make the peeing stop. I put a finger to my twitching eyelid. "Fine. Test him. Maybe the owner will pay me back?"

God, I was already tired tomorrow, just from today.

My cell phone pinged, and I looked at it wearily.

Kristen: Did the cop have that porn-stache they always have?

Ping.

Kristen: You should have cried. Machine gun sobbing always gets me out of tickets. Just sayin'.

I snorted. She was trying to make me smile. She and her husband, Josh, were on Sloan watch today. High alert, code red. Keeping an eye on me in case I flipped out or broke down.

It was probably a good idea.

Two hundred dollars and one expensive bladder infection later, we left with our dog antibiotics. On top of Tucker's vet bill, I bought a leash and a small bag of dog food. I needed enough supplies to at least get me through tomorrow in case this ended up being a sleepover. I also grabbed a chew bone and a ball to keep him busy. I didn't need this Tasmanian devil destroying my house.

I wasn't familiar with his breed. I forgot to ask the vet. He looked sort of like a small golden retriever. It wouldn't surprise me if he turned out to be half honey badger. He was a little wild. What dog jumps through a sunroof?

Whatever he was, he was not what I was supposed to be doing today.

Today I was supposed to be with Brandon.

Setting a bottle of Woodford Reserve against his headstone. Sitting on a blanket on the grass next to where we laid him to rest, telling him how much I missed him, how the world was worse for him not being in it, how hollow I was and it wasn't getting better with time like they said it would.

April eighth was the two-year anniversary of his accident. Not the date of his death—he lived a month before he succumbed to his injuries—but the date of the crash. That was really the day his life was over. *My* life was over. He never woke up. So today could never just be some day.

The year held a lot of days like that for me. The day in December when he'd proposed. His birthday. *My* birthday. Holidays, the date of the wedding that never happened. In fact, most of the calendar was a minefield of hard days. One would crest, I'd live through it, and then another one would roll toward me in the constant ebb and swell that was the year.

Another year without *him*.

So I had planned to distract myself today. Have my visit to the cemetery and then be productive. Get some paintings done. Eat something healthy. I'd committed to not sleeping through the day like last year. I'd promised myself I would ignore that the month of April smelled like a hospital to me now and reminded me of fixed pupils and beeping machines with tempos that never changed.

I glanced at my phone again.

Nothing.

CHAPTER 2

SLOAN

♪ AFFECTION | BETWEEN FRIENDS

Ten days. I'd had Tucker for ten wonderful, fur-on-my-bedspread, wet-kisses-in-the-morning, tail-wagging days.

I knocked on the door of Kristen's house, grinning from ear to ear. When she opened it, she stared. "You fucking did it."

"I told you I would." I beamed, edging past her into the house, not waiting to be invited in. Tucker and her little dog, Stuntman Mike, circled each other, tails wagging, noses to butts.

She closed the front door behind me. "You walked here? That's like seven miles, you crazy bitch."

"Yeah, I know," I said. My reemergence into daylight had been shocking friends and family alike lately. "I have to use your bathroom. Is Oliver awake?"

"No, he's down for his nap." She followed me down the hall. "God, you're really loving this dog thing, huh? Oh, which reminds me," she said, "I made him something." She disappeared and came back a second later holding up a dog tee that read I JUMPED ON SLOAN THROUGH A SUNROOF AND ALL I GOT WAS THIS T-SHIRT.

I snorted. Kristen ran an online business from her house that sold merchandise for dogs.

I went into the bathroom, and she tucked the shirt under her arm and leaned on the door frame. Josh wasn't home, so we fell immediately back into our old roommate habit of never closing doors between us.

"He's incredible. I've never seen an animal so well trained," I said. "Somebody must have really spent time working with him." I washed my hands and looked at my flushed face in the mirror, tucking some flyaway hairs behind my ear.

"Still no callback from that Jason guy?"

I hadn't heard a word from Tucker's owner. Tucker had spent the first two days peeing in my house despite his expensive anti-biotics, and I'd spent two days taking him outside as much as humanly possible to save my carpets.

It was miraculous how motivating a puddle of dog pee on your floors could be. Seriously. Better than a personal trainer. My Fitbit had never seen so much action.

I, of course, got no painting done at all while I was walking him. But this body had a tan for the first time in longer than I could remember, and I had to admit that the exercise felt good. So even after his infection was gone, we kept up the walks.

Today I felt particularly ambitious, so I decided to walk to Kristen's house to see her and the baby. I figured if I got tired, we could just call an Uber. But we made it, and the victory was glorious.

"Not a peep from Jason," I said.

I'd put up posters with Tucker's picture at the intersection where I found him, and I'd listed him on a few missing-pet websites. I'd even registered him as a found dog at the Humane

Society. And every day I left a message for Jason. I was beginning to think Tucker had been officially abandoned.

"Soooo, I saved your dog from certain death and he thanked me by jumping on me through my sunroof like a grenade. Give me a call to arrange for a pickup. I have so many questions."

"Hi, Jason. Sloan again. Your dog is peeing all over my house from the bladder infection he got from not being let out. It would be great if you came to get him so he can pee all over your house instead. Thanks."

"Sloan and Tucker here. While Tucker's love of expensive food basically makes him my twin separated at birth, I can't afford to keep feeding him. Think you might be able to call me back?"

I followed Kristen into the kitchen and gave Tucker a bowl of water with ice cubes in it. Then I sat at the granite counter, and she slid a glass of iced tea over to me. "Can I just say how happy I am that you're getting out?"

My mood deflated in an instant, and her steady brown eyes studied me.

"Kristen? Do you think it's weird Tucker showed up on the anniversary of the accident? I mean, it is, right?"

She waited for me to continue, stirring her ice around her glass.

"Tucker literally fell into my lap. And do you know what kind of dog he is? A Nova Scotia duck tolling retriever." I ticked the long name off with a five-finger tap on the countertop. "A hunting dog, Kristen. Ducks."

Kristen knew better than anyone the significance of that. Duck hunting had been Brandon's favorite sport. He'd fly out to South Dakota every year for it with Josh.

"What if Brandon sent him to me?" I said, a lump bolting into my throat.

She gave me a sympathetic smile. "Well, I do think Brandon wouldn't have wanted you to be this unhappy," she said gently. "Two years is a long fucking time to be this sad, Sloan."

I nodded and wiped my face with the top of my shirt. I stared bleary eyed at the high chair pushed up against the kitchen table. Kristen's life was a painful reminder of what mine should have been. If Brandon had lived and we'd been married like we planned, I'd probably have a baby of my own, taking him on playdates with Kristen and Josh's one-year-old son.

Kristen had been my best friend since sixth grade. Our worlds had been on the same trajectory since junior high. We'd done everything together. Our lives' milestones had always lined up accordingly.

Brandon and Josh had been best friends too. I'd pictured couples trips and having babies together. Buying houses next door to each other. And now Kristen had continued without me. Her life had kept its pace, and mine had crashed and burned when Brandon's motorcycle did the same. I was stuck in some sort of arrested development, trapped in a continuous loop I couldn't pull myself out of.

Until now.

Something had shifted in me. Maybe it was the routine that Tucker made me stick to, or the walks, or the sun. Maybe it was the thought that this dog was somehow a gift from the man I'd lost, a sign to *try*. I'd always believed in signs. It just seemed too unlikely to be a random thing. Of all the cars in all the world, Tucker ran in front of mine. It was like he *chose* me.

I pulled out my cell phone. "That reminds me, it's time for my call to Jason."

His steady voice had become a part of my daily routine. But this time when voicemail picked up, a robotic female informed me that the mailbox was full.

A sign?

I looked at Kristen, who watched me wordlessly.

That was it. My mind was made up. I thumbed through my phone and found a picture of Tucker and me that I'd taken a few days earlier. I attached it to a message to Jason and sent it off.

"You're right. Brandon would want me to be happy. And that Jason guy, if he ever shows up? He can go to hell."

CHAPTER 3

JASON

♪ MIDDLE OF NOWHERE | HOT HOT HEAT

The plane taxied toward our gate to the clink of seat belts coming undone. The air stopped coming through the tiny vents above us, and I got instantly hot. I peeled off my sweatshirt and plucked at the front of my black T-shirt.

Kathy leaned in and bounced her eyebrows. "You smell nice," she said in her thick Australian accent. Then she felt up my arm. "Ooh! Linea, cop a feel of his arm on your side, he's so muscly."

Linea reached across me to hit her friend with a rolled-up magazine. "The man gives up his first-class seat for that military bloke and to thank him you put your mitts all over him. You should be— Oh! He *is* muscly!"

I chuckled. I'd been the meat in a Kathy-and-Linea sandwich for the last four hours on my flight from New Zealand to Australia. Being jammed into a center seat had been well worth the sacrifice. These two strangers were fucking hilarious. I'd been highly entertained the whole trip. Better than a complimentary bourbon and a warm washcloth.

When we began to deplane, I stood in the aisle to pull down the ladies' carry-ons.

"Jason," Kathy said, in front of me, waiting for her bag. "I have a daughter who's single. She's a nurse. She'd love those blue eyes. Ya interested?"

"If she's half as gorgeous as you, she's out of my league." I extended the handle on her luggage and handed it to her with a wink.

She grinned up at me. "Cheeky bastard. Good luck with everything." She turned and started walking. "Thanks for the autograph. I'm gettin' on Twitter to keep tabs on you," she said over her shoulder, following Linea out of the plane.

I smiled after her as I grabbed my backpack from the overhead and stepped back into my empty row to dig out my phone. It had been dead when I boarded. I disconnected it from its portable charger and powered it on for the first time in two weeks. It burst into a vibrating symphony of chimes and pings.

Back to the real world.

Fifteen days of backpacking. I dreaded the crap I'd have to sift through after being out of contact for so long. I'd probably have a hundred messages from my agent, Ernie, alone.

I punched in my pin and started with my voicemails as I shouldered my bag. My mailbox was full. I was four messages in and waiting for a break in the line in the aisle to get off the plane when an unfamiliar female voice came through the phone.

"Uh, hi. I've got Tucker here? He was running around loose in the middle of the street on Topanga Canyon Boulevard? My name's Sloan. My number is 818-555-7629. Let me know when you want to come get him."

Shit.

I swung my backpack in front of me to dig for a pen. I wrote the number down on my hand and dialed it, doing the math quickly in my head. It was 11:00 a.m. in Melbourne. Six p.m. in Los Angeles.

Come on, come on, come on.

"Hello?" a woman said after three rings.

"Hi, is this Sloan? My name's Jason. I think you have my dog. Did someone come get him?"

There was silence on the other end for a moment, and I thought maybe I'd lost the call. I shuffled out of my row into the aisle and pressed for the exit in the crush of other passengers, hoping I'd get a better signal outside the plane. "Hello?" I said again.

"Yeah, I heard you." Her voice sounded edgy. "I still have him."

I flexed my jaw. Goddamn it. *Fucking Monique.*

I stopped in the stuffy Jetway and moved to the wall, holding the phone with my shoulder. I hovered the pen over my hand. "Give me your address. I'll send someone to pick him up."

"No."

Huh? "What?"

"No," she said again.

"What do you mean, no? No, you won't let me pick him up?"

"You know, you have a lot of nerve. It's been almost two weeks, and *now* you decide you want your dog?"

Two weeks? Tucker had been lost for *two* fucking *weeks?*

"I've been out of town. I didn't have cell service. I had no idea he was missing. I have no problem paying for a reward. Please, just give me your address and I'll—"

"No. He's not your dog anymore. If he'd been at the shelter, his hold would be up and he'd either have been adopted or

euthanized. I put up signs, ran his microchip, put him on-line, I left you a dozen voicemails. I did my due diligence. You abandoned him. So as far as I'm concerned, he's *my* dog now."

She hung up on me.

I stared at my phone in shock. I hit Send on the number again and it went straight to voicemail.

Cursing, I called Monique.

"You lost Tucker?" I growled, not bothering to lower my voice for the passengers still deplaning.

"Well, hello to you too, Jason."

The click of her heels came through the line. I could almost see her, holding her fucking skinny latte with those huge sunglasses she always wore, shopping bags on her arms while she *wasn't* looking for my dog.

"Tucker's been lost for two weeks? Why didn't you look for him? Or put through an emergency call to me? What the fuck, Monique? You're supposed to be taking care of him!"

"I work, Jason. And I did look. Sort of."

Then I heard a whoosh that sounded like a subway car. "Wait." Disbelief coursed through my veins. "Where are you?"

A pregnant pause.

"New York," she said quietly.

"How long have you been in New York?"

Silence again.

"Two weeks."

I clutched the phone with white knuckles. "We are done. Fucking done," I hissed.

"Jason, when Givenchy calls, you don't tell them that you can't be in their *Vogue* shoot because you have to look for your fuck buddy's *dog*. I'm sorry, okay? Don't—"

I hung up. I'd heard enough. She might as well have lost my

child and then run off to do a damn photo shoot. It was that unforgivable.

I tried Sloan's number again. Voicemail.

At a loss for what else to do, I stood by the gate going through the rest of my messages as rain pounded on the floor-to-ceiling windows overlooking the tarmac.

This Sloan woman hadn't been kidding. She really *had* tried to reach me. Every day for over a week she'd left me a voicemail about Tucker. I got more and more pissed off as the messages detailed Monique's complete and utter disregard for my dog.

He'd been in the middle of the street.

He'd had a bladder infection from not being let out.

This lady had posted all over, places Monique could have easily seen the signs had she bothered to stick around to look.

He'd dived into this woman's sunroof. What the hell was *that* about?

I rubbed my temples. Tucker hated kennels. Monique had been good enough with him, at least in front of me, and I hadn't had any reservations about it at the time. She told me she'd take him on her runs.

Stupid, stupid.

I should have flown him to Minnesota and left him with my family. I fucked up. It would have been a two-thousand-mile side trip, but at least Tucker would have been safe.

I raked my hand down my face and scratched my beard, tiredly. Fuck, now what was I going to do? This lady stole my damn dog.

When I finished my voicemails, I thumbed through my text messages and saw one from the 818 number I'd written down on my hand. I clicked it and a picture of Tucker popped up. It was great not knowing you.

The photo showed a woman with her arm wrapped around

Tucker's chest. I couldn't see her face. The top of Tucker's head covered her mouth. She wore black sunglasses and her hair was tucked under a hat. Her arm was covered in tattoos from shoulder to elbow. I tilted my head and studied them, zooming in on my phone. I made out the name Brandon on her arm. Then the screen shifted to an incoming call notification. The 818 number. I scrambled to answer it. "Hello?"

"If you love your dog, prove it."

"What?"

"I'm not feeling the greatest about keeping your dog if you really *do* love him. So if you do, prove it."

I blinked. "Okay. And how would you suggest I do that?"

"He's *your* dog, isn't he? Proof that you love him should be readily available."

My mind raced.

"All right, hold on," I said, getting an idea. I scrolled through the photos on my phone and selected several: Tucker and me at the beach, Tucker and me on a bike ride. Then I took a screenshot of my wallpaper, Tucker, sitting behind all my icons. I sent the photos through. "There. Check your messages."

Her phone made a shuffling noise. She went quiet for what I knew was longer than it took to see them all.

"Look," I said into the silence, hoping she could hear me, "he's my best friend. He came with me when I moved to LA from Minnesota. I left him with someone I thought I could trust. I love my dog. I want my dog back. *Please.*"

She was quiet for so long that again I thought the call had been dropped.

"Okay," she whispered.

I breathed a sigh of relief. "Great—thank you. And I'll reimburse you for your time and the vet bills—"

"And my ticket."

"Your ticket?"

"I got a ticket for parking in the middle of Topanga Canyon Boulevard when I stopped to get him into the car."

I moved the phone away from my mouth and breathed a sigh of frustration. Not at Sloan, at Monique and her ineptitude.

"Okay, yeah, no problem. Look, I'm really grateful for everything you've done for him. If you can just give me a few hours to find a kennel to take him I'll—"

"A kennel? Why?"

"I'm in Australia for two more weeks for work."

"Well, who was watching him while you were gone?"

"Somebody who will never watch him again," I said dryly. I collected my backpack and went to follow the signs toward customs.

"Well, I can keep him until you come back. I work from home. It's no problem."

I thought about her offer for a moment. My mind went to the picture she'd sent of her and Tucker and the voicemails about trips to the vet and walks he was going on. She seemed to really care about him. I mean, shit, she'd been ready to keep him. And she'd already had him for two weeks. He knew her. It would be better than a kennel. And there really was no one else. Besides Monique and Ernie, who wasn't a dog person, I didn't know anyone else in LA well enough to ask.

"You wouldn't mind?" I asked, stepping onto a moving walkway.

"No. I love him."

Something sad in her voice made me smile into the phone. Not that I was reveling in her unhappiness—I wasn't insensitive to the fact that just a half an hour earlier she'd thought Tucker was hers, and now she had to give him up. But it was nice to hear that the person watching him actually gave a shit about him.

"That would be great. I hate the idea of putting him in a kennel."

"He'd be miserable," she agreed, sounding a little miserable herself.

"Hey, can I call you back?" I'd been on a plane for four hours. I needed to find a restroom.

When I called Sloan back on my way toward baggage claim, we both seemed to have benefited from the break. Her voice sounded almost shy now. I thought for a second maybe she recognized me from my photos. Or maybe she just felt bad for being so pissed at me. Either way I was glad. If she was going to watch Tucker for me, we should at least be friendly.

We talked dog-sitting fees for a few minutes. Then I moved on to other logistics.

"Text me your address so I can send you a crate," I said.

"A crate? Why?"

"He sleeps in his crate at night. If he doesn't have it, he tends to destroy the house, as I'm sure you've noticed."

"He hasn't destroyed anything except for the belt of my robe on the first day. And he sleeps with me, in my bed."

I laughed. "I find it highly unlikely that he's not chewing your furniture to a pulp. It's his favorite pastime."

Chair legs, the armrest of my couch, doorjambs—Tucker demolished *all*.

I found baggage claim and waited with the crowd from my flight as the carousel started going around, empty.

"He hasn't chewed a single thing since the belt," she said. "He's a perfect angel."

"Really?" I said incredulously.

She snorted. "I wouldn't try and keep a dog who was destroying my house."

"Good point. Well, I'm glad he's being a gentleman," I said, checking the time and watching as the first luggage came down the ramp. I had rehearsal in two hours.

"I still have scratches from him jumping on me through the sunroof. Did you teach him that, by the way?"

"Uh, no. Did he really do that?"

"You think I'd make that up? Hold on." There was a pause. "Okay, go look. I just sent you my ticket."

A picture message came through my phone. It was a ticket from the LAPD with a flip-flop magnet over the recipient's information. The officer had detailed the entire event, sunroof and all.

I shook my head. "Unbelievable. He's never done anything like that before." He must have been out of his damn mind. "He's a little high energy."

"He just needs exercise."

He'd probably gone stir-crazy with Monique. "Are you sure you don't want the crate?"

"I definitely don't want it. He sleeps with me while he's here. That's a hard rule for me. And I'm not giving you my address either. You could be a creeper."

I snorted. "I'm not a creeper."

"Yeah, well, that's exactly what a creeper would say."

There was a *smile* in there.

"How old are you?" I asked, suddenly curious.

She scoffed. "Well, *that's* unnecessary."

"What? Me asking your age? It's the first thing I'd ask a dog-sitter in an interview," I reasoned, though that wasn't really what drove my interest. I liked her messages. They'd been kind of funny.

"Well, that would be illegal. You can't ask someone their age on a job interview."

I smiled. "What can I ask?"

"Let's see, you can ask what my background is."

"Are you in HR? You seem awfully knowledgeable about properly conducted interviews."

"See, *that's* a question you could ask."

Witty.

"And I thought I already had the job," she pointed out.

"You do. What? I can't know a little about who my best friend is sleeping with?"

I heard her snort and I grinned.

"Your best friend is sleeping with a young lady smart enough to know better than to tell a stranger where she lives and how old she is. Are you going to ask me if I'm home alone next?"

"Are you?"

"Wow. You're definitely a creeper."

"I've been called worse."

"I'll bet," she said. A pause. "I live alone."

"Okay. Any other pets?"

"Nope. Such a thorough interview. I have a feeling these questions weren't asked the last time you selected a dog-sitter," she said wryly.

I grinned. "I'm trying to learn from my many mistakes."

"I don't have any other pets. But I grew up with German shepherds. You have to exercise working dogs. They become destructive if you don't make them tired. Tucker's a birding dog. He's bred for high activity."

I knew this, of course, but it impressed me that she did. "And so you're keeping him busy?"

The sound of running water and the clink of dishes came through the phone. Then I heard her talking to Tucker quietly in the background and my smile broadened. She asked him if he was a good boy and if he wanted a puppy snack. He barked.

"Walking him five miles a day," she said. "My tan looks great."

"I'd love to see that. Send me a picture."

It was a joke—*kind of.* I did want to see what she looked like. I was curious.

"And now you've got a lawsuit on your hands. Sexually harassing an employee." She *tsk*ed. "You must be a nightmare for your human resources department."

"Nah, I'm only a pain in my own ass."

"Oh yeah? What do you do?"

So she didn't recognize me. That wasn't unusual—it was also something I was working very hard to change. My luggage came around the carousel. My guitar case sat a few bags behind it. "I'm a musician."

"Oh, one of those Hollywood types. In the biz, on tour or away filming a soundtrack for an indie movie overseas."

She wasn't far off. Jesus, was I really that cliché?

"Something like that. I am touring with a group. And there is a movie involved. But it's not an indie film."

The movie was kind of a big one, actually, but I didn't like to throw that around. Even though that seemed to be the LA thing to do, name-dropping made me feel like an asshole.

I lifted my luggage and guitar off the moving belt. Now both hands were occupied, and I had to hold my phone to my ear with my shoulder. I needed to get through customs and catch an Uber to my hotel, which meant I should probably hang up. But instead I wandered over to the bench just inside the entrance to baggage claim and sat down, setting my guitar case on the seat next to me.

"Hmm..." she said, sounding bored now. "Everyone's in the business here."

She didn't press me for more about the movie. She seemed uninterested. I was a little surprised. All Monique had cared about when I first met her was who I was and who I knew. Come to think of it, I'm not sure that ever really changed. It was refreshing to talk to someone who didn't give a shit what I could do for their career. Frankly, I was a little sick of talking about it.

I switched the subject. "And what do you do?"

"Nothing interesting," she said vaguely.

"How do you know I won't think it's interesting? You work from home and you have the time to walk five miles a day and rescue stray dogs. I'd like to know what gives you such a flexible schedule. You know, to gauge whether or not your lifestyle is conducive to dog-sitting."

She made a noise that I imagined went with an eye roll. "I'm an artist."

"And how is that uninteresting?"

"It just is. What I paint is uninteresting."

"Then why paint it? Can't you paint what you want?" I put my ankle over my knee and leaned back on the bench.

The running water shut off in the background, and she went quiet for a moment.

"What's your website?" I asked, feeling pretty sure she wasn't going to give it to me, but figuring I should give it a shot.

"I don't have a website. And if I did, I wouldn't give it to you."

I smiled. "You're consistent. I like that in a dog-sitter." Then I looked at my watch. "I need to get going here."

"Okay. Well, have a good trip, I guess."

"Sloan? Thank you. I can't tell you how much it means to me that you rescued Tucker and took such good care of him. And I really appreciate you watching him until I get back."

She was quiet for a moment. "Thank you for saying thank you," she said finally.

My lips twisted into a sideways smile. "We'll be in touch."

CHAPTER 4

SLOAN

♪ OCEAN EYES | BILLIE EILISH

I looked at the pictures of Tucker with Jason.
Again.

I'd been ogling them since he'd sent them to me yesterday. For all the crap I gave Jason, it turned out *I* was the creeper.

Jason was hot. No, he was *beyond* hot. He was bearded, thick brown hair, sexy smile, blue eyes *hot*. Six-pack abs on the beach *hot*.

I watched a lot of crime shows, and I'd gone full forensic psychologist on the screenshot of his cell phone home page.

The time on his phone was Australia's, so he *was* there, like he'd said he was.

The musician thing seemed true enough. He had a disproportionate amount of music apps. No Tinder or other hookup sites. There were Uber, Twitter, and YouTube. All the standard social media. Tons of notifications, but then he'd just landed, and he'd said he had been out of contact for a few weeks, so that made sense and actually gave his story credibility.

Overall, no glaring red flags that screamed pathological liar or mass murderer. And it was pretty adorable that Tucker was his wallpaper image.

I put a hand between Tucker's ears and tousled his fur. "Why didn't you tell me your dad was so handsome?" He leaned into me and let me kiss his head.

To say I was sad about losing Tucker in two weeks was the understatement of the year.

Tucker changed me. I felt good. Better than I'd felt in ages, actually. And I realized that somewhere along the line, the tiredness that comes with grief had turned into the kind that comes from inactivity and a crappy diet of caffeine and sugar.

Tucker got me moving. He gave my days purpose. And now he would be leaving me in a few weeks, and I felt panic at the thought of being alone again, like I wouldn't know how to keep doing this new and improved me if I didn't have him.

I had been so close to just keeping him. But after I'd hung up on Jason, I'd thought about what he'd said, that he'd been out of town and he hadn't known Tucker was missing. I wasn't a dog thief. If I had suspected for one second he was going back to a neglectful home, I'd have kept him and never looked back. But I couldn't take him from someone who truly loved him.

Josh wandered in from the direction of the garage, wiping his hands on a rag. "All done. Water heater's in."

I smiled at him. "Thanks."

"You should have let us buy it for you," he said, giving me a look.

Josh was like my big brother. Brandon would have been happy to know that his best friend took care of me like he did. But I didn't like to take advantage of it. It was enough that Josh fixed half the things that broke around here for free—he didn't need to buy the things too. I'd bought and had the water heater delivered before I even told Josh the old one had broken. Otherwise he would have just picked it up for me.

"It's okay. I have the money," I lied. "Took some extra commissions this week."

He studied me for a long moment, but I didn't break character.

"Okay." He glanced at his phone. "Well, I'm gonna head home and tap out the sitter. Kristen's already on her way over with dinner."

They liked to feed me. I think they thought if they didn't, I'd starve to death. Six months ago I'd put my foot down and only allowed dinner once a week now. They used to be here every day, but it had started to get ridiculous. They had a baby and their own lives, and I didn't want to feel like their responsibility. Kristen would never say it, but I think it was a relief. Either because she thought I was getting better or because she was glad she didn't have to schlep over here every day. I'd filled my freezer with Lean Cuisines and shocked them both when I didn't die from malnourishment.

"See you later." Josh gave me a hug, ruffled Tucker's ears, flashed me a dimpled smile, and left.

The dog laid his head back on my lap, and I peered down at him. I took my cell phone and hit the camera icon and snapped a shot. "I bet Jason would like to see some of your vacation pictures," I said, thumbing a text into the phone and shooting the photo off.

Sloan: All worn out after a six-mile hike!

I set my phone down and lolled my head back on the sofa. Then my cell pinged.

Jason: I bet he loved it.

Another ping.

Jason: No picture of you?

I rolled my eyes. Sexy or not, he was a stranger. I wasn't going to send him pictures of me.

Sloan: Do you think how I look is going to have any bearing on my ability to watch your dog?

The three little dots started jumping, letting me know he was typing a response. I smiled. I'd kind of liked talking to him yesterday. I sat up and tucked my feet under me as I waited for the reply. "Your dad's a flirt," I said to Tucker. He looked up at me with those soft copper eyes and then put his chin back in my lap.

Jason: You've seen pictures of me. I don't think it's that weird to want to put a face to a name. You're watching my favorite person in the world and I don't even know you.

I twisted my lips. He had a bit of a point. But still.

Sloan: You're a stranger. You could be a pirate.

The dots began jumping again.

Jason: Aye, that be true.

I laughed.

Jason: Do you like games?

Where was *this* going?

Sloan: It depends.
Jason: On?
Sloan: On whether someone ends up drunk or naked at
    the end of it. I don't like those games. I always end up
    the sober one, driving all the drunk, naked people home.
Jason: 😅 Not that kind of game.
Sloan: I'm listening.
Jason: Every day I can ask you one question to get to
    know you better. And if you don't want to answer it, you
    have to send me a picture.

I shook my head while I typed.

Sloan: What kind of questions are we talking about? The
    yes-or-no, check-a-box kind?
Jason: Lol! No, too elementary school. Real questions. I
    can ask anything I want, and you have to answer it
    truthfully.
Sloan: Do I get to ask you a question every day?
Jason: Of course.
Sloan: And if you don't want to answer it?

Jason: I'll answer it.

Sloan: How about if you don't want to answer it, you have to let me keep Tucker an extra day.

There was a pause between texts. The ceiling fan made a steady clicking noise above me while I waited.

Jason: Deal.

Sloan: Deal.

His questions were going to be perverted. I was almost certain. He wanted a picture, so he'd probably ask me things he thought I'd never answer. But the game was too alluring. And I liked the idea of asking this good-looking mystery man about himself. It was kind of fun.

Jason: Ready for my first question?

Sloan: Ready.

Jason: Why don't you paint what you want to paint?

I stared at the text. I hadn't been expecting *that*.

Had he asked it to throw me off? Had my weirdness over my art shone through in our brief conversation yesterday? I let out a deep breath. Now I kind of wished there were just yes and no boxes to check.

I decided to deflect him.

Sloan: Really? This question? Seems like a waste. You get a do-over.

Jason: Don't want a do-over.

And then,

Jason: Wouldn't mind a picture though.

My lips pursed. "Fine," I muttered to myself.

    Sloan: I haven't painted my own works since my fiancé
       died two years ago.

The dots started to jump. Then they stopped. Then they started again.

Jason: I'm sorry to hear that.

There was a pause between texts while he typed again.

Jason: Sometimes the hardest place to live is the one
       in-between.

I blinked at the message.
"Yes…" I whispered.
The dots started bouncing again.

Jason: Your turn. What's your question?

I was glad he was changing the subject. I didn't want to talk about this. I thought about my question and decided I'd have a little fun with it.

Sloan: How would you survive a zombie apocalypse?

The dots jumped for several minutes. Then a text pinged, but just three words came through.

Jason: I'm calling you.

The phone rang.

"Well?" I said, answering without saying hello.

"My answer is too long to text."

"You've given the zombie apocalypse that much thought, huh?"

"Haven't you? It's a serious situation," he said sternly.

"Only a matter of time, really."

I could tell he was smiling when he continued speaking. "Survival is all about going where there's the least threat of other humans and zombies. We'd have to get to somewhere remote."

"We?"

"You and me."

"How do you know that I'm qualified to be on your zombie apocalypse survival team?"

"Are you?"

I scoffed. "Of course. But you didn't know that. Do you always give out important jobs to people without checking their qualifications? It seems to be a thing with you." I pulled a blanket over Tucker and me and grabbed my iced coffee, snuggling deeper into the sofa.

"You're right. Totally right. Admission into my survival compound is contingent upon a satisfactory comprehensive interview, illustration of survival skills, and a thorough physical. I'll be conducting the physical personally."

I laughed, *hard*.

"Okay, so provided I've passed all of your tests, we'd be holed up in a rural—what? Cabin?" I asked, putting the straw to my lips, still smiling.

"Yes, on my property in northern Minnesota where we could live off the land until things blow over."

I raised my eyebrows. "Live off the land? Do you know how?"

"Did you think Tucker was just a pretty face?"

"You hunt? With Tucker?" I looked down at him. Brandon would have loved a hunting dog.

The phone shuffled, and Jason was quiet for a moment. "Check your phone."

A picture came through of Tucker wearing a life jacket at the bow of a small fishing boat on a choppy-looking lake. A shotgun rested against the boat bench, and a gray, cloudy sky loomed behind him.

Jason wasn't in the picture, and I felt a pang of disappointment. Then I felt disappointment in *myself*. I had become some sort of voyeur over this beautiful man.

It felt strange to be attracted to someone and even weirder to be attracted to someone I'd never met before. I hadn't really noticed another man since Brandon died. It kind of felt like cheating.

"And do you cook this meat that you kill?" I asked.

"The meat is eaten," he said, sounding somewhat evasive.

"You give it to your mom," I deadpanned.

He laughed. "She's an excellent cook. There's no shame in giving it to my mom."

"So you hunt. You're familiar with firearms. You've got a bunker in the woods. You *do* seem like a good candidate for zompoc survival," I allowed. "I might join your team. Not sure how I'd feel about holing up in northern Minnesota in the winter, though."

"You'd be surprised at how warm the cabin gets once the fire gets going. And we could always share body heat."

I arched my eyebrows. "You are *awfully* flirty for a man who's never seen me before. What if I'm hideous?"

"So you object to me flirting with you based solely on your personality?"

He had me there. "And what if I have a boyfriend?"

"Do you?"

I smirked. "That sounds like a question for tomorrow's round of truth or picture."

"Come on, you're not going to give me one freebie? It's a simple yes or no. Shouldn't I know if Tucker is spending time with another man?"

I snorted. "Really? You're going to make this about Tucker?"

"I just think we should discuss it if my dog is going to be around an unfamiliar male influence. I don't want to confuse him," he said in a mock-serious tone.

I rolled my eyes and laughed. "No, I don't have a boyfriend."

"All right. See? How hard was that? I'm single too. Now we can move on. So what makes *you* qualified to be on *my* zombie survival team?"

"Where are you?" I asked. "Don't you have a job? Aren't I keeping you from something important?"

"Are you avoiding the question? Is it possible that you've over-sold your ability to survive a zombie apocalypse? It feels like you're sidestepping. Answer the interview question, please."

God, he was fun.

"Oh, I'm qualified, believe me. I just wondered how you have so much time for phone calls during your fancy filming-on-location work trip."

"It's only eight a.m. here. I have something later, but not until noon. I've got time to hear all about how you'd make a good addition to my end-of-days squad. Stop changing the subject."

"How about this," I said, switching the phone to my other ear. "I'll send you a link that'll explain exactly why I'd make a good survivalist. But if I do, you have to give me an extra day with Tucker."

He sucked in air. "I don't know. I miss him pretty badly. Waiting an extra day to see him when I get back is a tall order."

"I think you'll really appreciate my skill set," I said, in my best salesperson's voice. "And there's a photo of me. It's old and grainy, but if you zoom in, you might get a rough, pixelated idea of what I generally look like."

"Pixelated, huh? Sounds sexy. Here's an idea, how about we share him on your extra day? Take him somewhere together."

Together? I wasn't sure how I felt about that. "Like where?"

"On a hike somewhere. You pick. You're the local. I don't really know anyone in LA, and I love the outdoors. It would be nice to have someone show me some good hikes."

I considered this. I wanted the extra day with Tucker. But the thought of going somewhere with Jason was a little daunting. It felt too much like a date. And I *liked* him, I realized. I liked talking to him. And that made going somewhere with him feel like a betrayal of Brandon. That was stupid and irrational, but it did. But I guessed I could always opt out if I decided against it when it rolled around. After all, it was *my* extra day.

"Okay. You have a deal. Give me a second to get to the page. Hold on."

I found the blog and sent him the link just as Kristen knocked on my screen. Tucker bolted up and ran to the door, barking.

"Hey, I sent you the link, but I have to go," I said quickly. "A friend just came over. I'll talk to you later, okay?"

CHAPTER 5

JASON

♪ GIVE ME A TRY | THE WOMBATS

Room service showed up with my breakfast right as I hung up with Sloan.

I poured myself a black coffee and sat on the bed with my plate on my lap and tapped the link she'd sent me. When the blog came up on my phone, I stared at it, my fork halfway to my mouth.

No. Fucking. WAY.

My thumbs couldn't move fast enough over my phone.

Jason: Are you trying to tell me you're The Huntsman's Wife?

I waited. The dots didn't appear, and I went back to the blog with my mouth open.

The Huntsman's Wife was a well-known website containing recipes for wild game. In hunting circles, it was the go-to for good wild meat dishes. Mom used it religiously when Dad, my brother David, and I brought home our hauls. Hell, *everyone* who hunted used it.

Tucker had scored The Huntsman's Wife as his dog-sitter? Un-fucking-believable.

I went right for the About tab and scoured the contents. It was brief.

If you're here, you're probably looking at some ridiculous amount of wild something or other in your freezer, wondering, "What the hell do I do with this?"

I laughed, hearing Sloan's voice as I read.

I'm here to help. My man is an avid hunter and I am an enthusiastic chef. Enjoy.

At the bottom of the About page, as promised, was a small picture of a smiling man in camo posing with a crossbow. A blond woman with tattoos down her arm stood on her toes, kissing him on the cheek. She wore light-gray capris and a white tank top with her braided waist-length hair in a pink bandana.

I tried zooming in and the photo distorted severely. I couldn't really make out her face. All I got from the picture was long hair and a nice figure.

I looked back at the man in the photo.

Mom had said, rather disappointedly, that *The Huntsman's Wife* hadn't been updated with any new recipes in years. Was it because the hunter in Sloan's life had died?

The site contained no other information to give me a clue as to who she was. She signed off on every post as "The Huntsman's Wife." No last name to google or search on Instagram.

It didn't escape me that I wanted to shamelessly google her, just like the creeper she accused me of being, but my curiosity about her had just gone from moderate to extreme. I was impressed. *Really* impressed.

I scrolled through the blog, looking at it with a new appreciation. I could taste some of the familiar dishes in my memory. Some of these were my family's favorites. The slow cooker Dr Pepper boar pot roast, the venison Bolognese, rosemary smothered pheasant. It was incredible to think I'd eaten Sloan's food without ever having met her in person, that she'd already been in my life in this way for years. It was like I already knew her.

Mom was going to flip. Shit, everyone back home was gonna flip. And I'd just weaseled my way into a date with her. I should play the lottery with my luck.

My phone pinged.

Sloan: So did I make the team?

I smiled.

Jason: Oh, yes. You're definitely on the team. Looking
    forward to the apocalypse.

CHAPTER 6

SLOAN

♪ FUTURE | PARAMORE

I must have looked guilty when I hung up with Jason so quickly because Kristen eyed me suspiciously as she let herself into my house.

"Who was that?" She dropped a bag from In-N-Out on my coffee table, flopped onto the sofa beside me, and ruffled Tucker's fur.

I debated lying to her. I don't know why. Maybe because Jason was a man and he wasn't Brandon and that made me feel guilty? But she'd see it on my face if I lied. She always saw through me.

"That was Jason, Tucker's owner."

Her eyebrows went up.

I shrugged. "It's nothing. He's taking Tucker back."

Her gaze softened. "He is? I'm sorry, Sloan. I know you really got attached to him." She dipped her head a bit to look me in the eye. "Now quit fucking with me and tell me what's really going on."

My eyes narrowed. "I don't know why I bother trying to keep things from you."

"I don't know why you bother either."

I let out a breath through my nose. "We've kind of been talking."

"Talking?" She grinned.

"Yes. Texting and on the phone." Then I scoffed. "And wait until you see *this*."

I grabbed my phone and went to the pictures Jason had sent me of him and Tucker. I handed it over to her and waited as she looked at them.

Her eyes flew wide. "*This* is Jason?"

"*That* is Jason. And he's nice. And funny. And really, *really* flirty."

"And he has a great dog," she said.

"Yes, and he has a great dog."

"Is he single?"

"Yes."

"Is he asking you things like whether or not *you're* single?" she asked.

"Yes."

She beamed, handing my phone back. "Have you met him?" Then she looked over at Tucker. "Why is his dog still here?"

"He's in Australia for work for a few more weeks. I'm keeping Tucker for him until he gets back."

My phone pinged and I glanced at it. It was Jason. My eyes shot up to Kristen, and she arched an eyebrow.

"Is that him?" she asked, smiling like the Cheshire Cat. "Is it a dick pic? Is it amazing?"

"No, it is not a dick pic. Ewww." If he ever sent me one of those, this little back-and-forth would come to an abrupt end. "He wants to know if *The Huntsman's Wife* is my blog."

Her eyes lit up. "Are you posting again?"

"No, it's a long story, how that came up." I pursed my lips. "Why do I feel guilty about this?"

"Because you haven't dated since Brandon. Because you're like a hermit. You remind me of those veiled Italian widows from the Old World, wearing black and lighting Virgin Mary candles, shuffling around with their rosaries and—"

I hit her with a throw pillow and she laughed.

"Seriously, Sloan. You're a hot *bombshell*. You're beautiful and talented, and you deserve to be happy again. This recluse stuff is bullshit."

"Wow, tell me how you really feel."

"No, I mean it, Sloan. Josh and I talked about this a few days ago. We're staging an intervention. We decided that once the two-year mark hit, we weren't going to let you continue to make your life a shrine to Brandon. Enough is enough."

I looked at her tiredly. "I don't choose to feel like this, Kristen."

"Like hell you don't. You used to be one of the most driven people I know. You had galleries *fighting* over your work." She looked around the living room, and when her eyes fell on my most recent commissioned artwork, she turned to me accusatorily. "This is the shit I'm talking about. What is that? A fucking astronaut cat?"

I had the sense to look abashed.

"You're a crazy-talented artist. Look at the crap you're painting. You *choose* this."

I sighed. She was right. She was right about all of it.

"Do shit that makes you happy. Why don't you paint something you like? Paint Tucker." She shook her head at me. "And that guy? You should climb him like a tree. Or at the very least shake his branches. See what kind of nuts fall out."

I laughed. Then I bit my lip. "Okay. You're right. I will *try*."

"You need to get laid. Find a guy who'll fuck you like he just got out of prison. Oh! Let's get you a Brazilian wax!" she said suddenly. "Let's vagazzle you! We'll make your vagina shiny and new!"

I recoiled in horror and her eyes danced mischievously.

"Oh my God, *no*."

"Yes. My treat. I want the cobwebs yanked off that thing."

My eyelid twinged. "You are awful."

"I pushed a small human out of this body. My vagina is destroyed. I have to live vicariously through your vagina."

We both giggled.

"If I agree, will you stop saying 'vagina'?"

~

Kristen stayed until almost 11:00 p.m. I'd sent Jason a quick text asking him if I'd made his zombie survival team. He'd said I had. That was the last of our back-and-forth for the day.

The next morning, Tucker woke me up at 7:30. That was another good thing about Tucker, he got me out of bed. He always wanted to be let out before 8:00 and he made sure I knew it. After I took him out, I couldn't ever get back to sleep, so I stayed up and started my day. I used to sleep until noon, sometimes later. I liked the earlier routine. It gave me more sunlight hours, and the sun perked me up.

To my surprise my phone vibrated at exactly 9:00 a.m. It was Jason.

I wondered if he'd waited until 9:00 on purpose, so he wouldn't text me too early. It made me smile to think he'd sat there watching the time, waiting for the exact moment it would be acceptable to text.

Jason: You up?

Sloan: I am. Your dog doesn't sleep in. What time is it there?

Jason: 2:00 a.m., Thursday. Just got back to the hotel. Wednesday there, right?
Sloan: Yup. Late night for you.
Jason: Rehearsing. So who came over?

He was fishing. I smiled.

Sloan: My best friend, Kristen.
Jason: Did you talk about me?

I blanched. Then I panicked. How was I supposed to respond to that? Yes, we talked about you? My best friend advised me to climb you like a tree in search of your nuts? And then we talked about my vagina? Of course I was going to lie. But I was too guilty to think up a believable one on the fly. I was weighing my responses when another text came through.

Jason: You totally talked about me.

My thumbs jumped into action.

Sloan: I did not.
Jason: Liar. If you didn't talk about me, what did you talk about?
Sloan: I may have mentioned you in a casual, very platonic way. Briefly.
Jason: Did you tell her about our date?
Sloan: It's not a date.

It wasn't. Right?

Jason: What would you call it?

I put my palm up in exasperation.

Sloan: An appointment.
Jason: Huh. How do I get it switched to a date?
Sloan: You don't.

I chewed on my thumbnail. The dots jumped, and I waited to see what he had to say in response to my rebuff.

Jason: When I tell my friends about it, I'm calling it a date. You can't stop me. There's literally nothing you can do about it.

I laughed. *This guy.* He did not lack confidence, that was for sure. I decided, in the spirit of keeping my promise to Kristen, to give him something small.

Sloan: I'm 26.
Jason: Another freebie! I'm 29. What high school did you graduate from?

I smirked. He was sneaky.

Sloan: Nice try. Then you'll Google my yearbook and figure out my last name.
Jason: I'll tell you my last name if you tell me yours.

Sloan: Nope.

Jason: It's a really great last name.

Sloan: I'm sure it is. Not gonna happen, though.

Jason: Truth or dare?

Sloan: No.

Jason: Spin the bottle?

Sloan: No!

I was giggling now.

Jason: Monopoly???

Sloan: Yes, I will play Monopoly with you someday.

Jason: Now things are getting exciting.

He wasn't wrong.

CHAPTER 7

JASON

♪ TALK TOO MUCH | COIN

The massive time difference between Melbourne and California was fucking with me. I wish I could say I was jet-lagged, but the real issue was that I had to put off texting Sloan so I didn't wake her up in the middle of the night. Poking her had become my new favorite pastime.

We'd chatted and texted on and off all day Thursday, my time, but I got slammed the whole day Friday with rehearsals and sound checks. She'd sent me a picture of Tucker and I'd shot her a one-word reply. After that I didn't get a second to breathe until after dinner. At 7:00 p.m. Australia time, it was 1:00 a.m. for Sloan.

When I woke up Saturday morning I felt for my phone on the nightstand. I typed in my message, barely awake.

Jason: It's a new day and I get a new question.

The jumping dots didn't appear, and when the phone rang in my hand, it was Ernie.

"Good morning, Down Under. I'm guessing by your context clues that you haven't checked your email today?" I could tell by the wind coming through the phone that he was in his coupé with the top down. "I'm going to need you to not lose your shit. It's a fifteen-hour flight to Australia and I can't be there to chokehold you off a ledge."

Fuck. I sat up in bed and put him on speaker. I opened the email and took one look at the attachment and shook my head. "No. I write my own lyrics. I *sing* my own lyrics, Ernie."

"I know. I know you do and this is a giant load of steaming horseshit, but we talked about this."

"We talked about someone else writing my music?" I squinted at the screen. "What the hell is this? It looks like a pop song. They rhymed *sweetie* with *teeny*. I'm not singing this crap."

A horn blared through the phone, and he told someone to go fuck themselves. Ernie drove like a madman. "Look, you need a strong crossover hit. I like indie rock. It's nice to listen to while I smoke a joint when I'm hiding from the wife, but that stuff doesn't go platinum. If you wanna get Don Henley famous like you said you *wanted* to, crossover hits for mass market is how you do that."

"Yeah, I get that," I said. "But *I* was supposed to write the music."

"Well, we tried it your way. You haven't written anything in six months and your label's getting itchy. They wanna know they're gonna get a return on their investment. You're in bed with these people now, it's time to tickle their balls a little. *Lie* to them. Tell them what they want to hear, that you'll roll over and sing what they ask you to, then write something that'll blow their fucking socks off and bait and switch them when you have it. Done."

I dragged a hand down my face. "Fuck," I mumbled. "And if I can't write something that'll blow their fucking socks off? Then what?"

"Then it's two songs on an album of ten and you do whatever the hell you want with the rest of it. Look, you and your label have the same objectives. To sell records. If you can't come up with the material to do that, they're gonna come up with the material for you. It's a partnership. I know you're an artist and this is your medium and the very suggestion that you sing something that you didn't write feels like picking which STD you want, but you went with the big boys and now this is big-boy time. It's time to put on your big-boy pants." Two swift honks. "You grin and bear it, and you know why? Because you are a goddamn *professional*." Another long, blaring horn.

I stared at my reflection in the black TV on the dresser at the end of my bed. I couldn't write. I was having some sort of lyrical performance anxiety. I'd never had to compose on demand before, and knowing they were waiting for it felt like an energy suck. I'd cranked out the soundtrack, but just barely, and the best stuff on the album was the three songs I'd written with Lola Simone— and that was mostly *her*. I'd taken those two weeks hiking in New Zealand hoping the solitude would kick-start my creativity again, but not even that had done it for me.

I wasn't opposed to collaborating. I wasn't even entirely opposed to singing something I didn't write—but the song had to be great. It had to sound like me, and it had to be amazing. And that's *not* what this was.

I pinched my temples. "I hate this."

"Yeah, well, let the money and fame console you."

I glanced again at the lyrics and cringed. I didn't even like the *idea* of saying I'd sing this. But what choice did I have? I didn't want to look uncooperative, and it wasn't like I had anything else to give them.

"Fine." I spit it out like the word tasted bad in my mouth.

"That a boy. Also, they're adding pyrotechnics and fog to your concerts."

"What?"

"I hope you like confetti. I'll let them know you're on board and you're thrilled. Hey! Pick a fucking lane—"

The call ended.

I let out a long breath. I sang on stage with nothing but a spotlight, a stool, and a microphone. I didn't do props and theatrics, and I sure as hell didn't sing some pop shit I didn't write.

Ernie had warned me about this. I'd known when I signed my record deal that this day might come, and I'd find myself compromising my vision for my work. But now it felt like more than that. It felt like I was selling my damn soul.

I tossed my phone on the bed and got up and took a shower. Then I made black coffee in the little coffee maker and went out to the balcony to drink it.

My room overlooked Marvel Stadium, where I'd play tomorrow. People walked around below like ants in the light drizzle, nothing but glass and wet concrete as far as the eye could see. No trees. Just the smell of damp asphalt.

This hotel was a nice one. All the amenities. Not that I was picky about where I stayed. I could sleep on a couch with my arm over my face. It was just a nice change—and one that came with having a big record label that had assigned me a personal tour manager. Per diems for room service, top-of-the-line recording studios, hefty advances, first-class flights—that I usually gave away, but it was a frill nonetheless.

I blew a resigned breath through my nose. Ernie was right.

It was a give-and-take. I'd been an independent musician for so long, I just wasn't used to being told what to do and how.

I'd have to get used to it.

Sloan still hadn't texted.

I leaned on the railing and checked my phone again, wondering if it had chirped and I'd missed it. I double-checked that my last text had gone through. It was marked read.

She'd never taken this long to respond before.

When a text came through from Lola with a picture of her licking her nipple, I was doubly annoyed. She had a new number. *Again.* I'd already blocked the last two. I was probably going to have to change *my* number since blocking hers wasn't making any fucking difference.

I deleted the picture, irritated, and decided to go to the gym.

I didn't have anything on my schedule. I'd actually been looking forward to today, when I'd be free to bother Sloan as I saw fit. It hadn't occurred to me she'd maybe not be available for that— or interested in it.

Between this, the Lola text, and the call with Ernie, my morning was a wash. I hadn't realized how much I looked forward to sparring with Sloan every day until it looked like she might stop accepting my challenges. She was funny. I enjoyed talking to her. I also liked hearing what Tucker was doing, though it occurred to me I'd be checking in on him a hell of a lot less if he were still with Monique.

I was tying my running shoes when my cell phone pinged. I tipped the screen toward me and smiled.

Sloan: Don't think you're getting two questions just because you missed yesterday.

I kicked off my shoes and got back onto the bed, sitting up against the headboard with a grin.

Jason: Do you have time for a phone call?

The dots started to bounce. Damn, I loved those dots.

Sloan: Sure.

I hit the phone icon and pressed my cell to my ear. "So you're going to rob me of a question because I was a gentleman and didn't call you at one in the morning to ask it?" I teased when she picked up.

"Seems to me that a gentleman who really wanted to get to know me better would have found time for a text with his question during reasonable hours."

"I was very busy yesterday."

"Sounds like you just weren't properly *motivated* yesterday. A text only takes a second. Now I have no choice but to penalize you."

Her tone was playful, but she wasn't going to cut me any slack. And was she maybe, just possibly, a little mad at me for not being more attentive yesterday? The thought made me smile to myself. "What can I do to make it up to you? Give me your address and I'll send you flowers. What's your favorite kind?"

"Sunflowers. And not a chance."

"I guessed you might say that."

"You *knew* I would say that. So what's your question?"

I didn't even have to think about it. "What did you tell your friend Kristen about me?"

She groaned. "I think I'd prefer to send you a picture."

"That bad, huh?"

"If I give you back your forfeited question, will you change this one?"

"Definitely not."

She let out a sigh and I snickered. Then I threw her a lifeline. "I'll tell you what, if you agree that our hike with Tucker is going to be a date, I'll ask you something else. Or you could keep calling it an appointment, and then you can tell me all about what you two ladies talked about yesterday. *Or* you could send me a picture. It's all a win for me. I can't actually decide which option I like best, they're all so great."

She laughed. "You are not going to give this up, are you?"

"Nope."

"You know what? I think I *will* tell you what I said. Because *I* said very little, actually. I showed her your picture. I said we'd been texting and talking. And I said you were taking Tucker back. That's it. You asked the wrong question. You *should* have asked what Kristen said in response to what I said. That was the juicy stuff."

"You showed her my picture?" I asked, grinning.

"Yes."

"Why?"

"She's my best friend and we were talking about you," she said.

"So you agree that having a picture of someone is helpful?"

"I see where you're taking this, and it won't work."

"I have a best friend too, you know. Cooper, the bartender downstairs, would also like to see a picture to accompany my stories about you."

"Well, Cooper is going to have to help you to think up much better questions, then, isn't he?"

I put my arm behind my head and grinned. "Make my picture your wallpaper."

"What? No!"

"Do it, I dare you."

"No. Tucker is my wallpaper. I *like* having Tucker as my wallpaper. Unlike his dad, *Tucker* is well behaved."

"Well, in all fairness, Tucker's got a date and not an appointment."

She laughed.

Housekeeping knocked, and I slid off the mattress to open the door and wave them off, slipping the *Do not disturb* sign onto the knob. I grabbed a bottled water from the minibar and climbed back onto the bed.

"So what did you do yesterday that had you so busy that you missed your daily question?" she asked.

"I had sound check and rehearsal. Then I had dinner with the group," I said, taking the cap off my water.

"Oh, you're in a group?"

"No, I'm a lone wolf. I had dinner with the group that I'm working with tomorrow night."

"And who's that?"

I was opening for The Black Keys on Sunday, but for Sloan that was embargoed information. I had officially decided not to tell her who I was or what I really did for a living. I didn't want it to distract her from getting to know me as a person. I'd learned a few lessons from my time with Monique. I wasn't going to lie, per se, I just wasn't going to volunteer things whenever possible.

"You've probably never heard of them," I said. Then I changed the subject. "So my mom's pretty excited I know The Huntsman's Wife."

"Really? Does she use my website?"

"Yes, religiously. I've eaten a lot of your food. Where did you learn how to cook?"

"My mom has a catering company. She has a food truck on the Warner Bros. lot. I grew up helping her."

"And does she serve a lot of wild game?"

I could almost imagine the smirk I heard on her lips. *Almost.* I really did wish I had a picture.

"No, but once you know how the meat tastes, it's not hard to work with it," she said.

I shook my head. "Yes, it is. That's why your page is so popular."

"Is it?"

"You're kidding, right? Everyone I know uses it. Why don't you update it anymore?"

She paused for a moment. "I cooked the meat that Brandon, my fiancé, used to bring home. He died in a motorcycle accident two years ago. Hit by a drunk driver. So I stopped blogging."

I could hear the tightness at the edges of her voice, and something protective in me twitched—which was weird. I barely knew her. But I didn't like that she'd gone through this. Why do all the bad things always seem to happen to good people?

"Do you still cook other things?" I asked, getting us off the topic.

"Not really. It kind of lost its allure for me."

"So if you don't cook, what have you eaten today?"

"Hmmm. Well, I'm still blowing through the gift cards I got for Christmas, so I went to Starbucks and got my coffee," she said. "Then I went to Kristen's house to go swimming. She has a toddler. We had watermelon and macaroni and cheese for lunch. Kristen made it, so the mac and cheese was *very* soggy."

"And where was Tucker? Did you leave him alone at home, heartbroken in a small closet?"

"Oh, you mean did I leave him in a crate?"

I smirked at the jab.

"No, he came with me and he went swimming too. And he got a puppuccino at Starbucks."

I wrinkled my forehead. "A what?"

"A puppuccino. A cup of whipped cream for dogs."

"That's a thing?"

"It is. There's all kinds of things you can get for dogs at restaurants. You can get ice cream at most places as long as it doesn't have vanilla beans in it. And there's a cupcake shop called Nadia Cakes that I take him to that has doggy cupcakes they make from scratch."

I arched my eyebrows. "Wow, he really *is* on vacation."

"There's a reason why you're paying me the big bucks for my dog-sitting services."

"I'd have paid more."

"I'd have done it for less."

I smiled and jammed another pillow behind my back.

"I'm going to put you on speaker. Hold on," she said. "I have to get some work done and I need my hands."

I heard shuffling.

"What are you painting?"

"Want to see it?" she asked, sounding slightly farther away than before.

"Yes, absolutely."

"Hold on, I'll send you a picture. It's really lame. You're gonna laugh. There."

I put my cell phone on speaker and clicked on the picture message she sent. "Is that…an astronaut cat?"

"I told you it was lame."

I zoomed in. "It's well done. It's just…a cat's head on an astronaut's body?"

"Yeah. I do freelance work for a company that takes your

pet's face and photoshops it onto different templates. Then they send it out to an artist to paint it. They're not all cat astronauts. Sometimes they're dogs playing poker." She laughed.

I tilted my head to study the picture. "It's pretty impressive that you can paint that, though. I'd love to see what you did on your own. You're obviously talented." I wasn't bullshitting her. It really *was* good.

"It got easier to paint something I was given than to find inspiration. I have an Etsy store too. It's all kind of mindless."

"You should paint Tucker. Paint him duck hunting in the boat," I suggested, grabbing the room service menu from the nightstand and starting to look over the breakfast options.

"Kristen said the same thing. You have an accent, you know that?"

I looked up. "I do?"

"Yeah, I can hear it when you say 'boat.' It's kind of nice. I like it."

She'd never said anything complimentary to me before. I'd lay on my Minnesota accent extra thick from now on.

"So what do you do while you paint? Do you listen to music?" I asked.

"I watch the ID channel. Real-life crime shows."

"Ahhhh, *that's* why you're so convinced I'm a murderer."

"How many acres of hunting land did you say you have?"

"My family owns two hundred acres in northern Minnesota," I said. "Why?"

"There you go. The perfect place to hide a body. I bet you have a hunting lodge that locks from the outside and everything."

I chuckled and crossed my legs at the ankle. "Do I look like a psychopath to you?"

"Ted Bundy was a good-looking guy. Charismatic too."

"I'll take that as a compliment since it sounds like you're saying I'm good-looking and charismatic. But aren't most psycho killers cruel to animals? I think Tucker would tell you that I've never raised my hand to him in anger."

"Hmmm," she hummed. "Well, that *does* go against the typical serial killer profile. Unless you use Tucker to lure your victims."

I smiled. "He is kind of a chick magnet, isn't he?"

"I bet the two of you make a killing."

"No, so far he's only brought home one girl, and he's been keeping her to himself."

There had to be an eye roll in the ensuing pause.

"Are you ready for my question of the day?" she asked, a smile in her voice.

"Shoot."

"What's the nicest thing you've ever done for a stranger?"

She had good questions, and this one was easy. "I donated my bone marrow."

"Wow. You did? That's a pretty big deal. How did *that* happen?"

Tucker walked around in the background, making a familiar clicking sound on the floor with his nails.

"I can hear Tucker," I said.

"Oh yeah, his nails are pretty long. I'm going to take him into PetSmart tomorrow and have them cut, actually. He's almost out of food too."

"Save your receipts so I can reimburse you."

"Yeah, yeah," she said. "So bone marrow, tell me."

"Right. I grew up in a really small town in northern Minnesota. Population three thousand. So everyone knows everybody else. There was a little girl in the town who got leukemia, so a lot of the townsfolk—"

" 'Townsfolk'?" She sounded amused.

"Yes, 'townsfolk,' we actually talk like that there."

She laughed at this. I liked her laugh. It was musical.

"A lot of the *townsfolk* registered on Be The Match because she needed a bone marrow transplant. She ended up getting one. Nobody she knew. But I was in the registry after that, and I ended up being the match for a guy with lymphoma. So I donated."

"Did they live?" she asked.

I nodded. "They did. I'm friends with the guy on Facebook. He's been in remission for four years now. And Emily too. She just graduated high school."

"Wow. That's... that's really generous."

I shrugged. "I just couldn't imagine being that sick and not having any options, you know? And maybe one day someone will do it for me. Or someone I love."

There was a little pause, and she was smiling when she started talking again. "So in this tiny town of three thousand, what kind of things did you do for fun?"

I ticked off on my fingers. "Ice fishing, dogsledding in the winter. Canoeing. I worked as a guide for trips into the Boundary Waters for ten years. My dad owns an outfitting company."

"And your mom? What does she do?"

"She stayed home. Worked at the outfitters in the summer when it was busy."

She laughed a little. "You really are a northerner, aren't you? Have you seen any moose?"

"I've seen moose, wolves, the northern lights—"

"Oh, I would *love* to see the northern lights. It's on my bucket list."

"Yeah? What else is on your list?"

She made a humming noise. "I want to eat soft-shell crabs.

Oh, and I want to visit Ireland. That's my biggest one. What's on your list?"

If anyone had asked me the same thing yesterday, I'd have answered, "Play the Hollywood Bowl." But today? "I want to take you on a date."

CHAPTER 8

SLOAN

♪ THIS CHARMING MAN | THE SMITHS

Tucker loved PetSmart. He started crying to be let out as soon as we got to the parking lot. He jumped from the car and pulled me into the store, choking himself in the process. His enthusiasm made me laugh, but that wasn't the only thing making me smile today. Jason had me in a good mood.

We'd talked all day yesterday. *All day.* When *Fight Club* came on the TV in his hotel room, I found it on Netflix and we watched it together, talking through it. I drained my cell phone battery three times and finally ended up lying in bed hooked up to my charger until we hung up a little after midnight.

It was official. I had a major crush on him.

He'd grown up stomping around in the woods, and I'd gone to a high school that had a student body the size of his town. He'd worked summers taking tourists on canoeing trips into the wilderness while I did beauty pageants until I was eighteen and worked at the mall. But somehow we clicked. We got along so well, it was crazy.

And it was scary.

Now I *hated* that he didn't know what I looked like. What if he didn't think I was pretty? What if he was like, "Oh" when he finally saw me for the first time? I wanted to just bite the bullet and send him a picture, but now I was too freaked out about it. And all through yesterday's phone call he'd kept asking me for a date.

It was 1:00 and I hadn't heard from him yet today, but it was still early in Melbourne. I'd spent the morning stressing about my appearance. I had a newfound urgency to undo two years of neglect.

Jason would be back in California in a week. That gave me seven short days to prepare. I hadn't cared about my appearance in so long I wasn't sure where to even begin. I always threw my hair into a bun, my toes went without polish, my skin got nothing except a splash of soap and water twice a day. And now this man was practically extorting me for a picture of myself, and I was in no way prepared to be examined.

"You're being dramatic," Kristen had said this morning when I called her in a half panic. "Your hair has never looked better. It hasn't been heat-styled in years. You're tan, and you've always had a perfect figure. Relax, you're a knockout. Believe me, I'd tell you if you were a hot mess."

This *did* make me feel a little better. She *would* tell me. She had literally no filter.

This morning I'd plucked my eyebrows and made an appointment to have my hair trimmed. I did a teeth-whitening strip and a mud mask, and afterward I felt slightly less despondent. But I was still *so* nervous. I hadn't cared about what a man thought of me since Brandon, and suddenly I was obsessed. I felt like I was shaking out a dusty party dress I'd left balled on the floor of my closet for two years, hoping it still fit and the moths hadn't destroyed it.

I walked Tucker to the grooming department at the back of the store and stood waiting to check him in at the counter, thinking of Jason and chewing on my lip.

A woman in a dark-blue PetSmart shirt greeted me. "Checking in?"

"Yes, he just needs a nail trim."

She leaned over and looked at Tucker. "No problem. And who do we have here?"

"Tucker."

Something flashed across her face. The groomer behind her jerked her head up to stare at me, and the two shared a look.

"Are you Sloan?" the first woman asked.

"Yeeeees," I said, looking back and forth between them, unsure what was happening.

"One moment." She grinned, putting up a finger. "Just wait here." Then she darted into a side door. When it opened again, a giant vase of sunflowers floated out.

"Oh my God," I whispered. "He *didn't*."

The woman heaved the vase onto the countertop. "These are for you," she said, beaming.

I stared at the arrangement in shock. "*How?*"

"Your boyfriend called us this morning and said he wanted to surprise you when you came in. We've been waiting for you all day. It's so sweet!"

My stomach flipped at the word "boyfriend." He wasn't, of course, but my stomach didn't care.

The flowers were stunning. Red roses were mixed in with the huge yellow blossoms, and flowering branches gave it extra height. It was easily the largest arrangement I'd ever gotten. It must have cost a *fortune*.

"There's a card," the woman said, turning the vase to the little white envelope.

I plucked it free and slid a shaking finger under the seal.

There were two square boxes drawn on the small paper, with the words "yes" and "no" written above them.

Sloan, do you like me? Check one. —*Jason*

I laughed out loud and had to slap a hand over my mouth.

I handed Tucker over for his nail trim and called Jason. He answered groggily, but I could hear the smile in his voice. "Good afternoon, Sloan."

"You are too much. How did you know where to send these?"

He sounded like he was stretching. "You said you were going to PetSmart. I know generally where you live. I googled it."

"They're beautiful."

"I was accused of not being properly motivated once, so I stepped up my game."

"You really did," I said, looking the flowers up and down. "But you shouldn't have done it."

"Did you read the card?"

I blushed. "Yes."

"Did you check a box?"

"Maybe."

"Are you going to tell me which one?"

"Definitely not."

"Then that's my question for the day," he said, the smile in his voice coming through the phone.

I sighed. "I checked yes."

"Good," he said. "I like you too."

CHAPTER 9

SLOAN

♪ A BEAUTIFUL MESS | JASON MRAZ

There was a small wet spot on my kitchen tile. "I think I've got a leaky pipe," I told Jason over the phone. I started pulling out all the cleaning products from under my sink and dabbed at the damp surface with my finger. "Ugh, it's definitely wet under here."

"I can have a look at it for you when I get back," he offered, a hopeful edge to his voice.

Jason was coming home tomorrow. He was packing his hotel room up as we spoke and heading to catch a flight in just a few hours. My stomach flipped again. It had been roiling for days in anticipation of meeting him in person. I was a mess. My eyelid twitched mercilessly from the stress.

"No, you're not coming over here," I said again. "I'll meet you like we planned."

"Come on, at least let me meet you at a restaurant. What kind of date is Starbucks?"

"It's not a date," I reminded him, sliding a bowl under the slow drip.

"Oh, that's right. It's an *appointment*."

We'd known each other for two weeks, and for the last week of that, we'd spoken daily, for hours a day. We texted nonstop when we weren't talking. I liked him so much it was ridiculous. I think I knew him better in a week than I'd known Brandon in six months—Jason was a lot less shy. But I couldn't bring myself to agree to a real date. Not until we met in person.

"I just don't want things to be weird," I said, turning and sliding down to the floor with my back against the dishwasher. I closed my eyes and put a finger on my spasming eyelid.

"Why would they be weird?"

Because you've never seen me before? Because we've talked constantly for the last week and you've never even been in the same room with me?

I didn't answer.

The long sound of a zipper closing on luggage came through the line. "Put Tucker on the phone," he said.

"What?"

"Tucker, put him on the phone."

"Like, put the phone up to his ear?"

"Yes."

I got up and found Tucker sleeping on the sofa. "Should I leave you two alone for this?"

"Yeah, this is just between us guys."

"Okay, here goes." I held the phone to Tucker's ear. He immediately perked up at the sound of Jason's voice. He cocked his head and listened and then bolted off the sofa and tore around the living room, barking.

I put the phone back to my ear, laughing. "What did you say to him?"

"I asked him to show you how excited I am to meet you.

Actually, I told him there's a squirrel outside, but I think he still illustrated my point."

I smiled into the receiver. Then I moved the phone away from my mouth and swallowed. "I made you something."

"You did? What is it?"

"Just something. I'm going to send it to you now. I hope you like it."

I attached a link to a text and held my finger over the little arrow that would put it into the universe. I took a nervous breath and sent it through.

No getting it back now. It was done.

"I'm going to go to bed early," I said. "Have a safe flight, okay? I guess I'll see you tomorrow..."

CHAPTER 10

JASON

♪ SOUL MEETS BODY | DEATH CAB FOR CUTIE

Sloan sent me a link to a YouTube video. I sat on the edge of my bed and watched it, maximizing the screen.

Someone held up a piece of paper in front of the camera that read, *My vacation with Sloan*. Then it began to show clips of Tucker. Tucker on hikes, Tucker swimming in a swimming pool. Tucker at Starbucks licking whipped cream out of a paper cup, and him at PetSmart with a blue plush doll in his mouth. Then he was in a bathtub getting a bath with his hair spiked into a Mohawk. Tucker chasing a green tennis ball on the grass and playing with other dogs at a dog park.

If I hadn't already liked Sloan, this would have done it. Tucker was my currency. It might as well have been me she was spoiling, it had the same effect.

I smiled down at my screen as I watched a clip of Tucker on his back, getting a belly rub. Then the frame changed, and he sat on a couch next to a woman. I bolted to attention and pulled the phone closer.

The woman smiled at him, and he licked her face. I could see the tattoos on her arm. She looked directly at the camera and reached up off-screen, and the video ended.

My heart thudded against my rib cage. *This* was Sloan. *This* was the woman I'd been talking to.

And she was fucking *beautiful*.

I played the video back. Then I played it back again. I paused it and took screenshots of her so I could look at them. I zoomed in and studied her. She had one of those broad smiles that radiated. Full lips, large brown doe eyes, long golden-blond hair. Jesus, she was gorgeous.

I was still watching the video when I got into my Uber. I called her.

Voicemail.

~

I texted Sloan last night, telling her how beautiful I thought she was, but all I got was a smiley face and didn't know how to interpret that. I think the stress of our meeting each other was getting to her.

It was getting to me too.

Even before I'd seen what she looked like, I'd liked her more than anyone else I'd met in a *very* long time. I went to sleep and woke up thinking about her. I fucking *dreamed* about her. I hadn't even looked at another woman sideways pretty much since the moment we started talking. And all that for a woman I hadn't even laid eyes on yet.

Now I worried that *I* would somehow not measure up—which was crazy. She'd seen enough pictures of me to know what to expect, and I was not an unconfident person by any stretch of the imagination. It was just that meeting her felt too important.

My flight had been smooth, and I'd gotten as much sleep as I could so I'd be fresh for our "appointment."

After I dropped off my luggage at home, I took a shower, threw on a T-shirt and jeans, and took longer than I care to admit trimming my beard and messing with my hair. Then I made my way to the Starbucks on Topanga Canyon.

I waited on the patio, bouncing my knee, opening and closing my hand the way I always did right before I played in front of a big crowd. I'd gotten there half an hour early and I sat there scanning the parking lot and sidewalks, completely nervous and laughing to myself because I *never* got like this—for anything or any*one*.

I didn't know what it meant that I felt like this already. All I knew was that I *did*.

She was eight minutes late when she called.

"Hey," I said, picking up on the first ring. "You said Topanga Canyon, ri—"

"Jason, I can't come, my kitchen is flooded!"

Chaos came through the line. Tucker barked in the background, and I could hear the sound of spraying water. "The pipe under your sink?"

"Yes! Oh my God, it's a disaster!"

I was already running to my truck. "Give me your address."

There was a pause.

"I...but..."

I had to laugh. Still? Even now? "Sloan, your *kitchen*."

She moaned. "*Fine.*"

She rattled off her address and told me not to knock.

Google Maps said she was just two blocks away, and I got there within three minutes and ran into the house.

I glanced around the living room, registering only momentarily that I was in Sloan's personal space. It smelled like vanilla. It was clean. The flowers I'd sent her sat by an easel with a half-painted canvas of a pug dressed like Napoleon on it. I darted toward the sound of distress and burst into the kitchen to madness.

Sloan was by the sink, soaking wet and panting, standing in an inch of water.

Our gazes met, and she hit me like a ton of bricks. My body's reaction to her was instantaneous. I could almost feel my pupils dilate as I took her in.

She was a woman who would have frozen me dead in my tracks anywhere. Absolutely showstopping.

I allowed myself two heartbeats to stare at her before I tore my eyes away to look around. She hadn't been kidding, this really *was* bad.

Towels and what must have been the contents of the cabinet were strewn all over the floor. The doors under the sink were open and water sprayed out. Tucker barked and scratched from behind a door off the kitchen.

I quickly rummaged through the open toolbox on the counter, hyperaware that Sloan watched me. Then I dove to my knees to look under the sink, kneeling in a pond of cold water and taking the spray right in the face.

Sloan had amazing water pressure. I was impressed.

The cutoff valve on the water inlet line was jammed. It took a few hard yanks, but I got it shut off. By the time I stopped the flow, I was completely drenched.

I shimmied out and stood, soaking wet, water dripping off the tips of my fingers. I turned to her, raking a hand through my damp hair. She looked at me, her eyes wide, and we stared at each other.

Wow. This is her.

"Hi," she breathed.

"Hello."

The short video clip and the tiny picture of her on *The Huntsman's Wife* had in no way prepared me for Sloan in person. She was like a 1950s pinup girl. All tattoos and curves. Long hair, loose around her shoulders, wet at the ends.

Smart, funny, and now *this*. I'd won the fucking lottery. Why she hadn't been throwing pictures at me right and left was beyond me. Maybe she didn't want me to know how good-looking she was for the same reason I downplayed what I did for a living? I didn't know, but this was a welcome surprise for sure.

Her wide, brown eyes moved down my chest and back to my face. The only sounds were the water still trickling out from under the sink and the thrumming of my heart in my ears.

The corner of her mouth twitched. Then she started to laugh, and I mentally assigned the image to every smiling moment I'd imagined on the phone.

Beautiful.

"I'm glad you didn't make things weird for our first appointment," I said. "Just a run-of-the-mill, no-stress, first-meeting *flood*."

She looked down at the water in her kitchen. "This is so messed up," she said, still giggling.

"Do you have a shop vac?"

"I don't know." She put a hand to her forehead. "Brandon might have had one."

"Where's your garage?"

She pointed to a door. I went into the garage and immediately noted the man cave–like interior. Professional tools and an impressive workbench. A few neon beer signs on the walls. A dusty man's jacket hung on a hook by the door and an empty open beer sat on the counter.

An old Corolla sat in the middle of the two parking spaces, with a duct-taped side mirror and a door that didn't match the rest of the car.

After poking around, I found a shop vac. When I got back into the kitchen, Sloan was sweeping water out the back door with a broom.

The next half hour was spent sucking water off the floor while Sloan wrung out towels and set up fans in the doorway. We worked without talking. The vacuum was too loud. But we kept stealing glances at each other.

I helped her carry a huge armload of wet towels to the washing machine. When the door to the laundry room opened, Tucker spilled out, and I dropped my towels and crouched on the floor, laughing and letting him lick my face. God, I'd missed him. He made crying noises at the sight of me and all I could think was, *This guy's getting a major finder's fee later.*

Sloan watched us with a smile and started the load. When she closed the lid and turned to me, I leaned in the doorway with my arms crossed. Tucker stood between us and looked back and forth with the same proud face he always made when he'd retrieved a duck for me and dropped it at my feet.

"Thanks for all your help." She looked up at me through her long lashes. "This house is a mess. It's really old. Things keep breaking." She seemed unsure what to do now that the crisis had been dealt with.

I smiled. "Go to dinner with me."

She blinked.

"Dinner, tonight, a *date*. Not an appointment, a date."

She studied my face.

"I want to take you out," I said. "Let me."

If she said no, I was pretty sure I was going to beg.

"Okay."

I grinned. *Good. Finally.* "I'll wait for you to get ready," I said. "We'll leave Tucker here and I'll get him when I drop you off."

"But what about you? You're soaking wet."

"You get ready, and then I'll drive us to my place so I can change."

She gave me a wide-eyed stranger-danger look and I laughed. So *that* was the face she made every time I asked her probing questions on the phone.

"Here." I pulled out my soggy wallet and fished out my ID. "Take a picture of my driver's license and send it to Kristen."

I handed it over and she looked at it. "You really *are* an organ donor."

"And not a creeper or a pirate. I hope you're not disappointed."

She laughed, and I couldn't even take my eyes off her.

She smiled up at me. "Give me a second to get changed."

CHAPTER 11

SLOAN

♪ NAME | GOO GOO DOLLS

This place isn't as crappy as I thought it was going to be," I said, loud enough that Jason could hear me through the door.

Jason lived in a silver Airstream trailer parked behind some music executive's mansion in Calabasas. An Olympic-size pool glistened within ten steps of Jason's front door, surrounded by birds of paradise and waterfalls. The whole place was green.

I could only imagine how much it cost to water everything in the drought. There were penalties for using too much water. My lawn was dead. I'd like to say this was due to my support of water conservation, but my sprinklers were broken and I couldn't afford the fix *or* the water to bring the grass back to life. Whoever owned this place must be loaded.

His trailer was small, but neat and comfortable. No frills. Kind of exactly where I would have expected Jason to live. He was a bit of a minimalist, from what he'd said to me during our talks.

He'd driven us over in his black truck, and that was practical and functional too. It was older but clean. Not like my car. I made a mental note to *never* let Jason in *my* car.

He laughed. "And why were you expecting someplace crappy?" he said from the other side of the bedroom door.

"Because you said Tucker chewed up everything."

I picked up a picture frame from the counter and studied the photo of Jason in thick winter clothes, smiling with his dog. A snowy backdrop as far as the eye could see spilled out behind them. Not my favorite shot of him. I liked the ones where I could see more skin. I set it down hurriedly as he opened the door of his room.

God, he was easy to look at. I felt my face flush. *Again.*

When he'd walked into my kitchen, my body had turned on like a house coming out of a two-year-long power outage. Everything switched on until the entire place was lit and all the appliances were running. Heart, cheeks, lungs, eyes, the tips of my fingers, the butterflies in my stomach, ringing in my ears, weakness in my knees. *All* alive, *all* buzzing with electricity.

He looked from me to the picture frame. "That's in Minnesota," he said, leaning on the counter, his arm almost touching mine. I swallowed hard. He smelled good. *Really* good. Something crisp and clean, like pine and fresh laundry. It made me want to lean in and take a deep breath.

His luggage sat in the small sitting area, and a guitar case rested on a bench by the tiny table. It reminded me how short a time he'd actually been back. He'd flown in, had about an hour to himself, then had gone to meet me.

"Aren't you tired?" I asked, peering over at him. "You just got off a fifteen-hour flight."

"I can sleep just about anywhere. I got enough rest on the plane."

He leaned well inside my personal bubble. I think he did it on purpose. I could actually feel the heat coming off his body. My conservative side, the side that couldn't forget I'd been engaged to another man, wanted me to take a step back. But the side that suspiciously sounded like Kristen ran out of breath yelling at me to hold my ground.

I held my ground.

I was single and was *allowed* to feel like this. I was permitted to flirt and get butterflies when another man stood too close. And I was *definitely* getting butterflies now.

"Are you here permanently? In LA?" I asked, trying to keep my voice from betraying my reaction to his nearness.

"For the moment. They wanted me here for the soundtrack I was working on. My recording studio's here, and it was just easier to coordinate everything with me living locally. Plus, it puts me close for the events I have to attend."

"What events?"

"Well, there's the movie premiere," he said. "And I went to the Grammys."

"You went to the *Grammys*?"

"Yeah, it was kind of a broad industry invite that I got in on," he said dismissively. He looked at my lips. "So, do you like my place?" he asked, somewhat distantly, talking to my mouth.

"I didn't know what to expect. I thought maybe there'd just be a hammock between some trees or something."

He laughed and his piercing blue eyes creased at the corners. I hadn't anticipated those eyes. There were some things photos just couldn't do justice to.

"When my label moved me to LA, they included housing. But I like my trailer. My agent, Ernie, offered a spot on his property. He's got a gym in the pool house and I have free run of the laundry room."

I smiled. "This place is a compound," I said. "Those are what? Thirteen-foot gates? Are you sure you don't want to ride out the zombie apocalypse here?"

He laughed. "I'll give you the gate code in case you want to drop by." He nodded to the back. "Come see the bedroom."

I *was* interested in seeing the whole place. He let me go first and I stood just inside the door and looked around. No bedspread, only gray sheets and a soft-looking blanket folded down at the end. He must sleep hot. Lord knew he put off enough body heat.

Simple beige curtains hung on the windows, and a cell phone charger was plugged in on the nightstand. The room smelled like him, and being in such a personal space made my heart flutter a little. It was weird to talk to someone so much on the phone and then realize he was a real person with nice smells and a *bed*.

Jason had come up behind me, and he leaned into the room with his hands over his head on the door frame. "Look, I got you in my bedroom on the first date," he teased, and I glanced over my shoulder and shot him a look.

"Is that where Tucker sleeps in his little dungeon?" I pointed to a crate wedged between the bed and the wall.

He chuckled. "I wonder how he'll take being back in his crate now that he's been spoiled by sleeping with a beautiful woman for so long."

I turned to him. "Are you just going to flirt shamelessly with me now that you're on this date that you wanted so much?"

"Of course." He grinned.

The room was small, and with him hanging in the doorway, I was backed up to the mattress. With his hands over his head like that, his arm and chest muscles pushed against his T-shirt.

He had *the* most amazing body. He wasn't bulky. He was lithe and toned and he stood easily a foot taller than me. He filled the room with his presence, even from the door.

My eyes flickered down. The bottom of his shirt had ridden up, and I could see a line of hair running down the middle of his stomach into the top of his jeans. My breath hitched, and I looked back up at his face quickly, hoping he hadn't noticed my wandering eyes.

His amused expression told me he *had*.

It didn't escape me that an hour ago I had been completely opposed to meeting him anywhere other than Starbucks, and now, if he took half a step forward, I'd have to sit on his *bed*.

I cleared my throat. "So, what if I hadn't agreed to this date?" I asked, looking up at him.

He gave me a mischievous eyebrow. "Then I was going to go with my backup plan."

"Which was what?"

"Same as my original plan, only with more subterfuge."

"Subterfuge?" I tilted my head.

"Yeah. I was going to take you on the date anyway, let you call it an appointment, and never tell you it was a date the whole time."

I laughed.

He nodded over his shoulder. "Come on. Let's go eat."

~

Jason wanted me to pick where we went, so I took him to a hole-in-the-wall Mexican place I liked down the street from my house. A red-boothed, small restaurant with trumpet-heavy ranchera music playing over the speakers and paintings of matadors on the walls. They gave us a quiet booth in a corner at a table with a sombrero hanging above it.

"I figure you haven't had Mexican in a while," I said. "Australia probably isn't known for its carne asada."

A busboy slid two ice waters in front of us.

"We don't have very good Mexican food in Minnesota," he said. "It's one of my favorite things about LA."

"What else do you like about California?"

"Well, the dog-sitters are hot," he said, winking at me over the laminated menu.

I narrowed my eyes at him playfully as I pulled my vibrating cell phone out of my pocket. "Oh no," I said, looking at the screen. "I have seven missed calls from Kristen. Hold on, it might be about Oliver." I must have not felt it going off when I was in Jason's truck. I pressed the phone to my ear. "Kristen? Is everything okay?"

"Please tell me that you googled Jason."

"What?"

"You *did* google him, right? You know who you're on a date with?"

My stomach dropped. *Oh my God.* I'd sent Kristen a picture of Jason's ID. She'd obviously found him online. Was he a registered sex offender? A *felon*? I looked up at Jason, who eyed me from across the table, looking concerned.

I cleared my throat. "Um...I need to take this. Excuse me for a minute?" I slid out of the booth before he could reply. I practically ran to the ladies' room and locked myself in a stall.

"Okay, I'm alone. What did you find? He wouldn't tell me his last name unless I told him mine, so I couldn't google him!"

My heart pounded. What had I *done*? He knew where I lived and everything. I'd given this stranger my address like an idiot!

I paced inside the stall. I almost deserved to be murdered, I was so stupid.

"You're seriously telling me you don't know who he is? I thought you guys talk like twenty-four seven. How did this never come up?"

"Kristen, *what*?"

"Uh, he's Jaxon Waters? The singer? The one with that 'Wreck of the *Edmund Fitzgerald*' animated viral music video you watched like two hundred times?"

My heart. Stopped. *Dead.*

"*What?*" I breathed.

"If anyone could make that song cool, it's that dude." Kristen snorted. "I'm on his Wikipedia page. Indie rock music. He got famous from that cover. Then his self-produced album went gold, and he got some big record deal. He's doing the entire soundtrack for that movie *The Wilderness Calls* with Jake Gyllenhaal. He got the Best New Artist award at the Grammys last year. Jason Larsen, grew up in Ely, Minnesota, birthday November seventh, six foot one. Mom is Patricia, dad is Paul, a brother named David—how did you of all people not find this shit out? You're like the most paranoid person I know."

I let out a quivering breath. "I mean, he told me he was a musician, but I just thought he played backup or something. He didn't tell me!"

"Wow. Major cyberstalker fail."

Josh spoke up in the background. "Tell her I hope she shaved her legs for this date."

"Yes, you need to get naked with that man," Kristen added.

I fanned my face with my hand. "Oh God. I'm freaking out. How do I act normal now? I have like seven of his songs in my playlist, *right now*. I'm a fan! I'm like a groupie! I cannot be cool, Kristen!"

"Okay, but did you shave your legs?"

"*No!* I *didn't*! I shaved none of the things! Because I'm not getting naked with him, nor did I have any plans to! How can I go back out there, Kristen? I'm going to have a panic attack!"

Jason had just been catapulted from a man I was really into to someone I was literally starstruck by. "I can't breathe. I stole his dog. He sent me flowers," was all I managed to say. My brain was misfiring, shooting off realizations as the information repositioned Jason in my mind.

"Uh-huh. Well, you have nobody to blame but yourself. You should have used the Google. Now get back out there."

"Have fun!" Josh shouted from the background, and they both snickered.

I made a pitiful groaning noise and hung up. Then I googled "Jaxon Waters" and hit Images.

There he was.

There were shots of him in a tuxedo on a red carpet. Then another picture of him sitting on a rock in the woods, playing his guitar. Oh my God. A still frame of him holding a Grammy. A fucking *Grammy*.

I grew up feeding celebrities out of my mom's food truck. They didn't fluster me. I rarely got nervous around them. But Jaxon Waters was different. His music *haunted* me. It spoke to my *soul*. It was ethereal and beautiful and I could not be nonchalant about this.

I came out of the stall with shaking hands and stood over the sink.

"Calm down," I whispered, willing my body to comply. It didn't listen. I think I would have been less panicked if I'd found out I was on a date with an escaped convict.

When I finally walked back out to the table, Jason smiled, a look of relief on his face at seeing me reappear. He'd probably wondered if I'd escaped out a bathroom window by how long I was gone.

"Everything okay?" he asked as I slid into the booth. "Do we need to go?"

"It's fine," I said, my voice a touch too high.

He raised an eyebrow. "You sure? What did Kristen say?"

My mouth had gone dry. I picked up my glass of water and downed it. He watched me with a mix of amusement and concern and I wondered if Jason found women who needed to breathe into their hands and lie down in restaurant booths sexy.

I set my glass down and cleared my throat. "I just got some news."

"What's wrong? Tell me."

"You're Jaxon Waters," I blurted.

The amused smile that crept across his face confirmed my accusation. "Have you heard of me?"

"You said you play *bass*." I glared, and my eyelid twitched ominously.

"I do." He shrugged. "I also play guitar, I sing…" His grin got wider in proportion to my growing eyes.

"But…but I went to your house!" I said breathlessly. "Where was your Grammy?"

Another shrug. "In the pantry?"

"Jason!"

He laughed. "What? It's a trailer. I don't have any shelf space."

Oh my God.

"Why didn't you tell me?" I demanded. "I…I…*why*?"

He'd done this on purpose. He'd purposely sandbagged this. I had been catfished, only the catfish was ridiculously good-looking and famous, and I was actually pretty impressed with what I'd reeled in.

This was too much.

Acting like a lunatic when nervous was my signature move, and I didn't disappoint today. My eyelid dove into a full-fledged twitching rebellion at the stress of the situation. I let out an exasperated sigh and pressed my finger to my eye. My face went either sheet white or bright red. Maybe the colors were rotating. There was no telling. I was so embarrassed. I don't think I could have looked crazier if I tried.

"My eyelid twitches when I'm nervous," I said miserably, trying to explain my weirdness.

Jason studied my face. "Don't you think I'm nervous too?"

I stared at him with one eye.

"I like you. And I get nervous around beautiful women I have crushes on."

Surely he knew this was not even remotely the same thing. The man had a *fanbase*. My face called bullshit and his eyes danced like this was the most fun he'd had all year.

We stared at each other in a Mexican-restaurant standoff of silence, and almost comically, the waitress dropped a basket of chips and salsa between us. It broke the tension and I launched into manic giggling. This made him laugh, and when I snorted, we both lost it.

It took us a minute to get a hold of ourselves.

"Jason, I listen to your music," I said a moment later, biting my lip. "A lot. I love it. Your last album got me through a really rough time in my life."

He wiped at his eyes, still recovering. "And I've eaten the food from your blog. I'm probably a bigger fan of yours than you are of mine."

"I doubt that. And at least I *told* you about my blog."

"Well, you had to or I'd have never let you on my zombie apocalypse survival team."

I scoffed.

"I didn't tell you who I was because it's not a big deal. I was still a bartender up until two years ago. My success is a very new thing, and I just wanted you to get to know me without it influencing what you thought of me. Besides, I'm not *that* famous."

I made a noise that indicated I disagreed. On a fame scale from one to ten, he was probably a solid seven. And anyway, it wasn't what everyone else thought about him that was freaking me out. It was the fact that *I* loved his music so much. God, no wonder I'd loved the sound of his voice from the very first phone call. *Ugh.*

I put my elbow on the table, still holding my twitching eyelid down. "I just need a little while to get used to this idea."

"Do you want me to sing something for you?" He grinned.

"Not unless you want to resuscitate me after."

He laughed. "That bad, huh?"

"Oh yeah. That bad. I may be one of your biggest fans, seriously."

"And yet you had no idea what I looked like," he deadpanned.

"Your viral video is Claymation. And you're not on your album cover! It's just a picture of that weird red-eyed duck."

"A loon?" He grinned. "You could have googled me."

"Come on, who googles pictures of singers? Your appearance has no bearing on your ability to make good music."

"Just like your appearance has no bearing on your ability to be a good dog-sitter?"

"Exactly."

～

By the time our food came, things were almost back to normal—as normal as a first date with your favorite recording artist *could* be.

The margarita I was having was helping immensely.

My strategy for dealing with this new Jaxon development was to try to forget who he was. Jason assured me he didn't get recognized very often, so hopefully that would aid in my attempt. If other people swooned, I was going to swoon in solidarity.

I was glad he hadn't told me. He was right—it might have changed things, mostly because if I had known sooner, my resulting weirdness would have probably scared him off.

"So do I still get one question a day?" he asked, taking a bite of his taco.

"Sure, why not?"

He swallowed and wiped his mouth with a napkin. "What does Kristen say about our date?"

I blanched. "Where to begin? Are you sure you're ready for this? She's pretty vulgar."

He picked up his beer. "I like her already."

"She told me to climb you like a tree."

He practically choked on his Corona.

"I was also advised to shake your branches. I'm afraid to think too much about that one. And all this *before* she knew who you really were."

He grinned. "And now?"

"Let's just say that both her and her husband are rooting for you," I said, talking into my margarita glass.

He looked thoroughly amused.

"She's been sending me texts nonstop for the last half hour," I said.

He nodded at my phone. "What do they say?"

I set my drink down and picked up my cell. "'Ask him if you can touch his guitar.'"

He shook his head. "That's not too bad."

"'Guitar' is in quotes."

His howl of laughter turned heads at the other tables.

"She wants to know if you smell like pine cones and flannel." I tilted my head toward him. "Do you see what I have to put up with?"

He beamed. "When do I get to meet her?"

"Hopefully never. She'll interrogate you the whole time. Then Josh will get you alone on the premise that he needs help grilling or something and he'll make threats about what he'll do to you if you hurt me. You're better off never meeting either of them, trust me."

He laughed. "I can't wait. Just let me know when. But it can't be this weekend, though, I'm going for a short visit to Minnesota on Friday."

"Oh." My face fell a little. "You just got here."

"Are you gonna miss me?" His eyes sparkled.

I held in my smile. "Who's watching Tucker while you're gone?"

"I was going to take him with me—unless my dog-sitter's available." He grinned. "But he's coming with me on tour, though."

I scrunched my forehead. "You have a tour? When is *that*?"

"June first. Four months, fifty cities."

He was leaving in *three weeks*? For *four months*? Well, *that* sucked.

"Will you come visit me when I'm on the road?" he asked.

"Right now, I'm just trying to make it through this meal without hyperventilating."

~

"Now, on to our next adventure," Jason said after dinner, starting the engine of his truck.

"Where's that?" I asked, rolling down my window.

"Home Depot."

"Home Depot? For what?"

"For parts to fix your sink," he said, backing out of the parking space.

I shook my head. "No. Definitely no."

"No?" He glanced at me.

"No. I can't let you fix my sink. That's ... just no."

He smiled over the steering wheel. "You'd rather let a stranger do it? You, who wouldn't even tell *me* where you lived until your kitchen was an inch deep in water?" He gave me a comical wide-eyed look and then turned back to the road with a grin.

I narrowed my eyes.

"Also, bonus, if you let me do it, Tucker stays over longer." He smirked, knowing he had me.

"Fine," I said, putting my mouth into my palm, not wanting him to see my smile.

"Anything else that needs fixing?" he asked.

"The whole house," I mumbled.

"It's not in good shape?"

The house had begun to feel like a sandcastle at high tide. It was crumbling around me.

"No. When Brandon and I bought it, he was going to fix it up. He was good at that stuff..." I said, trailing off, not knowing if I should be talking about my dead fiancé on a date. But Jason's expression stayed neutral.

"Give me a list. I'll do it," he said, turning onto Roscoe Boulevard.

I smiled. "You're a handyman in addition to being Jaxon Waters?"

"We're self-sufficient in Ely. I could build you a whole new house if you wanted. So what do you need done?"

"Jason..."

"What? I like fixing things. Besides, my dog likes you. I bet he'd like to come over. Come to think of it, *I* like you and *I'd* like to come over too."

His unrelenting flirting was going to give me a heart attack. But I couldn't really argue with his reasoning. The pipe *did* need fixing. Josh did two day shifts at the station, so if he had work tomorrow that would leave me without a kitchen sink until at least Wednesday— that was provided he dropped everything on his day off to come help me, which I hated. And frankly, I couldn't afford to pay for a professional to do it. I already lived paycheck to paycheck.

Brandon's fire station had set up a GoFundMe for me after Brandon died. That had helped bridge the gap until I was up to working again. I made okay money doing astronaut cats from the volume alone—I'd always been fast. But the ancient water heater just needed replacing and the month before that, the air-conditioning unit broke. Now my kitchen had flooded, and I wasn't sure if the floors were going to survive the damage. If I had to pay for a new kitchen floor, I wouldn't be able to pay my mortgage this month.

I should have sold the house after Brandon died. I couldn't afford it on a single income. It was too big for me and too broken. But I just couldn't bring myself to do it, the same way I couldn't bring myself to empty his closet or clean out the garage.

"Okay. But can I pay for your time?" I asked. "And I'll obviously cover the materials."

"I don't want you to pay me. Oh, which reminds me." He reached across me to open the glove box. His arm brushed my knee, and the sides of his lips twitched. He handed me an envelope. "Here. The money for watching Tucker. I know I don't have your receipts yet, but I guesstimated. And I added a reward."

I held the envelope and looked at it. I needed what was in it.

But now taking it felt weird. It was one thing to accept it from a stranger whose dog I was watching, a man who was taking Tucker away from me. That was a business arrangement. It was something else entirely to accept money from a guy I was kind of dating and who wanted to help me with repairs on my house.

I handed it back to him. "Why don't you keep this? You can fix the sink and we'll call it even."

He didn't reach for it. "I insist you take it. It's nonnegotiable." Something final in his voice told me the discussion was over. "As for materials, you have a lot of tools and parts in the garage. I doubt I'll need much else. I can get a lot done with what's already there."

I didn't reply. He parked the truck in the Home Depot lot and put on the brake. "We're here."

"You don't think this is a little weird? You fixing my sink?"

"The weird thing would be me not fixing it knowing that I can. Come on," he said, opening his door. "I wanna get my hands on your pipes."

Jason went through Home Depot with a surgical accuracy that told me he knew his way around a home improvement project. At the self-checkout stand, he wouldn't let me pay. "Part of our date."

"No, it's not," I objected, trying to swipe the items from him.

He pivoted and held everything over his head, out of my reach. I crossed my arms and glared at him. His blue eyes twinkled, and I marveled for the hundredth time at how handsome he was. His pictures had been great, but he was so much better set in motion.

"If I'd taken you to a carnival and won you a stuffed animal, that would be part of the date, right? Or if I'd brought flowers or paid for a movie?"

"Yes. But that's typical date stuff. Buying me parts to fix my sink isn't."

"So you want me to be typical?" He grinned.

He had this way of backing me into my own corners. He turned his back on me and continued his purchase, shooting a victorious look over his shoulder as the receipt printed out.

"One more stop," he said, grabbing the bag.

"What now? Are you going to change my oil or something?"

"I *can* change your oil if you want." He laughed, then took my hand and wove his fingers through mine as he walked me out of the store.

I *died*. I had to draw on some internal strength women probably use for childbirth just to close my fingers around his, because his touch made me lose control over the use of my hand.

Jaxon Waters is holding my hand.

I didn't even remember the walk to the truck. I think I blacked out.

"You're going to like the entertainment portion of this date," Jason said a few minutes later, pulling up to a gas station. "Let's go inside and get some dessert."

We made our ice cream selections from the deep freezer, and then I poured myself a small decaf and hovered over the coffee station, eyeing the individual flavored creamers. Jason came up behind me as I took seven hazelnuts and slipped them into my purse. I turned to him and he arched his eyebrows at me.

"What? They come with the coffee. And I love the little creamers. I keep them in my purse for coffee emergencies."

"Coffee emergencies?" He smiled down on me.

He was back in my personal space again. Just slightly closer than most people stood. It made me feel a little breathless.

"Yeah," I swallowed. "You can never be too prepared."

"And do you have a lot of these emergencies?" he asked. His eyes moved to my lips again, and he cocked his head a little like he was studying them.

"At least one a day."

He came back up and grinned. "Come on."

He took my hand as he led me to the register. He bought our desserts and my coffee, and he asked for twenty dollars' worth of lottery scratchers.

Once we were back in the truck, Jason drove us around to the car wash. "Ready?" he asked, leaning out the window to punch a code into the kiosk.

"Ready for what?"

"The entertainment. Rainbow car wash."

I laughed. "Oh my God, I *love* rainbow car washes! It's been so long since I've done one!"

"You don't wash your car?" he asked, driving in. Once the tires were taken over by the track, he leaned back in his seat and opened his ice cream.

I pulled the lid off of my sorbet and started poking at it with my spoon. "You haven't seen my car."

"The Corolla? I saw it in your garage when I was looking for the shop vac."

"Well, then you understand why I don't bother to wash it," I said, looking up at the windshield as water started spraying over the truck. The long strips of fabric began slapping back and forth across the hood and the nostalgic citrus smell of the underbody wash drifted in through the vents.

"We need a soundtrack for this." He fiddled with the radio. A mewing Lola Simone song came on and he quickly changed the channel. I hated her music too. Too Courtney Love for me.

He settled on KROQ, and when the foamy rainbow soap started to pour over the truck, we glanced at each other and smiled. We held the look for a long moment before staring back out through the glass.

I was so sensitive to him sitting there I could barely focus. It almost felt like neither of us was actually watching the car wash. Like our eyes were there, but our attention was on each other. At least *mine* was.

When the truck was done, Jason parked in front of the gas station and handed me ten dollars' worth of scratchers. "If we win anything, we decide what to do with the money together," he said, digging in his cup holder and producing a penny to give me.

"How do you think of this stuff?" I smiled, rubbing my penny on the scratcher. "I think this is the best date I've ever been on. First the guy saves me from a flood. Then he reveals he's my favorite recording artist. He gives me an envelope full of money and buys me hardware, followed by a show and some gambling."

"I could think of a few ways we could make it even better." He gave me a devilish grin.

"Just so you know, I don't even kiss on the first date," I said, finishing my scratcher. I won two dollars and held the card up to show him with a smirk.

"And here I am, getting the upgraded car wash for *nothing*."

I laughed.

I couldn't believe what a good time I was having. I always figured my first date after Brandon would be a painful milestone. A Band-Aid to tear off. But it wasn't. Jason made it easy.

Jason made it a lot of things.

"Can I see you tomorrow?" he asked.

I smiled. "You want to see me again?"

"I don't even want to drop you off at home tonight."

I blushed. *Again.*

But then I remembered what day tomorrow was. It was the two-year anniversary of Brandon's death. The day we'd taken him off life support. I had an agenda for tomorrow, a list of positive things I'd decided to do in his memory.

"I can't. I have plans tomorrow. How about the day after?"

He looked slightly disappointed, but he nodded. "Okay, the day after, then. It's a date."

I didn't object to him calling it a date, and he looked triumphantly back at the scratchers in his lap. He won five dollars.

"So what do we do with the money?" he asked.

I bit my lip, thinking. His eyes moved to my mouth again, and I smiled. "With seven dollars? How about we buy a chew toy for Tucker?"

"Great idea. We could take him to PetSmart on our next date." He put the scratchers into the drink holder.

A guitar intro I recognized came through the speakers. "Oh, I love this song," I said. "'Name' by the Goo Goo Dolls, right?"

He picked up my raspberry sorbet. "Yup. Can I try this?" he asked.

I nodded at his carton. "Give me yours."

We sat listening to the music and eating each other's ice cream. His was mint chocolate chip. We used each other's spoons. Something about knowing that the little plastic utensil had been in his mouth made my heart pound.

I couldn't believe this day.

We stared at each other unapologetically as we sat there. My eyes traveled from his sharp blue irises to his lips. I wondered if his beard would tickle if he kissed me. I'd never kissed anyone with a beard before. I moved down to his throat and watched his Adam's apple bob as he swallowed. I saw the pulse of his neck and the dip of his collarbone, the way his chest strained against his shirt, the rhythmic rise and fall of his breathing.

By the time I looked back up, neither of us was moving. I sat with my spoon upside down on my tongue, all the ice cream in my mouth long gone. He held his carton in his lap and just stared at me.

Jason had this way of looking at me. It reminded me of how people used to look at my paintings, back before the astronaut cats. A focused fascination that leaned in and searched the brushstrokes. He didn't even blink. It made me feel self-conscious, except I was pretty sure it meant he liked what he saw, which was good. Because I liked what I saw too. A *lot*.

And then suddenly he was moving.

Without breaking eye contact, he put his sorbet onto the dash. He took my spoon and my ice cream out of my hands and his fingers brushed mine in a split second of electricity before he set the carton down somewhere. Then he slid across the seat and slipped my cheeks into his warm palms, his fingers raked through the back of my hair, and he *kissed* me.

He barely touched me. Just a light brushing of his lips against mine, the slightest feel of his breath on my face.

It shot through me in milliseconds. The static crackling between us ignited, and I did exactly what Kristen said I should.

I climbed him like a tree.

CHAPTER 12

JASON

♪ ELECTRIC LOVE | BØRNS

Get a room!"

A hand thumped on the hood of my truck and Sloan scrambled off my lap and pressed her back to the passenger door with wide eyes. We sat there and stared at each other, panting.

Holy *shit*.

"Jason, I think you need to take me home," she breathed, biting her lip.

I wanted to take her home all right. I wanted to take her home and carry her into her bedroom. But unfortunately that wasn't what she meant. "Are you sure?"

She nodded.

I dragged my eyes to the windshield and got the truck started.

The tension between us on the drive home was like the arrow of a compass, turning to true north, the same way it had felt in the car wash, like it was work to *not* look at her. I kept glancing over at her, and every time I did, I caught her looking back at me.

"I don't think it's a good idea for you to walk me to the door," she said when I pulled into her driveway. "Seriously. Don't get out. Like, at all."

I put the truck in park. "What about your sink?"

Her cheeks were red. "You can fix it later or something. Stay here while I get Tucker." She let herself out of the truck in such a hurry that her sweater snagged on the lock. She spun to unhook herself and I reached out and put a hand on her wrist. "Sloan—"

"I don't trust myself around you right now," she said quickly.

I smiled for a long moment at her wide eyes and pulled her sweater free. She hurried to the house. She dropped her keys *twice* before she got the door open.

When she came back outside, I waited until she was almost to the truck and I got out. She stopped dead in her tracks and let go of Tucker's collar. He ran up to me and I pointed. "Get in the car, buddy." He jumped into the front seat and I closed the door, not taking my eyes off her.

Her motion sensor lights weren't working. She looked like an angel in the dim streetlight. The sky was dark and cloudless. No stars. Just her, her hair like a halo. The freeway breathed somewhere off in the distance and a breeze carried the faint scent of dirty, hot pavement.

I didn't want to smell pavement. I wanted to smell *her*.

I wanted to get close enough to breathe her in again. I walked toward her and for every step I took, she took a step backward.

"I had a really good time tonight," she said, biting her lip. Her back bumped into the garage and she looked up at me like a rabbit frozen in the grass near a fox, trying to decide if it should stay still or bolt.

I stopped two feet short, not wanting to corner her. "I'd like to kiss you good night, Sloan."

She didn't move, but her eyes dropped to my mouth.

The air between us felt charged.

The imprint of her still lingered on my skin. I could feel the press of her thighs, the weight of her soft body. Her perfume clung to me like fingers twisted into my shirt, drawing me toward her again.

"Come here," I said, my voice low.

The command activated her. She *flew* at me.

I caught her in a swirl of her floral scent, and she practically climbed me. My lips were on hers in a second. Warm and wet, mint and raspberries on her tongue. The smell of her skin drove me fucking insane. Sweet honeysuckle drifted up around me and ensconced us.

I hooked a hand under the leg she had hiked up against me and lifted her so she straddled my waist. She dragged her hands through my hair and when she gasped, I let her come up for air and trailed my mouth along her jaw and down her neck.

She tilted her head back and let out a soft moan and I almost lost it.

That guy at the gas station had been right, we *did* need a room.

I staggered us toward her front door. Then suddenly she was wiggling away from me, her feet back on the ground. She put her hand to my chest, making space between us. She panted and her wide eyes flickered back down to my lips, and it looked for a second like she might reconsider, but instead she launched herself off me, turned, and tore full speed into the house.

The door slammed, the bolt lock clicked behind her, followed by the rake of the chain, and I stood alone in her walkway for a whiplashed moment in my rumpled shirt, my hair a mess, catching my breath.

Jesus *Christ*. What the fuck just happened?

It was like I'd been sucked into a tornado made of animal

magnetism, tossed around, and then spit out alone in front of her house.

I had to adjust the front of my pants.

Goddamn, this woman had me. It was more than just physical. She fucking *had* me. I didn't even want to leave. I felt like scratching on her door like a dog wanting to be let in.

Tucker whined at the house through the open window of my truck.

"Yeah, I know, buddy," I breathed. "I wish I were in there too."

I drove home and poured myself a bourbon.

Sloan.

She liked my music. It hadn't even occurred to me how much that mattered until it came out. I wanted her to like it. Her opinion meant something. I wanted her to like everything about me.

This wasn't just some woman. I'd suspected it when we'd been talking on the phone, but now I knew it. This was big, different from anything I'd ever felt. It was like the first time I'd picked up a guitar, that same sense of certainty.

I stripped down for bed, climbed under the covers, and sat up against my headboard, my cell in my hand. Tucker was always the safest topic. I started typing.

Jason: Tucker misses you.

She didn't make me wait.

Sloan: He's just claustrophobic in that lunch box. Let him out.

I laughed.

Jason: I really enjoyed our date.
Sloan: Me too.

Then I decided to take a risk.

Jason: You're not mad I kissed you? I know you have rules
about first dates.

A long pause ensued before she replied. When the dots started
to jump, I sat up to wait for her text to come through, throwing
back the rest of my whiskey.

Sloan: I'm beginning to think the rules don't apply to you.
Good night, Jason.

CHAPTER 13

JASON

♪ MAKE YOU MINE | PUBLIC

I couldn't get Sloan out of my head, which was unfortunate, because I also couldn't get her on the phone. She didn't return my good-morning text until 1:00 in the afternoon, and when she did, all I got was a quick smiley face.

I unpacked and did laundry. Had a phone call with my new publicist, Pia, to schedule a meeting. I had a ton of media to do before my upcoming tour. TV, radio, magazine interviews. Sirius XM wanted an a cappella recording by the end of the week for its Coffee House channel. *Saturday Night Live* was biting, and I had to audition a drummer for the tour. The one I'd used on my album wasn't able to travel. Then I'd have to do rehearsals right up until hitting the road.

The next few weeks were going to be exhausting. Today was such a waste. I had nothing scheduled and I could have been with Sloan the whole day.

It had taken me twenty-nine years to meet someone I was this into, and when I finally did, it could not have come at a worse time. In three weeks I'd be gone for four months.

I'd meant what I said, that she should come see me on the road. But I knew even now that it wouldn't be enough. *Yesterday* hadn't been enough. I was already used to talking to her and texting her constantly and neither held a candle to seeing her now that I'd met her. Going cold turkey today felt like withdrawals.

I played with Tucker for an hour, sitting on a reclining chair by the hot tub, tossing a tennis ball into the pool. He seemed depressed, and I actually debated taking him to Starbucks for one of those puppuccino things to cheer him up. I think he missed Sloan, a sentiment I was quickly beginning to share.

I shot a text off to her with a picture of Tucker looking sad, his head on his paws. She didn't reply for over an hour.

Sloan: Awww. I miss him. Give him a kiss for me.

I typed, smiling.

Jason: He says for ME to give YOU a kiss from HIM. So what are you doing today?
Sloan: Just running errands.

It didn't feel like errands. She was too distracted today, almost evasive.

For a brief moment, I wondered if she was dating someone else. *Instant* jealousy.

We'd never discussed whether or not she was dating. She'd been so opposed to dating *me* I'd just assumed she wasn't on the market. But what if I was wrong?

Jason: What kind of errands?

She left me on read.

I used the gym in the pool house, trying to distract myself from my wandering thoughts about Sloan dating other people. Now I was shamelessly grateful she found my stage persona so impressive. I needed all the advantages I could get.

A few hours later I was sitting on a lawn chair in front of my trailer trying out a new capo on my guitar when Ernie made his way across the yard.

"How's my favorite squatter?" He tossed me a beer and plopped in the chair next to me.

Tucker was so depressed he didn't even raise his head to greet him.

Ernie loosened his tie. "Spent my morning with the bloodsucking lawyers. She wants her alimony adjusted."

I opened the beer with a *pith*. "Which wife is this?"

"Four." He grinned. "But I brought wife number five with me just to piss her off."

I chuckled.

He pulled his shoes and socks off and put his feet in the grass. "Excited about the tour?"

The funny thing was, I *had* been excited about it. But now?

"Hey, what do you think about taking girlfriends on tour?" I asked.

"Girlfriend? When did you get a damn girlfriend?" He took a drink of his beer.

"I didn't. It's just someone I like. I like her a lot, actually."

"I thought you wanted to be famous," he said. "Now you wanna have a girlfriend instead?"

I laughed. "What, I can't do both?"

He leaned back in his chair. "Nope. Not if you wanna do either thing well. This is not the time to be anchoring yourself with a girlfriend, my friend."

I shrugged and took a sip of beer. "I've headlined tours before."

"Not like this you haven't. You're touring with a label now. Your entire life is about to change, and in ways you can't even fucking imagine. Girlfriends are jealous and distracting, and they suck the energy from your soul. Trust me on this. You won't even have time for *you*."

He swatted at a bee buzzing around him. "Who is she anyway? Monique or Monica or whoever the fuck? Oh God, tell me it's not Lola. Man, you really screwed the pooch on that one—no pun intended. I mean, I get it, she's fucking hot, but damn is she nuts." He took a swallow of beer and looked over at me. "She still calling?"

I laughed a little. "Yup."

"She's never gonna give it up. You're gonna get a severed nipple in the mail, wake up chained to a bed in her basement."

I snorted. "Not funny."

He tipped his beer at me. "You hear she put a golf club through Kanye's windshield last week? Climbed the hood and then pissed into the crack in the glass. She's gone fucking *unhinged*. Talented as shit but completely off the deep end."

"Yeah, I saw that." I shook my head. "What the hell do you think happened to her?"

He scoffed. "She's a superstar, this business happened. The price of fame. If you let them, they'll bleed you for every damn drop, and once you're dry, they try fucking your corpse."

I looked over at him. "Do you think it's drugs?"

"Drugs, alcohol, a mental fucking breakdown. Who knows? She's been circling the drain for a while if you want my opinion. She's always been a bit of a paparazzi whore, a touch of Lindsay Lohan. It's a goddamn shame she turned out like this, though. What a waste."

I blew a breath out through my nose. I had to agree about the waste thing—my current situation with her notwithstanding. Lola was brilliant. A lyrical *genius*. I never met anyone that musically talented in my *life*. "You know she plays like seven instruments? And has a four-octave vocal range. Fucking effortless." I shook my head. "We got along too. She was cool—I *liked* her."

He snorted. "I bet you did. This is what happens when you mistake creative chemistry for *actual* chemistry. I did that once and ended up married to wife number three. Worst nine days of my life."

I scoffed. "Well, to say I regret it at this point would be an understatement."

I shook my head, looking out over the pool. I'd spent a week with Lola at her beach house writing, and she'd been perfectly fine the whole time. Focused, polite. Charming even. We'd hit it off immediately. We'd had some drinks to celebrate finishing the soundtrack, and one thing led to another—then it was like a switch flipped. Keeping me up until 5:00 in the morning while she wrote gibberish on legal pads, dragging me out to the beach to swim naked, not eating. Then sleeping for a whole day, and I couldn't get her out of bed.

I shook my head again. "I was so worried about her I'd called her manager to come get her. That *really* pissed her off. He got there and she completely lost her shit, started throwing furniture off the balcony."

Ernie snorted. "Well, to be fair, that guy's a dick." He bobbed his head. "Actually so is Kanye."

I laughed a little.

The day after the furniture thing, the harassment started, and once it started, it didn't stop. I didn't know what the hell to do about it. She was relentless. Calling all hours of the night, crying and screaming into my voicemail, then calling back to apologize, texting nonstop, showing up at my recording studio and causing scenes when I wouldn't buzz her in. Nothing I did would make her back off. I'd resorted to ignoring her, hoping she'd eventually get bored, but all she ever got was new phone numbers.

"God, what was I thinking?" I mumbled.

"You *weren't*. And that *song*. I don't know if I should feel sorry for you or congratulate you for your sexual prowess." Ernie held up an index finger. "You fucked her *one time*, and she's immortalized it in the Top Ten." He sat back and laughed into his beer.

My jaw flexed. "I'm glad *somebody* thinks it's funny."

Lola had written a fucked-up, piece-of-shit song about us having sex on a beach. It was everywhere. It had even popped up in the truck with Sloan during the car wash.

She didn't use my real name. She called me "Snow Bird," and she'd never publicly confirmed it was about me, but it made me fucking *furious*. The thing was like a leaked sex tape set to music. I grimaced even thinking about it. That's the moment when my concern for her finally turned to irritation. It had been half a year of this shit now, and I was officially over it.

Ernie undid the top button of his shirt. "So when did you meet this girl you're thinking of taking on tour?"

"Two weeks ago. I saw her for the first time yesterday."

He sat up. "Are you fucking *insane*?"

I shrugged. "What? I like her."

He set his beer down and faced me. "Here's the deal. Listen closely because I'm about to tell you something that took me five marriages to figure out. It takes a woman six months to show you her crazy. Six months, my friend. I don't recommend *ever* taking a girlfriend on tour, but if you absolutely must, it should be someone you've known longer than ten minutes."

I laughed.

"I'm not kidding. Listen to me, you're thinking like Jason right now. Jason likes this girl and Jason wants to take her on tour and Jason's all fucking twitterpated. You cannot be Jason at this point in your career. You need to be *Jaxon*. Jaxon is a stone-cold mother-fucker who wants to sell *records*. Jaxon doesn't have time for the emotional baggage that comes with that shit. Fame is a jealous mistress. She doesn't like to share." He shook his head. "Do *not* ask that woman to come with you. In fact, you should probably stop seeing her."

"Yeah, I'm not going to do that." I tipped my beer into my mouth.

He sighed. "Well, I can't say that surprises me. You're gonna do what you're gonna do. And what do I know, right?" He picked up his beer and stopped with it halfway to his mouth. "Just please, use a fucking NDA and condoms. Don't end up like that last idiot. What a fucking shit show."

I chuckled. "Still pissed about what's-his-face, huh?"

"Hey, *I* fired *him*."

I laughed. I loved Ernie. He was one of the best agents in the industry. He'd been a big-name musician himself in the eighties, so he'd seen it all. He was a little cynical when it came to women, though.

I checked my phone. Sloan still hadn't texted. I stared out over the pool. "This girl feels different."

"They all fucking feel different. See if you feel the same way next year when you've been on the overseas leg of your tour for six months and she's either back here riding your ass or with you on the road and riding your ass there. You do not need that shit, I'm telling you."

I drew my brows down. "Wait, what? What overseas tour?"

He gave me a raised eyebrow. "Didn't you get the email with the dates? Eh, Christ, my assistant is shit." He shook his head. "They're extending your tour to the UK. Adding two more months here, eight months there. Pia's working on the media blasts now. You'll be home for the holidays for five weeks." He looked over at me. "You're welcome for that, by the way. They wanted you singing in Paris for their Christmas thing and I told them to go fuck themselves so you could see your family. They might even keep that promise, though I wouldn't count on it," he mumbled. "They wouldn't put it in writing. Then you're off to Dublin and London and wherever the fuck else." He tipped his beer at me. "Congratulations and long live the queen."

I sat back in my chair with my beer between my knees. "Jesus. Fourteen months on the road?" I'd never done more than three without a long break between.

"I told you. Not a good time to have a girlfriend. They're gonna work you to within an inch of your life. You said you wanna be Don Henley famous and this is definitely the label to get you there, but they do *not* fuck around."

I dragged a hand down my mouth. Well, it was what I wanted. I'd dreamed of making it since I was five and I'd worked my ass off to get here. Ernie was right, though, the timing sucked. The timing *really* sucked.

He glanced at his watch. "I gotta get going." He stood and turned to me. "Hey, I don't mean to be a downer about the girlfriend thing. I'm sure it'll all work out and you'll ride happily into the sunset. I've just been around the block a few times and I've seen how hard this business is on relationships." He slapped my back. "But you guys are different. You two are gonna be fine. Just don't take her on tour."

I laughed, and Ernie made his way back to the house, his shoes dangling from his fingers. "Don't take her on tour, Jaxon!" he yelled over his shoulder.

Fuck, I didn't see how I could even if I wanted to. Fourteen months, minus the little break for the holidays—that was over a year on the road. That was a commitment. A *huge* commitment. A leave-your-life-behind commitment.

But I was getting ahead of myself. At the moment I couldn't even get a damn text back.

For the next few hours I just fiddled with my guitar, keeping my phone close in case Sloan called—which she didn't. Finally at 8:00 I bit the bullet and I just called her, even though she hadn't responded to my last text.

It went to voicemail.

Now I felt bad for every woman I'd ever left hanging, waiting for a phone call. This shit sucked.

Tucker and I were quite the pair. I was brooding and irritable and he wouldn't get up except to raise his head occasionally and whine.

When my phone finally rang at 10:30, I jumped for it. It was Sloan. Any thoughts of giving her a hard time for making me wait all day flew out the window. "Hey, you're alive." I smiled into my phone.

But there was no reply. Then I heard crying.

I stood. "Sloan? Are you okay?"

"Jason." She sniffed.

She was drunk. No mistaking the slur in her voice.

"Sloan, where are you?"

"Home."

I breathed a sigh of relief that she wasn't driving or somewhere unsafe.

"Jason? I was thinking about you today."

I felt the weight I'd carried all day in my chest lift. "I was thinking about you today too," I said gently.

"You don't want me, okay?"

"What?"

"You don't. Trust me, you don't. I'm messy. I'm a mess. I'm in an in-between."

I smiled softly. "I like your mess."

She didn't reply.

"Sloan?"

"Can you come over?"

I was in motion before she finished her sentence. I grabbed a backpack and started throwing things into it, cradling the phone with my shoulder. "I'm on my way. Sloan? You have to unlock the front door. Do it now, while I'm on the phone."

"Mmmkay," she said. A few moments later I heard the sound of a bolt lock being turned.

"I'm getting in my truck now. I'll be there in ten minutes." Tucker jumped in the cab with an enthusiasm that could only come from knowing where we were headed.

"Jason?" she said as I pulled down the driveway. She was crying again. "You make me want to cook for you."

I smiled at the compliment. I understood what that meant to her to say that. Then the line went dead.

She didn't answer when I called back.

Ten minutes later I pulled into her driveway and jogged to the front porch. Tucker had his nose pressed into the crack of the door, and when it opened, he tore into the house like he was retrieving a duck. But I stopped in the doorway with my mouth open.

The living room looked like a tornado had gone through it. Black trash bags everywhere and stacks of men's clothing strewn all over the floor. A knocked-over lamp and hangers in a pile, men's shoes scattered on the carpet.

Brandon's clothes.

A tumbler sat in a small clear spot in the middle of the mess with an empty bottle of tequila and wads of balled-up tissues next to it.

I followed Tucker's excited noises through a bedroom and into an adjacent bathroom. Sloan lay crumpled by the toilet on a white floor mat, her cell phone next to her. I crouched beside her and put a hand on her shoulder. "Sloan? Can you hear me?"

She groaned, but she didn't open her eyes. I sighed and scratched my beard. *Completely* wasted.

I got a damp washcloth and cleaned her face. She'd been sick at least once. I flushed the toilet and wiped the seat with toilet paper.

She'd thrown up in her hair. I lifted her and moved her to rest against the bathtub, pushing her shower curtain aside. A cotton ball was taped to the inside of her elbow like she'd had blood taken. I peeled that off and threw it away. Jesus, what had she been doing today?

I managed to wash her hair with a cup by letting it fall over the lip into the tub. Tucker sat in the bathroom doorway watching the activity. He seemed to know I was helping her. At one point she started to cough, and I turned her to the toilet and held her hair back while she threw up again.

She muttered some apologies, vaguely aware I was there. Then she went back under.

I towel-dried her hair and brushed it back as best I could, pulling it into a messy ponytail and carrying her to bed. She nuzzled her face into my neck and clutched my shirt and my heart pounded. I had to laugh. Even sloppy drunk, this woman had me.

Tucker jumped up and snuggled next to her as I tucked her in. She threw an arm around him and hugged him to her with a soft, "Tucker…"

No wonder he was disappointed to be home with me. If I got to sleep like that every night, I'd be pissed to be back with me too.

I walked through the house and locked up, turning off lights and collecting the empty bottle and tumbler, stepping around piles of her dead fiancé's personal effects. I got a bucket from the garage and a glass of water for her and left them by the bed. I collected her phone from the bathroom floor to plug into the charger on her nightstand, dropping a few pills next to her water for the morning. She'd need them.

Afterward I went out to my truck and got the parts for her sink. I went about fixing it so I could wash the dishes, checking back in on her when it was done. She slept peacefully.

A large photograph of Sloan hung over her bed. I couldn't stop looking at it. It was a portrait of her from the side, naked and balancing on the balls of her feet, with her tattooed arm covering her breasts. It looked like a professional photo, one from a tattoo magazine. Maybe she'd done modeling before. God knows she was good-looking enough. It was a fantastic shot.

Pictures lined her dresser. Mostly her and another woman, who I assumed was Kristen. Sloan looked like the colorful one of the two, even though I knew she was more conservative than her friend. One frame showed them at Disneyland wearing Mickey Mouse ears. Another was them outside the Pantages Theatre with a *Wicked* poster behind them.

There were photos of Brandon too. I recognized him from the picture on *The Huntsman's Wife*. He'd been a good-looking guy. He and Sloan had matched.

He had a Marine Corps tattoo on his forearm. In one picture he

wore a T-shirt that read BURBANK FIRE DEPARTMENT on it. There
was a photo of him with Sloan on a beach, standing in the surf.
Another one in a Tough Mudder frame showed him with Sloan,
racing bibs pinned to their shirts. She wore knee-high socks and
pigtails, smiling, covered in mud.

It was ridiculous to feel jealous of a man who'd been dead for
two years, but I did. I wondered how I measured up. I was a very
different person than he was. Just from these photos, I could see
we had lived very different lives.

I went back out to the living room and lay down on the couch
to spend the night in case she needed my help.

Who was I kidding? I was staying because I wanted to stay.

Something must have really affected her today, and I wondered
if I had anything to do with it. She'd said she'd been thinking
about me. I thought about what she said earlier on the phone,
that she was in an in-between. I didn't care where she was.

I wanted to be there with her.

CHAPTER 14

SLOAN

♪ MAYBE YOU'RE THE REASON | THE JAPANESE HOUSE

I woke up wishing I had died in my sleep. My head felt like a tomato that had been dropped from a second-story building.

I felt blindly along my nightstand for my phone to check the time. My eyes were puffy from crying, and my fingers knocked into a glass of water. I cracked an eye open.

Two Advils sat on the nightstand. My phone was on the charger at 100 percent. A bucket was on the floor next to the bed.

I prayed it had been Kristen. I scoured my blank, foggy, hungover memory for a drunken call to Kristen. Hell, I'd even settle for Josh. But then I saw Tucker curled up on the other side of the bed and I groaned. I looked at my last call, squinting at the impossibly bright screen. I'd drunk dialed Jason.

I. Drunk. Dialed. *Jason.*

I leaned back onto my pillow and put an arm over my face.

He wouldn't have left his dog here. At least I didn't *think* he would have since he'd just gotten him back, so I was pretty sure Jason was somewhere in the house.

I sat up gingerly, trying not to jostle my head. I downed the water and the pills, holding the glass with both hands. Then I stumbled to the bathroom and took the longest pee of my life. I brushed my teeth three times, practically drank mouthwash, and turned on the shower. When I went to pull my hair from its ponytail, I realized with horror that it was damp.

Someone had washed my hair.

Jason had washed my hair.

Sweet Jesus, just let me die.

After I'd showered, just to prolong the inevitable awkward first encounter with Jason since the hair washing, I turned on the faucet and ran a bubble bath.

Thank God for my new water heater.

I folded a cold wet washcloth over my eyes and sat in the tub with Tucker curled up on the shaggy bathroom mat.

Someone tapped on the door.

"Sloan? Mind if I come in? I have your coffee."

Jason.

The lock on my bathroom door was broken, like every other stupid freaking thing in the house. *Ugh.*

"The door's unlocked," I mumbled. The bubbles had me covered from the neck down. I dragged the washcloth from my eyes and lolled my head toward the door.

Jason let himself in, leading with a Starbucks cup. "I figured you wouldn't want to wait for this," he said, looking at the wall.

"Thank you," I rasped. "You can look. I'm covered."

He turned to me and put the coffee in my hand. Then, instead of leaving, he put the toilet seat lid down and sat on it, grinning at me.

I smelled the top of the cup. I didn't care what kind it was. It was coffee. I felt a caffeine headache lurking behind my hangover and I'd take anything. I took a sip, closing my eyes. Sweet nectar of the gods, it was *my drink*! A triple grande vanilla latte. How did he know?

"I saw an old cup by your easel. The drink was written on the outside," he explained. "When I heard the shower go on, I ran out to get it for you so it would still be hot."

I think I fell just a little bit in love with him in that moment. I got a murky vision of telling our grandchildren about the day Grandma almost drank herself to death and Grandpa saved her with espresso.

"This is the best thing I've ever tasted," I said, my voice husky in a way that told me I'd been vomiting.

"How are you feeling?"

Deathly? Mortified? Heartsick?

"I've felt better."

Jason wore a gray Muse T-shirt and jeans. He leaned forward with his elbows on his knees, his sky-blue eyes searching my face. I was puffy and hungover and this talented, sexy man had just brought me my favorite coffee after spending a night washing barf out of my hair.

Jaxon Waters washed barf out of my hair.

I was too sick for the embarrassment to truly settle in my bones. I accepted this information with a shallow understanding of how fucked up it all was and the knowledge that I'd dwell on it obsessively later while applying the appropriate mortification.

This was the end for us, I was sure of it. He had probably stuck around to make sure I didn't choke to death on my own vomit. Now that he'd seen that I was alive, he'd collect his dog and leave, and I'd never see him again.

I was a disaster, damaged, a hot mess, and now he truly knew it. My living room was covered in my dead fiancé's clothing, because yes, after two years I *still* had all his clothes. I'd called

Jason while sloppy drunk and said God only knew what. What was there to like?

"I'll make you some breakfast," he said, pushing up on his knees. "Take your time."

Then, to my shock, he leaned down and, with the biggest grin, he tipped my chin up and kissed me.

"Did you take the Advil?" he whispered, hovering just above me, looking at me with an amused smile.

"Um, yeah?"

"Good." And he kissed me again, lingering for a moment. Then he winked and walked out of the bathroom.

"Oh. My. *God*," I breathed, grabbing for my washcloth and dragging it back over my face.

I finally came out half an hour later, wearing a sweatshirt and leggings, no makeup, wrapped in a blanket and holding the bucket Jason left by my bed in a zero-fucks-given effort at not looking the way I felt. I figured I'd gone this far, why not go all in?

Jason sat waiting on the sofa. His face lit up when he saw me.

The scene was almost ironic. I would have laughed if I still didn't feel so crappy. There was Jason, surrounded by an ocean of Brandon's things, trying to be a part of my ridiculous, sad universe. And the funny thing was all this chaos was for *him*.

After our date and the kissing—which, let's be honest here, was so out of this world it had probably ruined me for all other men—it had occurred to me that at some point, I might want to invite him home. That if I ever wanted to ask him inside, he'd spend the night in my room and use my bathroom.

Then I looked at my life through Jason's eyes, and all I saw was Brandon. Brandon's clothes in the closet, Brandon's toothbrush still in the bathroom. The last beer he had, still sitting on his workbench in the garage, evaporated and empty. And I thought about what Kristen had said, about my life being a shrine to him, and I realized I was still living with another man.

And that man wasn't ever coming home.

So for the two-year anniversary of his death, I did the healthy thing. I paid my visit to his grave, gave blood in his memory, and started cleaning. I put on some upbeat music and tried to make it something positive.

Things had started well. I packed up all Brandon's hunting gear and brought it to Josh. That had been easy. I knew that's what Brandon would have wanted me to do with it. Then I threw away his toiletries and cleared out the medicine cabinet.

But when I started on his clothes, the situation went south.

Some of his clothes still smelled like him, and they reminded me of places we'd been together. Like the T-shirt he picked up in Venice Beach on our second date, and the jacket he wore when we rented that cabin in Big Bear that one winter. I started a pile for a few items I wanted to keep, things that had sentimental value for me, and after a while that pile was bigger than the donation pile.

So I grabbed some tequila, had a shot of liquid courage, and started moving items from the keep pile into trash bags. And I was actually getting through it, until I found a receipt in the pocket of his favorite jeans. A receipt from Luigi's, the stupid Italian place in Canoga Park we liked. The last place we ate together.

That's when I'd lost it. The rest of the night was a lot of drinking, crying, and, as evidenced by Jason's presence in my living room, drunk dialing.

I sat on the sofa with him and crossed my legs under me. Tucker jumped up next to me and put his head in my lap.

Jason smiled, handing me a weird silver package from the coffee table. "Breakfast."

I wrinkled my forehead. "Is this…camping food?" The

package read *Backpacker's Pantry, granola with milk and bananas.*
It was warm.

He handed me a spoon. "This is my favorite oatmeal. I buy it
by the case. It's great for a hangover. Plus, no dishes."

No dishes was good since I still didn't have a working kitchen
sink. The top of the bag had a zipper seal. I pried it open and
tasted it. "This isn't half-bad," I admitted. "I've never had actual
camping food before."

"You've never been camping?"

"Well, yes. But we drive in. There's an electrical hookup and
running water. We bring a cooler of food and we plug in the
griddle and cook on it."

He looked amused. "That's not really camping. That's hanging
out outside."

"Oh, I forgot. You're a camping purist." I smiled weakly, my
head throbbing. I closed my eyes as a mild wave of nausea rippled
through me, and I let out a breath through my nose.

"You'll feel better in a few hours," Jason said behind the
spinning darkness of my eyelids.

"So, what else do you cook?" I asked, picking up my bag of
oatmeal again.

"Grilling and boiling water for dehydrated food are about all
that's in my wheelhouse."

"Oh. Well, if you can boil water, you can make coffee."

"I make amazing coffee," he said. "I use a French press."

"Oooh, now you're speaking my love language. Say 'French
press' again," I mumbled.

He leaned over and put his lips next to my ear. "French
presssss," he whispered.

I gave him serious side-eye. If this hangover didn't kill me, his
shameless flirting was going to finish the job.

"Hey, thank you," I said, after a minute.

He smiled at me. "For what?"

"For coming. For taking care of me. For not letting…" I looked around the room at the mess. "For not letting *this* change things."

He didn't look at the clothes. His eyes never left mine. "Well, we have a date today. I waited all day yesterday for it. No way was anything going to stop me from seeing that through."

"Jason, I can't go anywhere today. I feel like crap."

"No, the date's *here*. We're on it now. ID channel and chill."

I laughed, and the sore muscles in my stomach reminded me I'd spent the night barfing.

Jason picked up the remote and turned on the TV.

God, he was *wonderful*.

Four hours into ID channel and chill and he'd only held my hand. Besides those quick kisses in the bathtub, he hadn't tried to make a move on me. I don't know if this was due to my hangover or the overactive flight instincts I'd shown him on the night of our first kiss, but he kept a safe distance. I think he knew that if he pounced me, I'd probably make him leave. He was right. And oddly, his reserved behavior just made me more comfortable, and it kind of made me want to pounce *him*.

I wondered if that was a strategy…

My hangover felt a million times better. I sat with my legs crossed next to him on the sofa, and my knee just touched his thigh. It was such a small contact, but it had been sending bolts of electricity through me for the last hour.

Being with him in person felt just as natural and easy as it did on the phone—except with sexual tension.

It was like we couldn't look at anything other than each other for more than a few minutes at a time. Our faces kept turning back to each other, and finally we just kind of gave up and ignored the show and talked instead. To his credit, he didn't seem to care how I looked at the moment and he appeared to be perfectly happy just sitting there with me instead of on a date doing something more exciting.

His phone chirped, and he picked it up and frowned.

"Everything okay?" I asked.

"I just have a lot of promoting to do. Ernie emailed my schedule for this week. I have to meet with my publicist tomorrow, and Ernie's found me a personal assistant for my tour."

"So you're busy tomorrow?"

"I have that meeting tomorrow at eleven, then a photo shoot right afterward. But I'd love to see you for breakfast or dinner. Or both."

"Both, huh?" I said, trying not to sound as satisfied as his suggestion made me feel.

His mouth drew up on one side and he put a hand on my knee. My stomach somersaulted. "If I want to see you, I'm going to ask to see you."

"And you want to see me twice in one day?" I teased.

"No. I'd rather spend the *whole* day with you."

Now I had the grace to blush.

"Hey, I really like that photo of you over your bed," he said, sitting back against the sofa, giving me a grin.

I raised an eyebrow at him. "I'm naked in that."

"I'm a photography enthusiast. I'm interested in it for purely artistic reasons."

"Uh-huh, I'll bet." I twisted my lips into a pleased smile. That particular image was something I was proud of for reasons he didn't seem to realize. I decided not to tell him just yet. Maybe he would figure it out. The fact that he liked it, and didn't know what it was, was a huge compliment on many levels.

I stretched. "Want something to drink?" We had a pizza coming and I had been a horrible hostess. I hadn't gotten off the sofa once since we started our murder marathon.

"Sure. Just water."

I got up and walked into the kitchen and froze. The kitchen was put back together. The fans were gone, and the counters and floor had been cleaned.

Openmouthed, I went to the sink and peeked into the cabinet underneath. Everything was put neatly away, and a shiny new pipe and knob had been installed. I closed the doors and turned on the water. It ran. The dishes had been washed. My tequila glass sat upside down in the sink, drying on the rack.

Gratitude pulsed through me.

When I came out, I handed Jason his water and nudged his knee with mine. "You fixed the kitchen."

"I said I would." He set his glass on a coaster.

"I'd like to cook you dinner tomorrow."

A grin crept across his handsome face. "I'd love that."

He kept beaming up at me.

"What?" I asked.

"It's just something you said to me on the phone last night."

"Oh God, *what?*" I said with horror.

He twisted his lips into a smirk.

"Tell me."

"You said I make you want to cook for me."

Ugh. Drunk me had no business putting that out there for sober me. She was such a gossip.

I flopped down next to him. "Well, thank God it was only *that.*"

"What else could it have been?"

"No clue. I have no access to the mind of drunk Sloan. That woman is a stranger to me."

"So what did you do yesterday?" he asked, putting the TV on mute.

I had hoped I wouldn't have to get into my day yesterday. It had seemed like maybe we were just going to sit among the remnants of Brandon's life and ignore it. That would have been my preference. But no such luck. And Jason had done more than enough to earn the right to ask.

"Brandon died two years ago yesterday," I said. "I visited his grave. I gave blood. And then I came home and decided to finally go through his stuff."

Jason's eyes took on a look of understanding. "That must have been very difficult for you."

"It was. It is. But it's time."

CHAPTER 15

JASON

♪ I WANT IT ALL | COIN

Sloan kicked me out last night at 7:00. She said she had some things she needed to do. I think she was going to finish packing up Brandon's clothes. I'd have offered to help, but it didn't really feel like my place.

I didn't like leaving her. I knew it was crazy, but I honestly wanted to sleep on her couch again, just to be near her. It felt like I was *supposed* to be near her.

My Minnesota trip was the day after tomorrow, and I wasn't going to see her the whole weekend. Fuck.

I'd been on my best behavior yesterday, holding back from kissing her the way I really wanted to, because I knew if things escalated like they had the other night after our first date, she'd kick me out. The last thing I wanted was to lose my newfound house privileges. I decided I would only kiss her on the porch, coming and going, until she was ready for more.

It wasn't easy.

She wouldn't see me for breakfast this morning, another disappointment. She said she had things to do. I looked forward to dinner, though. Having The Huntsman's Wife cook for you was an honor of the highest degree.

It was a brutal hour and a half in traffic to downtown LA. I called Sloan after I checked in at the front desk at my publicist's office.

Sloan answered, talking to someone else in the background. "What? Uh, *no*. But thanks." She sounded amused.

"Who was that?" I asked, thinking maybe she was with Kristen.

I sat in the waiting area drinking a Fiji Water. The entire place was white. Even the receptionist wore white. Framed photos of Pia with her famous clients were the only pops of color on the walls.

"I have no idea who that was. I think I just got hit on," she said, disbelief in her voice.

"What did he say to you?"

"It was weird."

I sat up. "Was it inappropriate?"

"What? No." She laughed. "He asked me for my number. Then he said if I don't give it to him, him and his friends are going to sing 'You've Lost That Lovin' Feelin'"? I don't get it."

I snorted. "Was the guy wearing naval dress whites, by chance?"

"How did you know?"

"You've never seen *Top Gun*?"

"No."

I shook my head with a chuckle. "Well, I know what *we're* watching later. So what are you doing today?" I asked, putting my ankle over my knee, leaning back into the couch. I checked my watch. My appointment wasn't for another ten minutes.

"I'm at the car wash right now. Then I have to go to Vons to get stuff to make dinner..."

"And what's for dinner?"

"I'm thinking chicken Provençal? I have to see how the produce looks. And then I need to go to the mall."

"The mall? For what?"

She paused. "Just...*something*."

She was being evasive, so my interest *immediately* spiked. "Something?"

"I'm not telling you. It's between Tucker and me. He and I are *not* friends right now."

I'd left Tucker at Sloan's house last night since I was going to be gone all day today and I was going over there later anyway. Besides, he liked it better there, and I didn't blame him.

"Really? I thought he was an angel."

She scoffed. "Turns out I was wrong about that."

"What did he do? Give me a hint."

"He just...He ate something he shouldn't have eaten."

Fucking Tucker.

"Can I pay to replace it?"

She laughed. "No, definitely not. I got it. He's going to spend a few hours in doggy prison thinking about what he's done."

"Doggy prison?"

"The laundry room. It's not Guantanamo Bay like the crate, but it'll do."

She was never going to stop giving me shit about the crate. "Okay, now you really have to tell me."

She sighed into the phone. "Your dog—"

"*My* dog? I thought we were coparenting?"

I could tell she was smiling by the pause. "No, he's definitely *your* dog today. *Your* dog ate about two dozen pairs of my underwear."

My burst of laughter made the receptionist look up from her white desk.

"He's been pulling them out of the dirty clothes basket every day to chew them up and stash them under the bed. I found his hoard this morning. I wondered where they were going..."

I was laughing too hard to respond.

She huffed. "Your best friend is a pervert and I feel like you're not taking this seriously."

"Well, I can't really say I blame him. He has excellent taste," I said, pinching the bridge of my nose, still chuckling. "So what store are you going to?"

"The lingerie department at Nordstrom."

I looked up and arched an eyebrow. "I think I should be allowed, as a responsible dog owner, to replace these damaged items. I'll need to approve everything, of course, for insurance purposes. Dressing room pictures would be best. In fact, we should probably Skype."

"You know, I've already forgiven Tucker for everything he'll ever do. You? Not so much."

"What? How am *I* the bad guy in this? Here I am, just trying to make you whole..."

"Uh-huh."

"I like red, by the way."

She snorted. "What makes you think that you're *ever* going to see my underwear?"

I grinned. "Unwavering, unrelenting persistence?"

"Speaking of persistence," she mumbled.

"Sailor boy's still there?" I asked, nodding back at a yoga pants–clad Jennifer Lawrence coming out of the floor-to-ceiling frosted doors of Pia's office.

"Yeah, he's smiling at me, standing by a giant bubble gum machine."

"Tell him you have a boyfriend," I said.

"Might work better if I tell him I have a *girlfriend*," she whispered.

My mind flickered to Sloan kissing another woman. "That will definitely *not* work better."

She laughed.

My suggestion made me realize that despite our two dates, Sloan *didn't* have a boyfriend. I had no claim on her besides just being some guy she was talking to. She could give this man her number and I couldn't say anything about it.

I didn't like that. At *all*.

"Whoa, there's more of them," she said. "Oh my God, I wonder if they're going to actually do it. They seem to be gathering. There's like five of them now and they're huddled. There must be a navy recruiting station around here."

"Does this happen often?" I asked.

"What? Naval officers?"

"You getting hit on."

"Actually, yeah, lately. It's weird."

I moved the phone away from my mouth. I didn't like that either. And there was nothing weird about it. She was beautiful. Of course other men noticed it.

I changed the subject. "So, did Tucker destroy any other lingerie? I feel like he probably did and we'll need to get some replacements."

"Oh, ha *ha*." Then she groaned.

"The naval crew still there?"

"Yup."

"Can you go outside? Get away from them?"

"I can, but I'll have to hang up with you. It's really loud out there."

"No, don't hang up with me," I said.

"They're turning around. They just looked at me," she whispered. "One of them just waved."

I dragged my hand down my face. "Are you *trying* to make me jealous?"

"No," she laughed. "Why? *Are* you getting jealous?"

"Of course." I said it like a joke, but it wasn't.

"You don't have anything to worry about," she said.

"Why? Navy guy isn't your type?"

"No, he's kind of cute, actually. It's just that I'm really into this other guy right now."

"Oh?" My heart picked up.

"Yeah. He's pretty amazing. Thoughtful. Took care of me when I was sick yesterday. Sexy northern accent. Doesn't scare easily, something I need in a man."

"Sick? Is that what we're calling it?" I was beaming. I knew she could tell.

"Yup. Sick. We don't need to elaborate. Oh no..."

"What?"

"They're coming over here. Oh my *God*..."

...Singing.

CHAPTER 16

SLOAN

♪ GIRLFRIEND | PHOENIX

When I opened the front door at 6:15, Jason stood there leaning on his arm against the door frame, *still* laughing.

I put my hands on my hips and glared playfully at him. "I'm glad one of us found that amusing. That was easily the most embarrassing thing to ever happen to me."

And so much recent content to choose from...

Jason had laughed so hard on the phone through the whole mortifying performance, you could hear him through my cell a foot away.

"I'm sorry, you're right. Can I come in?" he wheezed.

He looked sooooo good. Even slightly annoyed at him for laughing at me, I had to bite my lip in appreciation. He wore a green flannel with the sleeves rolled up, and his china-blue eyes were gleaming.

They were gleaming at my expense, but still.

I put an arm across the door. "I was musically assaulted today by a roving a cappella group in naval dress whites, and you think it's *funny?*"

He crashed into me, hugging me around the waist. I went limp in protest, dropping my arms to my side like noodles, and it made him laugh harder.

"You just don't realize the effect you have on musicians, Sloan Monroe. So...when do *I* get to musically assault you?"

I narrowed my eyes, but he kissed me, smiling against my unresponsive, protesting lips. Normally his close proximity made me swoon, but his laughing made me just indignant enough to hold my ground.

"I come bearing gifts," he whispered, an inch from my mouth, still cracking up.

"It better be good. I'm about ready to throw you into the laundry room with Tucker."

He let me go, picking up a plastic bag from the steps, and handed it to me, his eyes sparkling. I looked inside and gasped. It was full of tiny creamers.

"I bought five coffees for these," he said. "When I hit the creamer station, I felt like a Viking on a raid."

I beamed. "Jason, you pillaged for me? This is so sweet!" But when he leaned in, I turned my face to the side. "Where are my five coffees?"

"Gas station coffee? For a connoisseur like you? I wouldn't dare." Then he reached down, around the side of my front porch flowerpot with the petrified geraniums in it, and produced a warm Starbucks cup.

I looked at it and held my breath. "That's so thoughtful." I raised my eyes to his. "But I can't have caffeine this late."

He smiled. "I know. It's decaf."

I had to clutch a hand over my heart. "You realize that repeatedly bringing me my favorite coffee is comparable to feeding a stray cat, right? You might never get rid of me now."

"Good," he said, pulling me close to kiss me with an enormous grin. "I was hoping for something like that."

~

After dinner, we watched *Top Gun*. I rolled my eyes in the right place. Jason had his arm around me and we were snuggled deep into the sofa with a blanket over our laps. Tucker was curled up next to me, sleeping.

The living room was clear. I'd spent last night packing everything into the car. This morning I'd dropped it all off at Goodwill, bracing myself for the punch in the heart, but it never came. And I realized it was actually a relief to let it all go, like I'd been carrying it on my back all this time.

Then I washed my car, because, you know, *my car*. I couldn't let Jason see one more unattractive thing about me. I was sure he had a limit somewhere, and my Corolla was enough to make any man run screaming from the garage—not that Jason seemed to care what kind of dumpster fire I was. He'd never met the best version of me, and for some reason he still seemed to want to be here. I was a ghost, wandering the rooms of a museum of the person I used to be, and Jason was like one of the living who could somehow see me and decided to wander the place with me.

I *liked* that he was willing to wander the place with me.

He twined his fingers in mine on top of the blanket, and I put my head on his shoulder. He pressed a kiss to my forehead, and I could feel him looking down on me long after he finished. I smiled to myself.

Being with Jason in the house I'd shared with Brandon didn't feel strange. I'd lived here alone four times longer than Brandon had ever lived here with me. But I think the biggest part of it was that even when all his stuff had still been here, this place didn't feel like Brandon's. It didn't even feel like *mine*.

I'd realized something in the past two days. This house was a mausoleum. And not for the man I lost—for *myself*.

Once I took out everything that belonged to Brandon, all that was left behind was remnants of me—and it wasn't the me of now, it was the me of back then. The happy me who'd hung shadow boxes and cooked in the kitchen. The one who painted actual, dignified works of art that I was proud enough to hang on walls. These little mementos were all around me, small reminders of a woman I hadn't seen since Brandon took off on his motorcycle that morning and never came home. And the thing was I *wanted* to be that whole again. I *missed* myself.

I missed being *happy*.

Tonight was the first time I'd cooked anything that actually required effort in more than two years—and it made me wonder why I hadn't done it sooner. I *loved* cooking for people. And I loved seeing Jason enjoying something I could do as much as I enjoyed what he put into the universe.

Kristen was right. I'd chosen this life. And I'd had enough. I was going to make a concerted effort to get out of this in-between I was trapped in. I was going to actively pursue joy. I'd cook. I'd maybe start updating my blog again. I had too many paying commissions to be able to dedicate time to painting any of my own stuff, but maybe eventually I'd even get back to that too. And I was going to start *now*. Not for Jason. Not because he was here to reap the benefits. For myself. I should have done it a long time ago.

When the credits came on, I stretched and Jason sat up and hit the Power button.

"I need to ask you something," he said, turning to me.

"If you ask me one more time if I've lost that loving feeling—"

He laughed. "Not that." Then his face went a touch serious. "I'm not seeing anybody else. It occurred to me that maybe you might be dating. I just wanted to make it clear to you that I'm only dating you."

"Is that a question?" I asked, buying time while I processed what I'd heard.

Even though he hadn't said it before this, I knew innately that he was seeing only me. I just *knew*. But I guess it was good we were talking about it.

He smiled a little. "Are *you* seeing anyone else?"

I snorted. "No, of course not." The idea was almost laughable. Me? *Dating?* Besides, I liked him way too much to look at other options. But Jason looked...relieved, maybe?

"I would like it if you and I only dated each other," he said, looking at me intently.

I shrugged. "Okay."

"You agree?"

"Yes. I won't see anyone else. Just you."

He gazed at me for a moment, something soft playing around the edges of his smile. Then he leaned over and kissed me. It was a gentle, closed-mouthed kiss, and when it was over, he stroked my cheek with his thumb, looking in my eyes. My heart fluttered. Then my cell phone vibrated in my lap and we both looked down, reading the text at the same time.

Kristen: Tomorrow. Get here by 5:00. I want help with the sides. BRING HIM.

I groaned.

"What?" Jason asked.

"Kristen is conspiring to meet you. It's her birthday tomorrow, and Josh is grilling steaks. She wants me to bring you."

"Sure," he said.

I shook my head. "No. It'll be awful. They'll make you so uncomfortable. They're shameless. No."

"So you're just going to hide me from your best friend? Forever?"

"Yes. That's the plan. You don't understand, I can't even let her know you're over here right now. She'll show up just to show you pictures of me at my eighth-grade dance."

He laughed. "What time should I pick you up?"

"You really want to do this? It may test our relationship."

"So you admit it's a relationship," he said, smiling at me.

I narrowed my eyes at him, suspecting a trap. "Well, what would *you* call it?"

"That's exactly what I'd call it. But you have a tendency to rob me of the titles I'm due."

"Like *what*?"

"Like calling our first date an appointment."

I rolled my eyes. "Fine. We're in ... a *relationship*," I said, forcing out the last word. It was way early for that, but it kind of was one, I guess. He wasn't wrong.

"A monogamous relationship," he added.

"*Yes*, we're not dating anyone else, so I suppose that's also true."

"So that makes you my girlfriend."

I choked. "Jason!"

"What? What else would you call it?" He looked completely amused at how flustered I was.

"I don't know? We're seeing each other, exclusively. That's how I'd say it."

"And that would make me your boyfriend," he said, his eyes dancing.

He was right. And I was terrified.

"We've only known each other for two weeks," I said. "This is only our third date."

He shook his head. "I don't care."

I bit my lip. "Jason, I take that status really seriously."

"I hope so, because so do I. Look, I don't care what the rule books say we should be doing right now. I like you. You like me. We agree that we're exclusively seeing each other. And I want you to be able to tell random a cappella groups that hit on you that you have a boyfriend."

Then he leaned in and kissed me. "And your boyfriend should *definitely* know your best friend."

CHAPTER 17

JASON

♪ I FEEL IT | AVID DANCER

I could have written a love song about that chicken Sloan made for dinner. Hell, maybe I *should* write a love song about that chicken Sloan made for dinner. It would be better than the shit my label sent over, even in my current state of writer's block.

When it came time for me to go home, I wanted to stay again. I even considered asking this time if I could spend the night on the couch, but I figured if she wanted me there, she wouldn't be kicking me out, so I sucked it up and left. Stepping out onto the porch that evening, kissing her good night, and driving off in my truck felt as counterintuitive to me as anything I'd ever done, like leaving my guitar behind on a sidewalk.

No guy in his right mind ever did anything to fuck up a chance like this.

I was getting this shot with her on a technicality. I'd slipped in under some wire. She'd been isolated and grieving so no other man had gotten to her. I *knew* how lucky I was. And every moment I spent with her, I was more and more aware of it.

I wanted to do things for her. Bring her gifts that made her smile, hold her doors open. Take out the damn trash in her kitchen, watch her paint. I wanted to be useful to her and see what she looked like before she went to bed and watch her laugh at something on TV.

I definitely didn't want to go home without her, that was for damn sure.

When I got back to my trailer, it felt hollow and cold. I sighed and tossed my keys on the kitchen counter, taking off my jacket. I looked around and felt no attachment to any of it. It was my place, filled with my things, but it didn't feel like home. Oddly enough, Sloan's place did, and I had a feeling it had more to do with the company than the house.

Tucker, the Panty Bandit, jumped on the bed, and I let him. No crate for him tonight. We were in this together. Why make him any more miserable than he had to be, stuck here, with me instead of with Sloan, sniffing around my laundry basket instead of hers?

I showered and was rubbing my hair with a towel when I heard tapping. Tucker hopped off the bed and ran for the door, scratching and whining. I looked at my watch. It was almost midnight, a little late for Ernie to be wandering the yard.

I jumped into some sweatpants and opened the door to Sloan standing outside, rubbing her arms in the cold. Tucker spilled out of the trailer and circled her happily, jumping on her.

"Um...maybe I should have called first?" she said, patting Tucker's head and eyeing my bare chest. She bit her lip uncertainly and I broke into a grin.

"Get in here."

She climbed the step and I pulled her to me.

"I...I just missed you," she said, looking up at me shyly after I'd given her a proper kiss hello.

"You shouldn't have let me leave," I said. "I would have slept in the living room."

"You would?"

"Oh yeah."

I leaned down and kissed her again, standing there by the open door of the trailer. The kiss was a grateful one. She'd delivered herself to me like a gift.

"You're staying the night, right?" I asked, beaming at her.

I wasn't suggesting anything other than sleeping. If she didn't usually kiss on the first date, we weren't having sex on the third one, no matter how charming *I* might be. And I would never push her into it.

"Only if it's just sleeping," she said, eyeing me warily.

"Of course."

"Will you put a shirt on?" She glanced at my chest.

I chuckled. "Yes."

"And you promise to behave?"

"Absolutely."

She smiled, looking relieved, and nodded. I would have agreed to any demand she made if it meant she'd stay. I would have slept on a floaty in the pool if that was what it would take.

I tore myself from her. "You want some water?"

"Sure."

While I filled her glass, she wandered to the fridge and took down the tour itinerary I'd stuck there. "Is this your tour schedule?"

"Yeah." This one was for my US dates. I hadn't told her about the extra two months or the UK portion yet. Hitting her with, "By the way, I'm going to be gone for fourteen months" felt a little heavy for the first day of our official relationship.

She followed me into my room and sat on the edge of my bed

and studied the printout while I dug in my drawer for a shirt. "Wow. Do you even get a day off?" She looked up at me. "These concert dates are so close together."

Tucker pushed his face under her arm and she hugged him, watching me pull the tee over my head. She *really* watched me. Her eyes were nowhere near my face. I smiled. She was biting her lip and one of those blushes I loved was creeping up her neck.

I looked at her too. She wore a white tank top and some pink shorts. Her hair was in a messy braid. She looked like she'd been ready for bed before she came over. The tank top was low cut. Damn. I'd probably have to sleep with a pillow between us so I didn't press anything unwanted against her. It was definitely gonna be a problem.

"Tours are hard work," I said, taking the packet from her and dropping it onto the top of Tucker's crate. I got under the covers and held up her side so she could join me. She scooted in and put her head on my chest. I reached over, turning off the lights, then hugged her closer.

It wasn't close enough.

I put my nose to her hair and breathed in, and she slid a leg up over my thigh and snuggled in to me. I wondered if she could hear my heart pounding. She had to.

I cleared my throat. "'You never close your eyes anymore—'"

She hit me and I laughed, kissing the top of her head.

Tucker settled at the end of the bed and I shut my eyes, feeling a sense of calm, like everything I needed was in one place at the same time.

CHAPTER 18

SLOAN

♪ THE WRECK OF THE *EDMUND FITZGERALD* | JAXON
WATERS

Jason picked me up right at 4:45 to drive us to Kristen's to attend her trial by fire. I was hoping he'd get stuck doing some Jaxon Waters thing and have to cancel, but no luck. I argued we should take separate cars so he could escape if he needed to, but he wouldn't hear of it.

My eyelid was in a full-scale panic attack. The finger wasn't enough to hold it in place. I needed my whole *palm*.

Jason looked over at me from behind the wheel of his truck and laughed. "Come on, she *cannot* be that bad."

"Jason, there's probably a clone of her guarding the gates of hell."

The creasing at the corners of his eyes made me smile despite myself.

"I just never know what she's going to do. She's always scheming. And the baby's at his grandmother's house tonight, so who knows what she's got planned."

"Schemes, huh?" He chuckled.

"Yes, she loves messing with me. I can't explain her, Jason. She's too weird."

When we knocked on the door to Kristen's tan stucco house, I gave Jason one more I'm-so-sorry glance, and he winked at me.

Kristen threw the door open, grinning right past me at Jason like a lunatic. "You must be Jason!" She bumped into me theatrically and dove right in for a hug with my date.

I shook my head at her over his shoulder, and she gave me crazy eyes.

When he was released from her clutches, Jason handed her the flowers he'd brought, and she gushed, ushering us inside, where Josh waited like an accomplice, holding two beers.

Stuntman Mike bounced off Jason's shins, and he crouched and petted him.

Kristen leaned over and whispered in my ear. "He *does* smell like flannel."

"You promised me you'd behave," I hissed.

"What? What did I do?" she said, blinking at me with feigned innocence.

Jason stood and took the beer he was offered, shaking Josh's hand, introducing himself. Jason didn't look the least bit uncomfortable. Maybe he was used to overzealous, grabby, slightly inappropriate fans?

"Hey," Kristen whispered, nudging me in the ribs. "I told Josh to ask him if he can spell 'chlamydia.' If he can, he's gonna throw him out."

I blanched and she practically skipped across the room and hooked her arm in Jason's. "Let me give you the tour."

"I'm coming on the tour," I announced.

"Nope. It's a one-person tour. We're all booked up." She slapped the flowers to my chest. "Put these in water, will you? And, Josh, can you show Sloan to the kitchen, where there's a potato salad that needs putting together? *Thanks.*"

Jason looked thoroughly amused at my distress and allowed himself to be led away.

Huffing, I turned to Josh, who was smiling after his insane wife. "You know there's no stopping her when she gets an idea," he said.

"And what idea are we talking about, Josh?"

He took a swig of his beer. "I'm not telling you shit. I have to live with her."

I stomped to the kitchen to make the damn potato salad. Ten minutes later, as I was moodily squeezing mayo into a bowl and chopping celery, Jason and Kristen reappeared, laughing and chatting like old friends.

Jason sat on one of the leather barstools, sliding his half-empty beer on the counter. I glared at Kristen, then gave Jason a long look, trying to figure out if we were still dating or if he'd decided against it after spending a few minutes alone with my best friend.

"Kristen was just telling me about the time you won Miss Canoga Park," Jason said. "I didn't know you'd done beauty pageants. Why didn't you ever mention it?"

I stopped chopping and looked back and forth between them in disbelief. "*This* is what was on the tour? The scrapbooks didn't come out? No sleepover photos of me in headgear?"

Jason's eyes smiled as he lifted his beer to his lips.

Kristen scoffed dramatically. "Now why would I spoil those?" she said, cocking her head. "I'm saving them for the calendars I'm handing out at Christmas."

Jason laughed so unexpectedly he had to put a hand under his chin to wipe up beer. I slid my eyes back to Kristen and narrowed them.

"What?" she said. "I showed him the pictures of us at Coachella three years ago."

I stared at her. Seriously? The Coachella pictures? I was wearing a white macramé bikini with cutoff denim shorts and had flowers in my hair and I looked amazing.

Well, I'll be damned. She was wingmanning me. *Unbelievable.*

"I played Coachella last year," Jason said, still chuckling a little. "I wish you would have gone. I would have seen you from the stage. We could have met sooner."

I snorted, scooping celery into the bowl. "There are like two hundred thousand people at Coachella. You wouldn't have noticed me."

He looked me in the eye. "I would notice you in a crowd of a *million*."

He held my gaze and I could feel the weight of Kristen's stare as she watched the two of us look at each other.

The sliding glass door opened and Josh popped his head inside. "Hey, Jason, want to help me with the grill?"

"Sure," Jason said, flashing me a smile that said he remembered my prophecy of a grill-side interrogation, and he dutifully followed Josh outside.

"Have fun," I said after him before he slid the door closed. He gave me a confident two-fingered salute and disappeared into the yard.

Kristen looked at me and mouthed, "Oh my God."

"I know, right?"

"He is like seriously into you. I think he's in love with you. I'm not even kidding. It's all over his face. He's whipped."

I rolled my eyes.

"Have you had sex with him yet? Was it amazing? Tell me everything."

I shook my head. "No, we haven't had sex. But I slept at his place last night."

He'd snuggled me so hard. He never let me go once. I actually started smiling down at the potato salad thinking about it.

He'd also put a pillow between us at one point. That made me smile too.

"So third-base stuff, then?" she asked.

"Actually, no. We haven't done anything other than kissing."

She looked at me like I had two heads. "You haven't even touched his penis yet? *Why?*"

"Lower your voice!" I whispered, shooting a look at the door.

"I swear to God, if there isn't penis touching in the very near future, this friendship is over. That's what I want for my birthday gift."

"For me to touch Jason's penis?"

"Yes."

"Darn. I got you some lotions from Bath & Body Works," I said, turning out my lower lip in a mock pout.

The truth was, keeping my hands off him was getting harder and harder to do. The struggle was real. I didn't even want to admit to myself how quickly I'd decided to go to Nordstrom's lingerie department instead of Walmart to replace all the underwear Tucker chewed up. And I *definitely* didn't want to own up to how much red I'd bought.

"I like him," Kristen declared.

I went back to chopping celery. "I like him too." Then I set my knife back down. "Kristen? I *really* like him. Like, a lot. Oh," I said, remembering, "and he's officially my boyfriend by the way."

She reared back. "You have a boyfriend you've known less than a month? Wow. Does Jason know he's making history here? How did he get you to agree to *that?*"

I narrowed my eyes. "There was a lot of wordsmithing. It was all very confusing."

She grinned. "The flash-bang chaos campaign. My favorite. It's how Josh got me to marry him."

I snorted.

She picked up a piece of celery and waved it over my body. "Well, it works. You even look like a rock star's girlfriend."

I smiled. "I made him dinner last night. And breakfast this morning."

Her eyes flew wide. "You did? You're cooking again?"

"I am." I wrinkled my nose. "I sort of have to or we'll end up eating camping food every morning."

She laughed and she looked genuinely happy.

I took a deep breath. "I'm trying, Kristen. I really *am* trying."

Her eyes went soft. "Good. Keep doing it. And fall for him. And when you do, make sure you swing from every fucking branch on the way down."

~

At dinner Jason reached under the table and laced his fingers in mine. I wondered what had happened outside. I hoped Josh's questions hadn't been too invasive. It appeared my boyfriend still liked me, but the night was young.

Kristen tossed me a small bag of Doritos and I opened it and poured them onto my plate. But when I went to flatten the bag, she scolded me. "Uh, uh, uh. That's not how we do it."

I glared at her.

She dumped her own bag and then turned it inside out on her hand like a foil mitten. She waved it at me, waiting for me to do the same.

Ugh.

"If Jason can take you at your best, he can take you at your bag of Doritos," she said.

Josh snorted and went back to his corn on the cob. Jason eyed me and I let out a sigh. Technically Jason had never seen me at my best. Why start now, I guess, right?

I put my bag inside out on my hand and waited for Kristen to start. The least she could do was kick off the ridiculous practice. We'd been doing this since the sixth grade. It was kind of a tradition. When she began licking the bag, I started licking mine too.

"The inside of the bag's the best part," I said to Jason, lamely. "And it's her birthday. I have to."

He laughed and took my hand again, kissing it this time in front of everyone.

"Oh, I forgot to tell you!" Kristen said, holding up her bag hand like an idiot. "We have an activity tonight. Karaoke!" She looked back and forth between Jason and me with her "yay" face.

"Aaaaaand the shoe drops," I said, crumpling my chip bag and flinging it at her.

Kristen looked proud of herself and Josh shook his head, wiping his mouth with a napkin in his best I'm-staying-out-of-it performance of the night.

"Kristen, *no*. I'm sure Jason doesn't want to hear us sing. I'm sure that Jason doesn't want to sin—"

"I love karaoke," Jason said.

"He loves karaoke!" Kristen beamed at Jason.

"I'm going to kill you," I breathed, only half kidding.

After dinner, when the plates were cleared, Kristen and Josh went to fire up the microphones and I cornered Jason in the kitchen.

"I am so, *so* sorry," I said, putting my forehead to his chest. "I told you. I *told* you this would happen."

He smiled down on me. "What? Karaoke?"

"Yes!" I said, looking up at him. "She's trying to get you to sing!"

"I *do* sing professionally. This isn't particularly distressing for me."

"It's distressing for *me*!"

If he turned into Jaxon Waters in front of me, I was going to pass out.

"Why?" he said, tipping my chin up. "You don't want me to sing for you? Still a little traumatized by the car wash a cappella?" He smiled, doing that thing where he puts his mouth really close to mine and I can't focus anymore. He normally reserved this type of behavior for our good-night kiss on the porch. It was highly distracting.

"Uh-huh," I murmured, not remembering the question.

He pulled away a little, letting me get my wits back. "I'm having a good time. Relax. Josh warned me about the karaoke. He said he'd talk her out of it if I wasn't okay with it. It's totally fine."

"Josh told you?"

"He did. Also, I have no idea how to spell 'chlamydia.'"

I snorted.

He leaned in and whispered against my mouth again. "You're going to tell me *everything* Kristen said on the way home, right?"

"Uh...she said to swing from branches and touch your— *No*," I said, shaking myself out of my stupor.

"Touch my *what*?" he asked, grinning.

The sound of "Love Shack" began to spill through the doorway. Josh started the song and Kristen broke in with "Loooove SHACK!"

I rolled my eyes. "These two plan to close the place down."

He smiled. "Let's go in there before they think we've snuck off for a quickie."

"Kristen is all for me jumping your bones. It wouldn't surprise me if both our beers were spiked with ecstasy. In fact, don't drink anything she gives you."

"I don't need a drug to want to take *you* for a quickie," he said, sliding his hands under the bottom of my shirt so he held me by the bare skin of my waist. He put his mouth by my ear. "Will you come with me to Minnesota this weekend?"

I literally started choking on my own saliva. "To Minnesota? Like, to meet your parents? *Tomorrow?*"

"Yes, to meet my parents. And my asshole of a brother, David."

The asshole comment made me laugh. Then my eyelid started twitching.

He nuzzled his nose to mine. "I don't know when I'll be out there again, and I want you to come with me. It's really casual. My parents are very laid back."

I didn't want to go three days without him. But meeting his parents? Already? And wasn't Minnesota really, really cold?

"Jason, I've been your girlfriend for like five minutes."

"Yeah, and I already told them all about you."

I pulled my face back to look at him. "You *did*? What did you say?"

"The truth. That you held my dog ransom until I agreed to go out on a date with you."

I hit him and he chuckled.

"Come on. Don't make me miss you for three days. It'll be fun. Come with me."

He said he'd miss me. I melted.

"Okay," I said.

He beamed. "Yes?"

"Yes. *Fine.* Take me to Minnesota."

Screw it. Why not? What else was I going to do while he was gone besides wish I were with him?

He smiled and put his forehead to mine, pulling me closer to him. "I want something else," he said to my eyes.

I arched my eyebrow, but he just laughed.

"Not that. Although I wouldn't mind *that*," he added. "I want you to cook with my mom when we get there. It would mean a lot to her."

I rubbed my nose to his. "You couldn't stop me if you tried."

He smiled and was leaning in to kiss me when Kristen popped her head into the kitchen. We jumped like teenagers who'd just gotten caught making out on the sofa.

"Hey! Get a room!" she said, talking into the microphone so it reverberated through the house. Then she whispered into the mic, "Seriously, the guest room is all made up. Make yourselves comfortable." She bit her lip and bounced her eyebrows and then disappeared back into the living room.

Jason and I put our heads together and laughed.

"Come on. I want to sing a duet with you," he said.

I groaned.

"Need a shot of courage? I bet Kristen has some tequila." He grinned.

"Tequila officially tastes like the time I almost died. I'm going to have to go it sober."

He chuckled and dragged me into the living room by the hand. When "Love Shack" was over, Kristen roped me into singing "Hopelessly Devoted to You" with her. I died of embarrassment, but it was her birthday and Kristen was happy and that was what mattered.

Then the inevitable happened and Jason's turn was up.

"What do you want me to sing?" he asked Kristen. "Any requests?"

"'The Wreck of the *Edmund Fitzgerald*,'" she said, without even thinking about it.

It was for me. There was no question. I was going to *kill* her.

Jason put a thumb over his shoulder. "Hey, you know, I have my guitar in the truck. Would it be okay if I got it?"

Kristen's eyes flew wide. "Seriously? Yes. Yes, you can get it. Are you kidding me? Go!"

Jason got up and went out to the truck. Josh and Kristen looked stoked. And why wouldn't they be? They'd gotten a Grammy-winning musician to serenade them at their barbecue. I, on the other hand, felt a fine sweat breaking out across my forehead.

I was just getting used to the idea of having a boyfriend. I was still months away—maybe even *years*—from getting used to the idea that he was Jaxon Waters. The only way that I dealt with this fact was by doing my best to forget it. I was completely not ready for this.

Kristen and Josh sandwiched me on the sofa, elbow to elbow. Jason came back in with a guitar case and I felt myself being sucked into his vortex, just watching him pulling out his instrument. I was a complete groupie, it was embarrassing. I wondered if he could tell.

I picked up a *Parenting* magazine from the coffee table and started to fan myself while Jason stood in front of the TV, tuning his strings. That alone was enough to give me heart palpitations. But when he began to play...That was absolutely unreal. It was all over for me. I was officially in love.

He was *incredible*.

Jason had a voice like honey and coffee grounds, sweet and textured. It was so much better in person than on the album. It didn't even seem possible that it was this good. He was so talented. I wanted to slap myself for not wanting to let him sing to me sooner—and at the same time, I knew that if he *had*, I'd have confused my feelings *for* him with my feelings *about* him.

He was going to be famous. Really, truly famous. He had it all. The looks, the talent, the presence. I could see it as clearly as anything I'd ever known.

And *this* was *my* boyfriend. I said it over and over again in my mind. This man wanted *me*.

I felt flattered and lucky. Then I felt nervous and unworthy. I ran through a symphony of emotions as he played, and the whole time he sang, he smiled at me, like he was just happy I could see this side of him.

And I was happy too. Because Jason and Jaxon were *definitely* the same man.

～

When I jumped up to wrap my legs around his waist, the motion sensor activated and the floodlights poured over my porch. They used to be broken.

Damn Jason for fixing things around here like he'd said he would.

It was after midnight. My neighborhood was quiet, but I wasn't a fan of the full-fledged stage lights. He pressed himself against me, pinning my back to the front door as he kissed me. His hands gripped me under my thighs and his hips pushed between my legs, grinding into me.

God, what would this feel like horizontal?

The tension had been building between us the entire evening. Even Kristen's shenanigans and the awful duet Jason had forced me to sing with him hadn't lessened it. He'd been touching me and kissing me all night, right in front of Kristen and Josh. They didn't care. They probably handed him a condom on the way out.

As soon as he got me alone on the porch, we'd pounced on each other.

The light shut off and I smiled against his mouth. Then it came on again, dousing us in the brightness of ten thousand suns, and I grimaced.

"We could go inside…" he whispered, and his eyes came up to mine, his breathing hard.

Oh, hell.

I nodded and wrapped an arm around his neck. I felt around behind me for the knob, and when I turned it, the door gave way and we almost fell into the living room.

He staggered a few feet before regaining his balance. We laughed a little, but we didn't stop kissing. He kicked the door closed behind us and whirled me onto the sofa, sliding over me in the dimness, pressing himself against me.

All of him pressed against me.

I gathered the bottom of his T-shirt and tugged it up. "Take this off," I said breathlessly. I needed to run my hands along his chest, feel the outline of his six-pack under my fingers, trace the trail of hair that descended down into his pants.

He yanked his shirt over his head and was back on me in under two seconds. I was thoroughly impressed. "I have never seen a man take his shirt off that fast," I breathed as his lips fell on my neck.

"You should see how fast I can get yours off."

I snorted and his hand wandered up the bottom of my shirt. I didn't stop him. He hiked my leg up around him and I ran my palms over the curve of his broad, bare shoulders.

I wanted to feel the sear of my skin pressed to his. I scooted to sit up and peeled off my shirt and his fingers were around my back, unhooking my bra, before my top hit the floor. He poured over me, pushing me back down.

My body was alive, blood in my cheeks, my ears, my heart drumming in my chest.

His hands were everywhere. I actually looked down to make sure he only had *two*.

I wanted him. Sweet baby Jesus, I wanted this man. He knew what to do with me. I could tell. He would tune me and play me like his damn guitar. God, every inch of him was toned and solid. He was so strong and he smelled *so* good.

"I'm on the pill, okay?" I breathed. "For my periods."

"I got tested last month. I'm clean. And Kristen gave me a condom. So did Josh."

I laughed and it was drowned by his lips back on mine.

This was real. This was *happening*.

My breathing was ragged when I reached for the top of his pants and his breath hitched as I tugged at his belt. Then something in the familiar metallic clink of the buckle whipped me instantly back into the room.

Brandon. The last time I did this was with Brandon.

I sobered in a heartbeat. All the passion bled right out of me. I fell back onto the cushions, limp. "Jason, I can't."

His hands stilled immediately. All twelve of them.

"I'm not ready. I'm sorry," I whispered.

He hovered over me and put his forehead to mine and closed his eyes, catching his breath. His chest pressed into my bare breasts and I could feel exactly how much he wanted me, digging into my leg.

God, I felt awful. I should never have let him inside. The porch was safe. Bright as hell, but safe. The porch didn't come with expectations.

With *possibilities*.

He breathed against me for a minute, and I felt him cooling down.

"I just need more time. It's too soon." I bit my lip. "Don't be mad at me."

He opened one eye and looked at me gently. "I'm not mad. I could *never* be mad at you for that. Look at me." He held my eyes. "I get it. And I want you to be ready. You're not doing either of us a favor if you rush things. Okay?"

It was so earnest it made my heart melt. "Okay."

He smiled softly at me and kissed my forehead. Then he reached up and grabbed a throw blanket and pulled it over me, tucking it under my arms, and got up and put on his shirt.

I sat up on the sofa and clutched the blanket to my chest and I watched him as he went to let Tucker out of the laundry room. The dog bounded over to me and jumped into my lap, licking me.

Jason leaned down with a hand on the top of the sofa and kissed me. "I'll pick you up for the airport at five thirty. Get some sleep." He smiled at me.

"Thank you for understanding."

He shook his head. "You're worth the wait. You're worth everything." He winked and let himself out, and Tucker followed him, close on his heels.

CHAPTER 19

JASON

♪ MISERY BUSINESS | PARAMORE

Time to move. Lola Simone was sitting on the step of my trailer.

I slammed the door to my truck. "What the hell are you doing here?"

Tucker let out a low growl next to me.

She sat on the metal stair, lit by the lights of the pool, with her back against my door, smoking a joint. She wore a tiny silver dress and she spread her legs in answer to my question, balancing on the heels of her stilettos. She wasn't wearing panties.

"Oh, Jesus, come on," I said, looking away from her. "Enough of this shit, Lola. Get up." I looked back at her.

She didn't budge.

"Lola, now. *Leave*."

"Already? I just got here." She grinned up at me, her eyelids heavy. "Talk about a quickie," she muttered.

"Who the fuck gave you this address? I don't want you here. I'm *done*. Move or I'll move you myself."

Her eyes glinted and she shook her head.

Hot anger built inside me. I was so fucking sick of this. *Sick* of it. I'd been more than patient up to this point. I'd been a damn saint while she harassed me for months on end and dragged my reputation and my privacy through the music charts—but this was something else. Now I had to consider *Sloan*.

What if she had come home with me? Or shown up like she did last night? How would I even explain this shit? We were too new for this.

And what would Lola have done if Sloan had been here...

My jaw clenched. "I want you out of here. Let's go." I took her by the elbow and pulled her to her feet. I just wanted to get her out of my way so I could go inside, but I could feel the wobble of her body from the grip I had, and I knew that if I let go, she'd fall. Jesus, she was a fucking mess.

I nodded to the Hummer I'd seen parked outside the gate. "Call your chaperone to come get you."

She chuckled mirthlessly. "Awwwwww, are you mad at me?"

"You wrote a fucking song about me," I snapped. "What were you thinking? Were you trying to ruin my damn career? I have an image to maintain and you wrote me naked and drunk on a fucking beach!"

She grinned lazily, drawing again on her joint with her eyes closed, her bracelets clinking down her wrist. "Well, you inspire me, Minnesota. Never had something so clean before..." she slurred.

I shook my head at her. "I don't know what the fuck happened to you. I don't know what your fascination is with me, what you're on, or what your problem is, but I wish you'd figure it out and leave me the hell alone."

She blew her smoke sideways and smiled like a cobra. "So we're not doing this, huh?"

My nostrils flared. "No, we're *not*."

"You're something else, Jaxon. You snapped your fingers and I came all the way over here..." She dragged her eyes down my body and stared at my dick. "At least let me do that thing you like." She looked back up and sucked her bottom lip into her mouth.

I glared at her. "Don't *ever* come here again. Do you understand me?"

She smirked and yanked her arm down. The second I let go of her she teetered in her heels like a baby deer. She lost her balance and tumbled backward onto the lawn, laughing. I could see her bodyguard making his way up the drive, right on cue. She was cackling and giving me the finger when I scaled the metal steps with Tucker and slammed the door behind me. Two loud thumps that I guessed were shoes hit the side of the trailer.

I called Ernie. He answered groggily on the third ring. "If you're calling me with a cop car parked behind you, I'm going to need you to swallow the drugs," he joked.

"Lola was just in the yard."

He groaned. "Ah, shit. Give me five minutes."

By the time Ernie met me outside, Lola was gone. Her stilettos sat abandoned on the grass.

"I checked the security cameras," he said, meeting me by the pool in boxers and an open robe. "She used the gate code to get in. I don't suppose you gave that to her."

"No, I didn't. I also didn't tell her where I live," I said, dragging a hand down my mouth.

He blew a breath through his nose and looked around the yard. "Well, I can reset the code. That's not a big deal. But we have bigger problems. You're not gonna be happy." His eyes came back to me.

"What?"

He took a deep breath. "Due to the substantial financial commitment that your label is now making for your international tour, they would like to bring in another headliner. It's pretty standard. I've seen this before. It's not a lack of faith, it's more of an insurance policy to make sure they don't lose their fucking shirt."

"Okay…"

"They want to bring in Lola."

I dropped my arms. "No. Absolutely not."

"They like the tie-in. You've got three potentially hit singles with her on the soundtrack. They want you mainstream and Lola is as commercial as they come, so attaching you to her is beneficial. And say what you will about her, but everything she fucking touches turns to gold. And Jason, she wants it. She wants it *bad*. In fact, I think it was her idea."

There was no fucking way. It would be a shit show. Lola was a disaster. She'd be plastered the whole time, I'd be scraping her off the floor and propping her up on stage, peeling her off me like duct tape. "I'm not doing it."

"Yeah, well, I thought you might say that. I did what I thought you'd want me to do, which was to tell them to go to hell in the nicest way possible. I said if it ain't broke, don't fix it. Your US tour dates are selling out nicely and you don't need the help. And I made a point that Lola's a hot fucking mess and she's one overdose from a ninety-day stint in rehab."

I nodded. "Good. What did they say?"

"They thanked me for my feedback and said they'd take it into consideration."

I stared at him. "Can they do this?"

"They can do whatever the fuck they want. They're paying for it. This is just like the fog machine and the fucking pyrotechnics. It's their call."

I raked a hand through my hair. "No." I looked him in the eye. "If they dump her on me, I'm out."

"So now comes the fun part." Ernie ticked off on his fingers. "You walk, and they sue you for breach of contract. You have to pay back your advances, plus their expenses, plus any projected revenue from the tour. The damages will be in the millions. These guys don't fuck around. You could have a kid in the hospital and they'd expect you to be there, onstage as scheduled. Barring a mental fucking breakdown or a life-threating illness, you'll be there. Even in a *coma* you might be there. They're not above operating you like a puppet with their hand up your ass." He dipped his head to look at me. "And the icing on the bullshit cake? If you do manage to get a tour canceled for anything less than some medical emergency, you can kiss your fucking career goodbye because nobody's going to touch you after that."

I felt the color drain from my face.

"I don't understand," I breathed. "I don't fucking get why she's pushing this. Why *me?*"

He scoffed. "You're probably the only guy who didn't do lines off her ass and smack her around before he fucked her. She's gotta tour with somebody, so why not the guy who held doors for her?" He shook his head. "We are between a rock and a hard place, my friend. I gotta tell you, if you would have asked me a month ago who the worst person to bring on tour is, I'd have said a girlfriend. But Lola? She's my fucking tour nightmare. You see the shit in the tabloids this morning? She threw a beer bottle at a photog's *head.* She's like a rampaging hybrid of all my ex-wives, on cocaine."

Sloan.

A cloud of doom rolled over me as I realized for the first time just how far-reaching this was.

I wouldn't be able to bring Sloan on tour. I wouldn't even be able to fly her out to *visit*. It would be uncomfortable for her at best. At worst it would be downright dangerous. Lola had a history of instability and violence and some weird fucking fixation on me. Who knew what she'd do? Even locked gates couldn't keep her out. Even if I got Sloan a bodyguard, I couldn't guarantee Lola wouldn't get to her with more than a year of close proximity to try. Hell, Kanye had bodyguards too and a lot of good that had done. Not to mention all the lewd shit I knew she'd throw at my girlfriend just to piss me off. I couldn't subject her to it.

Fourteen months. Fourteen fucking months of Lola, without Sloan.

"What if I get a restraining order?" I asked, clutching at straws. "They can't force her on my tour if she can't get within a hundred feet of me."

He scoffed. "For what? Throwing stripper shoes at your trailer? Mentioning you on Twitter? Has she made any threats? Hurt you in any way?" Ernie put a hand on my shoulder. "Look, I don't want you climbing a ledge yet. I'm working on it. I'll get the lawyers involved if I have to. I didn't even plan on telling you until I had a definitive answer, but with this shit..."

"Fuck. No wonder she showed up here." I pinched the bridge of my nose. She'd probably hoped for some happy reunion between us, so I wouldn't fight it when I found out what she was trying to do.

But I *would* fight it. I would do everything in my power to make sure this didn't happen. Because if it did, it might cost me Sloan.

CHAPTER 20

JASON

♪ SUPERPOSITION | YOUNG THE GIANT

My feet were back on Minnesota soil for the first time since Christmas. I loved that Sloan had come home with me. Despite the shitty night I'd had, compliments of Lola, I hadn't stopped smiling all day. I was irritable right until I picked Sloan up and she bounced into my arms.

We walked with Tucker to the rental car counter at the tiny airport in Duluth. Sloan laughed at the single luggage carousel.

"So where is Minneapolis from here?" she asked, leaning down to pet Tucker. He sat pressed against her leg, looking up at her.

"The Twin Cities are two and a half hours south."

"And we're going..."

"Two hours north. Let me show you." I pulled out my phone and brought up Google Maps. "Right now we're here. And here's Ely."

She leaned over and I caught a flurry of her perfume as her shoulder pressed into my arm. Something seemed to activate between us. She turned her face slightly in my direction, her eyes moving to my lips, and I felt the same pull that had almost dragged us under last night tug me toward her again.

Sloan was moving slower in this relationship than I was. I didn't take it personally. I meant what I said: I'd wait for her. I'd wait as long as she needed. When she was ready, she'd let me know. And if I was doing my job as her boyfriend, making her feel safe—and making sure she wanted me enough—it would all work itself out eventually. There was no rush.

This was just a season, and there's beauty in all seasons. Even if you *are* looking forward to the next one.

"It's surrounded by so much green," she said, clearing her throat, and we both seemed to snap from our daze.

"It's on the edge of the Boundary Waters Canoe Area Wilderness."

"And you go in there?"

"I grew up in there," I said, tucking my phone back into my pocket.

She looked up at me with those deep-brown eyes and put her hands on my chest. "Thank you for bringing me." She stood on her toes and gave me a quick kiss.

When we broke away, she nuzzled her nose to mine. "And you're sure your parents are okay with me coming?" she asked again.

"Absolutely. My mom has probably been cleaning and recleaning the house in anticipation of your arrival. You're the first girlfriend I've brought home since prom."

She jerked her head back and stared at me for a second. "Please tell me that's a joke."

"I haven't brought a girl home in ten years."

Panic washed across her face and she wriggled out of my arms. "Why?!"

"Uh, because I haven't had one worth bringing?" I smiled. Flustering her was becoming one of my favorite hobbies. I totally got why Kristen did it. Sloan was so beautiful when she was blushing and biting her lip.

"But...you've had serious girlfriends. What about the one that you dated for three years?"

"Jessica? Yeah. That was my prom date."

"Jason!"

"What?" I laughed.

"What the hell? This is not what you sold me on!"

I chuckled and put my hands on her arms. "They're going to love you."

She put a finger to her eyelid and looked at me bleakly.

I shook my head at her. "You would make the worst poker player, you know that, right?"

"Jason, you made this sound like it's not that big of a deal."

"Would you have come if I'd told you the truth?"

"No."

"Well, then."

She glared at me.

"Would you prefer that you're just one in a long line of women that I've brought home?"

She narrowed her lone eye at me. "No."

"Well, then," I said again, proving my point.

She took her finger from her eyelid and hugged her arms around herself. "What if they don't like me?"

Impossible.

I tipped up her chin. "There's a very real possibility that they'll like you better than they like me."

Mom was flipping out. Not just because Sloan was The Huntsman's Wife, but because I didn't bring women home as a rule.

And bringing Sloan home meant *exactly* what Mom thought it did.

CHAPTER 21

SLOAN

♪ WHITE WINTER HYMNAL | FLEET FOXES

Jason had his playlist on the Bluetooth of our rental SUV. On the plane we'd shared his headphones, each of us wearing an earbud so we could listen and still talk to each other. We'd had our foreheads together the whole time. I think I'd learned every fleck in his irises on that flight.

Jason looked at me from behind the wheel. "So just to warn you, my mom's going to put us in separate rooms. She's kind of old-fashioned."

"Wise woman." It was probably safest to keep us separated, especially after last night.

"We could always get a hotel room," he suggested, giving me a wicked sideways glance. "Everyone *does* keep telling us to get one."

My cheeks heated.

I could count the number of men I'd slept with on one hand and have fingers to spare. And the last person on my list had been the only man I'd planned on sleeping with ever again. Even though absolutely *nothing* had felt wrong about what happened between Jason and me last night, Brandon's memory had been just enough of a buzzkill to pull me from the moment.

But I doubted I'd hesitate again.

Jason was slowly edging out all the things that froze me in time. He was thawing me from my nuclear winter from the outside in—and he was almost to my core.

He smiled at the road and I admired his profile from the side. The lines that creased at the corners of his eyes, the slope of his nose, a small freckle on his cheek, a square jaw and closely trimmed beard with its flecks of red, his Adam's apple.

My eyes followed his neck down to his arm. I took in the muscles of his biceps, then the hair on his forearm, his hand on the wheel. I thought of how his voice sounded when he sang, the way the calluses from his guitar felt on my bare skin, and how much talent was in those fingers. Those hands wanted to touch *me*.

No, next time *nothing* would stop me.

"This is Ely." His whole face lit up as we began to drive through the small town.

God, I wish I could be that excited to come home.

Mom had sold the house I grew up in years ago, after the divorce, and moved to a one-bedroom apartment with her new husband. Dad lived in San Diego with his new wife. I was an only child. Brandon's family and I drifted apart after he died. I was still friends with his sister, Claudia, on Instagram, but we hadn't seen each other since the funeral. Kristen was the closest thing I had to a sibling. It must be so great to be able to come home like Jason was.

The two-lane road ran right through the heart of the town. Restaurants and shops peppered the street on both sides. No Starbucks, but I could manage without it for three days.

We passed Jason's family's business and he pointed it out as we drove by. The building was cute. It was a log house with *Ely Outfitting Company* on the side. They'd used a canoe as a flower box under the window, and the railing on the steps was made from paddles.

We kept going fifteen more minutes beyond the town and turned down a one-lane dirt road with a mailbox at the entrance.

I craned my neck to see the house as it came into view. There wasn't another home in sight and there hadn't been for most of the drive since we left the edge of town. The single-story log house was nestled in the woods, surrounded by forest so thick I couldn't see the other side of it. The roof was green over honey-colored logs, and a porch with log banisters ran the length of the front. The smell of burning firewood filled the crisp air.

Jason parked and came around to meet me as I unbuckled myself.

"You ready?" he asked as I got out of the car. He stood with his hand on the top of the SUV, barring my exit from behind my open door. "I'm going to need one last good kiss from you. We might not get another chance until we leave on Sunday. I have a feeling we won't get much time alone." He smiled at my mouth.

"Oh, I *wondered* why you had me cornered here. You're saying goodbye to me for a few days."

"I'm only saying goodbye to your lips."

The passenger side of the SUV blocked us from the view of the house, so I wrapped my arms around his neck and kissed him, smiling against his mouth. Then a booming voice broke into our private moment. "Hey! Get a room, asshole!"

Jason shut his eyes and grinned. "*Fuck.*"

I turned around and looked through the windows of the car to see a man coming our way.

"David's here," Jason said, smiling.

Jason met his brother in front of the SUV. The burly, flannel-clad man held a bundle of firewood. He dropped it and gave Jason a hug as Tucker jumped up and down at their feet.

David looked to be around thirty, and he outweighed Jason by an easy fifty pounds. He was tall and bearded, like his brother, and looked exactly like a lumberjack. All he needed was suspenders.

"Look at you, you Hollywood big shot," David said, holding Jason away from him. "California turned you into a suit. Is that a fucking spray tan?"

"I can't believe Karen let you out this weekend. Did you barter your balls for your freedom?" Jason replied with a grin.

"Ahh, fuck you," David said, good-naturedly. Then he looked at me. "You must be Sloan. Nice to meet you." He put out a hand and gave me a firm shake. "This guy said he had a girlfriend. Of course, nobody believed it. Looks like I just lost fifty bucks at the office." He slapped Jason on the back. "So what's a beautiful thing like you doing with someone who won the Ugliest Man in Ely contest three years in a row?"

I smiled and channeled my inner Kristen. "It's purely sexual."

Jason snorted and David howled. "Whoooooaa, I like this girl!" He put an arm around his brother and knuckled his chest.

Jason beamed. "Where are the kids?"

"The kids are sick. Karen stayed with them. Colds or ear infections or something. I don't know. They get every damn thing in that school they're in."

David opened the trunk and grabbed my suitcase and Jason's backpack. Jason picked up his brother's firewood and nodded for me to follow them to the house. Tucker seemed to know where he was. He ran right to the front door and started to whine and scratch.

"Mom's pissed at you," David said ahead of us, wrangling my

heavy luggage like it weighed less than a gallon of milk. "You were supposed to be here hours ago."

"We stopped in Duluth," Jason said.

Duluth had been amazing. We'd walked along Lake Superior. It was so cool. I hadn't realized our sightseeing came at the expense of time with his family, however. He hadn't told me we'd been expected earlier.

David pushed open the front door and Tucker ran inside.

"Mom, they're here!" David called out, pulling off his boots by stepping on the backs of them with his feet. Jason did the same, not putting down his firewood.

I closed the door behind us and began taking off my shoes.

A woman came around the corner. She wore an apron and a red baking mitt on her hand. Tucker followed her and danced at her feet. She had brown hair pulled into a loose bun and soft hazel eyes. She gave Jason a sweet-looking scowl. "Jason! Why didn't you call me and tell me how late you were going to be?" she asked, looking more worried than pissed, as David had put it.

The entry of the house was a small room with coat hooks on the walls and a single step up into the hallway. Jason's mom stood on the step with her hands on her hips, still looking up at Jason despite the elevation. She put the hand with the mitt on his shoulder as he kissed her hello. Her eyes met mine over his back and she beamed at me.

"Mom, I said we were *landing* at one. I told you I'd make it by dinner. And you know I never get a signal on Highway One."

"Never mind," she said, waving him off. "I want to meet Sloan now. I'll deal with you later."

Jason turned to me, amusement on his face. "Mom, this is Sloan. Sloan, this is my mom, Patricia."

Having done his duty as far as introductions, Jason edged past his mother with his bundle of wood, leaving us to each other.

Patricia came down the step to greet me, her eyes alight. "Oh, you're beautiful," she said, giving me a hug. "Thank God I have another woman here this weekend. We're outnumbered." She held me out by the arms and smiled at me warmly. "Can you believe I never had a daughter? Just me and all these men."

"I bet they can eat," I said.

"Feeding them is a full-time job." She laughed. "Come on, let's go in. I was so excited when Jason said you were coming. I felt like I was getting a visitor just for me. The boys will be doing their own thing for most of the weekend, they always do." She led me into the house.

The home was thoughtfully decorated, with soft area rugs over the wood floors. The living room we passed was comfortable and rustic. A fire crackled in the fireplace and a deer head was mounted above the mantel. A huge bay window overlooked a lake.

Jason and David were already in the kitchen when we got there.

A man stood over the sink doing dishes. When he looked up, I knew *exactly* who he was. He looked like an older version of Jason. His beard and hair were salt and pepper, but his eyes were the same clear blue as his son's.

"Dad, this is Sloan," Jason said. "Sloan, this is my dad, Paul."

I was expecting a hand, but I got a hug and a kiss on the cheek instead. It took me by surprise. Jason grinned at me over Paul's shoulder.

Paul smiled at me. "We've heard so much about you, Sloan. The Huntsman's Wife! Very impressive. We've eaten a lot of your food over the years."

"I've heard a lot about you too," I replied, flustered by the familiar welcome. What was up with Larsen men and flustering?

"And what do you think of our state?" Paul asked.

"It's beautiful. I see why Jason sings about it."

Paul smiled at his son approvingly.

David sat in a chair at the table and Jason hovered over a pot, holding the lid.

"What are we having?" he asked, picking up a spoon and tasting the contents.

"Swedish meatballs." Patricia hit him with her baking mitt. "Get out of there," she said, running him off.

I smiled.

"Something to drink?" Jason asked me.

"No, thank you. You want help?" I asked Patricia, joining her by the stove. Jason smiled at me and grabbed a beer from the fridge and went to sit with his brother.

"Would you mind chopping some parsley?" she asked, pointing to a cutting board. "It's in the crisper drawer."

I dove right in, tying up my hair and washing my hands. I searched the fridge for the parsley and dug around for a knife and began to chop. Patricia looked on approvingly. I faced the brothers as I worked, while Patricia moved around behind me, dropping meatballs into a frying pan.

"Dad wants help putting the dock out tomorrow," David said to Jason.

"Already?" Jason asked, opening his beer.

Paul spoke over his dishes. "Ice is gone. Been warm this year."

"How's the dock?" Jason asked.

David looked over at his parents, whose backs were turned, and mouthed, "Fucked up."

"The dock is fine. Just needs patching," Paul said, not turning away from his dishes.

"Hey," David said, "Jason and I both offered to get you guys a new dock. One with wheels. That you can roll. That doesn't splinter."

Jason tossed his bottle cap at his brother. It hit David on the chest and he produced a stoic middle finger. I laughed to myself.

"You know your dad," Patricia said, not turning around. "He doesn't like to get new things if what he has can be repaired. And that's what he's got two sons for."

"It's fine, Mom. We'll get her out. We always do," Jason said. "What else needs to be done around here?"

Paul rattled off a list of projects. I saw what Patricia meant about the boys doing their own thing. They were here to *work*. That was fine by me. I wanted to get to know Patricia better anyway. I wanted naked baby pictures of Jason before this weekend was out.

Patricia and I served dinner like we'd been doing it together for years, plating things and chatting the whole time. I took a seat next to her at the table so we could keep talking. The meatballs were amazing.

When Paul discussed the long to-do list for tomorrow, nobody complained. Nobody cussed in front of Paul and Patricia, and Jason and David refrained from their ribbing of each other in their presence. I liked David. He worked in IT and lived in St. Paul. He didn't come up very often, mostly holidays. He had three small kids at home and his wife, Karen, worked full-time too.

All during dinner, Paul treated his wife with a reverence that made me smile to myself. He held her hand on top of the table during dessert and kissed her on the cheek both times he got up. It was adorable. It actually reminded me a lot of the way Jason was with me. Always touching me. Always turned to me somehow.

After dinner, the men cleared the table and did the dishes

while they went on about walleye fishing and some new lure Paul had.

Patricia and I had a cup of coffee in the living room while we waited for the guys to finish up. Tucker curled up between us on the sofa like he couldn't pick who he liked better. We were both sitting with a hand on his back, talking, as the men rejoined us in the living room. David threw another log on the fire and I smiled at Jason as he plopped next to me.

"Is that yours?" I asked him, nodding at a guitar propped against the side of the fireplace.

"No. My dad's. He plays too. He taught me."

"And your voice?" I asked. "Who gave you that?" Jason had an impressive vocal range.

"That's all his," Patricia said, looking at her son proudly. "No idea where it came from. Just a God-given gift. And Jason tells us that *you're* a talented artist," she said, putting her coffee cup to her lips.

"Oh, he did, did he?" I asked, giving him a raised eyebrow. "You lied to your mother?"

He smiled at me. "I've never actually seen one of Sloan's original pieces. But I've very much enjoyed the commissioned art I've seen her do."

"So you liked the astronaut cat?" I teased.

"Of course. Who wouldn't like an astronaut cat?"

"I paint for a few companies that outsource commissioned artwork," I explained. "I do some freelance stuff on Etsy too. Quick pieces. Birch trees, animal art. That kind of thing. Although, Jason, you *have* seen one of my original pieces. You did like it very much, actually. You just didn't know it was mine," I said, looking at him.

"When?" he asked, his brows drawing down.

"The self-portrait that you like at my house," I said carefully, looking at him, willing him to know what I was talking about without my having to say, *The one of me naked? In my bedroom, over my bed?* His family didn't need that visual.

When shock spread across his face, I knew he understood what I was talking about. "That's a *painting*?" he asked, his mouth open. "That's not a photograph?"

His reaction gave me a swell of pride. I'd forgotten that feeling, the satisfaction that my work brought me when I saw the way it affected others.

"No," I said, loving the surprise on his face. "I paint hyper-realistic art."

He sat up, staring at me. "Sloan, that's—that's incredible. I've looked at that dozens of times, up close. I had no idea that was a painting."

"Dozens of times? Up close?" I asked with a sideways smile.

Then I turned to his family, not wanting to leave them out of the conversation. "Here's one of my paintings that sold a few years ago," I said, swiping through the photo gallery on my cell phone. When I found the painting that I'd titled *Girl in Poppies*, I handed the phone around the room.

"I don't paint these anymore," I said. "They're very labor intensive. I have to take up to a hundred photos of my subject to work off of, and each one takes me up to two months. But this is what I used to do."

I didn't show my art off like this very often, but I sensed Jason wanted to impress his family, and I wasn't very proud of my current job, if I was being honest.

"Sloan, this is wonderful. You *have* to keep painting," Patricia said, genuine awe in her voice. "You have a gift. No wonder you two hit it off. You're both so creative."

She was right, I'd never thought of that. His voice was one thing, but his songwriting was something else. His lyrics were where he really shone. Beautiful and deep. They were what I loved the most about his music.

Jason looked at my painting photo last. When he handed my phone back, he stared at the side of my face. And he kept on staring.

CHAPTER 22

JASON

♪ EVERYWHERE | ROOSEVELT

Where's the bathroom?" Sloan asked.

"Second door down the hall," Dad said.

"I'll take you," I offered, getting up from the couch. I wanted to get her alone anyway. As soon as we were out of view of the living room, I spun her and kissed her against the wall.

"Jason, your parents are going to catch us," she whispered through a smile, looking back the way we'd come.

"I don't care," I breathed against her mouth. "Kiss me."

They loved her. I'd known before I'd brought her that they would. She made me feel proud to know her, like having a woman like her care about me was its own sort of achievement. When she and Mom went to the living room after dinner, Dad had told me she was remarkable and David had asked me where the hell I found her.

When I pulled away, we were both out of breath.

"Why didn't you tell me about the painting?" I asked.

God, how could she stop creating her own art when she had

so much talent? She made me want to unravel her, take her by a corner and undo her.

"I wanted to see if you'd figure it out. Besides, you didn't tell me you were Jaxon Waters, so now we're even," she said, biting her lip and glancing at my mouth. Then she looked back up. "Hey, what's a meat raffle?" she whispered.

I chuckled. "It's a raffle where you win meat as prizes."

"Oh, I wondered why your parents 'scored meat at a bar.' That makes sense now."

I loved seeing her experiencing my world. I wanted to show her everything. But it was more than that. I wanted to *share* everything with her. Like I didn't want there to be anything that she wasn't a part of. I wouldn't have come this weekend if she hadn't come with me. I would have stayed in California to be with her.

Distance from her was starting to feel like the tension on a bungee cord. The farther away I got, the stronger the urge to come back to her. And the cord felt like it was getting shorter. Like my threshold for not being with her was lowering.

What would I do if I couldn't see her when I was on tour? It would kill me. And how would I even explain to her why she couldn't visit? I messed around with some unstable, violent woman that I'm being forced to tour with? She might hurt you and I can't make you safe? Here's a song she wrote about me having sex with her, sitting in the Top 10? God, the whole fucking thing made me cringe. I was waiting to see if Ernie could get Lola off the ticket before I sat down to discuss the situation with Sloan. I wasn't coming at her with this until I had some sort of game plan.

"You better go," she whispered. "They're going to think something is going on between us."

I grinned. "Isn't there?"

She squeezed herself sideways and out from under me and

continued on to the bathroom as I watched her walk down the hall. She stopped in the doorway and made a shooing motion at me before she went in, smiling and shaking her head.

I stared after her, long after she'd shut the door, and I wondered offhandedly if this was what Dad had felt like when he met Mom...

And somehow I knew that it was.

CHAPTER 23

SLOAN

♪ INTO DUST | MAZZY STAR

Jason staggered into the kitchen at 7:00 a.m. with Tucker and found me not only awake and caffeinated but showered, dressed, and cooking with his mom.

Patricia and I had coordinated the start time for breakfast last night, and I took my cooking duties *very* seriously. Apparently we were expecting a large crowd.

"Good morning, ladies." He slid open the back door and let Tucker out. He poured himself a black coffee, looking unbelievably adorable with his messy hair in his eyes.

His plaid pajama bottoms and gray T-shirt made me want to wrap my arms around his waist to see what his chest smelled like. My heart picked up a little thinking about it.

He held his mug in his hand and came around to the stove and gave Patricia a peck on the cheek. Then he turned to me where I stood cutting a melon by the sink. "Did you sleep well?" he asked. Before I could reply, he leaned in and gave me a swift kiss too, only he put mine on the lips. In front of his *mom*.

I knocked over a container of blueberries.

Nothing was inappropriate about the kiss. It was kind of sweet, actually. I'd just been under the impression we were going to be totally hands off in front of his parents. He'd kissed me good night last night, but only after walking me to my room, and the hallway had been empty.

Patricia smiled down at her frying pan.

In typical Jason fashion, he grinned at the victory of catching me off guard. He popped a blueberry into his smiling mouth and then seemed to decide he'd embarrassed me enough for one morning and excused himself to take a shower.

"Sorry," I said to Patricia, picking up blueberries from the counter, my face hot. "It's like he has to fluster me once a day or a baby bunny dies somewhere or something. He's very committed to it."

She laughed heartily. "He learned it from his father. I think they like the color it puts in our cheeks."

I smiled. Hanging out with Patricia was my idea of a good time. I loved her.

A half hour later, Jason came back in and helped with dishes and cleanup as Patricia and I cooked. He found any chance he could to put a hand on my back or to stand close to me. Patricia totally noticed it. She kept smiling at us.

People started to filter in for breakfast around 8:30. Two cousins of Jason's, three of Jason's friends, and a neighbor were joining the Larsen men to do some work around the property, and the deal for free labor included food.

After the men went to work, I kept finding excuses to go outside to see what Jason was doing. I found him on the roof pulling shingles.

He wasn't wearing a shirt.

I was a lurker. His shirtless body had me creeping on him from the trees. I'd have used binoculars if I could have done it without being noticed. Broad, strong shoulders, six-pack abs, a defined chest that made me want to trace the contours with my fingers. I was my boyfriend's stalker.

When the men pulled on their waders and started putting in the dock, it was almost lunchtime. I liked the dock project because I could see Jason from the sliding glass doors off the kitchen, though he had a shirt on now, so it was slightly less exciting.

When Patricia and I brought sandwiches down, we set them right on the wooden planks so the men could stand in the lake and use the dock as a table. They descended on the food. Jason grabbed two sandwiches and a beer and we moved to the end, away from everyone, and I sat down with my legs crossed under me so I could be by him as he ate. He stood up to his stomach in water.

"Are you having fun?" I asked him, my chin in my hand.

"I am now," he said, smiling at me, taking a bite of a turkey sandwich.

I wanted to kiss him. He looked extra rugged and handsome today. Heaven help us both if he did one more sexy man-thing around here. If he took off his shirt and started splitting logs, I'd probably drag him into a bush and let him have his way with me.

"How cold is that water?"

He shrugged. "Forty-five? Forty-six degrees?"

"Wow. That's cold. But you're dry in there?" I peered into the front of his camouflaged waders.

"Want to put a hand inside and check?" His eyes gleamed.

I dipped the tips of my fingers into the lake and flicked him with water. He laughed.

The sun warmed the planks of the dock. A speaker played

Journey somewhere, and Tucker ran soaking wet back and forth along the shore with about half a dozen other dogs. Every pickup truck that had pulled onto the property this morning had had a hunting dog in the front seat.

"I have a confession to make," I said, drumming my fingers on my cheek. "I was checking you out on the roof earlier. I didn't really need to get anything out of the car three times."

He grinned at me over his sandwich. "And I had to talk myself down from sneaking into your room last night. Only the thought of my mom catching us stopped me."

"I locked my door last night. I figured I might have to protect you from yourself. I know how much of a risk taker you are." I ticked off on my fingers. "Kissing me on a first date, volunteering to meet Kristen and Josh, making out with me in the hallway with your parents in the other room. You have no self-preservation instincts."

"Not with you I don't."

I laughed.

He finished eating and I got up and grabbed him a fresh beer from the cooler. "Do you put in your parents' dock every spring?" I asked, sitting back down in front of him.

He put his hand on my thigh and rubbed it absently with his thumb. "I try to. They're getting older. They need the help." He took a drink of his beer. "You know, I got my stage name putting in the dock."

"Oh?"

"Yeah. It was a few years ago. David's oldest, Camille, was three and she couldn't say Jason. She used to call me Jaxon. I was standing in the lake and she pointed at me and said, 'Jaxon in the water.' I liked it, so I used it."

I gave him a smile. "I wondered about that. There wasn't

anything about it on your Wikipedia page. I was going to ask you."

"Nobody knows that but my family. And you."

I smiled, and we watched each other for a moment. "I wish I could kiss you," I said quietly. "I've been wishing I could kiss you all day."

A slow grin crept across his face. He put his beer down. "Well, I don't see how I can refuse *that* request."

He closed in on me, the lake swirling around him, and his fingers traveled past my jaw into my hair. He paused a moment, grinning an inch from my lips, and I inhaled him, his masculine smell, the hops on his breath, the faint intoxicating scent of his cologne mixed with his sweat. Then he closed his eyes and kissed me.

The hoots and whistles started almost immediately. Even the dogs howled.

"I'm gonna catch a ton of shit for this," he breathed against my smiling mouth, his eyes closed.

"Well, I hope it was worth it."

He answered by kissing me again, and even though the cheering got louder, I don't think either of us really heard it.

When he broke away, he put his hands around my face and held my eyes with his. "The reports say there's a good chance of seeing the northern lights tonight."

"Really?"

"Yeah." He glanced down at my lips. "It happens late, so we'll probably need a tent, some sleeping bags. I'll set us up." He looked back up at me.

My heart pounded. I knew what he was saying to me.

We would be alone.

~

After dinner, as soon as Jason got out of the shower, I took a quick one of my own. He'd instructed me to dress warmly, so I put on almost everything I'd brought.

He double-checked my layers and mumbled with a smile about his California girl getting cold. Not satisfied, he made me put on his bulky Twins sweatshirt. We said our goodbyes, left Tucker with Patricia, and made our way down to the rack of canoes outside the garage.

He handed me some paddles to carry, then lifted a canoe seat-side down onto his shoulders and walked it to the water. He tossed a large green pack inside.

Watching him carry that canoe so effortlessly was very, *very* sexy.

"Where are we going?" I asked, as he lifted me in and handed me a life jacket.

"Somewhere special." He pulled on his own life jacket and stepped right into the frigid water in his boots.

We slid across the lake as the sun started to set. The house fell away from view, and nothing but nature folded in on either side. The trees rose up like sentinels along the shoreline in an impenetrable wall of foliage. There wasn't the faintest hint of anything man-made, not a house, not a dock or boat. Not a single piece of trash or even a plane crossing the sky. It was just stillness and the sound of the paddle churning the water. Occasionally he would point out a beaver dam or a bald eagle flying overhead. But besides that, we didn't talk.

After a long ride he pulled up to some rocks on an island, banking the canoe sideways, expertly. He hoisted the pack, helped me out, and lifted the canoe from the water and set it on shore.

We hiked into the forest and up a rise, coming out into a rocky clearing overlooking the lake.

"We're here," he said, opening up the pack and pulling out a tent.

"This is where we're sleeping?"

"Yup," he said, laying down a tent pad. "This is the Boundary Waters. Two million acres if you combine the Canadian and American sides—some of the most pristine wilderness in the world."

I smiled as I helped him set up the tent. We blew up some sleeping pads and camping pillows, zipped our sleeping bags together so we'd both fit, and tossed them inside. He set up two camp chairs and got a fire going, and we watched the flames jumping as the last of the light faded.

I could see every star in the sky. I hadn't even known there were that many stars. This was nothing like any kind of camping I'd ever done. This was truly remote. No car sounds, no lights pricking in the distance. Nothing with you except what you carried in.

The wood shifted, sparks cracked and climbed, and I tucked my legs into my sweatshirt and hugged them. Jason sat with his elbows on his knees and his hands together, looking at the flames. He'd grown quiet. The air smelled like pine and smoke. It got colder and colder by the second. I looked out over the dark lake toward the distant sound of the lapping of the water on the shore. "I could paint this place. It's so breathtaking," I said.

"You should see it in the fall and winter." He nestled another log on the fire and sat back down. "Which reminds me, I have some news I wanted to tell you."

"Good news or bad?"

"Good. I mean, for my career it's great. I haven't told anyone yet, not even my parents. My label's extended my tour. Two more months here and eight months overseas. It's going to be worldwide."

I beamed. "Jason, that's amazing!" And then, almost as quickly as I said it, I realized what it actually meant. "Wait...you'll be gone for over a year?"

He shrugged, looking at the fire. "Yeah. But I get a five-week break in between for the holidays. And the first leg of the tour is local."

Local. He meant anywhere in America. Followed by what? Eight months where he'd be going to sleep when I was waking up? My heart sank, and I hid my frown behind my knees.

I'd been mentally prepared for four months. I figured if things were good between us when he left, we'd keep this going like we had when he was in Australia. I wasn't looking forward to it, but it was doable. At worst the time difference would be three hours. Maybe I'd drive to see him when he was playing in California and Vegas or fly out to be with him for a few days every once in a while.

But this? This was different. This was *very* different. This was over a year. And eight months of it would be a ten-plus-hour international flight somewhere if I wanted to see him. Massive time differences coupled with grueling schedules. I'd read his itinerary—it was ridiculous. And he'd already told me how different this tour would be from the last one in terms of his workload. That he was headlining and that meant he'd be responsible for all the promoting and that his sets and rehearsals would be longer. He'd be doing meet and greets with fans and he'd be on and off planes.

My parents had done the long-distance thing for years when my dad worked overseas. Kristen did it with the guy she dated before Josh. I knew *exactly* what this looked like. It was a slow death of a relationship. A separation that eroded everything, little by little, until it was stripped clean and you were practically strangers, lonely and attached to someone invisible.

I'd been lonely and attached to someone invisible for two years. I wouldn't do it again. I *couldn't* do it again.

Not that Jason *wanted* me to do it. We'd only known each other two and a half weeks, so I didn't in any way expect him to ask me to come with him—and even if he did, I wouldn't. It was too soon. I just didn't move that fast. I'd been with Brandon almost three years before I moved in with him. I'd been with Brandon a year before I even went on *vacation* with him.

Now I wondered if Jason had been preparing me for this over the last week. Every time he'd talked about the insane amount of work he'd be doing, was he setting me up to let me down gently when the time came? He had to know as well as I did that this would end us.

We went on listening to the haunting sound of the loons in the darkness. He didn't further the discussion and I was glad. I didn't want to have a breakup conversation around this campfire, and judging by his silence, he didn't seem to want to have one either. He probably wanted to enjoy this time. So did I.

When Brandon died, I'd wished for one more day. Just one more day to be with him and be happy. And Jason and I still had days. If all I was going to get was now and the next few weeks, I wanted to savor it, even if I knew it was going to end.

A shooting star tore across the sky and I looked back over at him to find him looking at me. He had his hands clasped, his cheek resting on his knuckles.

"What are you thinking about?" I asked.

There was a pause before he replied. "You. I seem to be doing that a lot lately." Another long silence. "What was Brandon like?"

"Brandon?" Jason had never asked about him before. I let out a long breath and put my cheek to my knees. "He was steady. Strong. He was the kind of person you could depend on. Loyal." I smiled a little. "He would always serve himself last. If we were at a barbecue or a party, he'd wait until everyone else served themselves before he'd make his own plate. He always wanted to make sure there was enough for everyone else before he ever thought about himself." My face went soft at the memory. "He was good like that. He was a good person."

Jason gazed back at me. "What happened to the drunk driver?"

I scoffed. "Not enough. She got two years. She gets out in a few months. Never even said she was sorry."

We looked at each other in the light of the campfire.

"Jason, I never told you this. Maybe you kind of figured. But you're the only person I've dated since him. Like, the *only* one. It's a big deal to me. *You* are a big deal to me."

He didn't say anything. He studied my face, the fire casting a warm glow that flickered in his eyes. I knew he understood what I was telling him. I hadn't been with anyone in two years. In any capacity.

"You're a big deal to me too," he said finally, holding my gaze.

We stared at each other and an eternity passed in the seconds.

"Cold?" he asked. "Want to get in the tent? I'll leave the rainfly off so we can still see the sky."

I nodded.

Jason poured water over the fire and we stepped inside the tent and took off our shoes. He hung a lamp from the top pole and zipped the door closed. Then we silently stripped off our heavy layers.

Jason stopped at his T-shirt and the thermals he wore under his pants. He probably didn't want to assume. But that's not where *I* stopped.

I took everything off but my tank top and my underwear. I undressed without looking at him. If I looked, I might be too nervous to go through with it. But I could feel his eyes on my body as I stepped out of my pants and stood in the tent in the red G-string I'd worn. I'd worn it on purpose. I'd worn it for *him*.

Once I'd taken off everything I dared, I climbed quickly into the sleeping bag, my teeth chattering. The slick fabric was freezing. "Hurry, it's so cold." I shivered.

He followed suit and took off his T-shirt and thermals, turned off the light, and got into the sleeping bag in nothing but his boxers. He gathered me immediately under him, caging me between his forearms and legs like a human heating pad. "Better?" he asked, looking down on me in the dark.

I nodded, biting my lip. "Better."

He was so warm. He smelled like soap and mint toothpaste and just a hint of smoke. I could feel the coarseness of the hair on his legs, rubbing against the naked smoothness of mine. The strong muscles of his thighs locking me in his firm embrace. His erection, growing harder with every breath he took, pressing into my stomach.

He caressed my cheek absently with his thumb. "You're shaking," he whispered, and gently, carefully, he kissed along my jaw, his beard scratching against my skin. I tipped my head back and he trailed his lips down, arching his body over mine as he worked his way to my collarbone.

He didn't move against me. While I could feel he was turned on, it was like he wanted me to know everything was on my terms and he wouldn't initiate anything unless I made it clear I wanted him to—it was *very* Jason of him.

He was always respectful of what I needed. I got the feeling that if I freaked out and told him to sleep outside, he would. He wouldn't even question it. He'd just kiss me good night and go. Having that control made me feel safe with him, like tonight would be whatever I was ready for it to be and he was okay with that.

He had no idea how much it furthered his cause.

His fingers tunneled through my hair and worked it from its tie, releasing my braid. He combed his fingers through the strands until they fell loose and free around me. He hovered over me, kissing me softly until the shivering stopped.

The forest sighed around us, and I explored him. I nuzzled his Adam's apple with my nose. Ran my palms along his chest, over his broad shoulders, around the back of his neck and up through his thick hair. I moved down his side and over his waist, brushing the ridges of his six-pack with my thumbs. I loved the scratch of his beard and the firmness against every part of me that was soft. He was so male—hard and hot and virile. Every time he moved, his scent shifted, an intoxicating pheromone that drew me in closer, made everything *him*.

It was like getting used to cold water. Climbing in a little at a time until you were submerged and warm and ready to swim.

And I was...

When my hands slid across his lower back, I pulled him into me and moved my hips against the length that lay across my stomach. His breath went ragged.

An instant electric tension rolled between us. Everything changed. His tender kisses turned serious, and I felt a surge of heat between my legs. I peeled off my tank top, and his mouth was on my naked skin before the shirt was over my head.

A calloused hand glided up my side and cupped my breast. Then he came back up to my lips and his tongue plunged into my mouth. I nipped at his bottom lip, and he bit me back, releasing me only to devour me again.

There was something more focused than the last time we'd found ourselves this close. That time in my living room had been playful. This was something else. There was something hungrier about it. Needier.

I wanted him.

I parted my knees and let him settle between my thighs. He shifted down so the tip of him pressed right into me through our underwear. The tease was a little maddening—and I think he *knew* it. It strained against me right where it would slide in effortlessly if there was nothing between us, almost like he was saying, "If we take these off, you can have this."

He didn't have to tell me twice.

I hooked my thumbs at the top of his boxers, yanking them down. He kicked them off and put fingers under the waist of my underwear. He paused breathlessly, waiting for permission, and I nodded against his mouth, lifting my hips.

I'd never been so turned on by the feel of satin sliding down my legs. There was something so carnal about him doing it. His fingernails scraped against my skin in his hurry, and it made me more turned on to know how turned on *he* was, like he couldn't get me naked fast enough.

His hand went down to guide himself into me, and I couldn't wait to feel him. I held my breath for the moment he would glide in—but he hovered over me and circled himself in the wetness along the outside of my opening instead, holding my eyes. Just the tip in, then out, teasing me for a flicker of a second in just the right spot. In, then out. Circle, repeat. Circle, repeat.

It felt amazing—and it also drove me *mad*. It made me want to claw at his back, pull him inside me.

Circle, repeat. Circle, repeat.

He watched me as he did it, like he wanted to see how much I liked it.

My breath launched, and I began panting.

I ran my hands up his chest, and he tipped his head down and sucked a finger into his mouth. Need ripped through me like a wildfire.

I realized suddenly that much like the Jaxon Waters thing, Jason had underplayed yet another one of his abilities. When we'd been making out on my sofa, I could tell that he knew things, but my *God* did he know things. He knew *exactly* how to touch me.

Circle, repeat. Circle, repeat.

An orgasm was building, but every time I felt close to coming, he'd pull away and it was just enough to stop my momentum. He had to know what he was doing. And every time he did it, I wondered if this would be the time he'd go all the way in or would he pull out again and start over, make me a fraction wilder than the last time? The anticipation was making my legs shake.

I thought I'd been ready for him a moment before, but now I realized I didn't know what ready *was*. I was drenched. I had no idea how he was maintaining this discipline. I could see how much he wanted me, feel how hard he was. All he had to do was let go.

"We don't have to do anything you don't want to, Sloan," he said, his voice husky. "We can stop at any time."

I couldn't stop, he *knew* I couldn't stop. He was teasing me within an inch of my sanity. I felt like some sex-crazed teenager.

This was the kind of turned on that clouded judgment. This was the level of horny that got a girl pregnant on prom night in the back seat of a car. I always considered myself immune to that kind of frenzy—mostly because I was usually too self-conscious for it, especially for a first time. My first times had always been slow and careful, getting to know someone's body. It was always a little awkward and weird, and so I'd expected *this* time to be a little awkward and weird—but all of that was out the window now. I didn't care anymore what noises or faces I made, I didn't care that he was hovering over me, openly looking down at my naked body. He'd pushed me beyond inhibition—and maybe that was the point. Now all I wanted was that tip to go all the way in.

That tip...

I wanted to do things to it. Taste the bead of moisture I knew he had there. Put it in my mouth, feel it bump my throat. I was already making plans for next time, imagining all the ways I'd make him crazy like he was making *me* crazy.

Why was he doing this? Why was he making me wetter and more frustrated when he could feel and see that I was ready? What did he want from me?

"I want you inside me," I breathed.

And that's what he was waiting for. I watched his control break. He crashed his lips down on mine and slid into me.

It was *instant* pleasure. A payoff bigger than anything I could have ever imagined, a wait beyond worth it.

His first thrust hit some inner wall I didn't even know I had. It sent shock waves of ecstasy through my whole body. Then he did it again. And again. And again.

I gasped under him, frantically rolling my hips against him.

I liked the way he circled between my thighs. I put my hands on his back to feel him moving, and I had the sex-clouded realization that I should have done this with him days ago. That I'd slept next to this man in his trailer and not taken advantage of what he could do to my body if I'd just let him. I wanted to go back in time and yank that pillow out from between us and climb onto his lap and ride him. I wanted to go back and let him take me on my sofa, let him carry me inside on our first date, the same way I wanted to go back and let him sing to me sooner. How many moments like this had I already missed because of my own stupid hesitations and rules and reservations?

And then it occurred to me that's why he'd taken me to this edge. Why he'd made me want him to the point of insanity, until the only answer could be yes. Because he *knew* how I was, and he was getting ahead of me now before my overthinking kicked in.

I would have laughed if I wasn't so out of my mind.

He hiked an elbow behind my knee and somehow managed to drive himself deeper. I let out a sound that made me grateful there was no one within two miles to hear it, and he released a moan of his own. I knew he was close. His body went rigid as he neared the end, and the orgasm that he'd been working me up to built and built on top of itself. And then, when he groaned and I felt the warm pulsing inside me, my climax tipped over and *decimated* me.

It was the fireworks finale on the Fourth of July, a dam breaking, an atomic *bomb*. I was leveled. I had nothing left after it. I couldn't even move.

I lay there, staring up at the sky through the mesh ceiling of the tent, seeing stars twinkle across my vision that had nothing to do with the galaxy.

His nose nuzzled my neck. "Are you okay?" he whispered, still out of breath.

I made a tiny squeaking noise, and he laughed. He leaned down and kissed me gently, closing his eyes, smiling against my mouth.

There was a reverence in the way he held me, and all I could think was how much I liked the weight of him on top of me. How safe and anchored and grounded I felt.

How *cherished.*

I never wanted to move from this spot.

There was nothing outside of this tent tonight. Nothing.

There was nowhere to be, no phone to check. No lights to turn off or doors to wonder whether I'd locked. Not even the faint white noise that comes with civilization. The only person I wanted with me was here, and the serenity of the lake and woods combined with Jason's gentle affection made me relax in a way I hadn't known was possible. Like I'd been tense my whole life and hadn't even known it.

All that was left was us.

A big scary world existed somewhere, where bad things happened and people you cared about died—or left you on fourteen-month tours around the world. But tonight there was only this. And I was happy, and *grateful*, to have it.

Even if it wouldn't last.

~

The next morning Tucker met us at the water's edge as we docked back at the shores of Camp Larsen. Jason grabbed my ass before he picked up the canoe and pack, and I giggled and hit him.

We were going home today, and we'd already decided that he was spending the night at my place tonight.

He carried everything to the garage, and I came in with him to drop off the paddles, both of us grinning. He hadn't stopped smiling since he opened his eyes this morning. Neither had I.

We never did see those lights. We'd been a little distracted—*all* night. I was sore and tired, and I couldn't have been happier.

Well, unless of course he wasn't leaving me. But that was something I wouldn't let myself think about right now.

I followed him through the garage with Tucker, looking around at all the toys. The Larsens were definitely outdoorsmen. They had *all* the things. Kayaks harnessed to the ceiling, three snowmobiles under covers, a wall of fishing gear. Even a motorcycle was parked in the left stall.

"Your dad rides?" I asked as I looked down at a carefully organized box of fishing lures.

"Oh, the motorcycle?" he said, shouldering off the enormous pack and putting it in the bed of Paul's truck. "No, that's mine."

I looked up and blinked at the bike.

His? Jason, on a motorcycle? I didn't know he—

Sand.

Invisible grains of sand began to fill my lungs. Every breath gave me sand. It poured down my throat, heavy and thick, taking up the space in my chest, robbing me of air, drying out my mouth.

Can't breathe.

Couldn't get anything past the weight of it. I gasped. Tears spilled down my cheeks. The panic spread, the sand coursed through my veins. I couldn't make it stop.

It drowned me.

CHAPTER 24

JASON

♪ BURN SLOWLY/I LOVE YOU | THE BRAZEN YOUTH

I had just slid the backpack into Dad's truck and slammed the tailgate closed when I heard Tucker's whimpers. I came around the driver's side and saw Sloan with her hands over her mouth, gasping for air.

I had her in my arms in an instant.

"Hey, hey, what's wrong?" I held her and tried to tip her chin up, but she buried her face in my chest and sobbed.

Her whole body shook. She was absolutely terrified.

My heart started to pound. "Sloan, what happened?" I could hear the panic building in my voice. "Tell me what's wrong."

She didn't reply.

I glanced over her shoulder and my eyes glided over the black wheels of my bike and then I realized... "Is it because of the motorcycle?"

She managed a nod.

Without another word I scooped her up into my arms and ran with her outside.

It had been two years since Brandon's accident. She must have seen thousands of bikes by now. There was only one reason this could be upsetting her. Because it was *mine*.

When I set her feet down on the lawn, I held her by the arms and dipped my head to look at her. "Sloan, we're going to work on your breathing, okay? Look in my eyes. In and out, slow and steady. Can you do that?"

She nodded and drew a careful, jagged breath through her lips.

"Listen to me," I said, holding her gaze. "Nothing is going to happen to me," I said slowly. "I'll sell it. Right now. You hear me, Sloan? I won't ever ride one again."

She let out a shuddering breath, and tears spilled down her beautiful cheeks. Tucker pressed himself against our legs, looking up at her, worried.

"I'm sorry," she breathed.

I shook my head. "Don't apologize to me, no. Shhhhhhh..."

She took a few more ragged breaths and when she started talking again, it was so quiet I almost couldn't hear her. "There was blood in his eyes, Jason. His skin was scraped off by the asphalt. All the way to the bone."

Her words came like a punch to my gut. *Jesus.* What do you even say to something like that?

I hated this. I just wanted to protect her, to keep her from ever having to endure anything else painful for the rest of her life. I wished I could wipe it clean. If I could take it from her and carry it myself, I would.

Every gasp and sob that came from her sliced at me like razors.

It was like my heart was split down the middle—I had one half and Sloan had the other. I knew without a doubt that from this point forward I'd have to care for her better than I cared for myself—because I could never be okay if she *wasn't*.

It took a few minutes, but she calmed down.

When the trembling stopped, I kissed her forehead and held her face in my hands. Her hair stuck to her wet cheek, and I brushed it aside and tucked it behind her ear.

"I can't watch another man die on one of those," she said simply. "Please. Don't ever get on one. You have to promise me, Jason."

"Never. I promise," I whispered. "I'm not going to leave you, Sloan. It's not going to happen again."

She nodded, took a deep breath, and let me walk her to the house, and the whole time my mind kept circling back to the same thought.

I was grateful that I'd been there for her through my music in her darkest hours. That I'd reached her and touched her and held her in my arms for years—even though neither of us had known it yet.

I wanted to reach her and touch her and hold her in my arms forever.

Because I was completely and *totally* in love with her.

CHAPTER 25

SLOAN

♪ 26 | PARAMORE

It had been three days since we'd come back from Minnesota, and every morning since, it had been a feat getting Jason out of bed and off to be Jaxon Waters.

"Don't you have to get ready?" I giggled. He was all hands today. "Zane's going to be here at seven."

He made a dismissive male grunt and trailed his lips down my naked chest, working his bare shoulders under the sheets. I smiled.

Jason's new personal assistant, Zane, had started on Monday. A tough-looking, no-nonsense woman with a pompadour, cuffed jeans, and a naked lady tattooed on her forearm. She spoke Spanish, was experienced, knew her way around LA, and she was *amazing*.

She drove him to his appointments so he didn't have to deal with traffic and she made sure he ate and got to places on time. Zane turned out to be exactly what he needed because his schedule had officially become ridiculous.

His soundtrack was being released on Friday, and he had

radio and TV interviews and photo shoots every day this week. The theme song for the movie was particularly promising. Next weekend he was even playing *Saturday Night Live*.

Jason started pulling my underwear down. I wriggled, tapping his shoulder. "No, no, no. Come on, get in the shower."

His head popped up from under the sheet and he gave me a sad puppy dog look.

I smiled at him. "I won't contribute to your delinquency. You have that KROQ thing today."

He let out a sigh and rolled off me onto his back, putting an arm over his face. "You make me insane. I can't keep my hands off you."

My cell phone pinged, and I leaned over with a grin and reached for it.

"Who's that?" he asked. It was barely 6:15 in the morning.

"Your mom."

"My mom? She doesn't text."

"She texts *me*," I said, flashing him the screen and then going back to typing a response.

"Unbelievable."

"Well, she's not going to call me and read me a recipe over the phone like a crazy person," I said. "It's eight fifteen there. She found a recipe in a magazine for sloppy joes she thinks you'll like. And she wants to know if I know how to make a compote."

"Do you?"

I snorted. "Well, *yeah*, of course."

He propped himself up on his elbow and looked at me and I set the phone down on my chest, smiling. "What?"

"Go on a date with me tonight."

"You mean go *outside*?"

We hadn't spent any time together out of bed since we'd come back from Minnesota. He'd spent the night at my house for the last three nights. I loved it. I loved going to sleep in his arms and waking up to him.

"Let me wine and dine you," he said. "Walk with you on the beach and hold your hand."

I put my arms around his neck. "Yes, I'll go on a date with you, my music man."

He kissed me deeply and I thought for a second I was going to have to remind him about his call time again. But he broke away and rubbed his nose to mine. "Hey, what do you think about me using that empty bottom drawer in the dresser? Maybe unpack my backpack? Hang it in the closet?"

The request hit me like a bucket of ice water. My response was so knee-jerk I didn't have time to rein it in. I bit my lip and shook my head. "No. I can't."

The light faded a little from his eyes, but he just smiled at me. "Okay."

He gave me a quick kiss, got out of bed, went to the bathroom, and closed the door.

I sat up and put my hands to my face. Feelings pinged off me, firing in all directions.

Why was he doing this to me? Pretending this relationship was going to be able to progress like any other one? This wasn't real life. This was just an in-between. He couldn't put things in drawers.

He was *leaving*.

I was doing everything in my power to try and enjoy this time. We had so little of it left. The start date of his tour loomed in front of me like a tidal wave. It was coming, and it would be the end. So then why did he want to put me through this? Emptying out a dresser again? I'd already done it once this year and it had been hard enough.

I threw off the sheets, put on my robe, and sat on the edge of the bed, staring at the guitar he'd propped on the chair and chewing my lip. The pipes knocked in the wall as Jason turned on the shower and I called Kristen. It was early, but Oliver always got her up at 6:00, and she answered on the second ring.

"Jason wants a drawer," I whispered.

The baby fussed in the background.

"Uh, then give him a fucking drawer?"

"Kristen, he's *leaving*. He *should* be living out of a backpack. That's exactly the nature of this situation. This relationship isn't a house. It's a tent. Why keep things here and act like it isn't all going to come to an end in two weeks?"

"*Is* it coming to an end in two weeks? I mean, have you guys even talked about it?"

I chewed my thumbnail. "No, not really. But it won't change anything if we do. I'm not doing the long-distance thing for fourteen months."

"What if he's planning to ask you to go with him? Why would he make you his girlfriend and take you home to meet his parents if he wasn't serious about this relationship?"

I shook my head. "I don't know. He didn't tell me the tour was extended until we were in Ely, so maybe he just found out? He probably went into all this with the best intentions, but his circumstances have obviously changed. And I'm not going with him even if he *does* ask. I've been his girlfriend for a week. I'm not running off on tour with him, and talking about it is just going to make the bubble pop. I just wanted to be blissfully ignorant for a few more days and then he went and brought up drawers."

I think Jason and I were both kind of pretending his tour wasn't happening. Who wanted to be the one to throw a wet blanket on this?

"Well, bubble or no, you need to fucking talk about it. And give the man a damn drawer. He's had his mouth on every inch of your body. He can't put socks in a dresser?"

I put my forehead into my palm and pushed back my hair. "I don't know if I can play house with him, Kristen. It's going to be too hard when we break up."

She snorted. "There's no way you're letting this dude go. You're like half in love with him already."

"Oh, I'm letting him go. I *have* to."

She scoffed.

I rolled my eyes. "I can't wait fourteen months for a man I've known three weeks."

"Why? At three weeks with Josh, I would have tattooed his name across my boob. You'll hang on to a car that's barely running just because you had your first kiss in it, but you won't stick out a long-distance relationship with a man who gives you multiple orgasms and makes you insanely happy?"

I shook my head. "Did you know that I kept a beer bottle in the garage for the last two years because Brandon drank out of it? Like, what kind of crazy is that? I am *so tired* of being more sentimental about everyone and everything in my life than I am about *myself*. For once I want to be the rational one, Kristen. I didn't even like losing Brandon to the fire station for two days in a row. Staying with a man who's going to be gone for a year will make me miserable—even if I *am* half in love with him. I'm in an in-between, and if I keep making decisions that bury me there, I'll never get out of it."

She made a whistle noise. "Wow. You really *are* on a self-improvement kick." The baby giggled in the background. "Look, I'm glad you're getting your shit together, Sloan. I really am. And if you think you need to end it when he leaves, do what you gotta do. But give the man a fucking drawer in the meantime. If you're giving him your vagina you can give him a drawer."

I snorted. "God. I'm a mess."

"Yeah, but you're the fun busted-piñata kind. That's why this guy's all over you. Look, I gotta go. Oliver's being a handful. I just got fire-hosed. Call me later."

When I heard the shower turn off, I knocked on the bathroom door to the sound of Jason's electric razor. He called me in and I leaned back on the sink next to him, my beltless silk robe falling open. He gave the slit an appreciative glance.

He wasn't mad at me.

The room was steamy and smelled like his cologne. He had a towel around his waist and he stood over the sink, trimming his beard.

Something about the casual routine stirred feelings in me. It felt so right to have him here. His presence didn't even feel new. It felt familiar and normal and it gave me a preemptive sadness that I suspected would grow with every day that brought us closer to his departure date.

In a few weeks, he would be gone. The bathroom would be empty. Tucker would go with him. Jason wouldn't come over anymore. And the clothes in the drawer he wanted would disappear.

Empty, *again*.

"Don't worry." He winked at me. "I'll clean the sink. You won't even know I was here."

The irony.

I gave him a weak smile. God, I was a nutjob. In the last week I'd shown Jason enough crazy to scare off anyone. He'd seen me blackout drunk and washed barf out of my hair. He'd sat with me, surrounded by piles of my dead fiancé's clothing, and watched TV.

He'd held me while I had a panic attack and even offered to sell his motorcycle so it wouldn't upset me. I was knee-jerk emotional responses, a minefield of bad days and walls to tear down, and they popped up at random, without warning.

And he didn't care.

For some reason this gorgeous man who looked like he could be in a damn electric razor commercial was all in—even if we were about to be all out—and I wouldn't even give him a fucking drawer.

I leaned there, watching him run the razor down his neck, and he glanced at me with those blue eyes and I missed him already.

"You're a very patient man, aren't you?"

He slid his eyes down my body and raised an eyebrow. "Well, it's paid off so far."

The breath that I blew through my lips was one of resolve. So it wouldn't last. Okay. But I'd give it everything until it ended.

I held up a key.

Jason froze and his razor clicked off.

I pressed the key to his bare chest, over his heart. "Use whatever drawer you want," I said. "Park your truck in the garage. No more ringing the doorbell when you come home. Okay?"

The smile on his face made my heart hurt. I don't know that I'd ever seen him look this happy.

"Okay," he whispered, putting his palm over the hand on his chest.

We'd have it all...right up until we wouldn't.

CHAPTER 26

JASON

♪ BROKEN | LUND

I typed in my text and heard the ping from across the store.

Jason: You're so fucked. One word: pleather.
Sloan: How do you feel about taxidermy?
Jason: How do you feel about the 70s?

A Talking Heads song played in the background, and I looked over the racks of the musty Santa Monica thrift store. Sloan glanced up at me from across the room and narrowed her eyes. I beamed back at her.

She'd had Zane drop me off at Goodwill so she could challenge me to a game on our date night. We each got fifteen dollars to buy something the other person had to wear for the rest of the evening. It was actually a pretty hilarious idea. But when I heard Sloan laugh all the way across the store, I knew it wasn't going to end well for me.

"Your bravery is about to be tested," she said outside ten minutes later. She was adorable.

"Nothing scares me."

"Really? I think *this* might scare you," she said, pulling out a long red cape with little tacos on it and holding it out by the corners.

I ran my hand through my hair and she laughed.

"Okay. It's a cape. I can do a cape," I said, a laugh in my throat. "I'm man enough."

"I tend to agree with you on that."

"Your turn." I'd hit comedy gold in there. I pulled out a footie pajama with a unicorn head for a hood. It even had a tail. She blanched and I started cracking up.

"Do I have to wear the hood?" she asked.

"Absolutely. *And* the belt." I produced a wrestling champion-ship belt made of gold plastic.

She made a face. "Fine. But I'm not done with you," she said. "Now, I know what you're thinking. You're thinking that you're this famous guy"—she made jazz hands—"and you can't get photographed walking around the Santa Monica Pier in this. That it would be bad for your image and Pia would lecture you and blah blah blah. But I want you to know I've made arrangements for this because I'm a very thoughtful girlfriend."

She turned away from me and put something on. When she turned back around, I howled with laughter. She wore flesh-colored plastic sunglasses that looked like hands over her eyes. There were gaps between the fingers to see through.

We both laughed so hard we were crying, and I grabbed her and pulled her into my chest.

I couldn't live without this. I wanted her to come on tour with me.

I didn't care what I had to do to make it happen—pay her bills, bribe Kristen for support. *Beg* her.

I was still waiting to hear back from Ernie on whether we could get Lola off the ticket before I talked to Sloan about it. But whichever way it went, I already had a plan to see her when I was on the road. If she couldn't go with me or visit because of Lola, I'd come to her as much as possible. And there was the five-week break for the holidays. We'd talk on the phone and we'd Skype. We'd done the phone thing before. We were good on the phone. We could do it again.

We put on our outfits. Sloan's needed some altering. We borrowed scissors from the thrift store and cut the feet off so she could wear her shoes. She said it was hot, so we cut the arms off too.

"There," she said, unzipping the front and pushing her boobs up, the crooked horn on her hood bouncing. "Sexy unicorn."

I looked at her through the plastic fingers of my new sunglasses. "Are you satisfied with yourself? Look what you've done to us."

"I *am* satisfied, thank you." She cocked her head at me triumphantly.

"You're nuts, you know that, right?"

"You're nuts too." She slipped her hands around my waist and hugged me, looking up at me with her chin to my chest. "Oh! We have to take a picture and send it to your mom."

We took a few funny selfies and shot them over. I loved that she and Mom had hit it off. I loved it so much.

We walked toward the palm-lined Third Street Promenade, holding hands as the sun went down. We elicited a lot fewer looks than we would have in Ely dressed like this. We almost went unnoticed, actually. I was grateful for the glasses. I'd brought a hat and some sunglasses so I wouldn't get recognized. I was doing a lot of appearances now, and more often than not these days, someone somewhere would know who I was. Santa Monica was touristy. The last thing I wanted was to end up signing autographs while out with Sloan. But I think the cape and the finger glasses did a better job of concealing my identity than my original plan. Nobody expected a taco cape–wearing Jaxon Waters.

Sloan stood at a shop window looking at a mannequin and I came up behind her and wrapped my cape around her. "Hey. I want to talk to you about something." I put a kiss on the side of her head and she smiled at me in the reflection in the glass.

"I was wondering where you wanted to spend my five-week break. We can be here the whole time if you want, but I know Mom would like it if we came for Thanksgiving."

I watched her smile melt.

She turned to face me. "Jason…"

Her voice was apologetic. My heart *sank*.

"Jason, I think we need to be realistic," she said gently. "You're going to be gone over a year. You'll be on the road the whole time, in different time zones—"

"Wait…" I blinked at her, not believing what I was hearing. "You want to break *up*?"

Her eyes went soft. "I don't *want* to break up. But I don't see how it's going to work either."

I shook my head. "Sloan, we've done it before."

"For two weeks. When you were opening. But you'll be headlining. You'll be so busy you won't even have time to think about me, let alone call me. Sometimes even back *then* you couldn't find time to call me."

I took off my stupid finger glasses and took a step closer to her. "We're not breaking up," I said. "No."

"Jason," she said softly. "I don't want what we have to be buried. I don't want to struggle to remember good days like this one."

I put my hands on her arms. "We won't. We'll have plenty of good days. We'll Skype, and I'll call you. I'll come visit you whenever I can. It'll be hard, but we just have to put in the effort." I shook my head. "Sloan, what did you think we were doing here? Did you just think this was some fling for me?"

"Of *course* not. That's not what it is for me either." She licked her lips. "But your circumstances have changed and, Jason, I know what this looks like. My dad worked overseas when I was growing up. It destroyed my parents' marriage. First we'll go a day without talking. Then two. Then a week. Then you won't even be able to remember the last time we spoke because not talking to each other is the new normal. And I know myself, Jason. I'll be a mess the whole time. You won't like who I'll become. I'll be paranoid because I won't know what you're doing and resentful that you're not making time for me, and you'll get frustrated that I want your attention when you're spread so thin. We won't know each other anymore, and we'll both be lonely, even though we're together." She put her hands on my chest and looked up at me, her beautiful brown eyes sad. "Jason, I spent so much time being lonely and unhappy. And I just can't do it again. I can't go from this to that. I can't. I won't."

The moment where I should have said, "Then come with me on tour" hung between us and then passed. Lola made it so I had no choice but to let it pass.

"Sloan, don't do this," I said, my eyes begging her. "*Please.*"

I studied her face. The determined set of her jaw, her steady eyes holding mine. Her mind was made up—and the worst part was I knew she was right.

It was one thing for me to want to stick it out. I wasn't happy about the way things would be long distance either, but I'd do it because the alternative was knowing she was out there without me, dating other people. And it was *my* fault it was happening because it was *my* job separating us.

But it wasn't fair to ask her to deal with this shitty situation. She'd been so miserable for so long I didn't even *want* her to have to deal with it. I wanted her to be happy.

I'd just hoped that being with *me* would be the way for her to do that.

I swallowed down the knot in my throat. "If you need to do this for you, then do it. But I'm waiting for you, and when my tour is over, I'm coming back for you." I took a step closer to her. "Tell me you'll take me back. As long as you're not with someb—" I had to stop for a moment to compose myself. I shut my eyes and let out a steadying breath before opening them again and looking down on her. "Please tell me when my tour ends that you'll let me come back."

"Jason, don't ask me to promise that. And you shouldn't promise to stay single either."

"Why?"

"Because then we're both just waiting for each other."

I shook my head. "Then let's wait. Better yet, let's not break up."

"I've given this a lot of thought." She paused for a long moment. "I can't replace the shrine I had for Brandon with a new shrine for you."

The words lingered between us and she held my gaze. "Let's just enjoy the time we have left and end it in a good place. And you're right. Maybe after your tour we'll find each other again. It won't be goodbye. It'll just be goodbye for now. Okay?"

It was amazing how much this hurt. The pain was almost breathtaking. I felt like I'd just been told I had two weeks left to live.

But could I expect anything different? Who the fuck was I anyway? Some guy she'd known less than a month?

Sloan was always two steps behind where I was in our relationship. I knew that. But if she could bear losing me, then maybe this really *was* one-sided. Because if she felt for me even half as much as I felt for her, she could never stomach letting me go.

And she *was* letting me go.

This wasn't the same reclusive, grieving woman I'd met on the phone. This woman would meet someone at the gym or at an art gallery opening, and by the time I came back around, she'd be lost to me. I was losing her already.

And there was nothing I could fucking do about it.

We ate dinner at an Italian place and then walked through the promenade toward the pier, dropping into some of the more interesting shops. The trees were lit with twinkle lights now that the sun had gone down. We threw pennies in the fountain and looked at the sculpted hedges. We got ice cream and watched a street performer sing and we dropped fifty bucks in his guitar case. Sloan bought Mom a tea party cookbook.

I tried to enjoy it. I laughed in all the right places and smiled so that it reached my eyes. But all I saw now was the ending.

We stood at a crosswalk on our way to the pier. Sloan hugged me from the side, pressing her cheek into my chest, and I looked down on her horned hoodie and suddenly I wanted to tell her I loved her for the first time, right there, on that busy intersection.

It was nothing like what they show in the movies. No romantic setting, no soft music playing. We had a homeless guy in a muscle shirt holding a Super Big Gulp a foot away from us. Some teenagers took selfies while a guy in a sauce-stained pizzeria apron impatiently pressed the crosswalk button. We weren't walking on the beach or sitting at the top of a Ferris wheel. She just wrapped her arms around my waist, wearing that stupid fucking outfit, and all I could think was that I loved her.

But now we were breaking up. What was the point in telling her how I felt? To make her feel guilty? Or like she had to say something back that she wasn't ready to say, or possibly didn't even feel?

The light turned green, we crossed, and the moment passed, and she probably had no idea it had even happened. But it *had* happened. And it was going to keep on happening. Every time I looked at her it would happen.

It would happen even when I couldn't look at her at all.

CHAPTER 27

JASON

♪ BLOOD IN THE CUT | K.FLAY

Lola roared up on her Harley in front of Grauman's Chinese Theatre, and the cameras fired up hungrily. She loved to make an entrance, and she always did it late. Fucking annoying.

"Forty-five minutes," I grumbled to Pia, looking at my watch. It was 6:47 p.m. God, I hated her.

Ernie was off the red carpet, on the phone with a finger in his ear. We'd been waiting for Lola to show for almost a damn hour. I was contractually obligated to promote the movie however the studio saw fit, and Lola and I had collaborated on the soundtrack, so unfortunately we were a package deal at the moment. They wanted red carpet pictures of me with her, so I'd been forced to stand around outside in the blazing Hollywood heat until she got here. It was eighty-five in the shade. Sweat trickled down my back. I slid my fingers into my collar and tugged at the neck of my tie irritably.

I'd had to tell Sloan I couldn't get a ticket for her so late—which was *true*. The seating arrangements had already been made. But I could have booted Ernie. Instead, I'd had to leave Sloan at home because Lola was going to be here, all over me, and I didn't know what kind of shit show it was going to be.

It had been three days since Sloan told me she wanted to break up when I left. We had thirteen days until my tour and every minute counted now. I didn't want to be here without her, wearing this monkey suit, waiting for Lola. I wanted to be in my underwear, tucked in bed with my girlfriend, watching TV. The fact that Sloan couldn't be here with me and the knowledge that Lola was to blame for that infuriated me. Not to mention this was a whole day away from Sloan when our time together was almost up—and that was Lola's fault too.

I wasn't doing well.

I hadn't been doing well since Sloan preemptively broke up with me. I couldn't fucking sleep, and I didn't feel like eating.

All of my wildest dreams were coming true. I was standing on a red carpet with superstars, promoting a major motion picture set to *my* music. I was about to leave on a massive worldwide tour. I was achieving all my career goals, and somehow I was about to end up losing the one thing that suddenly mattered the most to me. I actually *resented* my success now, wished I could just fucking walk away from it or take less of it in exchange for her.

I didn't care what Sloan said about not wanting me to wait for her—I wasn't dating other people during our split. I couldn't. The fact that she maybe *could* fucking killed me. I was trying not to think about it. And now I was here, wasting the precious time I had left with her dealing with Lola.

I looked moodily at her on her bike. She wore four-inch red heels and shiny black pleather skinny pants. Her nipples pressed into the red ribbon of fabric that she considered a shirt. She'd actually ridden here in that shit.

She took off her helmet and her red hair tumbled out to the

screams of fans behind the line stanchions followed by a strobe light of camera flashes.

I let out a controlled breath, making sure to keep my face neutral.

Pia put a hand on my arm. "Ready?"

"I will do as I'm told," I said unenthusiastically, looking away from my nemesis posing on her Harley.

Pia had coached me extensively on today. She knew all about my issues with Lola. My relationship with my publicist was a little like a relationship with a doctor or lawyer. I had to be honest, or she couldn't help me.

"Just remember to be diplomatic," Pia said discreetly. "You can't undo photos. If she touches you, don't react. Smile and look relaxed. Don't give them anything to speculate with. And don't let her work you up."

I nodded, my clenched fists the only thing revealing my mood.

Ernie finished his phone call and made his way back over. He was beaming. "Do you love me? Tell me you love me." He rubbed his hands together.

"What," I mumbled, watching Lola climb off her bike with a shaky coordination that told me I was *not* witnessing a moment of sobriety.

"I just got off the phone with your record label."

My head snapped.

"She's off the ticket."

It took me a second to process what I was hearing. "What? What does that mean? She's out?"

"I made the argument that she causes you undue stress and you'd be out with a stomach ulcer two weeks into it if they forced her on you. I may have *also* suggested that I'd hit her with trespassing for coming onto my property uninvited the other night if they wanted to push the subject. She's already knee deep in Kanye fallout and they need her to stay out of jail."

I stared at him for a solid ten seconds before I started to laugh. I couldn't even fucking believe it. It was the best news I'd had in years. I hugged him and he slapped my back.

"But listen," he said, putting an arm around me, his voice low. "And I need you to pay attention because there's stipulations. They said as long as you put asses in seats you can go it solo. But I had to agree that if you're struggling, they get to bring her in, no complaints from you, no questions asked. And I couldn't get them to bend on the fog machine and pyrotechnics. Those guys *really* like fireworks."

"Yeah, yeah. Not a problem." I beamed.

I was going to ask Sloan to come on my tour as soon as I got home. I'd plead with her. Fuck, I'd *kidnap* her if I had to. Everything was different now. *Everything.* The tour I had been dreading like a stint in a foreign prison suddenly looked like a fourteen-month dream vacation. "I'm asking Sloan to go with me."

Ernie eyed me. "So you're really doing this girlfriend thing, huh?"

I grinned. "Oh yeah, I'm doing it."

He let out a long breath and nodded. "Okay. Kinda thought you might. Well, I like her. She's a good one, you were right."

Pia spoke over her cell phone without looking up. "A girlfriend on tour? Not easy." She shook her head over her text. "Have you seen your media packet?" She looked up at me over her glasses. "They're keeping you busy, young man. Your attention is going to be extremely divided."

Ernie waved her off. "There's no talking to him. Isn't that right?" He slapped my back.

I grinned.

Lola saw me looking at her and she shoved a paper she'd been signing into some poor fan's chest and sauntered over to me. Her bodyguard, personal assistant, stylist, and long-suffering publicist followed close behind.

"Jaxon," she said, giving Pia and Ernie a cursory glance and then sliding her cat eyes back to me.

"Lola." I gave her a shit-eating grin. I couldn't help it.

"Jason, we need to start heading over," Pia said, checking her watch and nodding to the photo backdrop.

Lola fell in beside me as we made our way down the carpet toward the photographers, hooking her arm in mine. I didn't know how to shake her off without it drawing attention and fuck it, I didn't even care. This was the last time I'd *ever* have to deal with her. I couldn't stop smiling.

I wondered if she knew yet—probably not by how she was acting. I couldn't imagine she'd be taking the news with grace. It was better she didn't know. She'd probably just cause a fucking scene over it.

We came up on a crowd of supporting actors from the movie waiting for their turn in front of the cameras. A makeup artist I recognized from a *GQ* photo shoot earlier in the week swooped in and started dabbing at my face, and I took the opportunity to liberate my arm. Lola hovered over the woman's shoulder to watch me, looking bored.

"Hey, Jaxon. Long time no see," the makeup artist teased, talking to my forehead as she powdered it with a quick swipe of a brush. "So where's your girlfriend? Didn't bring her?"

Something almost predatory flashed on Lola's face.

"Couldn't make it," I mumbled, staring at Lola, trying to decipher the flicker I'd seen in her eyes.

"Aww, too bad," she said, finishing up. "All done, handsome. Have fun."

She moved, and Lola closed the gap in front of me. "A girl-friend, huh?" She bit her lip and ran a hand down my lapel. Her eyes raked down my body and then came back up and narrowed. "Have fun while it lasts." She yanked me to her by my tie, crushed her lips to mine, and slid her other hand over my dick.

I jerked back and smacked her hand off me. "Jesus Christ, Lola!" I shot a look over my shoulder. We stood in the huddle of our teams. Thankfully nobody seemed to have been paying attention. The photographers were focused on the backdrop, and even Pia and Ernie had their heads down over their phones.

I looked back at her and glared, wiping my mouth with my sleeve.

Her face had gone flat. "You're welcome."

~

I'd missed Sloan like crazy last night. In the theater, when my voice soared over a sunrise as the movie opened into the first scene, all I'd wished was that she'd been there with me.

I wouldn't have been able to handle it if things had ended at the start of my tour. There was no fucking way. My relief over the news I got from Ernie was a thousand-pound weight off my chest.

Pia and Ernie had stuck close to me all night. I'd grabbed a swag bag for Sloan at the after-party and taken pictures of the buffet because she'd asked for them. I rubbed shoulders like I was supposed to, stood for selfies, shook hands, signed autographs, thanked people, and stayed just as long as necessary to meet my contractual obligation.

Lola stayed away from me after the red carpet. In fact, I didn't see her for most of the night, much to my relief.

I'd gotten to Sloan's at around 2:00 in the morning and I'd

climbed into bed with her and passed out. I'd slept like the dead. It was like I hadn't truly relaxed since our breakup conversation. In reality, I probably hadn't.

When I woke up and glanced at my phone it was almost 9:00. Sloan was sitting against her headboard, staring at her cell. I smiled, looking at her, and scooted up and put a kiss on her thigh. "Hey, I wanted to ask you someth—"

"Jason, what is this?"

She turned her cell phone to me. My breath caught in my throat.

TMZ. A celebrity gossip site.

Sloan stared at me, confusion etched into her brow. I sat up and took her phone.

Someone had gotten a picture of Lola kissing me on the red carpet, with her hand squarely on my dick. It was like a camera had been trained on me, taking burst shots from somewhere behind the photo backdrop.

Another photo had us arm in arm like we'd come together and me grinning like a fucking idiot.

But that wasn't even the worst part. Not by a mile.

A grainy photo had me holding Lola by the elbow in front of my trailer last week. The angle made it look like I'd been leaning in to kiss her. A small blurb under the photo read, "Lola Simone and Jaxon Waters getting intimate in front of his home last week in Calabasas."

She must have had paparazzi following her. *Fuck.*

My heart pounded as I scanned the article.

Jaxon Waters and Lola Simone were extra close at the premiere of *The Wilderness Calls* last night with the two recording artists seen canoodling for much of the event.

But the real buzz started after Lola was seen grabbing the Minnesota native's canoe paddle right on the red carpet.

Ever since their collaboration on the soundtrack for the movie, rumors have been flying about the pair, especially after Lola Simone released her single "On the Water," a thinly veiled track about her sexual relationship with the northerner. While Lola will neither confirm nor deny that the graphic song is about Jaxon, last night's hands-on approach certainly does give us something to talk about during their upcoming joint international tour.

My mouth went dry.

"What a load of fucking bullshit," I breathed.

"Oh, I agree it's some bullshit. Especially the part about you *lying* to me and sleeping with another woman behind my back."

Her tone rendered me mute for a solid ten seconds and I stared at her. "Sloan, you can't actually believe this. It's TMZ."

I reached for her hand and she yanked it from me like my fingers burned. "Are you kidding me? There's *photos*. You kissed her, Jason. I'm looking at this with my own eyes."

"Wha— I wasn't kissing her in front of my trailer, it's the angle of the picture. And I didn't kiss her last night either. She kissed *me*, and she did it just to piss me off."

"She's going on your tour? And you took her to the premiere? Is that why *I* couldn't go? She was at your *house*? The night we went to Kristen's? And then the next day you just took me to Minnesota with you like nothing happened?" Her chest was heaving.

"I got home from your house and she was there," I said carefully.

"She was wasted and she wouldn't leave. I didn't tell you what happened because I didn't want to upset you. Sloan, I would *never* cheat on you."

She shook her head at me. "But you hid her from me. You hid *all* of this from me. There's like seven lies in this *one* article." Her stare drilled into my face. "Have you actually had sex with that woman?"

And here it was. I closed my eyes and puffed air from my cheeks. "Once. A long time ago."

Her disappointed expression gutted me. "Please tell me you're kidding." She let out a shaky breath. "You're kidding, right? You don't think this is something you should have told me about? My *mother* texted me to tell me that my boyfriend is sneaking around with his ex and I didn't even know what to say!"

Fuuuuck. Fuck, *fuck*. "Sloan, I'm sorry. I didn't know about the article until just now, or I would have gotten ahead of it. Lola was just a one-time thing and it was a mistake. Frankly, I'm embarrassed about it."

She pressed her lips into a line. "Great. Just a booty call mistake with Ernie's gate code. Even *better*." She threw the blankets off her and stormed to the bathroom.

"I didn't give her the gate—" She disappeared around the doorway. I got up and followed her into the bathroom. "I didn't give her the gate code," I said, coming around the corner. "I don't even know how she knew where I lived."

She scoffed and yanked a piece of toilet paper off the roll with her back to me and wiped at her eyes. "Right."

I threw up my hands. "Sloan, what did you want me to do? I have no control over what *they* write and how *she* behaves. This is what she does. She's famous for this shit. She does it for the attention."

She whirled on me. "This isn't even about her, Jason. This has absolutely *nothing* to do with her *or* them. This is about *you*. How about you have a little respect for me? Tell me when another woman has kissed you in front of dozens of cameras, so I can at least be ready for the TMZ article. Tell me when someone shows up at your house in the middle of the night for a booty call! This is humiliating, Jason! You *lied* to me!"

"I never lied to you," I said calmly. "I just didn't tell you about it. I didn't want to come to you with this until I had a solution for what to do about it. I didn't want it to give you any unnecessary grief. She's given me enough for the both of us."

She stood by the sink, glaring at me. "Lying by omission is still a *lie*. You've had some woman you have history with, who I didn't even know *existed* for you, showing up at your house in the middle of the night, writing songs about you, going with you to movie premieres. They're putting her on your tour and you let *magazines* write about it before you bothered to give me a heads-up about this double life you're leading. And you seriously have nothing to say about keeping this from me other than you were doing *me* some favor by lying to me about it?"

I looked her in the eye. "She's been kicked off my tour, and I was trying to *spare* you."

Her eyes flashed. "Okay. How about this? How about the next time an ex-boyfriend shows up here to have sex with me and grabs my ass I'll spare *you* and it'll just be my little secret."

Jealousy pulsed through me like an instant shot of adrenaline, and my temper ignited. "If anyone *ever* puts their hands on you, you better fucking tell me."

She gawked at me. "Oh, so now you get it, do you? That's not okay, but *this* is?"

"It's not the same thing," I said through clenched teeth. "She's a fucking mess. She's not worth any of this. You need to get over it."

She blinked at me. "Get *over* it?" She laughed dryly. "Wow. You're right. I should just 'get over it' so you don't have to be accountable for *anything* you just did. How inconvenient for you to have a girlfriend who demands *honesty*. I guess you're happy we're breaking up in two weeks so you can continue on with your double life without anyone nagging you about it!"

"That was *you* who wanted that! I don't want to break up, I never fucking did. It *kills* me that you don't want to be with me!"

We stood there across from each other, both of us breathing hard.

I combed a hand through my hair. "Look, I understand this is upsetting for you. I'm not thrilled about it either. This whole thing with Lola has been a fucking nightmare. She's been harassing me for months. *She* kissed *me*. This tabloid shit is going to happen. It comes with my career, and I can't do anything about it. None of this went down the way they said it did, and even if I told you every single thing, all the time, I cannot *possibly* prepare you for every story they might make up. They spin things, it's what they *do*. You're going to need a tougher skin and you're just going to have to trust me."

She let out a mirthless laugh. "You know, I was actually considering what you said the other day. That we should wait for each other."

I blinked at her. "You were?" I breathed.

"Of *course* I was. You think it's any easier for me to lose *you*? You think *I* want to see other people? I thought maybe you were right and we could just agree to focus for a year on our careers and stay faithful to each other and wait." She scoffed. "But I can't live like this. I don't even know what you're doing *here* and you wanted me to stay behind and wait for you while you do God knows what out there? You want *trust*? You don't even *talk* to me." Her chin started to quiver. "Jason, I think you need to leave."

My heart plummeted. "Sloan—" I took a step toward her and put out a hand. She smacked it away from her.

"I need you to leave before I say something to you that I'm going to regret." She hugged her elbows to her stomach and her eyes filled with tears.

Alarm bells went off inside me, all systems responding. I swallowed. "Sloan, let's just talk. Please. No fighting, let's talk."

"Jason, I want you to listen to me. I do *not* want to see you right now. I do not want to talk to you. I want you to leave this house. And you should know that if I'd understood how little respect you were going to have for this relationship, I would *never* have dated you."

CHAPTER 28

SLOAN

♪ A MOMENT OF SILENCE | THE NEIGHBOURHOOD

Jason: Sloan, can we please talk?

I stared at the vertical blinking line in the empty text box. I set my phone facedown on Kristen's kitchen island and put my forehead in my hand.

"Was that him?" Kristen asked, leaning on the counter.

Josh stood by the sink, giving Oliver a bath. He'd sculpted the baby's hair into a Mohawk and Oliver was giggling.

I had Stuntman Mike in my lap wearing his EMOTIONAL SUPPORT LUNATIC shirt. Tucker lay curled at my feet. Jason had called his dog to him before he left my house two days ago, but Tucker hadn't budged from the bed, so Jason had left him.

"Yes, that was him."

"What did he say?"

"What he's *been* saying."

"He wants to talk?"

I nodded. My eyes filled up again and she ripped off a paper towel and handed it to me. "Sloan, why don't you just talk to him?"

"About *what*? He doesn't get this, Kristen. He seriously thinks there's nothing wrong with any of this. He lied to me. He let my mom—my *mom*—be the one to tell me about Lola. He just stood there shrugging like, 'Well, nothing I could have done to prevent this. Sometimes famous recording artists show up to fuck me, I didn't want to bother you with the details.'" I pressed the towel to my eyes.

"Well, he *is* a rock star..."

I did a laugh-cry.

Josh rinsed the baby's hair with a cup. "Nah, he's not a rock star. I didn't get that vibe from him. That guy's pretty grounded."

Kristen peered at me. "Do you think he cheated on you with her?"

I sniffled. "No. I believe him. But he should have at least *told* me about her."

Josh lifted Oliver into a towel and handed him to Kristen for a diaper. Then he kissed the side of his wife's head on his way to the fridge. "Look, I'm gonna be honest. I like him, and I think you need to cut him some slack." He grabbed a beer and pulled up a stool at the counter. "Did he handle the situation badly? Yes. But no guy wants to tell his girlfriend about the women he's slept with, believe me."

I shook my head at him. "So he should just get a pass for this? He was about to go on a year-long tour with his old hookup and I didn't even know about it."

Josh opened his beer. "I know what a man looks like when he's in love with you, Sloan. I saw the same look on Brandon's face once, and I'm telling you, this guy's serious about you. Give him a break. He fucked up and he knows it. He's probably losing his mind right now."

He's losing *his* mind? Jason felt like a stranger to me with some torrid past and secret double life. Like the Jason I'd known was a different person from the man who'd lied to me and hooked up with Lola Simone.

Maybe the bad guy was Jaxon.

"Did you even listen to that song?" I asked, looking back and forth between the two of them. "Did you?" How many times had I heard that nasty Lola Simone song and not realized it was about Jason? It was like I'd just found out my boyfriend had starred in a lyrical porno that everyone had seen. The whole situation was so cringy.

Kristen shrugged while she fastened Oliver's diaper. "I listened to it. So he got drunk and fucked her on a beach. Then she wrote a song about it. It's messed up, but that just makes her a bitch. It doesn't make him anything less than a guy who was exercising his God-given right to make bad choices six months before he knew you."

I let out a breath. "What about the lying?"

Kristen sucked air through her teeth. "He didn't really lie. He just didn't tell you. I mean, that doesn't make it okay, but I gotta be honest, I kind of get it."

I stared at her, incredulous.

"What? Jason's a nice guy," she said, pulling a onesie over the baby's head. "He's the kind of person who donates his fucking bone marrow to a stranger. He didn't want to make you insecure. Was he really going to tell you that a gorgeous rock star showed up at his house in the middle of the night to fuck him when the two of you had only been dating for three days? How would that have gone over?"

She did have a point.

She put the baby in his high chair. "And when she grabbed him, same thing. He probably thought nobody saw it and he was sparing you the visual of a famous train wreck touching his dick. And he's not special, believe me. She's always doing shit like that. She'd give the pope a lap dance." She sat on Josh's knee and put an arm around his neck.

I mopped at my nose. "You know, maybe I wouldn't be so upset with him if he'd told me about this without letting TMZ pick it up first."

"You guys don't have typical problems, I'll give you that," Josh chuckled, pulling on his beer. "Just tell him that from now on he needs to be honest with you so you don't get blindsided when stuff like this happens."

I clutched my damp wad of paper towels, miserable. "I *did*. He said he can't prepare me for every story the tabloids might make up. He sure as hell could have prepared me for this one, though," I mumbled.

My phone rang. I picked it up and looked at the screen.

It was him.

My gaze shot to Kristen. I hovered a finger over the Answer Call button. I wanted to hear his voice. Talk to him. But I wanted the old Jason. The one from before. I thought about how he'd been so oblivious to how he'd let this happen, how he'd purposely hid all this from me and how dismissive and unapologetic he'd been.

I sent his call to voicemail and shut off my phone. What could he possibly have to say that would change my mind? The only thing that could make this different was complete and total transparency in our relationship, and he'd made it very clear he had no intention of participating in that.

Kristen shook her head at me. "You only have ten days, Sloan.

That's all you get before his tour. Are you really willing to let this be the thing that breaks you guys up? You can end it now, like this, or calm the fuck down and give him a chance and at least enjoy the time you have left."

I shook my head. "It's bigger than that, Kristen. This isn't just about the next ten days. It's about whether I'd even consider dating him again when his tour is over. He wants me to wait for him. And you know what? I was actually considering it. I figured, what's the harm? It's not like I'm gonna be dating anyway. We can just put our relationship on hold, do what we have to do, stay faithful to each other, and get back together when his tour's over. And all I can think now is, how much crap will I learn about him this way while he's gone?"

I wiped at my nose. "Even if I forgive the lying—the *omissions*, which he didn't even seem to be sorry about—what about the next time? And there *will* be a next time. He was right, this shit is going to happen. I don't know if I'm strong enough to do this with him again and again while he purposely keeps me in the dark. I mean, if he didn't feel like Lola Simone and the song sitting at number two on the damn music charts warranted mentioning, what else isn't he telling me? Am I just going to find out about his skeletons with everyone else when they hit the celebrity gossip circuit?" I shook my head. "I'm not cut out for this life and I don't think I really realized it until today."

Kristen and Josh looked at me like they felt sorry for me and didn't know what else to say.

"I've been able to compartmentalize this whole fame thing because I didn't ever see the Jaxon side of him. And now all of a sudden it's this enormous, glaring spotlight on everything," I said, waving my paper towel around.

My chin started to quiver. "He'll do nothing to protect me

from the tabloid onslaught. He'll keep doing things behind my back. I'll get no warning, just like this time. Then when the inevitable happens and some story breaks, he'll tell me I need a tougher skin. He'll brush it off, justify hiding whatever it is from me, take no responsibility."

I'd be a lunatic. I would be twitchy and worried, waiting for the other shoe to drop the whole time he was away.

Stuntman Mike peered up at me from my lap.

My eyes filled with tears again and I looked back and forth between Kristen and Josh. "I have to break up with him," I breathed. "I have to do it now."

The finality of it crushed me. Tears came again and I sobbed into my paper towel.

He'd given me no choice.

CHAPTER 29

JASON

♪ MESS IS MINE | VANCE JOY

She sent my call to voicemail again.

I put my palms over my eyes and let out a ragged breath. It was almost midnight. I'd been calling and texting her all day.

"She still not talking to you?" Ernie stood in his kitchen and dropped ice into a tumbler behind the darkness of my eyelids.

"I fucked up," I muttered.

"Yeah, you fucked up. Your first mistake was arguing with a pissed-off woman. You should have backed away slowly and agreed with everything she said. Pissed-Off Woman 101."

I looked up at him as he set down the bourbon he'd poured me on the coffee table.

He plopped into the couch next to me and crossed his leg over his ankle, holding his own glass.

I felt haggard. The last two days had been *hell*. I was at the point that I'd apologize for being *born* if it meant she'd speak to me. I just wanted this to be over. She'd brought me to my damn knees on silence alone.

"I think she's going to break up with me." Even saying the words out loud made the lump bolt into my throat.

Ernie let out a long breath. "You guys were breaking up anyway."

I shook my head. "No. Not like this. Not because she didn't want me, not because I fucking disappointed her. And I would have never let it happen. I would have begged her to come with me." I put my forehead into my hands. "It can't end like this."

Fuck, I should have told her everything. Why didn't I tell her everything? I had no idea how to navigate any of this. Lola, my tour, my fame. All of it felt like some giant snowball, gathering momentum and destroying my life on its way down.

"You know, maybe she's doing you both a favor," Ernie said.

I took my forehead from my hands and glared at him.

He swayed his whiskey at me. "How fair was any of this gonna be for her anyway? Think about it. She stays behind and she's alone for fourteen months while you travel the world. Or she goes on the road with you and she doesn't see her friends or family the whole time, doesn't sleep in the same bed for more than three nights in a row. She can't work, can't even fucking unpack. Either way, she's doing nothing but living for *you* and you're living for your career. You really want that for her?" He took a swallow of his drink, the ice clinking in the glass. "You're getting famous, and what is she getting? It's a little selfish."

I looked away from him.

I was supposed to marry this woman. I'd known it the moment I thought I might lose her. She was it for me. The thought of being without her was as unacceptable to me as never seeing daylight again, never picking up another guitar.

If I'd fucked this up for good, I would suffer for it for the rest of my life. I'd never get over it. I needed to fix this and then put a ring on her hand and let every man who looked at her know there was already somebody hopelessly in love with her.

And they *did* look at her. I was going to need a very big ring.

I dragged my hands into my hair and squeezed. "Fucking Lola. I hate her."

"I gotta tell you, none of this Lola shit sits right with me. My Spidey senses are tingling." He tapped a finger on his tumbler. "And you're sure you didn't give her the gate code?"

"I didn't give it to her," I mumbled.

He squinted out at the fireplace like he was thinking.

Fuck this. I got up. "I'm going over to Sloan's. I can't sit here and do nothing."

I'd given her space. It had been two fucking days. If she was going to break up with me, I'd rather she swing the ax now instead of leaving me kneeling with my head on the block. Not knowing was killing me. I couldn't do this anymore.

The drive to her house felt like I was delivering myself to my own execution. I sat in her driveway rallying my courage to even get out and try my luck at getting in the door.

It was midnight. The house was dark.

I had my key, but Sloan always put the chain on. I'd probably have to ring the doorbell and wake her up. And would she even let me in? Or answer it after she looked through the peephole?

I had to be braced for the very real possibility she would break up with me tonight. That I'd had all I was going to get. I imagined her asking me to leave, taking my key. Making me empty my drawer and then never seeing her again.

My heart would break. It would fucking shatter.

The floodlights came on when I got to the porch. I put my key in the lock and turned it under the judgmental glare. I pushed the door open an inch, then another, and the moment when the chain would have gone taut came and went and Tucker spilled out and jumped on my legs.

She didn't put the chain on.

It was the first ray of hope I'd had in days. I stood with my forehead to the open door and my hand on the knob for a solid minute.

She didn't lock me out.

I prayed this meant something. That it wasn't just some oversight. And I hoped that this wouldn't be the last time I ever spoke to the woman I loved.

CHAPTER 30

SLOAN

♪ HOLOCENE | BON IVER

The dip of the bed jostled me from my sleep. Somewhere in my misery I'd drifted off. Familiar hands wrapped themselves around my waist from behind and pulled me in.

Jason...

The scratch of his beard brushed the side of my neck and then in a husky voice, "I'm sorry."

None of it mattered suddenly. *None* of it. The change in my brain was so fast it gave me whiplash. All my plans disintegrated. My mind flipped in a single heartbeat. I rolled over in the circle of his arms and kissed him. Even if there hadn't been an apology, I'd have kissed him. He was forgiven, and I immediately became whole again.

He held my cheeks in his warm hands. "Sloan, I'm so sorry. I should have told you everything. I don't know why I didn't."

"I'm sorry too," I whispered. "I missed you so much. I don't know what I was thinking. I should have trusted you, I just got so in my head..."

"It was my fault," he said. "I was just afraid you'd think less of me or wouldn't be able to handle it, and I thought I was protecting you. It was stupid."

He put his forehead to mine. "You didn't put the chain on," he whispered.

I shook my head. No, I hadn't put the chain on. I couldn't speak to him, but I couldn't lock him out, even though I didn't think he would come home. Not after the way I made him leave.

But Jason never did have self-preservation instincts when it came to me, did he?

He brushed the hair off my forehead in the dimness. "Don't ever take yourself from me again. Promise me. Please."

His beautiful deep voice sounded like suffering. The room was dim. The only light came from the glow of my alarm clock on my nightstand. But I could see the dark circles under his lids and the hollow look in his eyes and my heart broke a thousand times in a single beat and I knew instantly that I would never have been able to break up with him when he left for his tour. Never. His plane would have still been sitting on the tarmac and I'd have been calling him, begging him to take me back. Fourteen months of being separated was nothing compared to nothing at all.

"Jason, I don't want to break up when you go on tour. I can't."

"I love you."

The words sucked the air right out of my lungs and I blinked into the darkness.

"I love you, Sloan."

"I love you too," I breathed.

He let out a noise that sounded like a mixture of joy and relief, and I wrapped my arms around him and buried my face in his beard.

He held me so tightly I couldn't breathe. "Sloan, come with me on my tour. Please."

I laughed into his neck from happiness. "Yes."

"Yes?"

I nodded. It was crazy. It was so not the kind of spontaneous thing I did. But it wasn't even a question. I had to.

I wanted so much to be me again. I'd promised myself I would chase joy, climb out of my in-between, live a life of happiness that was worth living—and the only life I wanted to live was with *him*.

"I'll pay your mortgage," he said into my hair, a grin in his voice. "I'll give you as much as you need."

I pulled away so I could look at him. "No, I can't let you do that. Maybe I can rent it?"

"It needs too many repairs to rent," he said, his hands on my face. "Why don't you sell it?"

Sell it?

"When we get back we can buy a new place," he said. "Something better. Close to Kristen and Josh."

I smiled at him. "You want to live with me?"

His eyes moved back and forth between mine. "I want *everything* with you."

Screw it. If I was going to do this thing, I was going to do it. And I wanted to start over. I wanted to start over with *him*.

I nodded. "Okay. Let's do everything. Let's do it all."

He paused and beamed at me. And then he smothered me with kisses. My mouth, my cheeks, my neck, telling me over and over and over again that he loved me, and I laughed and clutched him.

Every time he said it, the words filled me up. They wrapped themselves around me like warm, strong arms and made me feel safe and cherished, pushing out every doubt that his past and his fame had made me feel.

He loved me.

And I loved him back.

This was why we could weather his fame. Why I could trust him, always, no matter what came up. He belonged to me and we were in it together. How could I ever question it?

We were in love.

CHAPTER 31

JASON

♪ DIAMONDS | BEN HOWARD

I bought a ring. A very, *very* big ring.

CHAPTER 32

SLOAN

♪ BIG JET PLANE | ANGUS & JULIA STONE

Are you sure you don't want to come with me? *Saturday Night Live* is kind of a once-in-a-lifetime deal," Jason said. He talked against my lips as he kissed me goodbye on my porch. His guitar case sat next to us and his hands twined in the hair at the nape of my neck. His eyes practically smoldered.

He did this on purpose, of course, because he knew how defenseless I was when he sucked me into that vortex of his.

I had to be strong. I had too much to do.

"If you want me to be ready to leave my whole life behind in less than a week, I can't give you three more days," I said, nuzzling his nose with my eyes closed.

It was actually a good thing he was leaving for New York. The man was highly distracting. I couldn't get anything done when he was home—well, nothing that required clothes, anyway.

"I'm going to miss you," he breathed.

"I'm going to miss you too." I kissed him, wrapping my arms around his neck. "But mostly I'm going to miss being the other woman for a few days."

He snorted.

"I'm going to frame it," I said. "Maybe Kristen will put it in the Christmas calendar."

Yesterday a picture of me and Jason holding hands at Trader Joe's ended up on the cover of the *National Enquirer*. JAXON WATERS CHEATS ON LOLA SIMONE! was plastered all over the front. I'd been wearing sunglasses and a baseball cap and my tattoos were covered, so only I recognized myself. But it was still really funny.

"They called me a mystery woman," I said, smiling against his lips. "I've always wanted to be mysterious."

He chuckled. "I've always wanted two women. This is working out for both of us."

I hit him, and he laughed, tickling me by nibbling my neck.

It had been three days since we made up, and things between us were on a whole new level. There was no more end date. We weren't breaking up, we were going on his tour and then moving in together. The future of our relationship was clearly laid.

And we were ridiculously in love with each other.

He'd told me everything. About Lola, the song. Why he didn't ask me on tour earlier. *Everything.* And I'd listened and understood and when it was over, I felt like we were allies against the world.

Zane idled in my driveway, waiting for him. I could tell he didn't want to leave me and it made my heart happy, but I had to be practical. "Go, you're going to be late for your flight. Text me from the car."

"Look at me."

I gazed up and drowned in his blue eyes.

He put his thumb over my lips, pressing them shut. "I love you," he said. Then he moved his thumb, kissed me swiftly, and jogged down the steps with his guitar before I could reply.

My heart could barely take it. I don't think I could ever get used to him saying that. I leaned on the door frame, Tucker at my feet, and watched Jason get into the car, smiling. I blew him a kiss as they pulled out of the driveway and my cell phone pinged with a text message from him before Zane's Tesla cleared the end of the block.

Jason: I miss you already.

Ping.

Jason: Sext me.

I laughed.

God, we were so adorable, even I could barely stand us.

I got to work. In the next seven days I had to contact the company I painted for and tell them I was quitting, and I had to put my Etsy store on vacation. Three paintings needed to be completed. I had to rent a storage container, put my house on the market, and start packing. Things needed to be pulled together for a quick yard sale.

And I still had the hardest thing of all to check off my list: telling Kristen I was leaving.

We'd never been apart for more than a few days before. *Never*, going as far back as the sixth grade. There was no telling how she would react. I half expected her to tell me not to go. She'd been a huge Jason fan so far, but agreeing to go on tour with him after only two weeks as his girlfriend sounded crazy, even to me. And then to explain I'd be selling my house and moving in with him too? On paper it was nuts, no matter how right it felt to *me*.

I'd made plans to meet her and the baby at the park, and I drove over with Tucker at noon. Kristen had Oliver in his jogging stroller and was already making a circuit around the running track when I got there. I walked the wrong way until I met up with her. When I fell in beside her, she didn't waste any time calling me on my agenda.

"So what do you need to tell me?" She looked determinedly ahead, speed walking.

God, how does she do that every time? Knowing exactly what I'm up to within five seconds of seeing my face?

I didn't bother drawing it out. "Jason's asked me to go on tour with him."

Kristen didn't take her eyes off the running track. "And you said yes?"

"And I said yes. But there's something else. I'm selling the house. And when we get back, we're moving in together."

Kristen stopped walking so fast I outpaced her by three steps before I noticed.

She panted and stared at me for a moment. "Let's go sit," she said carefully, giving me a look I couldn't decipher.

Ugh. This wasn't good. I *so* wanted her to support me in this. I was going to do it whether she wanted me to or not. But I really had hoped she was going to back me because the news hadn't gone over well with my parents. At *all*.

My dad thought my running away on tour with my "rock star" boyfriend of two weeks was some kind of crisis I was working through. He'd given me a long speech about the perils of dating musicians and ended it by telling me he disagreed whole-heartedly with my decision. He'd even thrown around the word "disappointed."

He'd loved Brandon. They were both ex-military and they'd

played in the same poker league. Dad didn't even want to meet Jason. He said he'd put money on it being over by Labor Day and if it wasn't, maybe he'd meet him at Thanksgiving.

Maybe.

Mom tended to be more of a romantic, but after Jason's minor tabloid scandal, she thought I was crazy to even consider staying with him, let alone going on his tour and selling my house to move in with him. She'd agreed to meet him, but was so unenthusiastic I opted out.

Jason's family had embraced me so much I think it killed him to know how mine felt.

Not having anyone be as happy about this as I was sucked.

We found a bench in the shade, walking in a heavy silence until we got there. Kristen parked the stroller and handed Oliver his sippy cup before sitting to face me.

I dove in. "Before you even start, I know it's only been a few weeks, and I know—"

"I'm glad you're going."

It took me a few moments to process what she'd said.

"You...you *are?*"

"Yes. And I'm glad you're selling the house. You should have done that a long time ago."

I blinked at her. "You're not upset that I'll be gone so long? You don't think I'm crazy?"

"Sloan, there are some things I need to say to you."

She pushed her hair behind her ear and licked her lips. It took her a while to begin. She seemed at a loss for words. Kristen was *never* at a loss for words.

"I know that you'll be away for a long time. But I've gone longer without seeing you." She paused for a long beat. "These last two years, the Sloan I grew up with has been missing. I was afraid she was buried at Forest Lawn with Brandon and I was never going to see her again. Then you decided to live, and you know what? My Sloan came back." She shook her head. "I missed my friend. And if I thought that you were only okay because you have a man in your life again, I'd tell you not to go. But I think you have a man in your life *because* you're okay. I don't think this is some rebound thing. I think what you two have is real. And goddamn it, if he wants you to go on his tour, *go*. Because I haven't seen you this fucking happy in a *very* long time."

The tears were falling before I even knew they were coming. "Thank you," I whispered.

"I'm glad he finally figured out how bad it would suck if he went without you. Honestly, Josh and I were worried about what might happen when he left, and we were wondering what was taking his ass so long to ask."

"Seriously? You guys talked about it?"

"We're your emergency response team. Of course we talked about it. Did drills and everything."

I laughed out of relief and hugged her. This made it real. It gave it validation to have her support this—both of them, her and Josh. They saw it too, what I had with Jason.

"Sloan, it makes me so happy to see you make these choices. Go, have adventures, fall more in love, shake a tambourine, be a fucking groupie and say cliché shit like, 'I'm with the band.'"

I snorted, wiping at my tears.

"I'll be here when you get back. And so will you. Finally."

Kristen and I walked for forty-five minutes, talking about the tour and Oliver. Then I had to get back to the house and get started on my to-do list. I hugged her goodbye and made my way up the stairs to the parking lot.

I was texting Jason. He'd just sung "Name" into my voicemail on the way to the airport. The song we had our first kiss to. I melted.

I was typing with my head down, telling him I loved him, so I didn't notice my car until my feet were already crunching over glass. I looked up and froze with a hand to my mouth.

My windows were broken. *All* of my windows were broken.

My windshield was caved into the front seat like someone had stood directly on the hood to smash it in.

All four tires had been slashed. My side mirrors had been broken off and lay scattered in the parking lot like candy from a busted piñata.

And the words *Jaxon's Whore* were spray painted over the door that didn't match the rest of the car.

CHAPTER 33

JASON

♪ DO I WANNA KNOW? | ARCTIC MONKEYS

The cameras in the parking lot were broken—but *I* fucking knew who did it.

Lola was pissed about being booted off my tour, about seeing me in the tabloids with another woman, and she'd gone after Sloan. I had no doubt in my mind it was her.

I was fucking furious. I'd called Ernie immediately after Sloan told me about her car and he'd gone down and gotten her. I'd almost flown back from New York, but both of them insisted I stay and do *SNL*. Ernie promised he'd keep her safe and deal with the police—and he did.

But the car wasn't the end of it. Not even close.

Sloan's social media accounts were suddenly bombarded with trolls. Fake accounts set up with no other purpose than to comment on her photos and slide into her DMs and harass her. It was so bad she had to delete her Instagram page and even Kristen and Josh had to lock down their accounts.

Then the phone calls started.

Vulgar texts and voicemails from strangers to Sloan's cell,

all hours of the night. It ran the gamut from calling her names to making threats of violence. And it was all made *very* obvious that this was about me. Jaxon's whore, Jaxon's bitch. None of it was traceable. All the numbers they called from were spoofed.

I had no idea how Lola had gotten Sloan's number. But then I had no idea how Lola had gotten the gate code either.

It was like she'd hired a fucking army to come after my girlfriend.

I'd never felt so much hatred for someone in my *life*.

Ernie urged me not to confront her, that any engagement would just encourage her. He was right. There was no fucking point. It's not like she listened to reason. All I could do was control the damage and try to keep Sloan safe.

I wasn't taking any chances. We changed Sloan's number and I wouldn't let her off Ernie's property alone or anywhere near her house. I'd hired a moving company to finish the packing, and I'd had Zane oversee it. We canceled the yard sale. I didn't need Sloan outside dealing with strangers when there was someone out there who'd taken a baseball bat to her car.

The whole thing was a stress neither of us needed because our lives were hard enough as it was at the moment.

I'd been back from *SNL* for three days. My tour started in two. Everything was chaos. I'd had to dive right into rehearsals the day after I got back from New York, with the backup band I'd hired for the tour. I'd been working sixteen-hour days, juggling that and the media. I was being pulled in a thousand different directions and so was she.

And now Ernie had me up and waiting for him in front of the pool house at 6:30 in the damn morning. Sloan was asleep with Tucker in the trailer. *I* should have been asleep with Tucker in the trailer. But Ernie's text had said it was important and that it couldn't wait.

He came out the back door of the house and made his way past the pool. He was in his suit, even this early. "Hey, my friend. Sorry to rouse you. I know you need your beauty sleep." He put his hands on his hips. "It's important, or I wouldn't have called."

"What's up?" I asked, yawning.

"Someone paid off my fucking housekeeper."

I rubbed the back of my neck. "Huh?"

"Someone gave her a thousand bucks to give up the gate code so Lola could get in here that night. Ten years she'd been with me, and I have to find a new housekeeper. I'm doing my own goddamn laundry. And I haven't even told you the crazy shit yet." He looked me in the eye. "The person who paid her wasn't Lola or any of her people." He paused. "It was *your* people."

My hand dropped, and I stared at him.

"I had to do a shit ton of digging. Had to give Lupe another thousand bucks to get her to talk and I had to ask the Swansons across the street for their surveillance video, but I got the plate for the guy who bribed her. He's some low-level lackey for *your* label."

"*What?*" I breathed.

"Yeah." He scratched his cheek. "Here's what I think. I think your label set you up for those photos with Lola. I think they did it so they could leak that shit. I think the whole TMZ thing was planned and they wanted the rumors circulating so when they stuck Lola on your tour, the two of you would be all over the tabloids together, nice and fucking neat."

I stood there speechless for a long moment. "*Why?*"

"They're manufacturing your hype. They want everybody talking about you. The Lola-Jaxon singles on the soundtrack are on fire. Everybody's fucking grabbing for you. Pia can't even keep up with all the press they want you to do. That's why they pushed your tour out ten more months. They're posturing to mass-produce you. The writing's on the wall, my friend. You've got all the makings of a superstar."

Ernie wasn't one to make declarations like that. He was more of a manage-your-expectations kind of guy, so I didn't take any of what he said lightly. I should have been happy that he had this much faith in the future of my career, but instead the most peculiar sense of foreboding overcame me. That little stunt with Lola had almost cost me my girlfriend and they'd given my harasser access to where I lived? What the *fuck*?

He went on. "At this point I wouldn't even put it above them to drop Lola on your tour no matter how well your tickets are selling. It works for you both. She gives your image an edge and keeps you in the gossip mags and you give her a tour she can be on that'll keep rolling even if she drops dead with a needle in her arm."

My face went hard. "No. I'll walk before that happens. I don't give a shit, let them do what they need to do."

He put his hands on my shoulders. "Look, I don't want you worrying about Lola. She's not coming anywhere near you for the time being. You just keep up your end of the bargain and book up those shows. And as for right now, just be braced. I hope both you kids got plenty in the reserve tank because this tour's not gonna be easy." He slapped my shoulder. "Congratulations, Jaxon. You've officially made it."

CHAPTER 34

SLOAN

♪ YES I'M CHANGING | TAME IMPALA

I woke up alone with Tucker in Jason's bed. My boyfriend's side of the mattress was cold.

My house was empty and on the market. I'd quit my job and liquidated my life. And I was exhausted. We both were. Which was why it was weird he wasn't sleeping when he had the chance.

We were living in Jason's trailer until we left on tour in two days. In the last week my entire life had been reduced to a single large suitcase and a carry-on. My car was gone. The insurance company declared it totaled because apparently four tires, some windows, and a coat of paint would cost more than the whole vehicle. Got fifteen hundred for it and I felt like a bandit.

I wandered out to the bathroom wrapped in a blanket. Jason wasn't in the trailer. I peeked out the blinds and saw him by the pool house talking to Ernie.

I slid down onto the sofa with Tucker to wait for him to come back in and turned on the TV. I was sitting there, flipping through channels, when an email came through to my phone with a ping.

Every time my phone chimed I jumped a little, even though I'd changed my number and deleted my social media accounts. The Lola onslaught had been horrible. I was so glad it seemed to be over.

I clicked on the little envelope icon. My heart leapt.

It had been over two years since I got a message to this account. It was the one I used back when I painted hyperrealistic art, the one on the business cards the art galleries handed out—or used to, back when I did that sort of thing.

It was so random, for a split second I worried it was more trolling, but I recognized the name. It was a gallery curator in Laguna Beach. A well-known one.

I pored over the email.

She had a client who'd seen *Girl in Poppies* and wanted a painting of his daughter. He wanted it by Christmas and he was willing to pay $4,000 for it.

A commission.

I let out a puff of air.

This was the kind of order I used to *pray* for. My paintings usually sold, but they hung in galleries for months before they did. Not only to have someone love my work enough to commission it, but to have the painting sold before it even existed? God, it was my dream!

And then the reality pummeled me.

I was leaving on tour. And there was no way I could paint where I was going.

The disappointment hit me right in the heart.

I was ready to get serious about my art again. But I'd been bogged down with Etsy and astronaut cats so I hadn't been able to actually attempt it. And now that I'd shucked all those responsibilities and had this incredible opportunity dangling in front of me, I couldn't take it.

I put my phone away and went back to watching TV, depressed. I guess I should be happy that I'd gotten to the point where I wanted to pursue things that I used to be passionate about. Even if I couldn't do them.

Jason clomped into the trailer twenty minutes later and looked surprised to see me up. He put his hand on the back of the sofa to lean down and kiss me. "Good morning. Coffee?" He smiled, but he looked weary.

"Yeah. Hey, did you see this?" I said, nodding at the TV. I was watching E! News.

"What is it?" He went to the kitchen and opened the cabinet and pulled out the bag of grounds.

"Lola's suing her manager. I guess he embezzled all this money from her."

He spooned coffee into the press. "She was probably too wasted to notice," he mumbled. He put water in the microwave. "Speaking of Lola, Ernie thinks the photos of me and her were staged by my label."

I scrunched my forehead. "Really? Why?"

"Publicity." He leaned on the counter with his arms crossed while he waited for the microwave. "He thinks they might put her on my tour even if my shows are sold out."

I shrugged. "Okay. Well, she doesn't scare me. Just so you know."

He smiled and walked over to turn off the TV. "Hey, I got you a gift."

I grinned at him. "You did?"

He opened a cabinet in the kitchen and pulled out a large blue

polka-dot gift bag and put it in my lap as he sat down. "I thought
you might like this," he said.

I reached in and pulled out a small table lamp. It had a gear
for the base, a twisted metal neck, and an old scuffed-up curved
license plate for the shade.

"It's from your car," he said. "I had Zane get the parts from the
junkyard and send it to a guy who makes lamps out of refurbished
auto parts. I had to place a rush order to get it before we left, but
I really wanted you to have it. I know you liked that car."

I beamed. "Jason, this is so thoughtful!"

I *loved* it.

I leaned over and hugged his neck. "Thank you."

He pressed his cheek to the side of my head. "We can keep it
here until we come back from tour and get a house."

I nodded, wiping under my eyes with my thumb. *This* was
Jason. So thoughtful.

"You ready for breakfast?" I sniffed. "Pancakes or bacon and
eggs? Both?"

He sighed, and his hand went up to rub his forehead. "I'm
sorry we can't go out to eat."

He'd been getting recognized. A *lot*.

The Wilderness Calls was a blockbuster. Once the movie came
out and *Saturday Night Live* aired, his soundtrack had blown up.
The music video for the theme song had over fifty million views
as of yesterday, and unlike with his Claymation one, he was in it,
front and center.

At the last minute they gave him the cover of *GQ* magazine,
which didn't surprise me one bit. The man took a good picture.
And Lola's little tabloid scandal had actually seemed to work to his
advantage. His website crashed the day it came out, so I guess the
publicity stunt succeeded—even if it *did* almost ruin our lives.

Jason liked his fans. He liked signing autographs. He was personable and outgoing. But I don't think he'd quite expected this level of celebrity. There was no shutting it off.

He was a neon sign. People took pictures without asking, came up to him at the store and the gas station. Followed him. We had gone out to a late-night dinner a few days ago and we hadn't had a moment's peace. And even if he wasn't being approached, he was being looked at. *Stared at.*

On top of all of that, he was super on edge after the Lola thing. He said he felt like he couldn't protect me with random strangers coming up to us at every turn.

I climbed into his lap, straddling him, my shirt bunching up around my hips. I wasn't wearing shorts and my G-string was red. He glanced down and arched an eyebrow.

"We'll just have to change the way we live a little," I said. "Order room service in bed instead of going to restaurants. That kind of thing." I kissed him and he gave me a weak but grateful smile.

His head lolled back on the sofa. "What are you doing today?" His hand absently caressed my thigh.

"I have to go to FedEx and ship out the last of my commissions. Then I need to drop off a few bags at Goodwill and turn the house keys in to the real estate office. I'm stealing your truck."

"First she steals my heart, then she steals my truck," he said tiredly.

"Technically, I stole your dog first."

He chuckled, looking down at me over his nose, not lifting his head from the back of the sofa. "Any chance you might be able to do the girlfriend thing and come watch me rehearse today?"

I smiled. "Where?"

"Century City."

"I think I can fit that into my day."

He beamed, looking truly happy for the first time this morning, and leaned in and kissed me—but he knew my lips too well. He pulled his face back. "What?"

I let out a sigh. "I just...I got an email—not a bad one," I said quickly, when I saw the instant worry on his face. "For a painting. A real one. Not Etsy stuff."

He beamed. "That's great! What do they want you to paint?"

I tucked my hair behind my ear. "It's a little girl on a swing. And they're offering me a lot of money for it."

He pulled me into him by my thighs and smiled. "Of course they are. You're incredible."

I smiled weakly. "I miss creating. Feeling like I'm reaching my full potential. I totally want to do it and I can't."

He wrinkled his forehead. "Why not?"

I shrugged. "We'll be touring. I can't paint on a bus."

"When do they need it by?"

"Christmas."

"So do it on our break."

I shifted on his lap. I hadn't thought about that. "Five weeks isn't very long to finish something like this."

"Leave a little early," he said. He leaned in and kissed me. "And I'm glad this came up because there's another gift in the bag," he whispered to my lips. "You missed it."

I pulled away slightly and looked at him.

"Go on."

I leaned over and picked up the bag again, pulling out the tissue paper. A gift card sat at the bottom.

It was to an art supply store.

For a thousand dollars.

"Jason! This is too much!" I gasped. "I can't take this!"

He wrapped his arms around my back and put his lips to my

ear. "I just think you're so sexy when you paint," he said, trailing kisses down my neck. "And now that there won't be any more astronaut cats, I figured you might want to go back to painting your own stuff. You'll need supplies, and I want to support you like you support me."

Something hard in his lap was supporting me at the moment.

"Thank you," I whispered.

He nipped at my lip. "You're welcome."

Then he got up and threw me over his shoulder like a caveman. He slapped my ass and I shrieked, giggling as he turned us for the bedroom.

CHAPTER 35

SLOAN

♪ LITTLE BLACK SUBMARINES | THE BLACK KEYS

Fourteen weeks later

The alarm on Jason's phone went off. Even Tucker whined from the end of the bed.

Jason moved next to me to flick on the light and I winced. "It should be illegal to get up before the sun," I mumbled.

He laughed a little and propped himself up on his elbow, his hair messy. "How you feeling?"

"My ears are stuffy."

A cool hand was pressed to my cheek, and I closed my eyes. "You don't feel hot," he said.

"I think it's just allergies or something." I sniffed. "I'm okay."

Jason scooted up on his forearms until he was hovering over me. He gave me one of his amused smiles, which meant my hair was probably crazy.

"Don't kiss me," I said. "I don't want you getting sick." If he did, they'd just make him sing through it.

He grinned and nuzzled into my neck instead.

"What city are we in?" I asked, yawning.

He shifted to look at his hand. "Last night was Atlanta. So I'm thinking Memphis?"

Zane always wrote the city on Jason's hand before he went onstage so he wouldn't thank the wrong place.

"Aww. I've always wanted to see Memphis," I pouted. We'd be gone by tonight.

"Why don't you skip sound check and go sightseeing with Jessa?" he asked, looking down on me.

Jessa was the lead singer of his opening band, Grayscale. She was also *very* good friends with Lola. I didn't hold it against her. Jessa was actually pretty nice, and we seemed to have an unspoken agreement that we didn't discuss Lola, which helped. Zane was super close with Jessa's personal assistant, Courtney, so we all hung out a lot. We always got rooms next to one another so we could go in and out the connecting doors and borrow curling irons and watch TV together.

I shook my head. "I'm not going sightseeing without you. If we're not seeing Memphis, we're not seeing it together."

He kissed my forehead and smiled, his blue eyes creasing.

I put a hand up to his cheek. "I hope our kids get your eyes."

His smile got deeper. "And their mother's artistic talent." He took my hand and curled it up in his.

I sighed. "I haven't done anything talented in a while."

He narrowed his eyes. "Well, maybe not artistically. But there *was* that thing you did with your mouth on the bus last week."

I gasped and hit him, and he chuckled.

"You know how I knew you were the girl for me?" he asked, pulling me into him, his forehead to mine. "When I saw you licking that chip bag. I said to myself, 'That's her, Jason. She's the one.'"

I giggled, and he started to tickle me. I shrieked and tried to wriggle away from him, and he laughed. Then his alarm went off again and all the fun abruptly stopped. We both let out a sigh and got up and wandered to the bathroom.

He handed me my toothbrush and we stood over the sink brushing our teeth in our well-practiced routine. I stared at myself in the mirror. God, I looked like hell. Like I needed to be dipped in a full-body moisturizer or something. I had dark circles under my eyes and I was pale again. Even though most of our hotels had pools and spas, we didn't have time to use them.

Maybe we needed to drink more water. I made a mental note to make Jason do that with me—even though *he* looked great.

Jason was born for this life. None of the traveling fazed him. Not to mention it was in his contract that he had to do at least an hour at the gym with a personal trainer four times a week. So while I was getting puffy and pale, he was getting toned and hotter than he already was. It was so unfair.

I let my eyes follow the line of hair down Jason's six-pack stomach into the waistband of his pajama bottoms. When I looked up, he was smirking at me with his toothbrush in his mouth. He bounced his eyebrows, and I laughed and spit. "Don't let it get to your head just because you're still gorgeous despite this marathon we've been running."

He spit too. "Well, I have to be equal to my beautiful girlfriend, don't I?" He winked.

I scoffed. "Yeah, right." My eyes were bloodshot from coughing. I was bloated and exhausted.

I did *not* adjust to change well. I hadn't known this about myself until change was all I did.

We'd been on the road three months. And none of it was at *all* what I'd expected. There was nothing glamorous or vacation-like about anything we were doing.

Bus, hotel, venue, flight. Radio station, news station, photo shoots, fast food, six hours of sleep, four hours of sleep, back in the bus. Perpetual motion, all the time. It was so constant my body couldn't catch up.

The crew got two days off a week—but we didn't. There was always some sort of media thing they needed Jason doing. He was too afraid to *not* do it. If he didn't sell out his concerts, they'd bring in Lola. It was exhausting.

I'd been fighting this cold for forever. My stomach was a mess too. We were eating nothing but junk—and there really wasn't much of a choice. Jason's tour manager had him on such a tight schedule, stopping for anything longer than gas and whatever restaurant was in the adjacent parking lot was all we could manage. We ate at all different hours of the day. Sometimes we had dinner at five before his show, sometimes we didn't eat until midnight. I was jet-lagged and we weren't even out of the United States yet.

I was *living* for our five-week break. Counting down the days. It was September fourth and we had ten more weeks of this until the time off for the holidays. I hadn't seen Kristen in months. Jason kept offering to fly her and Josh out, but there was no point. We almost never stayed in the same place for more than two days and the baby wouldn't do well with all the traveling.

So the plan was to spend a week in Ely with his family for Thanksgiving, and then a month in California so I could paint and see Kristen and my parents. A month wasn't a lot of time to pull off the piece that had been commissioned. But I didn't want to leave him early and honestly, I was so excited to do it I didn't care if it meant I had to paint fourteen hours a day just to finish it in time.

I missed painting like a penetrating ache in my *soul*. I'd never gone this long without doing it in some capacity. Now, over three months without a paintbrush in my hand and I craved it. Not to mention I wanted the work. I'd made a nice chunk of change from the sale of my house. I had my own money to spend—not that Jason would let me. But I wanted a purpose. Something that wasn't just being Jason's girlfriend.

Someone knocked on the door and I put on my robe and went to answer it. This was part of our system now. I got the door and Jason got out of sight in case someone passed by and saw him inside.

We'd learned to do this the hard way. If someone spotted him in the room, we had to move or we'd have fans or cameras waiting for us when we came out—or worse, knocking and waking us up.

I opened the door to Zane holding our coffees and the room service guy with the cart standing there at the same time.

"Hey," I said, letting them both in.

I breathed in the warm smell of pancakes and bacon as the cart pushed past me into the room. At least I could count on a semi-decent meal when we stayed in a hotel with room service. But even that had lost its luster months ago. All the menus were the same. The same five or six options for every meal at every hotel. I had never thought I'd be bored of room service, but here we were.

I'd pictured we'd eat at all the signature restaurants in the cities we would visit. Barbecue in Kansas, deep-dish pizza in Chicago, cheesesteaks in Philadelphia. But we didn't really visit the cities we were in. We drove through them. Sometimes so fast we didn't even know we'd been there.

Zane handed me my Starbucks latte and put Jason's black

Sumatra drip next to the TV. She pulled a folder out from under her arm. "Here's the schedule. They booked him in the six o'clock slot."

I groaned. "They couldn't prerecord it?"

"Nope. Live. Sorry."

Ugh. This meant that instead of any kind of sit-down dinner tonight, he was going to run right from the news station onto the stage. Again.

I sighed, mopping at my nose with a tissue and scanning the rest of the timeline for the day. After the concert tonight we were making the three-hour drive from Memphis to Nashville for a festival tomorrow. So we'd check into the hotel at 2:00 a.m. Sound check at 8:00. Festival at noon.

Another crappy schedule.

Zane seemed to sense my weariness and signed the room service slip for me.

"You okay?" she asked, after she let the guy out.

Jason was in the shower. I could hear the water running.

I rubbed my forehead. "Yeah. I'm just so tired."

"Go get your nails done or something. Skip this shit."

I looked down at my hands and the chipped polish on my fingers.

It was funny, because when I was grieving Brandon, I didn't take care of myself and it was exactly like that now too.

"Want me to get you somethin'?" she asked.

Zane was great. She was like our life raft out here. We were so isolated. Jason couldn't even get off the bus half the time or he'd end up signing autographs. He couldn't even go into a CVS and pick his own deodorant. Zane did everything for us. Our laundry, our errands.

"I'm fine," I said, coughing into my elbow. "Thank you, though."

"You just gotta get used to the road," she said, leaning down to grab the bag of dirty clothes where we always put it by the door. "You'll be a pro by the next one."

I scoffed. "At least I'll get a few years to recover from the one I'm on."

She flung the bag over her shoulder. "You wish."

"Ha. He's done after Brisbane," I said, wiping my nose.

She looked confused. "He gets a three-month break after this one and then he's back on the road. He didn't tell you?"

I blinked at her. "No…"

"They've been sending around the paperwork to the crew to extend their contracts. I just got mine yesterday. Maybe he didn't know yet."

My stomach dropped. "Are you sure?"

"Very sure. Looks like he's pretty hot in Tokyo. I hear they're sending him there and then Brazil, Chile, Panama, Argentina. It's good. Means he's big."

I completely deflated. Another tour? Three months off and then more of this? "Oh my God…" I breathed.

Zane patted her leg. "Let's go, Tuck. Walk time."

Tucker jumped off the bed and let Zane leash him. "I'ma bring up some DayQuil. Text me if you want anything else."

I let them out and put my back to the door after it shut.

The disappointment crashed into me like a whole new wave of exhaustion and my eyelid lurched into spasms.

I didn't know what I'd expected. I mean, they'd have him doing *something* when this tour was over. But I'd just thought it would be writing and recording his next album, home, with me, in a house somewhere. It had never even occurred to me that they'd have him do this all over again, right after the last one.

So was this what it was going to look like? On tour, off tour, and then back again? *Forever?*

The water shut off in the shower.

I took another second to compose myself and went back into the steamy bathroom.

"Everything all right?" he asked, looking at me as he tied a towel around his waist.

"Did you know they're scheduling another tour for you after this one?" I asked.

He froze. "No. Where'd you hear that?"

"Zane said they're renewing the contracts for your crew. That you're getting three months off and then you're going back."

I saw the tic in his jaw. "What time is it?"

"Too early to call Ernie," I said, already knowing what he was thinking.

Jason picked up his phone from the sink, dialed, and hit Send anyway.

He stalked out into the bedroom and I followed him. "Jason, it's like four a.m. there."

He turned and put the call on speaker and held it between us.

Ernie picked up on the second ring. "Good morning, kids. Calling me from Graceland?" he said groggily.

"Are they putting me on another tour?" Jason asked.

There was a pregnant pause.

"Eh, fuck," Ernie mumbled. "Give me a second."

Ernie muttered something muffled to his wife. A few moments passed and then a door shut in the background. "Who told you?"

"Is it true?" Jason asked.

"Look at it this way, you have job security."

I shut my eyes for a long second and when I opened them, Jason's face looked like an apology.

"Technically it's not a new one," Ernie said. "It's the same tour, extended. It's a good thing. Means you're in demand. I was fighting for another soundtrack for you to keep you in LA, Patty Jenkins fell through, though, and the deal got fucked. You're not writing and you're not recording. They're not gonna let you sit pretty and do nothing, my friend. And you're hot in Tokyo right now."

Jason and I looked at each other, having a silent exchange. He dragged a hand down his beard. "Ernie, I can't do another one of these. This schedule's fucking ridiculous. I haven't been able to rest my voice in months, we're exhausted."

I stared at him. *He* wasn't exhausted at all—this was 100 percent for me. And it was the first time he'd really admitted that he wasn't happy with what was going on.

"Yup, well, it's bullshit," Ernie said. "But unfortunately it's what you signed up for. If you give them an album, I can get you six months off the road instead of three to produce it. They're only giving you the three in hopes that you actually write something, otherwise they'd just keep you going."

Jason's eyes went sorrier still, and he sat heavily on the edge of the bed.

He couldn't write. It was bad before we went on the road, and now it was the worst it had ever been. I don't know how they expected him to summon creativity under these conditions.

"And since I have you two on the phone, I gotta tell you something else," Ernie said. "And I'm gonna warn you, you're not gonna like it."

Jason looked up at me and we waited.

"They booked you in Amsterdam for Thanksgiving. And you're going to Paris for Christmas."

What little was left in my tank bled out.

CHAPTER 36

JASON

♪ I DON'T KNOW WHAT TO SAY | BRING ME THE HORIZON

The light drained right out of Sloan's eyes. She blinked at me wordlessly for a few seconds, then turned and walked slowly into the bathroom.

"Ernie, I gotta call you back."

I hung up and followed her. She was sitting on the closed lid of the toilet seat with her face in her hands and I crouched in front of her. "I'm sorry, Sloan."

I didn't know what else to say. I *was* sorry. I was sorry every fucking day out here.

This wasn't a life. She was run-down and bored. She missed her friends and her family. I did what I could to make it fun for her, but being on the road was just fucking brutal.

She didn't take her face from her hands. "I just need a minute to process this," she said quietly.

She'd been looking forward to going home. She missed Kristen, and she wanted to do that commission. It was all she talked about. And now it had just been ripped out from under her.

What kind of fucked-up cosmic joke was it that my passion

involved constant motion and travel, and hers required total and complete stillness?

"Hey." I put a kiss on her knee. "Maybe we can go see the Louvre?" I said hopefully, knowing that they'd probably have me running to the next thing and it wouldn't happen.

She must have known it too. She didn't reply.

"Sloan…"

She took a deep breath and pulled a piece of toilet paper from the roll and wiped at her nose. "Okay. It is what it is." She sniffed. "We can't change it. So how much longer?" Her beautiful eyes were bloodshot. "How long is your contract? When it's over, Ernie can renegotiate your terms, right? We can ask for better schedules? More control?"

"Yes, but…" My heart sank at what I was going to have to tell her.

When I got my record deal, I'd been ecstatic. Most musicians got a single album offer with an option to renew if the artist did well enough. You got offered two albums if the label had faith in you. Very few got the offer I did—and I'd gotten it because they'd accurately foreseen what was happening to me now: stardom.

Ernie had warned me it would tie me to them, but I didn't care. I'd landed one of the top labels in the world. I *wanted* to be tied to them. I wanted to be Don Henley famous.

I wasn't afraid of the work. I couldn't even imagine the scenario in which I wouldn't want to be represented by one of the most powerful forces in the music industry. Ernie had negotiated great royalties and perks—my advance was more money than I could have imagined in my wildest dreams. I knew they'd push me hard, but I was single, I was used to being on tour, the road didn't bother me, and writing had never been an issue for me, so I had no doubts that I could produce what we agreed upon.

And now *everything* was different.

I couldn't write. There was Sloan to consider. Lola was hanging over my head like a fucking guillotine. This record deal was crushing me under its weight, and all I wanted now was something in the middle. Manageable fame and success that would still give me the possibility of a life—because that was *not* what this was.

She waited. "How long?"

I shook my head. "It's not a set time frame, Sloan. My contract is for four albums. The soundtrack was one. I need three more."

"All right. And how long will that take?"

I paused before I answered her.

She licked her lips. "Six months? A year each? What are we looking at?"

"The average time between albums for most musicians is three years."

The news hit her like a smack. She actually recoiled from it.

"Three *years?*" she breathed. Her red eyes dropped to her lap, moving back and forth. "Three years, Jason?" Her gaze came back up to mine. "*Each?*"

"I know it's a lot—"

The color drained from her face. "And you can't write," she whispered, the reality of our situation truly sinking in. "It could be nine more years of this? *More?*" Her eyes begged me to tell her it wasn't true.

And I couldn't.

With nothing to say, I got up, feeling like I had to do something to make this better, but there was nothing to do. "I'm starting a bath for you."

I ran the water in the Jacuzzi tub and poured in the hotel soap. "You're staying here today. You're sick."

She didn't argue with me like she usually did when I tried to get her to leave me to do something for herself, and I couldn't tell if that was a good sign or a bad one.

I stood her up and started to undo the belt of her robe. She looked dazed. She wouldn't make eye contact with me.

Her blond hair was tied in a sloppy bun on top of her head. She never wore it down anymore. She rarely put on makeup, she didn't get her nails done. I didn't care one ounce how she looked. She was beautiful to me no matter what—but I cared what it *meant*. She wasn't taking care of herself.

She was deteriorating out here. I felt like I'd taken an orchid on a road trip and it wasn't thriving. I was watching it wither, its petals falling off, and there was nothing I could do about it except take it back home and plant it. And now that wasn't going to be possible.

She coughed miserably and I managed to actually feel worse than I already did.

"I'll bring your breakfast in here," I said. "And then you're going back to bed. Come on."

I helped her into the tub and went to the room, grabbed the chair from the desk, and rolled it into the bathroom so she could use the seat as a table. Then I ran her food in and set it up. The whole time I was looking at my watch because I was already running late. I needed to be here for her, take care of her—at least be around when she was ready to talk about what had just happened—but I had to be at a fucking radio station instead.

I kissed her forehead goodbye before I left and she didn't say a word. She didn't even lean into it.

Zane drove and I called Ernie from the car. I cradled the phone with my shoulder and tried to rub the encroaching headache from my temples.

He picked up on the first ring. "Did you know that you can

see the sunrise right through the sliding glass doors of my living room if my wife makes you sleep on the couch?"

I pinched the bridge of my nose. "I shouldn't have called so early. I'm sorry the wife is mad."

"One of my wives is *always* mad. It's how I know I'm alive. How's Sloan? She taking it okay?"

I peered out through the window at the rainy streets of Memphis. "No, she's not. She's sick. She's tired. She's not happy."

He scoffed. "What the fuck's there to be happy about? This road shit sucks."

I rubbed at my eyes tiredly. "It's like I've wanted this my whole life and now I have it and I just want it to fucking be over."

I pictured him doing his head bob. "Well, you're a victim of your own success. You have to tour while people wanna hear you play." He let out a long breath into the phone. "You know, you *do* have choices here, my friend."

"I'm not breaking up with her."

"Well, that's definitely a choice, but that's not what I was about to say—and I'm a little offended you think I'd suggest that at this point. That's your first wife we're talking about."

I snorted.

"You can bite the bullet and record the bullshit they wrote for you."

I groaned.

"Hey, it'll get you started. Speed up the end date. It's that or the other thing, and you definitely don't want the other thing. There are only two ways out of a contract. You fulfill it, or you get dropped. And they're only gonna drop you if your career's gone to shit. I don't see that happening, unless you have some kitten-drowning video out there that I don't know about."

I closed my eyes and lolled my head back on the headrest.

"Look," he said. "Give her a break. Send her home for a few weeks."

I lifted my head. *Send her home?*

Even the thought of being on the road without her made my stomach plummet. She was the only thing keeping me sane out here. I was a prisoner of my fame now. Trapped in a bus or a hotel room unless I wanted to sign autographs—which I didn't. The shine had worn off that months ago. I didn't mind being sequestered with Sloan, but without her? She was my whole world. My best friend. Sending her away sounded like a jail sentence.

"What does Sloan like to do?" he asked.

I squeezed my temples. "She likes to cook. Paint. See Kristen."

"Okay, then that's what you arrange. She needs a vacation from this shit. The burnout is real, and you're not even overseas yet. You drag Sloan to the UK like this and she's jet-lagged and miserable, and she's gonna end up going the way of my second wife, packing up and leaving your ass for your drummer while you're at sound check somewhere in Berlin."

I nodded wearily.

"And she's sick?" he asked.

"She's been sick for weeks," I admitted. I probably should have made sure she went to urgent care, but she hadn't had a fever and it wasn't exactly easy to get away.

"I'll send a rock doc over to have a look at her."

"A what?"

"A rock doc. A musician's physician? They're on call for tours. They come to you. There's a guy in Memphis I like. I'll get him over there. He'll patch her up—antibiotics, a shot of B12, she'll be right as rain. I'll do that and you figure out how to get her home for a few weeks."

I let out a long breath. "I guess it's a good idea."

"Of course it is. All right, I gotta go. I gotta bring the wife a mimosa and a credit card in bed or my back might never recover from this couch."

"Why don't you just turn off your phone?" I asked tiredly.

"Because I need to be there when my clients call. What you're doing is a hell of a lot harder than what *I'm* doing. If I would have had an agent who answered the phone to give me relationship advice when I needed him, I might still be married to my first wife. And that was the *only* wife I ever shoulda been married to."

There was a serious pause in the silence. "Take care of her, Jason. You won't get another one."

CHAPTER 37

SLOAN

♪ KEEP YOUR HEAD UP | BEN HOWARD

Zane brought DayQuil and NyQuil. I took the NyQuil. I needed to sleep. I needed to not think about what Jason had just told me. It was too enormous and far-reaching to even comprehend in my current state.

A decade.

This would be our life for the next *decade*.

I wouldn't see Oliver grow up. I wouldn't paint. I wouldn't even have a home. What would be the point? We'd never be there for more than a few months.

And there was no other choice. I wouldn't ever leave him. That was the most final thing of all. Our fates were bound—what happened to him happened to me.

The way my body cried for sleep after this news scared me because it felt like before, when I used to sleep through my depression. Only this time I hadn't lost anyone but myself, swallowed whole by Jason's career.

I waited until it was 6:00 a.m. in California, and I called Kristen.

"God, you sound like you have the black lung," she said, when I launched into a coughing fit instead of saying hello.

"I know. I've been super sick." I wiped my nose with a tissue. Tucker pushed his face under my arm on the bed like he knew I needed it.

She snickered. "Did Jason offer you the penis-cillin yet?"

"Uh, what?"

"Men think their penis is the cure for everything. I swear to God, I could have some terminal disease and Josh would be over here bouncing his eyebrows like, 'Gurl, I know what you need.'"

My snort of laughter thrust me into another coughing fit.

"So how's the groupie life?" she asked once I'd recovered.

I gave her the recap of the last week since I'd talked to her and told her what had happened this morning.

"Damn," she said. "That sucks. What are you gonna do?"

"Nothing. What *can* I do? It's his job."

"The guy's like a nomad. You're just going to walk the Earth with him for the next ten years?"

"It won't be the *whole* time," I said defensively. "We'll get breaks."

"I should have known when you told me the dude lived in a trailer that this wasn't a put-roots-down kind of guy." Oliver fussed in the background. "You do *not* travel well either. Remember in the ninth grade when Mom took us to Coronado and your nose bled the whole time?"

I snorted. "And she kept saying, 'This is truly unacceptable, Sloan,' like I was doing it on purpose?"

We fell into laughter again and my mood lifted a bit.

"Look," she said. "If this was Josh, then I'd go full nomad too. If you love him, do what you gotta do. But try and take better care of yourself."

"I don't even know *how* to take care of myself out here." I swallowed the lump in my throat. "And I miss you guys."

She paused for a long moment. "We miss you too."

We talked for a few more minutes and then the NyQuil kicked in. When I hung up with her, I did feel a little better.

Maybe she was right. Maybe Zane was right too. I had to figure this out. I needed more sleep. I needed to exercise and eat better.

Ernie had really pushed for driving at night instead of the day and sleeping in the bunks on the bus. Jason thought it was a good idea too, but we'd tried it a few times and I couldn't get used to it. My mind couldn't relax knowing I was in my pajamas on a freeway somewhere. It was just weird. And I could feel the braking and turning into parking lots and I kept waking up.

But if we did that instead of staying in a hotel every night, we'd have the days free of travel to actually *do* things. We'd wake up in our city instead of running out of hotel rooms at 5:00 a.m. and driving all day to get there. Maybe we could even sightsee now and then, go to restaurants. Then we'd eat better and I could get moving again.

I let out a sigh as I climbed under the covers and bunched the pillow under my head. I'd tell him when he came back that I wanted to give sleeping on the bus another try. I couldn't keep doing the same things and expecting different results.

I fell into one of those cold-medicine slumbers. The kind where you float through the black and don't dream.

When I woke up, Jason was there sleeping next to me, an arm draped over my waist.

It took me a few moments to blink away the confusion. The room was pitch-dark, but I could see the sunlight etching the sides of the curtains. He was supposed to be gone until tonight, running around doing media and then at his sound check.

I sat up on my elbows. The clock said noon. I'd slept five hours.

Jason stirred and opened his eyes. "Hey, you're up. How are you feeling?"

"Groggy. What are you doing here?"

He brushed the hair off my forehead and kissed it. "I canceled my day."

"You canceled your *day*?" Ugh. His publicist was going to be so pissed. "Jason..."

"Don't worry, I didn't cancel my concert. But we're staying in today. We're going to lie in bed and watch crime shows. Zane's picking up food from the highest-rated restaurant in Memphis, and I have a doctor coming to see you in an hour."

It was a punch to my heart. My chin started to quiver. "Jason..."

He put his forehead to mine. "Sloan, I haven't been taking very good care of you and I'm sorry. I'm going to do better."

I sniffed. "This isn't your fault, Jason."

"It's *all* my fault." His eyes held mine. "There's nothing that I want more than for you to be happy. Do you understand? I would do *anything* to make you happy."

"I *am* happy."

But his eyes told me he didn't believe it.

Two hours later the doctor had come and gone. I had bronchitis and a double ear infection. When the doctor announced it, Jason looked like someone had kicked his dog. I think he felt guilty that I hadn't seen someone sooner, but it wasn't *his* fault. I could have gone to urgent care while he did what he had to do, but I'd just thought I'd get over it on my own.

The doctor gave me antibiotics, a shot of vitamins, prescription cough medicine, and a breathing treatment. And after that, Jason and I stayed in bed. God, we needed it. It was amazing that even though we were almost never apart, it was like we hadn't seen each other in months. Nothing we did out here was quality time.

We lay there talking about everything but Jaxon. I was *so* tired of Jaxon—and I think he was too.

It felt like another person was in our relationship. One who was demanding and required our constant attention. Our entire life was spent in the pursuit of Jaxon's needs, and now for the first time in months we were finally taking time for us. It felt good.

Maybe *this* was the trick. The thing I had to chase. And maybe if we slept in the bus, our waking hours would be more like this and less like what it had been so far.

But even as draining as the touring had been, there was good in it too. I'd fallen so much more in love with Jason over the last three months. I'd always been in awe of him—even before I knew who he was. But now I loved him for a hundred more reasons.

I'd learned he was kind and polite to everyone, from the people who checked us into our hotels to the cashiers at the gas stations. I learned he'd stay until every single person who wanted to meet him got the chance, no matter how tired he was. He was generous. He tipped well and took care of the people around him. He always helped bring in his gear, even though his crew was supposed to do it. I knew he carried around spare guitar picks to give to little kids who wanted autographs. And most of all, I knew he cherished me. I felt like the center of his gravity. Like wherever I was, he was orbiting me. It was an honor to be loved by him and it made all of this worth it, even though it was hard.

We were lying there with our heads on the same pillow, looking at each other. He reached out and brushed my hair behind my ear as I studied him. I'd memorized every freckle in his eyes. Every line. "I could paint your face from memory, you know that?" I said quietly. "You are burned into me, Jason."

He smiled gently. "Sloan, I did something for you."

I bit my lip. "What?"

He let out a breath. "You can say no if you want to, but I put a lot of thought into it and really think you should do it."

"I put a lot of thought into something too," I said. "I think we should try sleeping on the bus again. You're right, it's more practical. I'm just going to have to get used to—"

"I want you to go to Ely and stay a few months with my family."

I bolted up straight. "*What?!*"

He sat up and put out a hand. "Hear me out, okay? It's not as crazy as it sounds. I want you to do that commission," he said. "And I think my parents' house would be the perfect place to do it. You could paint by the bay window overlooking the lake. You could take Tucker with you and he'd have all that space to run after being cooped up with us for so many months. My mom's freezer is full of wild game and you could cook and maybe start updating your blog again. Mom loves you and she wants to get to know you better. Minnesota is central, so no matter where I am in the US, you could fly out to see me and be there within three hours and the time differences won't be that bad. And I called Kristen. Her and Oliver are going to come and stay with you there for two weeks."

I blinked at him. "You . . . you called *Kristen*?"

His blue eyes held mine. "Yes, I did. You could go to California for Thanksgiving and see your parents. And if you leave now, you'll be done with the painting in time to join me in Paris for Christmas. The timing is perfect."

I was speechless.

"Jason, I don't want to leave you . . ."

He shook his head. "Look, we have to figure out how to make this work for *both* of us. It's not going to end anytime soon. You need to have something that's for you." He looked me in the eye. "I want you to go. I want you to do this."

We stared at each other, my chest rising and falling a little too quickly and him looking levelly back at me. It was so thoughtful and sweet. Really, it was. But I couldn't... could I?

After losing Brandon, I'd found joy in nothing. Everything stopped for me. My world was a bleeding watercolor in the rain. And now it was a stark white canvas, begging for me to paint on it—and my hands were tied behind my back.

I was in an in-between again. I'd set up a new shrine without even realizing I was doing it, only this one wasn't for Brandon *or* Jason. It was for Jaxon.

I wanted to do that commission so badly it was a physical craving. I had to go somewhere else to paint it. That was the simple truth of it. There was no other choice.

And Jason was right. I needed a break.

If I went overseas like this, I was going to fall apart. I was physically exhausted, and the UK leg was even longer than this one and I'd be jet-lagged on top of it. If I was worn down now, how would I be then without a chance to recover first? I could come back, reset, and be ready to take all this on again, and we'd try the bus thing and maybe it would be a game changer.

And there was something else too.

If I said no, if I didn't take him up on this offer, he'd feel worse than he already did. He needed this solution as much as I did so he wouldn't feel helpless to make things better for me. I couldn't let him carry that guilt.

I licked my lips. "When were you thinking I'd go?"

"Tonight."

I blanched. "*Tonight?* As in a few hours?"

"If it's too fast or you're not up to it, you can stay here for a few days and rest. But there's a flight to Duluth at seven thirty. And if you left today I could even go with you to the airport. I already talked to Dad about picking you up."

I shook my head at him. "Why is every trip to your parents' house pitched to me with less than twelve hours' notice?"

He smiled gently at me and waited for my answer.

I held his eyes. God, but two whole weeks with Kristen and Oliver! And the luxury of unpacking, sleeping in the same bed until I was ready to wake up, no alarms going off or flights to catch. No more bus or endless Taco Bell. *Painting.*

"Say yes, Sloan."

I let out a breath. "Okay."

"Okay?"

I nodded.

He looked almost relieved. His face went soft and he ran a thumb along my cheek.

There was something so tender in the way he touched me it made me forget to breathe. He looked at me like I was the most beautiful woman in the world. I was sick and gross, but he didn't care. I was everything to him and he made me know it, every single day.

And now he was going to be without me for weeks. Maybe even months. And he was doing it all for me. *I* was his sacrifice. Just like he was mine.

I pulled down his hand and looked at it, holding it between us, touching the calluses on his fingertips. "I love your hands." His instrument. His talented, capable, loving hands.

"Have them. They're yours," he said.

I smiled. "You're giving me your hands?"

"My hands, my voice. My back to do your heavy lifting, my arms to carry you to bed when you've had too much tequila. My money, my time, my heart. It's all yours, Sloan."

I could feel the love in his words. It was so earnest, it made my heart ache so much, tears pricked my eyes. "If I didn't know any better, I'd say you sing love songs for a living."

He shook his head. "It's just how I feel. I'm yours. All of me. I think I always belonged to you. Even when you belonged to someone else." His eyes moved back and forth between mine. "Tucker knew it. He took one look and he saw the other half of me inside of you and he brought you home."

Two hours later we said goodbye at the airport. And I watched him pretend not to be sad.

CHAPTER 38

JASON

♪ BOTTOM OF THE DEEP BLUE SEA | MISSIO

Five weeks later

I was playing in Vegas. I was sitting on a cold metal folding chair backstage drinking my second Red Bull of the night when Sloan called. It was loud. Grayscale was almost done with their set.

It had been five weeks since I'd last seen her. I missed her so much it made me physically ill. I couldn't sleep and I was getting headaches. Probably grinding my teeth, who the fuck knew.

This whole thing with Sloan was a complete and total transfer of energy. She was happy and light and rested, and now *I* was a mess. Saying goodbye to her had fucking wrecked me.

"Hey, babe. What's up?" I said, rubbing my forehead.

"Did you get the cookies?"

I could hear the smile in her voice. She was always smiling now. I tried not to dwell too much on what it meant that she was so much happier *not* being here.

"Yeah. Thank you."

"Your mom gave me the recipe," she sang.

I arched an eyebrow. "Did she?" I set the empty can down and waved at Zane, pointing at it for another one.

"Yup. I can make them for you now whenever you want."

I actually smiled a little, despite the throbbing in my head. "She must really like you. She doesn't give that to anyone."

She laughed. "Well, I had to barter for it. I let her post her favorite grouse recipe on *The Huntsman's Wife* in exchange."

"So she *can* be bought." I chuckled dryly.

Mom loved her. Everyone did. Dad raved about my girlfriend every time I called home. But I'd actually been regretting sending her there instead of an Airbnb on the beach or something because my parents, though well intentioned, were a distraction.

Sloan wasn't getting her work done.

I missed her. Every time I talked to her, all I wanted to ask was, "How long?" How much longer until she came back?

Her paintings took months. I knew that. And I didn't want to rush her. She needed to focus, and me constantly asking when she'd be done with it wasn't going to help things. So I never poked her. It was my number one rule. I inquired about how it was going, if it was coming out the way she wanted. But I never asked how long.

And then last night she'd sent me a picture.

It wasn't even half-finished.

My heart had crashed and burned in my chest.

I don't think she even started until Kristen left, so that was two weeks of zero progress. Mom was taking her antique shopping and to meat raffles. Dad was bringing her on hikes and having her over to the outfitter. I'd been right about the cooking thing—Sloan had started updating her blog again. But she and Mom together were a dangerous combination. They could be in the kitchen all day long if left to their own devices—which they *were*.

Under normal circumstances, I'd be thrilled that my family had embraced her. But these weren't normal circumstances. I wanted her back.

I'd rather Sloan get two hours of painting done and come home to me two hours sooner than I get a delivery of Grandma's cookies to my hotel room—even if they *were* my favorite.

"You want to hear something funny?" Sloan said. "Your mom says the next time we're here together, we can share a room." She sounded triumphant.

"Wow, that *is* big," I mumbled. The bass from the stage vibrated from the floor to my brain and I squeezed my eyes shut.

"I think she's hoping you'll get me pregnant so she can keep me."

I snorted. "Sounds like a good enough reason to me," I said tiredly. "Let's do it. Stop taking your pill."

She laughed. "Wow, your tour has officially made you insane."

"What?" I pinched my temples. "You want to raise kids with Kristen, don't you? Let's knock you up."

She giggled. "How romantic. But pregnant? And then with a baby? On tour? That's crazy."

I squinted out at the curtains. "How is that crazy?"

She snorted. "Are you kidding?"

"Why would I be kidding?" I frowned.

"Pregnancy is hard, Jason. Look how run-down *you've* been, and you're not carrying a baby. We can't do that on tour."

I shook my head. "Sloan, there's always going to be a tour. We know that already. We can't let that stop us from living our lives."

"Jason, we don't need to have kids right now. We can wait until it's better."

I shook my head again. "It's not going to *be* better. We have to work with what we have."

"Uh, by doing something nuts like dragging myself around the globe pregnant? And then what? Breastfeeding behind stage? A crib in the dressing room?" She sounded amused.

"Yeah, why not?"

"Are you serious?" She laughed. "Have you ever actually *met* a baby? You do realize that they require a routine, right?"

My jaw flexed. "Sloan, I'm not joking about this. If we want to have kids, we should have kids."

There was a beat of silence. "You don't even get days off, Jason." The humor had suddenly left her tone.

"So?"

"So I get pregnant and then what? Deal with morning sickness *and* jet lag? When would I go to the doctor? And would you even be there with the way they're running you? What if I needed to be on bed rest? What if I went into labor on the road in a foreign country? What if the baby got sick or—"

"I would make sure you're taken care of," I said slowly. "You *know* that."

"You can't even take care of *yourself* out there. You've been having headaches for weeks, you're not sleeping. And we both know how *I* do on the road."

I tried to steady my breathing. "So you're just what? Not going to have kids with me?"

"I didn't say that," she said carefully. "I just said I wouldn't do it right *now*. It's not practical."

"Sloan, this is the best I can do. I can't change it."

"I know. But that means you have to be realistic about what you can have—what *we* can have—until this situation improves. Lots of couples put off having kids while they focus on their careers. It's fine."

But it *wasn't* fine. Not to me and not to her either, no

matter what the hell she said to try to make me feel better about it.

The background music from the opening band came to an end. We both heard it. Zane handed me my Red Bull and held up a hand, letting me know I was on in three minutes.

Sloan's voice softened. "Look, you have to go on. Let's talk about this later, okay? You don't need to be worked up about this before your show."

I put my fingers on my temples. "Sloan—"

"Call me tonight, Jason. I love you."

The line went dead.

I set my phone on my leg and put palms to my eyelids.

This separation was killing me. I was fucking unraveling out here. I couldn't keep doing this.

It was nothing like it had been when we met. Talking on the phone wasn't enough anymore, and at the rate she was going with her work, I doubted she'd even be able to meet me in Paris. And now this? How many more things was she going to have to give up?

I dragged myself onstage and went through the motions, but I couldn't stop thinking about our conversation.

I took a quick break halfway through my set and called her.

"Hey," she said, picking up.

"I need to know you'll do whatever it takes for us to have a life together," I said without preamble.

"You want me to tell you I'll be pregnant and dragging after you like a groupie while you go be a rock star?" she said, finally irritated with me. "*Really?* Why are you so dead set on arguing about this?"

"Why are you so dead set on making sure this won't work? I'm a *musician*, Sloan. You knew this was what you were signing up for."

"*I* signed up for touring with you. *Me.* Not babies who will grow up in hotel rooms. Not little children who won't even be able to play unless it's in a bus. It's not fair to them. I wouldn't even bring a *puppy* into this. Not until you have some balance."

"I would have balance if you were *here*," I said through gritted teeth.

"I can't be your balance, Jason. I'm not doing it, I'm not further reducing the quality of *my* life just so you can check something off your list," she snapped.

"Sloan—"

She let out a shaky breath. "Jason, I have to go."

She hung up on me.

I hurled my phone against the wall.

Zane, who stood by the emergency exit texting, got pelted with shrapnel. "You know I'm not going to be able to replace that until tomorrow, right?" she said calmly.

"*Fuuuuck!*"

I clawed my fingers down my face and then turned my wrath on the nearest inanimate object and kicked over a fog machine. "No more goddamn motherfucking *fog!*"

My backup band milled around the water fountain, waiting for me, and they looked at me now like I'd lost my damn mind.

Maybe I *had.*

I yanked out my in-ear monitor and stormed off to the bathroom to splash water on my face. I leaned on the sink, trying to catch my breath.

So now what? The price for being with me had gone even higher? She had to trail after me for years on end, sick and exhausted, missing her friends and family, not painting, and now I was taking motherhood from her too?

I just wanted her to tell me that all of this was all right. That we'd figure it out. Get through it, do whatever we had to do. And she *wouldn't*.

And why the fuck would she? *None* of this was all right.

Zane came in. She didn't scatter after my rampage, which made me think either she didn't have any self-preservation instincts or she thought raging, chronically exhausted, asshole rock stars were par for the course.

Fuck, maybe they *were*.

"Can you send Sloan some flowers?" I muttered, without looking up.

"You know what I bet Sloan would really like?" she asked. "For you to not be a dick."

I looked up and glared at her. She had her arms crossed over her white T-shirt.

"You doing okay?" she asked dryly.

"Fine," I muttered.

"You don't look fine. You look like shit. And you sound like shit too, come to think of it."

I narrowed my eyes at her through the mirror, but she leaned on the wall and crossed her legs at the ankle, unperturbed. "You're taking an Ambien tonight and I don't want to hear any crap about it," she said matter-of-factly. "You're taking one every night until Sloan gets back. You're not sleeping and it's making you an asshole."

I looked away from her and let out a long breath. "I'm sorry. I just... I just miss her."

"I know. She misses you too. But you need to get it together. Pissing her off isn't gonna fix anything."

Nothing was going to fix anything.

Last week I'd talked to Sloan about recording the bullshit my label had sent over. I was getting desperate. I needed to start working toward an end date and I still hadn't been able to write anything worth a damn. But she'd blatantly refused to let me do it. She was so upset about it I'd had to swear never to bring it up again. She said she didn't want me singing astronaut cats, that she'd be deeply disappointed in me if I ever compromised my music like that.

So then what was I supposed to do? What was the out? It was like no matter what I did, I was making her unhappy.

I squeezed my eyes shut and counted to ten. Ernie's words, that I couldn't have my fame and have Sloan, streamed through my head like a prophecy come to fruition. And I didn't fucking know how to fix it. There was no solution to this.

"Can I use your phone?" I asked, looking over at Zane.

She pushed off the wall, pulled it from her pocket, and slapped it into my hand. "Don't fucking break it." Then she left.

I called Sloan.

She picked up on the third ring. "Zane?"

"Sloan, it's me. Don't hang up."

"What do you want, Jason?" And then she started to cry.

It was the kind of crying that didn't sound like it was beginning. It was the kind that sounded like it was *continuing*. My heart shattered into a thousand pieces. I felt like the biggest asshole on the planet. My chest got tight and I had to clutch it with my free hand. "I'm sorry," I said. "I'm so sorry, Sloan. You're right. I shouldn't be asking you to do more than you're doing."

"I hate this," she sobbed. "I hate fighting with you."

"I know. I'm sorry," I said, a lump growing in my throat. "I just can't handle hearing you won't have kids with me. I already feel like I'm ruining your life...I just...I have to know we're gonna be okay."

I wanted to walk out of that bathroom and take the next flight to Minnesota. If I hadn't been in the middle of a concert, I would have already been out the door, even if I got to see her for only an hour before I had to get back on a plane.

"You're not ruining my life, Jason." She sniffed. "I know what you want me to say to you. You want me to tell you that we can have everything. And you know what? Maybe we *can't*. Maybe we just have to accept that our life isn't conducive to certain things right now and be okay with that."

How? How the fuck was I supposed to be okay with systematically taking everything from her?

I squeezed my eyes shut and forced myself to say what I'd been thinking for a while, the thing that had haunted me incessantly since the first time I noticed she wasn't handling the road well. "Sloan…have you considered that maybe us being together isn't the best thing for you?"

She went silent on the other end for a long moment. "Why would you say that to me?"

"You're miserable."

I heard her swallow in the silence. "Jason, I don't want to hear you talking like that again. We're *not* breaking up. How can you even suggest that?"

I put my forehead in my hand. "You want kids."

"And we can have them. When we can offer them more stability."

I shook my head. "When? Ten years from now?"

"I'll only be thirty-six," she said. "I won't exactly be an old lady. You know, life doesn't always give you what you want, Jason. Being in a relationship means compromise."

I scoffed quietly. The only one compromising was *her*.

We went quiet. The audience began to chant my name. They were getting restless and I was going to have to go back.

Fuck it, let them wait.

"Why did you call me from Zane's phone?" she asked.

"I broke mine," I said, not volunteering the details.

She sighed. "Jason, I love you. I *choose* you. And I know you feel guilty because of the way things are and you don't have to."

I shook my head, even though she couldn't see it. "I want you to have a *life*."

"I *have* a life. With *you*." She laughed a little. "Also, you should know that the number one reason I wouldn't have kids with you right now is because we're not married. Until you make an honest woman out of me, I'm not open to any negotiations."

I could hear the smile in her voice. She was trying to cheer me up. Make light of this.

There was nothing funny about it.

I had the ring, but I wouldn't ask her.

I didn't want her to be like me, trapped in a long-term contract that she'd grow to regret.

CHAPTER 39

SLOAN

♪ FUL STOP | RADIOHEAD

The second I'd hung up with Jason, I'd darted around my room and packed my things to leave. I grabbed Tucker, said goodbye to Patricia, and had Paul drive me to the airport in Duluth so I could catch the next flight to Vegas. I didn't tell Jason I was coming. He was so low, I wanted to surprise him. I'd told him good night when we hung up and he wasn't expecting to hear from me until the morning.

The last five weeks had been torture. It was great seeing Kristen, and I loved cooking with Jason's mom. I'd gotten sleep, I'd gotten healthy—and none of it compared to being with him. Not even a little.

It was going to take me at least another month to finish the piece, and I didn't have another month in me without him. I'd already been debating coming back to the road early when we'd had our argument, and that was the deciding factor.

What he'd said scared me.

I knew this separation had been hard for him. That's why I'd made it a point to always be happy when we talked, so he'd know his sacrifice wasn't a waste. But now I thought maybe I *should* have let him see how awful it was without him. Honestly, I couldn't even focus on what I was here to do. I spent most of my days trying to distract myself from the fact that I felt too in a funk to paint.

We were simply no good without each other. This separation had been the proof. We were both miserable. I had to go back. I wanted to fall asleep in his arms tonight and every night from now on.

Every step I took to getting back to him—getting off the plane, climbing into an Uber, walking into the hotel—made me feel elated, like I was coming home.

The *road* was home.

It was miraculous that I felt that way after how much it had worn me down—but it was true. Home was wherever Jason was, and knowing this gave me the world's biggest second wind. This time was going to be different. *Very* different.

So much of what I'd struggled with on tour was mental. I'd kept thinking about all the things I wasn't able to do and looking forward to the day it would be over instead of appreciating that every minute out there was time with *him*. And now that I'd seen what being apart was like, my brain had done a complete 180.

I could do this. I could do the *crap* out of this.

I'd learn to sleep on the bus. That was the very first thing on my list. I'd figure out how to eat better. I'd go with him to the gym and exercise when he did. I'd get a Crock-Pot and make us dinner so we could eat real food. I mean, the bus had a kitchen. Why not?

And why couldn't I paint on the road if we drove at night? That would mean during the day the bus would be parked. I could paint during his sound check. I'd have to be careful, figure out a way to make sure the canvas was secure when we were moving, but it wasn't impossible. I didn't have to lose myself in Jason's career, I could *find* myself here. Reinvent myself. Evolve.

He was going to *marvel* at the new me.

And you know what? Maybe we *could* have kids. If we got the bus outfitted with the right sleeping setup, had help? We could do anything.

I was going to channel my inner nomad. Make this work for both of us and turn these years into some of the best of our lives. Reclaim myself and support him at the same time, learn to love it. Because making him happy was the only way *I* could be happy— and I knew he felt that way too. That was what was bothering him about all this. He thought he was robbing me of a life. But he *was* my life—and we could have it all.

I stood outside Jason's hotel room with Tucker, beaming, ready to tell him all my plans, ready to start over and do it right this time. I knocked, practically bouncing.

But when the door opened, my entire world came to a crashing halt.

Lola stood in the doorway.

I was frozen. I couldn't even breathe. My eyes had to adjust to it like someone suddenly turning the light on in a dark room.

She wore nothing but underwear and a white Jaxon Waters sweatshirt. The room was dark behind her. She looked like she'd been sleeping.

"Yeah?" she asked lazily.

I just stared at her. I couldn't believe it. I literally couldn't believe it. I probably should have been afraid. She'd been harassing me and she beat up my car, but I was too shocked for afraid.

What was she doing here?

My mouth opened and closed like a fish out of water.

Maybe I had the wrong room? Maybe she was in Vegas for some reason and maybe they were putting her on Jason's tour and he hadn't told me yet because he didn't know yet and somehow their rooms got swapped and...

The fact that I'd sent cookies to this exact room number not twelve hours ago glared like neon in the back of my mind.

I swallowed. "Is...is Jason here?"

She looked drowsily over her shoulder. "Sleeping," she said, peering back at me.

The wind was knocked out of me.

I didn't understand. Why would she be here? Everything we *did* was about keeping her from being here. We *hated* her. Jason didn't want her anywhere near us, and now she was in his *room*?

Tucker growled low next to me, and Lola's eyes dropped to the sound. "I'll take him," she murmured, reaching clumsily for the leash.

She was drunk.

I yanked him back instinctively. "No."

I stared at the woman between me and the man I loved.

She was shorter in person than I'd expected. Prettier. She had wavy red hair that hung almost to her navel. Sharp green eyes with long fake eyelashes and perfect wing-tipped eyeliner.

Her lips were bare.

A lump started to build in my throat. "What are you doing here?" My voice shook.

She looked at me, bored, and leaned her head on the door frame. "What do you want?"

I blanched.

What do I *want?* I *belong here.* My chest started to heave.

This was the person behind all the bad things in our lives. She was the reason I'd had to ghost myself on social media, change the number I'd had when I was with Brandon. She'd had us running ourselves into the pavement to keep her from being forced on us. She was why we didn't get days off.

And now she was in *my* boyfriend's room half-naked.

A small surge of anger-fueled bravery kicked in. I pushed past her.

She made a leisurely laughing noise as she fell back into the wall, like this was all hilarious to her in slow motion.

And there he was.

I don't think I would have truly believed it if I hadn't seen it with my own eyes. But there was Jason. He was in nothing but his underwear, sleeping on top of the bedspread.

I stood there dumbfounded for a moment before I darted to the mattress and grabbed his shoulder. "Get up!" I shook him. "Jason, wake up!"

He groaned into the pillow.

Tucker jumped onto the bed and started licking his face. Jason didn't even push him off.

I looked around, mouth open, tears filling my eyes. A bottle of bourbon sat on the nightstand. *Two* glasses.

He must be shit-faced, I thought with disgust. There was no way he could sleep through this otherwise.

Was that what had happened? He was upset with me so he got wasted and slept with *Lola*?

The finality of the situation smacked me in the face. How was this happening? *How?* None of it made sense.

"You should probably go," Lola slurred from behind me.

I didn't need more prodding. I'd seen enough.

I turned and left without looking at her. She clicked the door closed and Tucker pulled at his leash back toward the room the whole way to the elevator as I dragged my luggage behind me, gasping.

I burst from the smoky casino and walked vaguely in the direction that I'd come in my Uber from the airport. When I felt like my lungs couldn't give me the air I needed to continue, I stopped at a closed cafe on the strip and sat at one of their dirty patio tables. I blocked everyone. Zane, Jessa, Ernie—Jason. I didn't want anyone trying to talk me out of what I knew I'd seen—or telling me more. I knew enough.

Then I sobbed into the phone to Kristen.

She told me to come stay with her. She said Josh was going to murder him. She told me to get off the streets of Vegas at 1:00 in the morning and that I was too good for him and I deserved better.

I didn't want better. I wanted *him*.

I was alone, homeless, and devastated. And now I was adrift again, waves crashing over me, water filling my mouth.

CHAPTER 40

JASON

♪ ABOUT TODAY | THE NATIONAL

I woke up like I was coming out of a coma. Layers of unconsciousness peeled themselves back, one at a time.

I probably shouldn't have taken that Ambien with bourbon, but I'd already had one glass when Zane showed up with the pills. I'd needed a drink after three Red Bulls and the conversation with Sloan, and frankly I'd forgotten I'd promised to take the damn thing.

I looked between the two glasses on my nightstand for the one that had water and not whiskey in it and gulped it down. Then I felt around groggily for the hotel phone and dialed Sloan, rolling away from the window and the blinding light coming in from the crack in the curtain.

It went straight to voicemail.

Man, that Ambien was no joke. I'd been knocked out without even getting under the damn covers. I didn't even remember getting undressed. Hell, I didn't even remember getting on the *bed*.

The wireless hotel phone rang in my hand. I rubbed my eyes and hit the Answer button. "What's up?"

"Have you talked to Sloan?" It was Zane.

I scratched my beard. "Not today. Why?"

"I'm on my way up, open your door. Sloan showed up last night and Lola was in your room."

I bolted up straight. "*What?!*"

"It's not good news. I'll be there in a second."

I leapt off the bed and jumped into pants.

Zane pounded from the outside and I ran to let her in. She barged in talking. "I was at the breakfast buffet and Courtney told me. Lola came down last night. She was in Jessa's room, and Sloan was knocking on your door. You must have left the adjoining door between your rooms unlocked because Lola came in and answered it."

She grabbed the knob and sure enough, the door on my side creaked open into the room.

Fuck, I could have done *anything* last night and not remembered it. I was half-drugged on sleeping pills and whiskey.

I dove for the phone and dialed Sloan again and it went to voicemail. Mailbox full.

I moved to the connecting door between our rooms and pounded on Jessa's inner door. "Jessa! Open up!"

She opened it, still half-asleep. I could see Lola passed out on the bed behind her. She was wearing nothing but one of my merch sweatshirts and underwear. *Jesus Christ*, was this what Sloan had come home to?

"Did you let Lola in my fucking room last night?" I asked.

Jessa pushed the side of her pink hair up and yawned. "Yeah. Some crazy bitch was banging on your door at one in the morning."

"That crazy bitch was *Sloan*. What the fuck were you thinking?"

Jessa's eyes went wide. "It was Sloa— Oh, shit. I...dude, it was *loud*. We thought it was an emergency. Lola tried waking you up first, but you were knocked out. She kicked your bed and everything."

I didn't let her finish. I slammed the door in her face.

"Shit!" I paced. "I have to find her. We had a fight, we weren't okay."

Zane was calm. "Any idea where she might have gone? Any family in Vegas? Friends?"

"I don't know. I don't think so." Panic descended on me like black flies, swarming.

I ran all over the room, tripping over my shoes, putting on a shirt and socks, holding the phone to my ear with my shoulder, calling her voicemail uselessly. She had to be out of her mind. Fuck, what would I think if I'd seen that?

"Okay," Zane said. "We'll start calling hotels. I'll see if Courtney can go to the airport and look for her there. You stay where you are in case she comes back."

If she was in the city, we'd never find her. It was Vegas—there were literally thousands of hotels. She might have gotten a car and driven back to California. She'd go to Kristen's, but I didn't have Kristen's or Josh's number because my fucking phone was in a million pieces. I couldn't remember where they lived either, I'd only been there once.

The phone rang and I dove for it. It was Ernie. "Did you really stomp a fucking fog machine to death last night? What's next? Trashed hotel rooms?"

"Ernie, I can't find Sloan." I dropped into a chair and put my palms to my eyelids trying to catch my breath. I told him the whole story. I hadn't thought to call him, thinking there was nothing he could do, but he offered to track down Kristen and go over there and look.

At least I felt like *something* was happening. I didn't even know if Sloan was texting me or leaving me voicemails because I didn't have my cell.

I was afraid to move in case someone got a lead on her, so instead I paced like a caged animal, dialing her number, hoping one of the calls wouldn't go straight to voicemail.

I was pulsing with anxiety. It was almost unbearable. I had a deep, gnawing claustrophobia about the walls around me.

She had no house, no job. She could disappear into the world without a trace, and I wouldn't know where to find her.

Two hours later and nothing.

I was sitting in the desk chair just waiting when someone pounded on the adjoining door from Jessa's room.

I got up quickly, hoping it was news. When I opened the door, Jessa looked up at me wide-eyed. "Jason, Lola's in the bathroom and she won't come out."

I stared down at her. "Are you fucking kidding me? Do you think I give two shits about what *she's* doing at the moment?" I went to close the door.

She threw herself against the knob. "Jason, I know you're pissed, but you seriously need to come. Like, it's bad. Just come on!"

"*No.*" I pushed again.

She braced herself against the door. "Jason!"

I gave up and let go, throwing out a frustrated hand, and Jessa stumbled into the room.

This was all I needed. I didn't even have the patience or the energy to process what it meant that Lola was here in the first place. Was she on my tour now? Was this how they were letting me know? Just dumping her in my damn lap to babysit without so much as a fucking phone call?

I couldn't even care. All I could care about was Sloan. That was all I had in me. "Have somebody else deal with her," I said, drop-ping tiredly into a chair. "I can't fucking do this right now."

She bounced nervously. "Jason, come on, stop being a dick. That court thing with her manager happened yesterday. She's totally triggered."

I rubbed my brow. "What court thing?"

She huffed impatiently. "It was all over the news? He stole all this money from her? Yesterday they ordered him to return it, but it's already gone. He had like a gambling addiction or something. She's never going to get it back. She's all broke and bankrupt and she's totally fucked. I left for like twenty minutes, and I came back and she was locked in the bathroom. And look." She darted into her room and returned a second later with a handful of long red hair. "She cut her hair off. Like, all of it."

I scoffed. "A publicity stunt. What's new?"

She scowled at me and smacked the hair onto the TV stand. "What the hell is wrong with you?"

I glared up at her. "What's wrong with *me*? I don't know, let's see, she wrote a fucked-up song about me and then set me up for paparazzi photos, groped me on a red carpet after harassing me for months, and now this shit with Sloan? She's tried to ruin my life a hundred times over. She can go fuck herself."

Jessa snorted indignantly. "A song she never once said was about *you*? And what, you don't write about real life? I didn't see you complaining about those red carpet photos when you were trending on Twitter. She made every woman in the universe wanna know what your name was. She was trying to *help* you."

I laughed mirthlessly. "So I'm supposed to thank her for grabbing my fucking dick?"

She shook her head at me. "She likes you, Jason. Does she have a fucked-up way of showing it? Yeah, she does. She needs *help*. She's relapsed and off her meds, and *nobody's* trying to do anything about it but me. The asshole who was supposed to be taking care of her screwed her over and did his best to keep her like this because it made it easier to do it. She's broke, her label's two seconds from dropping her, and *you* kicked her off the tour. She was here to ask you if you'd let her come back. She wouldn't try to piss you off."

I clenched my teeth. "If she thinks that she's coming on this tour after what she fucking did to Sloan before we left—" I growled. "*Never.*"

"What?" Jessa blinked at me. "She didn't do anything to Sloan."

"Bullshit. She smashed her car windows, popped her tires, had people leaving fucked-up voicemails—"

She laughed. It was so out of nowhere it actually surprised me. Little tinkling bells of amusement.

"What?" I asked, irritated.

"Get over yourself. She doesn't care about your girlfriend. Seriously. It was *them*."

I shook my head at her, annoyed. "Who?"

She waved her arms around. "Them. This. This industry. These *people*. It's a thing. They run off your girlfriends. Or boyfriends. Whatever."

"What the fuck are you talking about?"

She rolled her eyes like I was an idiot. "Why would they want *you* with Sloan? How does that sell records for them?" She cocked her head. "Once, on her second tour when I was opening for her, Lola was all in love with this backup dancer Matthew? They didn't like that. They wanted her with someone who would boost her career. Lil Wayne or somebody. First they offered Matthew a better job. He didn't take it, so then they threatened him. And when that didn't work? He ended up 'accidentally' "—she put her fingers in quotes—"getting his knee shattered in a mugging in Moscow. He'll never dance again. She hasn't seen him since. It's what they *do*. They don't want their up-and-coming superstars with some nobody they can't sell. You and Lola?" She leaned forward. "*Think* about it. *Everybody* wants to read that story. The free press alone."

I stared at her. "No." I shook my head. "They wouldn't."

She smirked. "Uh, yeah, they *so* would. These industry people are *shady*. You have no *idea* how gross they are. I've been with Lola since the beginning. You don't even know what I've seen them put her through." She ticked off on her fingers. "Starvation diets at sixteen until she got an eating disorder, they leaked her sex tape to the tabloids, bullied her into plastic surgeries, gave her shitty agents and managers so they could control her. They even had her own assistant calling the photogs on her. And you think they wouldn't vandalize a *car*?"

I held Jessa's serious stare for a long moment.

"I didn't know about this or I would have told you months ago." She shook her head at me. "You should know that unless the public suddenly wants you and Sloan together more than they want pictures of you dating celebrities, she's always going to be a target. You're worth too much money to them now. Honestly, I'd break up with her. Just saying. No offense to Sloan."

I stared at her before I looked past her toward her room, where I knew Lola was barricaded in the bathroom.

Was it possible?

Then something occurred to me. It clicked in my brain like a clock striking midnight. Something so painfully obvious I don't know why I hadn't thought of it right out of the gate.

Lola was crawling with paparazzi. All the fucking time. How would she have vandalized a car in broad daylight without paparazzi catching the whole thing on camera and it ending up all over TMZ?

She was capable of drunken acts of vehicular destruction. No fucking doubt about it. But she wasn't organized. Lola was impulsive. Careless and reckless. Spoofing dozens of phone numbers to harass Sloan anonymously wasn't something she'd even know how to pull off, especially in her current condition.

And something else...

That night at my trailer.

I knew my label had been the one to give Lola the gate code. But all this time I'd thought she was in on it. That she'd set me up for those paparazzi photos, or at the very least showed up to harass me. But now I remembered something.

Lola had said I'd *asked* her to come. That I'd snapped my fingers and she'd come all the way down there. I didn't think much of it at the time, she was so fucking wasted. But now...

They lied to her.

They *sent* her.

My mouth went dry.

"My own fucking label," I whispered.

It wasn't Lola. It was *never* Lola.

The whole room started to spin.

It was them all along. My personal life was an agenda. Something to sell—and Sloan didn't fit into the narrative. I'd put her in danger. I'd put her in danger because I'd made a deal with the fucking devil.

And Lola...

Trapped on this merry-go-round since she was sixteen years old. Exploited and manipulated, nobody to protect her. No Ernie or Zane to watch her back. Sick and no one to help her get better.

She wasn't the enemy. She wasn't out to get me. She was a pawn.

Just. Like. *Me.*

I got up and ran past Jessa to the bathroom in her room. "Lola?" I tried the knob. "Lola, let me in."

Nothing.

I pounded. "Lola, I need to make sure you're okay. If you don't open the door, I'm breaking it down."

Silence.

I looked over at Jessa. She stood there, chewing on her lip.

"Stand back." I backed up and slammed my shoulder into the door. It took four hard hits until the lock gave out and the door swung into the bathroom.

My stomach dropped.

Lola sat by the toilet with her knees drawn up to her chin. A bloody pair of scissors lay on the white tile next to her. Her hair was hacked to pieces, all the way down to the scalp. Spots of blood soaked through the white sleeve of her sweatshirt on her left arm. Jessa darted to her friend, and I crouched in front of Lola among half a dozen tiny empty vodka bottles from the minibar scattered around the floor. "Hey," I said softly.

Her puffy eyes stared straight ahead, and long streaks of black mascara ran down her cheeks and met under her chin.

She let me take her wrist and carefully pull back her sleeve. A slew of thin, inch-long cuts raked up her arm. They were superficial and already scabbing over.

I looked at Jessa. "She's okay."

Her eyes were wide. "Jason, I can't do blood."

"All right. I'll take care of it. You get her a coffee and a water bottle."

She nodded and disappeared.

I turned back to Lola. "I'm going to clean this up, okay?" I said gently. "Let's get this off you."

Her green unfocused eyes settled on me, like she was just realizing I was there.

She let me remove her hoodie like a tired child being undressed for bed. She wore a tank top underneath, and I took off my flannel and draped it over her shoulders. Then I took a warm washcloth and dabbed at her wounds while she sat there, dazed.

She wouldn't answer my questions, so I worked in silence. It was a couple of minutes before she said anything to me. "I have nothing," she said quietly.

My hand stilled and I looked up at her. She stared out blankly into the room. "I have nothing to show for anything. I don't even have a place to live."

Fuck. So it was as bad as Jessa said.

I couldn't imagine suffering through all this work to end up empty-handed in the end, without even the money to console me.

No wonder she'd tried to climb onto my tour.

Tours were where you made the money. And Ernie was right, she wasn't capable of her own. Hell, *I* was barely capable of it, and I had my shit together. There was no way her label would make a tour investment for her in her condition. But latching on to me? That was easy. Three duets on my set and she was done for the night. And if she bailed, the show went on.

It was the perfect solution to her problem. It was probably the *only* solution. What other choice did she have? She couldn't even quietly slip into obscurity, get a job doing something else. She was Lola fucking Simone.

"Have you eaten today?" I asked.

She shook her head.

"Okay," I said. "Why don't we get you into bed and order some lunch."

She studied me with those fractured green eyes I barely recognized, like a beaten dog, bracing to flinch.

I stood and put my hand out to her. "Ready to go?"

She looked at my outstretched palm, my small white flag, and her chin quivered. Then she folded over, put her face into her knees and cried.

I sat next to her and wrapped an arm around her. "Hey, it's going to be okay," I whispered. "You just start over again. Start now."

She sobbed uncontrollably and I sat there, holding her on the cold tile.

Jessa came back in with a coffee and a water and sat on the other side of Lola until she calmed down.

"Lola, look at me." I waited until her glassy eyes held mine. "I will do *whatever* I have to do to help you. Do you understand? If we can get you into rehab, will you go?"

She paused a long moment before she nodded at the floor. Then she blinked up at me with wet eyes. "You can't tell them where I am. They'll send cameras. Will you take me?" The question was so childlike it made my heart constrict.

"Of course I'll take you. And I won't let them know where you are. I promise."

I ordered her a sandwich and sat with her while she ate it wrapped in a blanket while Jessa made a call to a private rehab center she recommended.

There was still no word from Sloan. Courtney came back empty-handed. Sloan wasn't at the airport and we were all still going to voicemail.

I got my clippers and buzzed the rest of Lola's head for her. Then I handed her off to Jessa and Courtney so they could clean her up before we left for the rehab, and I went back to my room.

As soon as I sat on my bed, someone knocked on the door. I ran to open it without checking the peephole.

Sloan stood in the hallway with Tucker.

I grabbed her in my arms and dragged her inside without a word. The second I had her, I was instantly whole again.

"I'm sorry," she said, crying. "I was so upset and I didn't know what to do and then I thought about it and I knew you'd never cheat on me..."

My fingers raked into her hair and I clutched her to my chest. I felt like I was collapsing at a finish line. Tucker whined and cried, jumping at my legs. I put my forehead to hers with my eyes closed. "Sloan..."

"I drove halfway to Kristen's and then I drove back because I knew you had to have an explanation. I'm sorry, Jason, I should have trusted you."

"You didn't finish your painting," I whispered.

She shook her head. "I'm not going to. I'm staying to be with you."

Every breath I took of her, I held. I broke away to look at her. Her red nose, her puffy eyes. The most beautiful woman I'd ever seen. The woman I was supposed to marry but never got the chance to ask because my job had robbed us of romantic evenings and perfect moments and finally a life worth sharing. My soulmate.

And someone I needed to let go.

It was going to take everything I had in me to do it. But I *would* do it. The price for being with me had officially become too high.

She wasn't safe. I knew that now. It would only be a matter of time before they tried to separate us again. There was no telling how they'd do it, and I couldn't protect her. Maybe next time their warning would be a violent one. They'd break her hand and she'd never paint again.

This wasn't some deranged fan that a few armed bodyguards and a house in a compound could take care of. The threat came from within. They knew where I was at all times—where Sloan was. They had access to us. It could be a roadie they paid off. The person who cleaned our hotel room, anyone. And the more famous I got, the bigger the incentive to do it. There wasn't even anyone I could confront about it. Who was the face behind this? I would never know.

And this wasn't a life.

All the sacrifices were hers.

This wasn't what I'd promised her and it never would be. We'd never have a house near Kristen and Josh because we'd just be transients, living in a bus. We'd never raise our kids with theirs. We'd never have anything normal.

I wanted her to have everything. I wanted her to be able to cook and update her blog, sleep in the same bed for more than two nights in a row. I wanted her to be the great artist I knew she was, to have children she wouldn't have to raise alone or take on the road for them to know their father. She deserved it all and more.

And I could never give it to her.

I knew she'd never leave *me*. Her standing there was proof of it. She'd abandoned her painting, half-finished, to be here so I could keep dragging her around the country like luggage. And if I leveled with her, told her the truth about the danger she was in, she'd just say they didn't scare her and she wouldn't let them run her off.

I was nothing but an indentured servant. I'd never get away. But I wouldn't condemn her to one more dangerous minute of it.

I took one final breath in, let it out, and began. "Sloan, we need to talk."

She blinked up at me with teary eyes. Those beautiful eyes I wouldn't see again after today.

My heart held the lie I was about to tell like a shot of poison I was braced to drink. But if I didn't do it this way, she'd never accept it. She'd never move on. She was too sentimental. It was going to be cruel, but it had to be something final. Something horrible.

Something she'd *never* forgive.

"What?" she asked. "Jason, what? What's wrong?"

"Sloan, I'm sorry."

"Sorry for wha..."

I didn't have to say it. Understanding flickered across her face.

She took a step back, dropping her hands away from me, and I registered briefly that that was the last time she'd ever touch me.

"You..." Her voice was shaking. "You actually *slept* with her?" she whispered.

I dragged a hand down my mouth. "I didn't plan what happened last night with Lola. It just happened."

I knew I would never forget that look on her face. Never. Not if I lived to be a hundred. It was the moment after shattered glass. The tinny buzz in your ears after a loud noise. A plunge into glacial waters, frozen, unable to breathe.

I looked her in the eye. "Sloan, this wasn't going to work out between us. I think we both knew that. I need to be single, I'm not in any position to be a boyfriend right now."

She put a trembling hand to her mouth and I wanted to shout that it was a lie. I wanted to close the distance between us and kiss her, tell her it was bullshit, beg her to forgive me for not being what she needed, for not being able to protect her. Instead I picked up the hotel phone and dialed Zane.

I marveled at how calm I was. How collected and matter-of-fact.

"Zane? I found her. She's here. Can you come down here, please?"

Sloan had backed up to the wall. She was staring at me, unblinking. Tears were streaming down her face. Tucker looked up at me and made a whining noise like he was crying with her.

"I'm going to have Zane take you to the airport," I said, tucking the phone in my pocket. "I'll buy your ticket. Ernie will pick you up. Oh," I said, like I'd just remembered something. "And can you keep Tucker? I don't have time for him."

He'd take care of her. She wouldn't be alone.

I gave her the last of my heart to take with her.

She stared at me in horror. "How...how could you do it?"

But I didn't have to answer. Zane knocked on the door and I let her in.

She stepped inside and looked back and forth between the two of us in confusion. Sloan crying. Me stoic and dying inside.

"I need you to get Sloan to the airport," I said. "A first-class flight to Burbank. Get yourself a ticket so you can wait with her at the gate."

I felt Zane's disapproving glare, but I didn't pull my eyes from Sloan to see it. This was the last time I'd look at her, and I didn't want to turn away, even though the stare she gave me was pure hatred.

Sloan let Zane take her arm and allowed herself to be led away.

The door closed after them, and I fell to my knees as my world shrank around me, suffocating me, the edges turning black.

An hour later, with Lola dressed in my flannel and one of Jessa's hats so the cameras waiting outside the hotel wouldn't see what she'd done to her hair, I climbed onto Lola's motorcycle with her sitting behind me, and I drove her to a rehab facility an hour away.

I could have taken an Uber. I could have called a black car or had Zane drive us. But I needed something that could outrun the paparazzi so they wouldn't know where she went. I did it knowing that Sloan would see this in the tabloids and it would add a final blow to the already-mortal wound I'd inflicted.

I remembered the fear in her eyes that day in Dad's garage and how I'd vowed never to get on another motorcycle.

The last of my promises, broken.

I checked Lola into a private room, gave the rehab facility my credit card, and had Ernie send them an NDA. Then I stopped for a new phone, and when I got back to the hotel, I blocked Sloan's number and deleted it. Erased all her messages, all her pictures. Deleted her on social media. All traces. I wouldn't know where she lived now or have a one-click way to reach out to her in case I had a moment of weakness.

And then, with the final thread between us severed, I lost my fucking mind.

I destroyed my room. I threw a lamp, pushed over a table, and punched a hole in the wall. Then I got drunk. Blindingly, sloppy drunk.

When Zane showed up again, coming into my fog like an apparition, I sat with my back against the closet of my trashed hotel room, holding an empty bottle, with a washcloth wrapped around my bleeding knuckles.

She crouched down and peeled away the blood-soaked towel and I watched her dispassionately. She shook her head at me in that unfazed way she had. "Well, this looks pretty bad. Let's go. Hospital time."

When the doctor came into the ER with his clipboard, I couldn't even remember how Zane had gotten me there.

The doctor pulled up an X-ray of my hand on the monitor, and I stared at it, bleary and shattered, from the edge of the paper-covered exam table, the smell of rubbing alcohol stinging my nostrils. "Well, it's not broken. Pretty bruised, but not broken. Ice it, take some ibuprofen, and you should be able to use it in a few days."

But Zane shook her head. "Naw, Doc. It looks broken to me. He probably needs at least a couple weeks to rest up that hand. I'm thinkin' severe exhaustion and dehydration too. Maybe some other stuff you just missed." She nodded at his clipboard. "We'll need a medical report. Something to show his record label since he'll have to cancel some tour dates."

The doctor looked at her and they shared some sort of silent exchange. He glanced at me, and he must have seen the wear on my face, the despair behind my eyes. The crevasse across my heart.

"You know, you're right. There does seem to be a break there, along the proximal phalanx. Funny I didn't notice it before. I'll uh, write something up."

Zane packed my things. She made all the necessary phone calls and had all the needed conversations. My intoxication moved into a hangover, and then into grieving as I processed what I'd lost. And I vowed to feel every fucking second of it.

The plane ride was torture. Just me and my thoughts and a hangover. I couldn't even put in my earbuds. Music chipped away at my soul, every song about her. Every lyric haunted me. The smell of coffee on the drink cart made tears squeeze from my eyes.

When I landed, Ernie called. I answered without saying hello.

He blew a deep breath into the phone. "Girlfriends on tour..."

I laughed a little, despite myself. "It must be hard to always be right."

"This is one time, my friend, that I really wish I had been wrong."

The ride from Duluth to Ely with Dad was the worst of all. Long and quiet, tense with judgment. When he pulled into the garage, he put the truck in park, but he didn't get out. He held the wheel and looked over at my bandaged hand, his eyes sad.

"I'm sorry, Dad," I said with my forehead in my palm.

He looked at me, the pity on his face. And something else.

Loss.

He lost a daughter. I'd lost her for everyone.

My guilt and grief tripled, crushing me. I couldn't look at him. I couldn't look at anyone. How would I face Mom? Sloan was a member of this family now, and I'd ripped her from their lives. I put a hand over my face and felt the wave of nausea and sorrow surge again.

Once I got inside, Sloan was everywhere and nowhere to be seen. I felt her in every inch of that house. She was grocery lists in the kitchen, tiny creamers in the fridge, and a stray blond hair on the couch. She was an abandoned shampoo in the shower and polish on Mom's nails.

The sadness in Mom's eyes.

The absence swallowed me whole and left nothing behind but emerging chords and painful lyrics that bubbled from a crack in my heart so deep it was fathomless.

I couldn't stay there. I couldn't be anywhere. So I went where I would be nowhere.

I slipped into the mouth of the wilderness with my canoe and my guitar and I abandoned the world, that world without Sloan, behind me.

CHAPTER 41

SLOAN

♪ IT'S NOT LIVING (IF IT'S NOT WITH YOU) | THE 1975

Three months later

D o you want me to meet you at the cemetery, Sloan?"
Kristen was worried about me.

"No, I'm not going today," I said, sitting back to take one final look at the painting that had been drying for the last two weeks on my easel.

I gave it a soft smile. It was beautiful. It looked like a photograph.

It was the fifth one I'd finished over the last three months. Another addition to the collection in the gallery that had picked me up. I'd completed the commission I'd started in Ely, the little girl on the swing, and shipped that two months ago. Three more had sold, and this one in front of me was leaving today.

"You're not going to the cemetery?" she asked. "It's the anniversary of the day you met Brandon."

I picked up the remote to turn off my crime show. "How do you remember this stuff?"

"I have reminders in my phone."

I laughed, collecting my brushes. "Are you serious?"

"Uh, yeah, I'm serious. I have to watch you like a hawk."

I slid off my stool. "I'm fine. I'm just finishing up some work before the thing."

"Are you sure you're up for this? I mean the dude's hot as fuck, but we can skip this double date. It's not a big deal."

Josh's cousin Adrian was in town from St. Paul. He was a lawyer, single, and, according to Kristen, the perfect rebound for me. He lived out of state and was only here for a few days. I think she thought it would be distracting or boost my shattered self-esteem or something.

"I don't know what you expect me to do with him," I said. "I don't even kiss on the first date."

"You need someone prescreened to tell you you're pretty and hand you free drinks. And he's got all the things you like. He's tall, he's bearded, and he's from Minnesota."

I rolled my eyes. "Ha *ha*."

"Seriously, Sloan, we can call it off if we need to. I mean, he's excited to meet you but Josh can just take him out instead. I figured you might need to hit something with a bat today so I made a piñata full of mini alcohol bottles and Starbucks gift cards. I could be there in a half an hour."

I rinsed my brushes in the sink. "Nope," I said, tapping the water off them. "I'm fine. It'll be fun."

It would not be fun.

"Look at it this way," Kristen said. "If you guys hit it off, you'll end up a Copeland. Then our kids would be related. *And*, what if Josh's enormous penis is hereditary? I'm just sayin'."

I snorted. "God, I do *not* want to think about Josh's penis, thank you very much."

There was a pause on the other end. "You're sure you're okay?"

I nodded. "I really am fine. I'll visit Brandon on his birthday from now on, and that's it. It's time I stop living my life in the past. It's what he'd want."

Another pause. "And the other thing going on today?"

I took a deep breath. "It's time I move on from that too."

Jason was in town. He was playing the Forum in LA tonight.

I *forbade* my eyelid to start twitching today.

This day had loomed in front of me like an impending invasion. Jason had been in the UK for the last few months, as far away from me as humanly possible. And now he was going to be less than an hour from my loft.

I'd debated several options for dealing with this event. A sleepover at Kristen's. A trip to literally anywhere as long as it was far enough to put a couple hundred miles between us again. But when Adrian decided to visit, from Minnesota no less, and Kristen had suggested this double date, it had seemed like the universe was sending me a message. So I agreed to it, and I had about as much enthusiasm for this outing as I did for going down to check the mail.

"Okay," Kristen said. "Well, we'll be there in a half an hour to get you. What are you wearing? You better make an effort. I'm gonna be pissed if I talked you up for the last three days and then you show up looking half-homeless."

"I'm wearing the red dress. I have makeup on. I've done my hair. I won't bring shame upon your house."

"Good. Don't wear underwear. Goodbye."

I snorted and hung up, shaking my head at the Verdugo Mountains through the window in my living room.

My new apartment was nice. It had a pool and a hot tub, and I had my own washer and dryer. It was newly remodeled too. I didn't have things breaking all around me, which was a pleasant change. There was a dog park nearby and a Starbucks on the corner.

I was doing okay. I went to the gym, I got my nails done. I was tan. I took Tucker on walks and went to art shows and had Josh and Kristen over for dinner once a week—and *I* did the cooking. I did all of the things—and I was proud of myself.

I'd never gone to grief counseling after Brandon died. Kristen had begged me to go, but I had no interest in learning how to be okay without him. I didn't want to talk about his death or share it with strangers. I didn't need to bond with other people going through it to know I wasn't alone. People died every day, unfairly and prematurely. My tragedy wasn't anything special. I just wanted Brandon's hold to let me go when it was ready to let me go. I wanted to feel that grief in its most organic way, like trying to take the edge off it would somehow be dishonoring what he meant to me. But somewhere along the line, it *had* let me go, and I hadn't noticed because the tired listlessness that comes with grief had shifted into the kind that comes from losing yourself through depressing life choices—and I wasn't repeating that mistake.

I *wanted* Jason's hold to let me go. I was desperate to shake it. I wanted to do everything I could to make it stop—because he didn't deserve any grief.

I'd allowed myself exactly one week of falling apart at Kristen's before I pulled myself up through sheer will, found myself an apartment, and started painting. I slept. I updated my blog. I did yoga. I decorated my apartment and did things I loved—and I chose happiness.

There was a certain dullness to it, though. My "happiness" wasn't always the real thing. Most of the time it was a fabricated, forced version that cracked around the edges if examined closely enough. But it was the *choice* that was the accomplishment. I'd finally found the me I'd lost before. I was strong—heartbroken, but stronger than I'd ever given myself credit for. Especially under the circumstances.

It was hard to come to terms with something that didn't make sense, like a tragic untimely death or a breakup that came out of nowhere. How can you be at peace when you don't know what you did to deserve it or what you could have done to make things different? I couldn't wrap my brain around how I'd misjudged Jason to such a high degree, how I could think he was that in love with me, when clearly he *wasn't*. It made me question my entire sense of self. Like finding out your hero isn't a hero at all and you're just too blind to know the difference.

Right after it happened, I'd had a moment of disbelief. Even though I'd seen Lola half-naked in his room with my own eyes and he'd confessed right to my face, my heart simply wouldn't accept it, and I'd almost called him. Then I saw the picture of him with her on the motorcycle.

Jason had broken every single promise he'd ever made me. That was *his* choice. And mine was going to be to thrive despite it.

You can't control the bad things that happen to you. All you can do is decide how much of you you're going to let them take. I would be fooling myself if I said I didn't still love him. I think I'd *always* be in love with him. But I refused to mourn him or give him a shrine.

Everyone around me knew talking about Jason was off-limits. No one ever mentioned what he was doing. Not even Ernie, during his many visits to check in on me. But a few weeks ago, curiosity had gotten the better of me and I googled him.

I wished I hadn't looked.

Apparently Jason had gone full rock star since our breakup. He'd trashed a hotel room—kicked in a bathroom door and everything. Then he'd hurt his hand somehow. The tabloids said a fist fight with a roadie. Jason's crew loved him, so I doubted it. But the article also said he'd broken a fog machine in a rage and Ernie had accidently confirmed it when I overheard a phone call with Jason's tour manager, so who knew who Jason was these days. He'd ended up canceling three weeks of concerts due to exhaustion and dehydration, and there was speculation that he was abusing drugs and alcohol. I'd seen him passed out myself, and concerts didn't get canceled unless there was a legitimate medical emergency, so I didn't know what to believe.

I was worried about him, so I'd asked Ernie. The only time I'd ever asked him about Jason. Ernie told me to let *him* worry about Jason and to just take care of myself. Judging by how evasive he was, it was pretty clear that at least some of what I'd read was true.

And the Lola/Jaxon rumors were back in the tabloids in full force—only those, I knew for sure, weren't rumors.

The whole thing made me sick. I wanted to bleach her from my brain. I couldn't forget her standing there in that doorway in her underwear, so smug. And the universe wouldn't let me forget it either. Her music, *his* music, constantly popping up in the grocery store and the gym. I'd started wearing earbuds everywhere, just so I wouldn't be randomly accosted by it.

It was the most peculiar form of torture.

Jason was capable of things I never could have imagined. He was someone I didn't even recognize now. Maybe he finally became Jaxon.

The painting that I was going to deliver to the gallery today had been therapeutic. Proof that the six months I'd spent with him had been real. At least at the time.

At least for *me*.

But it was time I rid myself of the visible reminders of the man I lost. I had enough invisible ones to deal with.

I'd drop off that painting and then I'd go on my first date since my breakup. Kristen and Josh would be there to carry the conversation when this guy bored me, which he probably would.

And I'd get through it—I had to. Because I chose happiness.

I wrapped the painting in brown paper, leashed Tucker, and went downstairs to drop it off and take the dog for a walk.

Twenty minutes later, we were coming back up to my door when I saw a courier standing outside waiting for me. "Are you"— he looked at his device—"Sloan Monroe?"

I wrapped Tucker's leash around my hand. "Yes…"

"I have a package for you. You need to sign."

"A package?" I scribbled my name on the digital screen. I wasn't expecting anything. Kristen maybe?

I took the flat white envelope and let myself into my apartment, examining the outside. There was no name on it.

Kristen. She was always sending me something crazy. Last week she'd mailed me a crocheted tissue holder that looked like a vagina. She was so weird.

I dropped my keys on the credenza and sat on the sofa to open it. Tucker stood in front of me, tail wagging like there were dog treats inside it. "Maybe it's something for you, huh?" I grinned at him as I pulled out the contents.

And then my smile fell.

I knew the handwriting on the paper instantly, even before I read a word.

A hard lump built in my throat as I scrolled through the letter.

I reached back into the envelope and a shaking hand pulled out the real reason for the delivery.

Two front-row, VIP tickets to a Jaxon Waters concert at 7:00 tonight.

CHAPTER 42

SLOAN

♪ FRESH BRUISES | BRING ME THE HORIZON

I read the letter Zane had sent me a hundred times. Stared at those four words at the top of the page until they were seared behind my eyelids. *Jason lied about Lola.*

Zane and Courtney were close.

The letter went on to explain that Courtney had told Zane she had been there the night Lola showed up. That Jason had never been alone with Lola except for the few seconds when she'd walked through his room to answer the door for me. Jason had taken a sleeping pill and had no idea Lola had even been there until he woke up.

Then Zane said that Lola had a breakdown and hurt herself, and Jason was only on that motorcycle to take her to rehab. She told me nothing in the tabloids was true and that Jason had told Ernie explicitly to let me believe it if I asked.

Zane wouldn't lie. She was the most brutally honest person I knew. And if Jason knew she'd done this without his permission, he'd fire her. She was risking her job to send me that message.

I couldn't breathe.

Why? Why would he make that up? Why would he say something so horrible to me and want me to think so many awful things about him?

I immediately called him. The first time in three months. It went straight to voicemail.

Jason had never, in the entire six months I'd known him, had his phone off. Ringer down, yes. Phone off, no.

My number was blocked.

So Jason didn't want to talk to me. He didn't want me calling him. He was here, in LA, and he hadn't come looking for me. And he'd never once reached out to me in the last three months. So why was Zane trying to get me to go over there? He clearly didn't want to be in a relationship with me if he'd fabricate a story like this just to get out of it. He'd gone to extremes to make sure it was over between us.

And now I was angry.

When he'd first done what he did, I was devastated. Then, when I saw the pictures with Lola, I'd been hurt and disappointed. I'd spent the last few months in various states of numb confusion. But now that I knew that he'd lied to me, I was *furious*.

So he'd wanted to break up and he'd thought destroying me would be the easiest way to do it?

I called Zane. I thought it was going to voicemail, it rang so long before she picked up. "Hey, what's up?" she whispered.

Jason must be there.

There was something heart wrenching about knowing he might be just on the other end of that line. Maybe I'd even hear him. My knees suddenly felt weak. I hated that he still had that effect on me, that I still loved him to stupidity.

"Why would you send me that, Zane? He obviously doesn't want to see me."

"Just...can you give me one second? Just hold on."

I heard shuffling. Then a few moments later she came back. "Are you coming?" she asked, her voice low.

"No. He doesn't want me there."

"Yes he *does*," she said. "He's fucked up, Sloan."

I laughed, incredulous. "*He's* fucked up? He lied about sleeping with another woman and then he put me on a plane and never spoke to me again."

Her voice went lower. "Look. Just come. I don't know what the fuck his problem is. All I know is Jason loves you."

I shook my head. "I think Jason loved me once, Zane. But he's Jaxon now."

I hung up on her.

My eyelid bounded into a full-scale attack. I paced in my living room with a palm to my eye, breathing hard.

Why? *Why*, Jason? I thought about those last few days and what might have made him do it. He'd said he felt like he was ruining my life—so to fix it he'd ruined my life? I scoffed.

Maybe I was too much maintenance. Maybe those weeks I'd been in Ely had shown him how much taking care of me on the road had taken a toll on him. Maybe he'd figured that I was unhappy anyway and he didn't have the energy for it and letting me believe what I saw was a win-win. He *did* say he wasn't in a place to be a boyfriend. I guess he thought he was doing me some kind of favor.

The only thing I knew for sure was this: He didn't love me. A man who loved me wouldn't do this. He wouldn't light a match and set my world on fire.

My phone rang. It was Kristen, probably calling to tell me they were outside. I picked up and she started talking immediately. "Okay, don't be mad."

"Oh God, what?" I breathed. I couldn't deal with Kristen's shenanigans right now. I couldn't deal with *anything*. I didn't want to go anymore, I didn't want to stay. God, I hated my life.

"Adrian's on his way up there alone to get you himself."

I groaned. "Are you kidding me?"

"Everyone was getting out of the car to come up and he was all like, 'Stay here,' in this really deep, very authoritative voice. It was a super alpha male move. Even Josh froze up."

I could hear Josh laughing in the background.

Someone knocked on my door.

"I'm going to *kill* you guys," I hissed, hanging up on her.

I slumped in the middle of my living room with palms to my eyeballs. How was I going to get through tonight? I couldn't do this.

My hands were shaking. Not because my blind date was standing outside, but because of Jason. I took a deep breath and tried to steady myself.

Adrian knocked again. That playful, musical knock that friends do when they come over.

"Hold on, one second," I called, hearing the trembling in my voice.

I took another deep breath. I shoved the envelope with the tickets and Zane's letter into my purse and smoothed down my dress, took one more moment to compose myself, and then I opened the door.

The man standing in my hallway wore a dark-green V-neck sweater with the sleeves rolled up and jeans. He was holding a piñata shaped like a cupcake. "Hi," he said, giving me a dazzling smile. "I'm Adrian. You must be Sloan."

Well, Kristen was right. Adrian Copeland was gorgeous. Green eyes, close-clipped beard, a nice body.

I was 100 percent not interested.

He held out the piñata. "I was told to bring this up?" he said, looking amused.

I rolled my eyes. "Of course you were," I mumbled, taking it and setting it on a table inside the door.

Tucker spilled out into the hallway, jumping excitedly on Adrian's legs. He crouched down to pet him. "Hey there, little guy." He smiled up at me while he ruffled my dog.

He was checking me out. *Big-time.* He wasn't even trying to hide it. His eyes dropped down my body and came back up with a grin.

A fierce blush roared up my neck.

The letter had me so flustered I couldn't even think straight. All I could think about was what Zane had said. I wasn't in the right headspace to deal with what I'd just learned, let alone this stranger who was trying to date me, here in my doorway, shamelessly ogling me and playing with my dog—*Jason's* dog—Jason, who was here in my city and hadn't come to see me because he broke up with me and didn't want me anymore.

My other eyelid twitched once, just to remind me that today could still get worse.

"I'm sorry," I said, reaching for Tucker's collar. "He gets really excited when people come over. Tucker, let's go."

"It's fine," Adrian said. "I like dogs." He let Tucker lick his chin.

God. I was two seconds from maniacal cackling.

Tucker finally finished with him and ran back into the apartment and Adrian stood.

Time to get this over with.

I grabbed my purse and slung it over my shoulder. Then I stepped out into the hallway and closed the door.

"I'm glad I have you alone for a minute," Adrian said from

behind me as I bolted the lock. "I actually wanted to talk to you before we went down."

"Okay." I turned to him.

My eyelid was having a seizure. I squeezed it shut and stood there looking up at him with one eye. I was positive I looked insane. My face was bright red and I had to cross my arms and tuck my hands into my armpits to keep them from visibly shaking.

But he smiled at me anyway. "I heard some of Kristen's phone call with you earlier. I know you just broke up with someone and this date's a little jarring for you."

Oh God. I shook my head. "It's not—"

He put up a hand. "It's fine." He gave me a smile. "I'm only in town for a few days and I'm just grateful for the opportunity to have dinner in Los Angeles with a beautiful California woman—even if she *is* unavailable. I just wanted to let you know that this is a zero-expectation situation. I've already been told that if I even so much as shake your hand tonight without your express consent, I'll be punched in the forehead."

I snorted, my face going soft, and I tucked my hair behind my ear. "Josh is really protective of me."

"It wasn't Josh." He gave me an arched eyebrow. "So does Kristen hit hard, or..."

He actually managed to draw a laugh from me.

Adrian dipped his head to look me in the eye. "Look, let's just have a good time," he said. "Let me buy you some drinks and see if I can't make you have some fun. Deal?"

He waited patiently for my reply. I relaxed a little. Taking the pressure off this date was at least something. My eyelid took mercy on me and relented and I gave him a weak smile. "Okay."

He nodded toward the stairs. "Ladies first."

We started walking. "You know, I have to be honest," he said, holding the door to the stairwell for me. "Your pictures don't do you justice."

I scoffed. "Let me guess, Coachella?"

"Uh, no, actually." He jogged down the steps behind me. "Headgear?"

I pushed the door to the sidewalk open, laughing.

Kristen and Josh were parked a few feet away. Adrian ran ahead and opened my car door for me. He put a hand to my back as I got in. I didn't like it. I didn't like any man touching me who wasn't Jason.

Jason would never touch me again.

It was like I could feel him in the air now that he was here in California. He was all around me, like the sun on my face. It actually made me peer out the window, looking for him.

I let out a long breath, trying to release him from my mind.

It didn't work.

CHAPTER 43

JASON

♪ SOMEBODY ELSE | THE 1975

It wasn't hard to find the ones that were Sloan's. I just looked for the paintings that looked like photographs.

Three hung in the gallery, and they all had sold signs on them, marked by red dots. I stood there, staring, studying every inch of the artwork, making out almost-invisible brushstrokes.

She touched these. Her hands had created them, her eyes had looked on every inch of canvas, and the art had sprung from her beautiful mind.

Pride filled me. I took a deep breath. I missed her. I missed her every second.

The click of heels on wood turned me to the approaching gallery curator, a polished gray-haired woman in glasses and red lipstick. "You must be the gentleman who called."

I looked back at the paintings. "Yes. You said you had a Sloan Monroe available?"

"It's in the back. Your timing is excellent. It was just dropped off. These don't stick around for long."

My heart swelled. I couldn't take my eyes from the wall. "She's very talented," I breathed.

I hoped she had used the gift card I'd given her to buy the supplies to make these. I wanted to be a part of this. I wanted to be a part of it all.

It wasn't over. It would *never* be over. At least not for me.

It had been ninety-four days since I'd last seen her, and I was nothing but a husk of myself now. My world was dim. All was faded. And the more time that passed, the darker it got. Life without her was a sensory deprivation of my soul.

My tour had brought me back to California. I'd been braced for how hard it would be to breathe the same air as her. Look at the same sky. But then it was hard everywhere, wasn't it?

I hadn't told anyone where I was going when I left the hotel. I'd had to sneak out a service exit by the dumpsters in a hat and sunglasses, evading Zane like a zoo animal that had escaped its keeper. She and Ernie would have advised against it. But I'd had to come see these.

I'd told Ernie if the paintings didn't sell within the first week of going up to buy them for me—without Sloan knowing, of course. But they'd sold. She was gifted. She didn't need a guardian angel.

I'd been busy too. Besides the tour, I'd actually been able to write. I'd composed six songs during my three weeks in Ely while my hand was healing. And they were *good*.

They were good because they were about *her*.

Nobody would ever hear any of them. If I put these on an album, Sloan would know they were about her, and I could never let her know how destroyed I was. Those songs were just for me.

No, the next new thing I recorded would be some pop garbage

written by a hired gun my label picked. And I couldn't even muster up the passion to give a shit.

The clicking heels led me to the back room and when the woman went to remove the brown paper from the canvas to show it to me, I put up a hand. "I'll take it. I don't need to see it."

I couldn't spare the extra minutes it would take to wrap it back up. Every second I was here was playing with fire.

Sloan lived in the loft upstairs. Ernie had told me. He was the one who'd told me where to find her artwork too. I'd asked him to take care of her once she was back in LA, and he had.

He also told me she hated me. That she couldn't stand to even hear my name.

I'd accomplished everything I'd set out to do. She rued the day she met me, just like I'd needed her to. And my success was my greatest regret.

I finished my purchase. With any luck I could sneak back into my room without Zane ever knowing I'd been gone. I was walking to the door with the painting under my arm when I froze.

Kristen and Josh were parked in a black Honda just outside the gallery.

I darted behind a sculpture in the entry—and just in time.

She came out of nowhere, like the sun peeking through the clouds. If I'd been two seconds faster, I would have crashed right into her on the sidewalk.

Sloan.

Everything slowed.

She was just twenty feet away. We were separated by nothing but a sheet of glass.

My heart was a thumping bass in my rib cage.

I stared out at her from my blind. She looked even more beautiful than I remembered. She had on a red dress with bright-red lipstick. Her hair was down around her shoulders, and she was tan. She looked healthy, like she was taking care of herself like I'd hoped she would.

She was smiling at someone behind her, out of my line of sight. A beaming, radiant smile like the ones she used to give me when I'd sing to her.

My heart broke a thousand times every second that I looked at her.

I was going to go out there.

I didn't even have control over it. My body had taken on some involuntary reflex in response to her sudden presence. The pull was so strong it felt like my very existence had just tipped in her direction and everything was sliding toward her. I took a step...

And then some fucking guy was opening her car door for her and helping her in with a hand on her back.

CHAPTER 44

JASON

♪ IF I GET HIGH | NOTHING BUT THIEVES

I don't even know how I made it back to the venue in one piece. I'd tempted Fate by going to the gallery, and Fate had called my bluff. I was fucking destroyed.

Seeing her with somebody else tore through my heart like a hot knife. It took the wind right out of my lungs.

Men had always looked at her, even when I held her hand. I went mad thinking of someone else touching her. Of her smiling at their jokes or cooking them dinner.

I'd been following the updates to *The Huntsman's Wife*. I checked it every day. It was the only direct link I still had to her. She'd started posting regularly while she was living in Ely and she was cooking the game Dad had in the freezer. But a few weeks ago she'd posted a recipe for wild boar.

Dad didn't hunt boar.

I didn't think much of it at the time. I thought maybe it was something old, from when Brandon was still alive, that she hadn't gotten around to sharing. But now that I knew she was dating, my mind went crazy wondering if she was seeing someone who hunted, obsessing about who she cooked for, who she was spending time with.

I knew she hadn't been ready to date when she met me, so I'd hoped, for my own selfish reasons, that she would stay single for a while, that maybe we had been a special circumstance. It was the only thing that had kept me halfway sane all these months. But she wasn't waiting. She was seeing someone.

Nobody would ever love her like I would. She would never find the same devotion, even if she looked for a lifetime. I knew that with every cell of my being. She'd never know about it, but it would always be there. When she married someone else, had children, when she grew old, I would still be out there in the world, cherishing her in secret. If she ever needed anything, I'd make sure she had it. It would be my penance for the rest of my life for not being able to do it in person.

Three hours after the gallery, I was in my dressing room, sitting with my head in my hands, like I had been for the last hour. Jessa was on and I had about thirty minutes to showtime. I'd go through it like the puppet I was now. My label finally had its marionette. Everything would be an act from this point forward because I had nothing real left to give. All my joy in life had been drained out of me.

Someone knocked on my door. I didn't move. I didn't even look up. "Yeah?"

"Um, it's Courtney. Can I come in?"

I let out a tired breath and dragged myself to my feet to open the door.

She stood there biting her lip. "Um, Lola's here."

My face brightened into one of my rare smiles. "Really? Where?"

She threw a thumb over her shoulder. "She's in Jessa's dressing room. She came to see you. I didn't want to tell her where your room was in case—"

"No, it's fine. Can you bring her?"

She nodded.

I was actually excited to see her. I wanted to see how she was doing. I'd called her a few times in rehab. She'd never come to the phone or called me back.

A moment later someone knocked on my dressing room door. I opened it, and when I did, I stood there, staring.

The woman standing there was nobody I knew. Even as I recognized her, it *still* was nobody I knew. The transformation was so shocking it disarmed me completely.

She smiled. "Hello."

Her hair had grown out a bit. It was brown, not red. She wasn't wearing any makeup, and a scattering of freckles I never knew she had peppered her nose. She had a red tote bag on her shoulder and she wore a baggy T-shirt, leggings, and flip-flops.

She looked five years younger. She wasn't a rock star three months into rehab, she looked like a college student studying for finals. A babysitter after the kids had gone to bed, waiting for the parents to come home.

"Hi," I breathed. "God, you look...you look different."

She laughed a little, sucking her lips together. "Can we talk? Is that okay?"

"Yeah. Yes. Sure." I let her in and closed the door behind her. She sat on the couch and I took the chair across from her. I couldn't stop staring. I didn't even blink. How was this the same person from all those months ago? The same woman who'd shown up at my trailer, three sheets to the wind and staggering across my fucking lawn?

The gaunt, sharp edges of her cheekbones were gone, and so was the death she'd carried behind her eyes the last time I saw her.

Her clear green irises settled on me. "Thank you for seeing me. I wouldn't have blamed you if you didn't want to."

"No, I'm glad you're here," I said. "How have you been? You look good."

Her hand went self-consciously to her head. "When it gets a little longer, I can get extensions." She laughed nervously. "I actually kinda like it because I don't get recognized."

She put her hands into her lap and stared down at them for a long moment. "I wanted to apologize to you. And to Sloan. I was messed up for a really long time. I wasn't myself and I'm not proud of how I acted."

When I didn't respond, her eyes came up to mine. "I didn't know that was your girlfriend that night. I'd never seen her before, and Jessa had said Sloan was in Minnesota. I thought it was your assistant or something walking your dog." She swallowed. "This is the first time I've really been sober and stable in almost three years. I know that's not an excuse, but—"

"It's okay," I said, putting up a hand. "I accept your apology. If you accept mine."

Her face went soft. She let out a long breath as if she'd been holding it. "I've been talking to Ernie about representing me. I need someone honest, you know?"

I smiled a little. "He's a good one."

She nodded. "Most of them aren't. You're really lucky."

I studied her while she seemed to struggle with what to say.

"I, um...I was wondering if you would ever consider letting me tour with you? I mean, it doesn't have to be full-time or anything," she said quickly. "Maybe just the biggest venues? Or holiday specials?"

I leaned forward with my elbows on my knees. "There'd have to be rules," I said. "You'd need to stay sober."

Hope flashed across her face. She nodded.

"Stay on your medication. And if you fall off the wagon, you exit yourself. You don't make me do it."

She nodded again and I sat there, searching her face for the old Lola.

I didn't see her.

I put out a hand.

She looked at my small olive branch, and her chin quivered. Then she took my hand and shook it.

I let go of her and reached across the coffee table to pull some tissues from the box. I handed them to her and she held them, staring down at the tips of her toes, smiling through tears.

I sat there, watching her in silence. I felt like I should tell her I was proud of her. I knew how hard it was to battle against yourself. To wrestle your desires down every single day of your life to do what you know is best. But I didn't have the strength to talk about it.

I probably never would.

Sometimes the hardest place to live is the one in-between. And sometimes in-between is all you'll ever get.

She wiped at her nose. "I should go," she said after a moment, starting to get up. "I don't want to cause any more problems for you with Sloan."

I laughed a little and sat back in the chair. "Sloan and I broke up. The night you left."

She blinked at me, perched on the end of her cushion. "Was it... because of *me?*"

I shook my head. "No. Not really. I just couldn't give her the life she deserved."

Lola sat there, clutching the wads of tissues I'd handed her. "I'm sorry, Jaxon. But you know it's probably for the best, right?"

"I do," I said quietly.

"This business isn't the greatest for relationships." She looked away from me for a moment. "I never told you this but..." Her eyes came back to mine. "When I met you, you kinda reminded me of someone." She shook her head. "Just someone I used to know. A dancer..."

She trailed off and it was a long moment before she continued. "I think that's why I was always drawn to you, you know?"

I let out a small laugh through my nose. "I get it. If I ever met someone who reminded me of Sloan..."

I'd probably never meet someone who reminded me of Sloan.

I just wasn't that lucky.

Lola wiped at her nose with a tissue. Then she looked around her like she'd just remembered something. She reached down and picked up her tote bag. "I forgot to tell you. I brought you something." She sniffed as she pulled a folder out. "Feel free to say no. It's just Ernie mentioned that you're having a hard time writing, and I thought..." She took a deep breath. "Here." She handed it to me.

"What is it?" I asked, taking it.

She gave a one-shoulder shrug. "I wrote some music when I was in rehab." She laughed again. "I wrote a *lot* of music. You inspired me, Minnesota."

I snorted, despite it being a bad joke.

I opened the folder and looked at the sheets inside.

"If you sing them, I'll get royalties," she said. "And I need the money. I wrote them just for you, and Ernie says they're good..." She trailed off when I didn't look up to answer her.

My eyes pored over the verses. The music danced around my

mind like lightning bugs. I flipped the pages, hearing the songs in my head.

They *were* good. I mean, they'd need a few tweaks here and there to make them mine, and some of them weren't finished, but . . . they were *amazing*.

I looked up at her. "How many are here?"

"Twenty-two?"

I almost choked on the laugh. "Twenty-two songs," I breathed. I had to put a hand over my mouth. It was almost three albums' worth.

My freedom. She'd just handed me my freedom.

"Thank you," I whispered.

"You'll take them?"

I nodded, my eyes tearing up. "Yes. Of course."

"'Cause I know you write your own songs and you—"

"Lola, it would be an honor to sing these." I looked her in the eye and she stared back at me almost shyly.

"My name is Nikki."

I tilted my head. "What?"

"My name. It's Nikki. Not Lola. Will you call me that from now on?"

I had to muscle down the knot in my throat. "Yes. Yes, I'll call you that. And you call me Jason." I paused for a long moment. "It's nice to finally meet you."

She smiled. "It's nice to finally meet you too."

I looked back down at the music in my lap and a jab of sorrow overcame me. I had my way out now. I'd need a couple more songs, but that was nothing. Hell, maybe Lola would help me. My label would stagger the releases. Probably one a year and a tour to support each. But three more years wasn't ten.

But it didn't make any difference for me and Sloan.

Lola peered around the room like she could tell I was broken and she didn't want to stare at the cracks. "What's that?" she asked, nodding to the paper-wrapped painting I had propped against the wall.

I cleared my throat. "It's just something I bought."

"Oh. Can I see it?"

I nodded and she got up. When she peeled off the brown paper to look, she gasped. "Wow. That's a really cool photo of you."

I looked up and had to clutch a hand over the punch to my heart.

It was me.

Sloan had painted *me*.

I stood in the lake, in my waders. It was that day in Ely when I'd been putting in the dock. It was the moment right before I'd kissed her.

Tears threatened, and I had to put a hand on my mouth.

She'd painted this from memory. It was like seeing the moment through her eyes. This was how she had seen me that day, smiling and happy.

I'd been happy because *she* was there.

And I'd never be that happy again.

She wanted to get rid of it. She'd dropped this off to be sold and then left on a date.

The tears in my eyes rolled down my cheeks and I let them.

"What's wrong?" Lola asked.

I shook my head. "My life is a mess," I said, talking to the canvas.

She laughed a little. "Someone smart once told me you can start over again. Start now."

But it was too late for starting over. I still couldn't make Sloan safe. Not unless the public was suddenly more interested in buying magazines with pictures of me and her in them instead of me and Lola. And I'd done my job too well. Ernie said she hated me, that he couldn't even mention my name without her face going hard. She was dating. She was moving on.

The damage had been done.

CHAPTER 45

SLOAN

♪ PROOF | JAXON WATERS

Adrian had two hands behind his back. "Pick one." He smiled and his green eyes creased at the corners. We were sitting in a steakhouse waiting on appetizers.

Adrian held open doors for me. He pulled out my chair and ordered me a glass of wine that he seemed to know a lot about. He was funny, charming, and engaging. Intelligent, successful, and attractive. And he was trying *very* hard to show me a good time.

It totally wasn't working. I couldn't stop thinking about Zane's letter.

Adrian waited for me to pick a hand. I pointed unenthusiastically to the left one. He put a full-size bottle of vanilla creamer on the table in front of me. I cracked a small smile. We'd stopped at the gas station on the way over and he'd caught me putting a few single-serve creamers in my purse.

"Smooth," Kristen said from across the table. "But she likes the little ones."

He smiled. "Well, I can't help you there."

Kristen kicked my shin under the table.

Adrian was flirting with me. Hard.

And I. Felt. *Nothing.*

If the complete and total lack of butterflies in my stomach wasn't depressing enough, I kept looking at the clock. One hour until Jason's show. I felt like I was going to burst into tears. The moments that he was in town were ticking down before my eyes. Running out like sand in an hourglass. And instead of being where he was, I was on a date with someone amazing who couldn't even hold my attention because I was too damaged and in love with somebody else to even entertain it.

"Excuse me." I got up. "I need to use the ladies' room."

Kristen's chair raked against the floor as she got up to follow me. As soon as the door closed behind us she pounced on me. "Damn, that dude wants to eat you alive. I think you should let him."

"And I think you need to see *this*," I said. I dug in my purse and pulled out the letter. I unfolded it, handed it to her, and watched with my arms crossed as she read it.

The longer she looked at it, the deeper her frown got. "Oh my God…" She looked up at me. "Do you believe what she said?"

I sniffed and nodded. "She wouldn't lie. And the Lola thing never felt right. That's why I came back to his hotel room that day. There was something off about it from the very beginning. Why would he lie about it, though?"

She pursed her lips. "I don't know, Sloan. Maybe he had to lie to you to break up with you. I mean, you know how you are."

I narrowed my eyes at her. "How *am* I?"

She shrugged. "You don't like to get rid of things that aren't good for you. You know this. Brandon's stuff, your shitty car, your dilapidated house? You don't exactly have a history of making rational, sensible life choices. You're sentimental to a fault. You've always been that way and I bet Jason knew that."

My chin started to shake.

"Maybe he knew you wouldn't take his logical reasoning for whatever it was, and he needed to do something extra. Because let's be honest, what he did was *really* fucking extra."

I leaned over the sink and snatched a paper towel out of the dispenser. "So what's your theory, then?" I asked, blowing my nose.

"I don't know. But my gut tells me that dude fell on a sword. If Zane is saying he's all fucked up and she thinks you should see him…I don't know. Even Josh is giving him the benefit of the doubt, and you know Josh."

I sniffled. "Really?"

"Yeah. You know what he said that really got me?" She crossed her arms. "When I came back from visiting you in Ely and I told him how in love Jason's parents were, he said he could tell that's what Jason came from. That Jason was a guy, just like him, who grew up in a small town seeing two parents ridiculously in love with each other. Guys like Josh and Jason don't do shit like this. It's not how they were raised. It's not in their DNA. They mate for life. They fall in love and they worship the ground that woman walks on. They don't cheat and they don't fucking leave. If Jason left, he had a reason."

I mopped at my nose. "Maybe the fame finally changed him."

She scoffed. "Do you really believe that? Come on."

No, I didn't believe that. I didn't know *what* to believe.

"So what are we doing?" she asked. "Going to see him? Beating the shit out of that piñata? Double-dating? What?"

Jason didn't want to be with me. He didn't want to *see* me.

But it didn't change the fact that I wanted to see *him*.

I was almost angrier with myself about this than I was at him for breaking me in half. But I did. I wanted to see him.

Not up close. Not one-on-one. But in a crowd, where he wouldn't know I was there?

When I'd seen him for the last time, I hadn't known it was going to be the last time. It happened so fast and I was so in shock.

Maybe seeing him again, on my terms, would give me closure—even though I knew I was fooling myself. If anything, it would probably thrust me back to week one and I'd be over at Kristen's bawling my eyes out by tonight, beating a piñata with a baseball bat.

But I had to go. If Zane's letter hadn't stirred up my shit, I would have held strong today. I would have dug in and tried to have fun with Adrian, had a few too many drinks with Kristen, and gotten through the night. But now all I wanted was to be where I knew Jason was. Barring me being so far away it was impossible to make it, I was going to end up there. It became true the second I'd read what Zane wrote.

I sniffled. "I want to see him."

She shrugged. "Okay. The heart wants what the heart wants. Let's go." She marched out of the bathroom.

"What about Adrian?" I whispered, following her.

"He'll be fine. I'll tell Josh to take him to a strip club or something." She walked up to the table and tapped her husband's shoulder. "Give me the keys."

He dug in his pocket and handed them to her. "What's up?"

"Sloan doesn't feel well. I'm taking her to a Jaxon Waters concert. You guys can get an Uber. I love you." She gave him a swift peck on the cheek, hooked my arm in hers, and turned for the exit.

I waved lamely at Adrian as Kristen dragged me through the restaurant. "I had a really good time," I called. "It was nice meeting you."

He looked amused and gave me a wink.

We hopped in the car. "If we're creeping on him we need to have disguises," Kristen said, putting the car in reverse and backing out of the parking space. "There's a party supply store a block down. We'll go there first."

Five minutes later she was handing me a pair of 1980s glasses from a Halloween clearance shelf.

I shook my head. "I am *not* wearing that."

"His crew knows you, right?" she said, putting a hand on her hip. "You want someone recognizing you and telling him you're there?"

I crossed my arms. "No..."

"Then you're wearing this. You're either blazing in like, 'I'm here, bitches,' or you're going deep undercover. And if we're undercover, we can't sit in the front row. We'll have to switch tickets with someone."

I took a deep breath and let her slide the enormous glasses on my face.

"You need to hide your hair and your tattoos. Take my sweater," she said, peeling it off and handing it to me.

I stared at it in my hand. "Is this crazy?"

She picked up a brown wig. "Maybe. But my job is to help you with your crazy. Make you the best, most magnificent crazy you can be."

I snorted.

Kristen prepared me for the concert like I was a sacrifice delivering myself to an altar. I was fussed over and garbed.

I ended up wearing the hideous glasses and a beanie since we couldn't get all my hair to stay under a wig—not to mention the wig made me look like a lunatic.

Kristen, on the other hand, *did* look like a lunatic.

Nobody but Jason would recognize her, but that didn't stop her from going all out. She was wearing a mullet and some fake braces she'd bought. It was so funny I couldn't stop laugh-sobbing the entire way to the Forum.

I was a mess. My whole body was shaking. My eyelid was in full revolt. When we got there, it took me ten minutes to gather the courage to even get out of the car.

Walking into the Forum felt off. I didn't come into venues this way anymore. I came in the back, through service entrances, with the band. I hung out while they set up. Watched shows from backstage.

Now I was in the crush of the crowd. I had to go through metal detectors and get my tickets scanned. I was a spectator. A fan. Just one of his millions. No different from anyone else. And I guess that all made sense. After all, I was here to see Jaxon, not Jason.

I wasn't even sure Jason existed anymore.

Kristen tried to get me to eat something, but I couldn't. I let her buy me a bottled water and I waited by the merch tables for her while she ran to get it. I stared at the posters for sale. "I was with him when he took those pictures," I said to Kristen when she came back. "I'd been standing there right off camera at the photo shoot."

But there were other posters now too, pictures I hadn't been there for. He didn't want me there anymore. He'd ejected me from this life.

The betrayal surged back and I almost lost my nerve.

Zane's expensive tickets weren't a hard sell. We found a couple in the tenth row to trade us for our front-row seats. Now we were close enough to see him well, but too far for him to notice me from the stage.

I was nervous and jumpy through the whole opening act.

When Grayscale did their last song and Jessa did her "Make some noise for Jaxon Waters!" I panicked and *did* debate leaving before he came out.

Maybe this was totally self-destructive. Maybe if I saw him, knowing that he'd never cheated on me, it might make things worse. I might have a harder time accepting that we weren't together anymore if I wasn't fortified with my pure rage.

"God. I can't believe I'm doing this."

Kristen dipped her head to look me in the eye. "We can go anytime you want. Okay?"

I nodded. But I wouldn't go. I would see this through. I had to.

We stared up at the two Jumbotrons, one on either side of the stage, with the words "Jaxon Waters" rotating over an image of a loon.

I knew what was going on backstage. I could imagine every activity that was bringing him closer to coming out. He was walking out of the dressing room. Zane was handing him a water bottle. A production manager was jogging in front of him, stepping over thick black electrical cords, speaking into a headset so the rest of the band would know it was time to gather by the curtain. Jason would put in his in-ear monitor and hand his water back to Zane. He'd open and close his fists to warm them up the way he always did before he went on. He wouldn't be nervous. He'd be loose and light, and getting brighter the closer he got to going on, like he drew his energy from the pulse of the crowd.

And then there he was.

He burst onto the stage through fog and fireworks in a white T-shirt with a navy velvet jacket over it. His hair was longer than I remembered on top, but it looked good. I could almost see the blue of his eyes.

I clutched Kristen's arm with my left hand. His voice was beautiful and strong and my heart gave out.

I loved him.

Even now, after everything he'd put me through, I loved him. Even if he *was* Jaxon.

And Zane was right. He was fucked up.

He came out with the same energy as always. But I knew him. Performing was the thing he loved most in life. No matter how tired he got, his eyes always lit up when he hit the stage. He could always summon it for his fans. But he was dark somehow. Faded.

A copy of a copy.

Everyone was screaming around me, pulsing with the music. His voice boomed through my whole body until I was saturated. He came in through my eyes, my ears, the vibration in the floor. I could taste the memory of his sweat on my tongue, smell the warm masculine scent of him after a show when he'd peel off his shirt and slide over me, his heart still racing from the adrenaline of the crowd.

How could I go home after this?

How could I get this hour and a half of him and then leave with everyone else who'd come to see him? And then the world would just swallow him up once more and he'd disappear.

I'd probably never see him again. Not in person. I did what I'd come to do, but I could already feel my heart paying the price for this visit. It was as unhealthy as spending all my time in a cemetery. It was a cold, one-sided devotion and I couldn't put myself through it again.

Kristen put a hand over the one clutching her arm. It felt like it had when I'd sat in that hospital room with her by Brandon's bedside. I could see the man I loved. He was there, but he was gone, beyond my reach.

The feeling was crushing. A helplessness no one should ever have to know.

And now I'd known it twice.

Kristen pulled tissues from her purse and put them into my hands. "Thank you." I sniffed, pressing the tissue under my eye. "God, I would have never left him," I said, shouting over the music. "No matter what. I would have followed him around the world like a groupie for the rest of my life."

Kristen paused a minute and then leaned into my ear so I could hear her. "Did you ever think maybe he wanted more for you than that?"

"I *know* he wanted more for me than that," I said, too quietly for her to hear.

The song ended and I knew Jason would do what he always did after the first one. He'd thank the crowd and welcome them to the show. Say something personal about the city.

How inconsequential was this place to him now? I wondered if he even knew where he was, or if he'd had to look at his hand before he hit the stage.

He put his lips to the mic. "Thank you, thank you. It's great to be back in LA."

Everyone cheered and I waited for him to say something about the beach or Disneyland or traffic on the 405.

But then something weird happened. He just stopped.

It started slow. The slight downturn at the corner of his lips, the loss of humor around his eyes. And then he changed suddenly and all at once, like a mask had come loose and fallen off and underneath it he was deeply sad.

He paused. He paused so long the crowd started to murmur.

"Actually, no," he said, his tone suddenly serious. "Being back in LA has been a little rough for me. I'm sorry. It's just...something happened today, and it's been hard." He glanced down at the stage and shook his head. His eyes came back up and looked over his fans. "You guys don't know this, but I met the love of my life in Los Angeles."

I sucked in a shock of air and my heart stopped dead in my chest.

The crowd whistled and hooted, but Jason put a hand up. "No, no. It's not who you probably think it is. The tabloids get it wrong most of the time. Lola Simone and I are just colleagues and good friends. No, this woman…" He seemed to struggle with it. "She was incredible. She found my dog, actually. That's how I met her. Wouldn't give him back. Said I had to prove I loved him first." He laughed a little and the crowd laughed too. ·

He went on. "We fell in love really fast. I know people say love at first sight—but it really was. Hell, I loved her before I even laid eyes on her. She came on tour with me. She's this amazing artist, and she couldn't paint on the road." He clutched the microphone stand with both hands. "Being on tour isn't easy. It's exhausting. And she was willing to do it because she loved me, even though it meant making a lot of sacrifices. But there were some bad things going on that I couldn't tell her about. Really scary stuff. And it got to a point where I realized that being with me wasn't good for her. I couldn't give her a life or protect her. So I let her believe something terrible about me so I could end it with her."

Kristen squeezed my arm. "Are you hearing this? What is he talking about?"

I shook my head, tears starting to well in my eyes. "I don't know," I breathed.

He chuckled a little. "The funny thing is, I got what I wanted. I wanted her to get over me. And you know what? She did." He dragged a hand down his mouth. "Yeah. She's on a date tonight. I saw her. Went down to her art gallery and saw her with some guy when I was about to come out. It fucking killed me," he whispered. "I thought breaking up with her was hard. But seeing that…"

My mouth went dry. I couldn't even breathe. "Kristen, he was there." I was afraid to take my eyes off him to look at her. "He was there," I whispered. "He came."

This time he didn't recover as quickly. He went quiet for a long moment and the audience simmered to a hush. Cell phones hovered over heads, recording video. You could have heard a pin drop in the arena. They were *hanging* on his words.

Jason squeezed his eyes shut and when he opened them, his tone was sad. "You think you know what love looks like. You think the fairy tales and the romantic movies prepare you. And then you finally, really truly find it and you realize you never knew a thing about it until her." He shook his head. "She was every love song I've never been good enough to write." His voice cracked on the last word.

"Sloan," Kristen whispered. "Everybody's crying…" She tapped me. "Look."

I tore my eyes from the stage to look around. The woman next to me had her hand over her mouth and tears running down her face. Everyone did.

Jason wiped at his eyes with his thumb and picked up his guitar. "I'll never get her back. It's too late for that. But this song is for Sloan anyway. It's called 'Proof.'"

My fragile heart shattered. I completely lost it. I leaned forward, hands over my mouth, and sobbed.

He sang.

It was poetry about a woman who was every season. She was the muffled moment when snow started to fall. A soft, beguiling spring fog over a glass lake. The full moon, white and unmarred in an inky-black summer sky. An autumn so vibrant you can die feeling peace because your eyes have seen it.

It was the most beautiful thing he'd ever written. It was the most beautiful thing I'd ever *heard*.

And it was *mine*.

I wasn't surrounded by thousands of captivated Jaxon fans. Kristen wasn't sitting next to me. Jaxon wasn't even there. This was *Jason* singing. And every word was a declaration of unrivaled love, an apology, and a plea for forgiveness—to no one. Because he didn't even know I was here. He thought it was nothing but a cry into the void to a woman who'd moved on.

He was so, *so* wrong.

When it ended, the crowd went insane. I'd never heard them like that. Not even after his most popular songs.

His sad eyes scanned his screaming fans like none of it mattered to him. Like he didn't care one way or another whether they liked it because he was too broken to feel anything but the emptiness that I'd been feeling for the last three months.

And then he stopped cold.

He put a hand up to block the lights and squinted out over the crowd.

"Oh. My. *God*," Kristen breathed next to me.

He just stood there, staring.

At *me*.

It wasn't possible.

I was one face in the thousands on the floor. I was buried in the crowd. I had a hat on and glasses and the lights were in his eyes. But he was looking right at me. He was looking at me so intensely people started turning around to look at me too.

I couldn't move. I was frozen to my seat.

And then Jason dropped his guitar and jumped off the stage.

A laughing sob burst from my lips. Kristen grabbed at my sweater, yanked my beanie and glasses off. "Go! *Go!*" She spun me and shoved me toward the aisle.

"Let me through!" I started to push my way out of the row. "Please!"

I managed to get to the aisle, but once I did, my progress stopped. I wasn't the only one trying to get out.

Bodies surged toward the front. Fans folded in around Jason on all sides, and I lost sight of him. I only knew where he was because they kept the Jumbotrons trained on him as he tried to make his way through the throng.

It was complete mayhem.

He didn't have any security with him like he usually did. He'd stage dived before they knew what was happening. There was nobody to keep the swarming fans back.

"Jason!" The chaos drowned out my voice. Everyone was pushing in the same direction I was, trying to get closer to the same man. I wasn't moving.

I looked around frantically. I had to get higher. I climbed a seat and stood on top of it, people bumping into my back and legs. He was still fifteen feet away, but he saw me. "Sloan!"

As soon as he pointed me out, the camera for the Jumbotron panned back and then zoomed in on me. I could see myself, twenty feet tall in my red dress and tattoos, tears running down my face.

That's when people seemed to understand what was happening. The crowd began to make a path to let him through and gentle hands guided me down to the floor and toward him. It felt like the ebb of the ocean. A riptide sucking me out to sea. They parted for me and then folded in after me, pushing me forward. And then suddenly the only person in front of me was him.

We both paused for a breathless second before we dove for each other. I jumped, wrapping my legs around his waist, and he caught me.

The floor shook with the cheers. Camera flashes came off of a thousand cell phones and someone backstage released the confetti meant for the finale of the show and it burst over the crowd and fluttered around us.

He buried his face in my neck and I could feel the racking of his gasps as he held me to his chest. Hands touched us, people swayed against our bodies with the surge of the crowd and it didn't even matter because we were alone. It was just us.

Nothing was left but us.

His lips went to my ear. "I think we just figured out how to make them want pictures of us together."

I didn't know what he meant, but I didn't care.

"How did you see me?" I whispered.

He came up to look at me. He had tears in his beautiful, blue eyes. "I told you, Sloan. I'd notice you in a crowd of a million."

And then, in front of fifteen thousand cheering Jaxon Waters fans, *Jason* kissed me.

EPILOGUE

SLOAN

♪ THE HUNTSMAN'S WIFE | JAXON WATERS

Three years later

Tucker watched with a wagging tail as our long-suffering stagehands lugged my giant recliner backstage and set it up in my usual spot where I could watch my husband play.

When he first bought me this monstrosity, I'd refused to use it. It was beyond ridiculous. It had the massage features and a remote and everything. It weighed like half a ton and needed an extension cord to power it up.

For the first few weeks he'd had to plop me in it before every show and command me to stay, threatening to punish me for moving by dragging me onstage to introduce me to the crowd. *Again.*

The album he'd dedicated to me, *Sloan In-Between*, had gone platinum. Actually, all of his last three albums had gone platinum. Not to mention I was a media darling and had been ever since Jason's dramatic stage plunge at the Forum three years ago. The video of Jason's confession and him kissing me in the crowd had gone viral and suddenly everyone had wanted to know who I was. I had almost as many Instagram followers as he did. People loved my photos of life on tour, so my onstage cameos were always a crowd pleaser, even though I was completely mortified every single time he did it. I didn't know how he could stand out there in front of all those people and not be nervous.

I felt different about my chair these days, though. Now that my ankles were starting to swell, I actually appreciated being able to put my feet up while I watched my husband perform.

We'd been on the road for eight months this time. The Hollywood Bowl was our last stop before we went home—for good.

This show was the last one with this label. Jason was signing with a smaller independent one after this. The money wasn't quite as good, and they didn't offer as many frills, but the life balance we'd have would make it worth it, and they gave Jason complete control over his work and his schedule.

Jason was doing his sound check, so I sat down, hoisting my pregnant belly. Tucker plopped by my chair. Zane pulled up next to me as I extended the leg rest and handed me a warm Starbucks cup. She turned a metal folding chair backward and straddled it, crossing her arms over the backrest. "Ernie told me to tell you he's on his way and he has the cupcakes."

"He got lemon drops, right?" I asked. I was addicted to Nadia Cakes, and my pregnancy cravings were serious.

"Placed the order myself. Couldn't let Ernie fuck that up. I didn't want you pissed at me."

"Like either of us could ever get pissed at *you*." I smiled.

She smirked and we sat and watched Jason adjust his microphone stand. He sang a few verses to test his equipment and he tipped his head toward me, his lips to the mic, and winked. I blew him a kiss and his grin got so big I could hear it in his voice.

Lola—Nikki—joined him for the big cities, by our invitation. She'd be here tonight. She was actually pretty cool. She was mostly producing these days and doing really well. She only performed with Jason, and the two of them collaborated on writing most of his songs—except for the ones he wrote about me. Those just poured out of him.

He set his guitar down on its stand and walked over to us, pulling out his in-ear monitor. He put his hands on the arms of my chair and leaned down to kiss me. "Are you comfortable, sweetheart?"

"Yeeeess." I smiled against his lips.

He put a hand to my belly and I moved it to the left, where the baby was kicking, and his eyes gleamed.

"She likes the music," I said.

He held his hand to my wiggling stomach and grinned. "Are you hungry?"

"Always."

"Almost done." He leaned down and kissed my stomach. "Twenty more minutes," he said to my baby bump. He reached down and ruffled Tucker's head, then jogged back out to his sound check.

Zane chuckled after him. "You know, it wouldn't kill you guys to be slightly less adorable."

I smiled at her. "Probably not. But why risk it?"

We survived our last show of the tour and had a late dinner with my parents. Then we headed home—well, *our* version of home. A mini mansion we rented in Woodland Hills. It was close enough to Kristen and Josh for when we were in town between tours. It was gated and safe and we had a place to keep our stuff while we were on the road.

Both of us preferred Ely to LA. Jason's fame was harder

on us in California. We couldn't really go out without getting approached.

Ely was small, and nobody there cared who he was. Everyone there had grown up with him. There was no paparazzi, and I'd gotten really close to Patricia over the past three years. With the baby coming, it would have been nice to live near her. But Kristen and Josh took priority for me, and whatever took priority for me took priority for Jason. So Woodland Hills it was.

Jason smiled at me from the limo seat across from me. "I have a little surprise for you." He grinned.

I narrowed my eyes at him. "What surprise? I didn't like the last one."

He chuckled. "What? When I told you I want to get pregnant again right away?" He crossed over to sit next to me and leaned in to kiss me, putting a hand on my belly. "I just love you like this," he breathed against my lips.

I jerked my head back. "And did you love all the barfing?"

"Well, no. But look how sexy you are right now…" He put his face into my neck and trailed his mouth across my skin.

"There is nothing sexy about this, Jason. I'm swollen and starving. I have to pee constantly."

He laughed into my neck. "I think I can convince you."

Yes, he was very good at convincing me to do things. Like getting me to agree to marry him just forty-eight hours after we got back together. I'd been wearing a ring since two days after the Forum.

"What if I had said no?" I'd asked.

"Then I was going to go into plan B."

"Which was what? Subterfuge? Tell me I'm just your girlfriend but really we'd be engaged the whole time?"

He'd laughed. "No. Unwavering, unrelenting persistence."

I hadn't said no, of course. But I'd made him wait a year to marry me. I didn't want something rushed. I wanted a real wedding—*and* I'd kept my last name. I wanted my own identity.

We'd gotten married at the Glensheen mansion in Duluth, on the shore of Lake Superior—home of the wreck of the *Edmund Fitzgerald*. Tucker had worn a tuxedo Kristen had made for him, and he sat at our feet as we'd said our vows. Oliver had been our ring bearer. Ernie, David, Zane, and Josh had stood next to Jason, and Kristen had stood next to me—the way it was always going to be.

"So what's your surprise?" I asked, closing my eyes as he kissed my neck.

"It's at home."

We stopped at Forest Lawn like we always did when we came to town so I could visit Brandon. Jason usually stayed behind in the car to give me some privacy, except for one time, right before we were married. He'd asked to have some alone time at Brandon's grave.

He'd spent a half an hour there while I watched from the car. He didn't tell me exactly what he'd said. Only that he was thanking him, and letting him know he was going to take good care of me.

It meant a lot to me that he'd told him that.

Jason and I both gave blood on Brandon's birthday, a tradition we vowed to keep for the rest of our lives.

When we pulled up to the curb in front of the house, Kristen and Josh were out front with their kids and Stuntman Mike. "My surprise?" I beamed at Jason. We weren't supposed to see them until tomorrow.

He winked.

I got out and Kristen ran to me. I hadn't seen her in five months.

"Look at you and your sex injury!" she said, putting her hands on my belly. "Does Jason know what this baby is about to do to his favorite playground?"

"Yes. And can you believe he wants to do it again right after this one comes out?"

She arched an eyebrow. "That's eighteen months without raw cookie dough and real coffee. Has he met you?"

We both laughed.

Jason and Josh hugged, slapping each other on the back. They saw each other as much as I saw Kristen. The guys flew out to Minnesota for the deer and duck openers and we'd all spent a week in Ely right before the tour so he and Jason could go ice fishing. They were practically best friends. Kristen said they were having a bromance.

I hugged Kimmy and Sarah, Kristen and Josh's adopted daughters. They were nine and eleven now.

Two years ago Josh had gone on a fatal heart attack call at work. The man who'd died was the grandfather and sole guardian of his two granddaughters. Kristen and Josh stepped in as emergency foster parents. The girls' adoptions had been finalized just a few months ago. They were amazing kids.

"How have you guys been?" I asked, scooping Oliver up into a hug.

"Oh, you know, just doing the married thing, eating tacos with that one special person for the rest of our lives. How was the tour?" Kristen asked.

"Piece of cake. Glad it's over, though." I straightened from my hugs with Oliver and put my hands on my lower back as I walked to the gate.

"Are you gonna autograph my cookbook for me?" Kristen asked.

I laughed. "Sure."

I'd published a cookbook. *Slow Cooker Recipes by The Huntsman's Wife.* I'd developed most of them in the bus, on tour. All the recipes had conversions for wild game. And I painted on tour too. I had a two-year waiting list for my artwork.

I'd made the road my home. Being on tour was as easy to me now as breathing.

I started to punch in the code to the gate, but it wasn't working. I wrinkled my forehead. "This thing's broken."

"You're at the wrong house," Jason said from behind me.

I looked back through the gate. No. This was the house. The same one we'd rented for the last three years.

I turned around, confused. Kristen was beaming at me. I looked over her shoulder at Jason and Josh, watching me from the curb. They stood next to each other and grinned like conspirators.

"What's going on?" I asked, looking back and forth between them.

Kristen looked giddy. "You moved."

"What?"

She smiled. "So did we."

"You moved? When? Where?"

The three of them looked at each other like they were trying to decide who should answer me. Jason volunteered. He stepped up and took my cheeks in his hands and kissed me. "To Ely."

I gasped and whirled on Kristen. "*What?*"

Jason grinned. "We bought houses next to each other. A hundred acres combined. Private. Safe. A room with a lake view for you to paint and a recording studio for me."

"We needed the bigger place," Josh said, putting an arm around his smiling wife.

Kristen looked at her husband and he grinned at her. "Josh quit the fire department. He got a job with the Forest Service in Minnesota. And…" She paused. "Our surrogate's pregnant."

"What?" I breathed.

"She's due in three months," she said, beaming.

I put my hands over my mouth. "We get to have babies together?"

She nodded, her eyes tearing up. "I'll be able to snowshoe to your house in a blizzard to borrow a cup of frozen milk."

I laughed, taking turns hugging them all through tears. I ended with my husband and put my face into his chest. He put his lips to my ear, his arms wrapped around my back. "Trying to keep all my promises."

All I could do was nod. The baby kicked between us, and I felt so much happiness my heart threatened to burst.

When I pulled away, he kissed me, his eyes a little misty. "Come on, we have a plane waiting. It's time to go home."

A NOTE FROM THE AUTHOR

*The identifying details of the following have been changed out of respect for privacy.

I have a very close childhood friend who was widowed in her twenties when her young husband passed away suddenly.

Before the tragedy, my friend was fiercely driven and independent. She was working in a career she adored and was thriving. Two years after her husband's death, she was still withdrawn and isolated. She'd stopped doing things she loved. She couldn't hold down a job. She had anxiety and panic attacks. She'd disappear for weeks at a time in her isolation, and I couldn't get her on the phone or get her to open the door. She didn't have any close friends anymore, and her relationships with her family were strained. She refused to go to counseling.

It seemed like so much of the state of her life had some colossal ripple effect. The lack of self-care, the refusal to socialize or seek therapy, the junk food she ate because she couldn't bring herself to cook for one, the unhealthy habits she picked up to cope with the stress and anxiety of her loss.

I now know that my friend was most likely suffering from a condition called complicated grief, also known as persistent complex bereavement disorder. It's most common when the death is unexpected or particularly traumatic and the person lost is very close to you.

When I started writing *The Happy Ever After Playlist*, I never in my wildest dreams thought I'd get it published. Writing was just a hobby, and this book was more for *me* than anything else—a cathartic exercise, my own way of working through the confusing, shattered aftermath I was witnessing, a way to make my friend better, even if it was just fiction—because nothing I did in real life seemed to help her. I felt like a helpless bystander, and I wanted so much for something or someone to reach her beyond the wall of sadness she'd put up around herself. So I made up a fictional universe and a fictional widow who lived behind a wall of grief, and I sent in Tucker to retrieve her. But the rest had to be *her*.

It took active participation on my friend's part and people around her who never gave up trying to make her whole again, but just like in the book, eventually she decided to pursue healing and happiness. She's finally found joy in life again. I wish it would have happened sooner—but I'm grateful it happened at all. Because for a *very* long time, I was afraid it wouldn't.

According to Bridges to Recovery, it is estimated that between 10 to 20 percent of those who have lost a loved one will experience an extended period of complicated bereavement. Complicated grief can affect you physically, mentally, and socially. Without treatment, complications include depression, suicidal thoughts, PTSD, increased risk of heart disease, cancer, or high blood pressure, and substance or alcohol abuse.

Getting counseling soon after a loss may help prevent

complicated grief. Hospice will have resources available. Talking with others and seeking support from friends and family and support groups may also help. Medications are available to assist with depression and sleep disorders associated with the condition.

If you or anyone you know is suffering from unresolved grief, please seek help—it *can* get better. My friend wants me to tell you that.

♫ *THE HAPPY EVER AFTER* PLAYLIST

1. ♪ In the Mourning | Paramore
2. ♪ affection | BETWEEN FRIENDS
3. ♪ Middle of Nowhere | Hot Hot Heat
4. ♪ ocean eyes | Billie Eilish
5. ♪ Give Me a Try | The Wombats
6. ♪ Future | Paramore
7. ♪ Talk Too Much | COIN
8. ♪ This Charming Man | The Smiths
9. ♪ A Beautiful Mess | Jason Mraz
10. ♪ Soul Meets Body | Death Cab for Cutie
11. ♪ Name | Goo Goo Dolls
12. ♪ Electric Love | Børns
13. ♪ Make You Mine | PUBLIC
14. ♪ Maybe You're the Reason | The Japanese House
15. ♪ I Want It All | COIN
16. ♪ Girlfriend | Phoenix
17. ♪ I Feel It | Avid Dancer
18. ♪ The Wreck of the *Edmund Fitzgerald* | Jaxon Waters

19. ♪ Misery Business | Paramore
20. ♪ Superposition | Young the Giant
21. ♪ White Winter Hymnal | Fleet Foxes
22. ♪ Everywhere | Roosevelt
23. ♪ Into Dust | Mazzy Star
24. ♪ burn slowly/i love you | The Brazen Youth
25. ♪ 26 | Paramore
26. ♪ Broken | Lund
27. ♪ Blood in the Cut | K.Flay
28. ♪ A Moment of Silence | The Neighbourhood
29. ♪ Mess Is Mine | Vance Joy
30. ♪ Holocene | Bon Iver
31. ♪ Diamonds | Ben Howard
32. ♪ Big Jet Plane | Angus & Julia Stone
33. ♪ Do I Wanna Know? | Arctic Monkeys
34. ♪ Yes I'm Changing | Tame Impala
35. ♪ Little Black Submarines | The Black Keys
36. ♪ i don't know what to say | Bring Me the Horizon
37. ♪ Keep Your Head Up | Ben Howard
38. ♪ Bottom of the Deep Blue Sea | Missio
39. ♪ Ful Stop | Radiohead
40. ♪ About Today | The National
41. ♪ It's Not Living (If It's Not With You) | The 1975
42. ♪ fresh bruises | Bring Me the Horizon
43. ♪ Somebody Else | The 1975
44. ♪ If I Get High | Nothing But Thieves
45. ♪ Proof | Jaxon Waters
46. ♪ The Huntsman's Wife | Jaxon Waters

ACKNOWLEDGMENTS

The biggest of all thank-yous to my agent, Stacey, for reading the query for this book and knowing it was something special the second she laid eyes on it. It was the start of a whole new chapter of my life! And thank you to Dawn Frederick of Red Sofa Literary for letting me be a part of your author posse.

Thank you to my incredible editor, Leah, for not only knowing what this book needed, but knowing how to explain it to me in a way I understood so I could make it the fabulous read it is today.

Estelle, you're a fucking marketing genius.

All the love to the team at Forever who beta read this, championed it, worked on the cover, figured out the title, and helped it reach readers: Beth, Amy, Lexi, Elizabeth (I adore this cover!), Mari, Mary, Ali, Rachel, Suzanne, and all the many others.

A huge thank-you to my crit buddies on Critique Circle and beyond: Joey Ringer, Hijo, Tia Greene, Shauna Lawless, Debby Wallace, J. C. Nelson, Jill Storm, Liz Smith-Gehris, G. W. Pickle, Dawn Cooper, Andrea Day, Lisa Stremmel, Lisa Sushko, Michele Alborg, Amanda Wulff, Summer Heacock, Stacey Sargent, George, Jhawk, Abby Luther, Patt Pandolfi, Bessy Chavez, Mandy Geisler, Teressa Sadowski, Leigh Kramer, Stephanie Trimbol, and Kristyn May.

Waves at Lindsay.

Thank you, Patty Gibbs, for giving me some publicist behind-the-scenes info, and Jason from Ely Outfitting Company for letting me use the name of your outfitter (yes, it's a real place! Go see it and let them show you the most pristine wilderness in the world!).

An extra big thank-you to Kim T. Kao (Book Bruin) and author Leigh Kramer for beta reading this in the eleventh hour.

A special mention to Dawn Cooper for being my number one! This book has changed a lot since the first draft and you were there for all of it, in every way possible. Not only would this book not be the same without you, but I would not be the same author without you. Those plot walks are everything.

To my oldest daughter, Naomi Esella, the musician, who got a big mention in the last book's acknowledgments and who said I'd probably forget to thank her for all the music stuff she helped me with in this one—thank you! (I showed you *again*, you salty bitch.)

And lastly, thank you to my husband. He's my number one fan and none of this would be possible without his patience, support, and love.

Many thanks to all these wonderful supporters!

Kristina Aadland	Shirley Allery
Andrea Aberle	Kristol Allshouse
Dara Abraham	Jenny Andersen
Jes Adams	Ashlee Anderson
Kerri Allard	Marcie Anderson
Jennifer Alleman	Laura Andert
Kimber Allen	Diane Andrajack
Natalie Allen	Megan Andrews
Tami Allen	Margaret Angstadt

Lisa Arnold
Iqra Arshad
Lisa Ashburn
Elena Austin
Katie Baack
Cheyenne Baca
Cathy Bailey
Janean Baird
Melisa Bajrami
Elizabeth Baker
Marci Baker
Marie Bakke
Mandy Baldwin
Jenny Ballman
Gina Barboni
Michelle Barbra
Kristen Barker
Kimberly Barkoff
Dayna Barta
Talia Basma
Kelly Bates
Jennifer Battan
Elizabeth Baumann
Ashley Baylor
Angelina Beaudry
Heather Beedy
Kristine Bemboom
Jessica Bennett
Michelle Bennett
Christine Benson
Maria Berry
Linda Berscheit
Stefany Besse
Carol Bezosky
Maggi Billingsley
Lori Bishop

Marion Bishop
Betsy Bissen
Tim Blaede
Jamie Blair
Lisa Blanchar
Corrie Block
Rachel Blust
Helen Boettner
Abby Bohrer
Carrie Bollig
JoLynn Bonk
Amy Bonner
Tyler Bonneville
Shana Borgen
Sandy Borrero
Breanna Bouley
Jen Boumis
Hannah & Jenn Bowers
Kathryn Boyer
Roclyn Bradshaw
Marjorie Branum
Ashley Brassard
Kimberlee Brehm
Jessika Brekken
Crystal Bremer
Taryn Breuer
Elizabeth Brimeyer
Kathryn Brimeyer
Suzanne Brown
Larissa Brune
Paige Brunn
Sharon Bruns
Elissa Bryden
Jennifer Buechele
Melissa Bump
Kat Bunn

Therese Burrell
Melissa Bussell
Stacey Busta
Kelly Butler
Cheri Buzick
Kristin Cafarelli
Danielle Calderoni
Bree Campbell
Acacia Caraballo
Lindsey Cardinal
Elizabeth Carter
Lenore Case
Alexa Cataline
Shelly Caveney
Andrew Oakes
  Champagne
Christina F. Chavez
Kris Christenson
Alyssa Cihak
Veronica Clampitt
Heidi Clayman
Jammie Clement
Olivia Clements
Heather Cmiel
Leanne Colton
Michelle Comstock
Katie Connelly
Katie Connors
Michelle Conrad
Samantha Coogan
Heather Cook
Patty Cooper
Peggy Coover
Jessica Corcoran-Lacy
Kristen Corser
Robyn Corson

Sylvia Costa
Liz Cote
Deana Crabb
Laura Crane
Megan Crawford
Mallory Credeur
Cholie Crom
Kristin Curran
Anna Dale
Lynn Dale
Lindsay D'Angelo
Brandi DaVeiga
Anna Davenport
Mandi Daws
Laura DeBouche
Denise Delamore
Katie Delano
Amber Delliger
Pamela Demaree
Jayme DeSotel
Laura Diallo
Katrina Diaz
Kendall Diebold
Brandy Dillon
Kimberly Dobo
Wendy Dodson
Melinda Doncses
Alyssa Doss
Tricia Downey
Allison Doyle
Rose Drake
Kim Droegemueller
Heather Dryer
Nicole Duff
Stacey Duitsman
Meggan Duncan

Lindsay Dupic
Deidre Easter
Victoria Edgett
Precious Edmonds
Joanne Ehrmantraut
Ashley Eisenberg
Tiffanie Elliott-Stelter
Alison Ellis
Casey Ellsworth
Melissa Elsen
Korissa Emerson
Brittany Emmert
Lindsey Engrav
Lisa Eskelson
Megan Eskew
Jen Eslinger
Jennevieve Evers
Rebecca Falk
Ashley Faria
Christina Ferdous
Veronica Ferguson
Krystina Ferrari
Robert Finch
Dianthe Fleming
Emily Foltz
Re Forest
Angie Forte
Kimberly Foth
Larice Fournier
Stacy Fox
Jacqueline Francis
Becky Freer
Kayla Freitas
Jenni Friedman
Jenie Fritz
Ashley Fultz

Sheila Gagnon
Emma Galligan
Rena Galvez
Jesse Garber
Adilene Garcia
Melissa Garcia
Melissa Garrity
Stephanie Garuti
Emily Gaspers
April Gassler
Pamela Gedalia
Amanda Gilbert
Heidi Gilbert
Peggy Gipe
Karla Glass
Katrina Gliniany
Sarah Gocken
Jennifer Godsey
Kristin Graham
Toni Graham
Kathryn Greenwell
Nikki Greer
Deborah Gregory
Trish Grigorian
Joseph Griner
Ashley Grittner
Kaylene Grui
Catherine Guilbeault
Gina Haars
Jeannie Hackett
Tina Hackley
Christina Hager
Gwen Hagerman
Rachelle Hall
Susie Hall
Judi Halpern

Casey Hambleton
Lyndse Hamilton
Joan Hammond
Alyssa Handevidt
Jenny Hanen
Kristin Hannon
Kristyna Hanson
Melody Hanssen
Erin Hardy
Debra K Harper-Grodin
Susan Hart
Shannon Harte
Kelsey Haukos
Sarah Hawes
Angela Helland
Travis Hellermann
Angie Hendrickx
David Henkhaus
Melinda Hennies
Carmen Henning
Sawyer Hennlich
Brielle Herbst
Ivonne Hernandez
Bridget Heroff
Ashley Herro
Stephanie Heseltine
Ashley Hester
Katie Hileman
Lisa Hilgendorf
Bekki Hince
Keri Hinrichs
Timika Hite
Katrina Hodny
Ann Hoff
Alyssa Hoffman
Amber Hoffman

Shanna Hofland
Tiffany Hokanson
Misty Marie Holder
Elizabeth Hollingshead
Sarah Holmes
Erin Holt
Liz Kruger Hommerding
Jessika Hoover
Jennifer Hopkins
Jennifer Hoshowski
Cassie Hove
Livia Huang
Karen Hudak
Tonia Hufnagel
Elizabeth Huggins
Melissa Huijbers
Danielle Inagaki
Kayla Innis
Rebecca Irizarry
Nicole Jackson
Raelyn Jackson
Gabrielle Jendro
Michelle Jenkins
Brigette Jennings
Angie Jensen
Gina Jenson
Jeanette Jett
Jefre Johannson
Adrienne Johnson
Amy Johnson
Holly Johnson
Kim Johnson
Leah Johnson
Nicole Johnson
Rachel Johnson
Stacey Johnson

Alina Johnston
Carly Johnston
Meghan Jones
Elise Jordan
Mary Ellen Joslyn
Amy Juelich
Amanda Jules
Kim Kao
Cheryl Karlson
Kate Kehrel
Alison Keil
Kelsey Keil
Noel Kepler-Gageby
Vanessa Kern
Judith Kesner
Bex Kettner
Judy Keyes
Tej Khera
Soleil Kibodeaux-Posey
Andrea King
Shannon King
Donna Kiolbassa
Kristin Kirk
Leslie Kissinger
Sarah Klatke
Dani Kline
Jennifer Klumpyan
Rebekah Knebel
Shylah Kobal
Nicki Kobaly
Clare Koch
Amanda Korent
Julie Kornmann
Kelly Kornmann
Dawn Kosobud Johnson
Amanda Koval

Amy Krajec
Holly Kramer
Emily Kremer
Molley Kroska-Stock
Traci Kruse
Jessica Kudulis
Anne Kuffel
Stephanie Kurz
Kelly Laferriere
Patty Langasek
Jessica Langer
Jennifer Langlois
Amy Larson
Elizabeth A. Larson
Jaimie Larson
Beth Lee
Bethany Lee
Kari Lee
Meghan Lee
Tamara Lee
Amanda LeMarier
Brooke Lemcke
Dana Lenertz
Patty Lester
Carmela Chavez
    Liberman
Teresa Limtiaco
Samantha Lindner
Ginia Lindsey
Caitlin Litke
Monique Little
Katie Lloyd
Felicia Loeffler
Ariana Lopez
Ara Lotzer
Lindsay Loyd

Ashley Lubrant
Krissy Luce
Kelsey Lucero
Shannon Ludwig
Andi Luedeman
Jessica Lulic
Brandy Lulling
Brian Lyon-Garnett
Alyssa Lyons
Katie Maas
Niki Mackedanz
Jennifer Maddigan
Leigh Ann Mahaffie
Kelley Majdik
Cynthia Maldonado
Karleen Malmgren
Tarah Malmgren
Marcella Malone
Faith Marie
Wendy Marik
Jill-Ann Mark
Chelsea Markfort
Heidi Markland
Rosa Marrero
Michelle Martin
Jennie Martinez
Lucinda Martinez-Carter
Tracy Mastel
Emily Mayer
Debra McCormick
Karen McCullah
Summer McGee
Callie McGinn
Margaret McLean
Tamara McNelis
Laurie Mease

Edlyn Medina
Jennifer Meiner
Chynna Mesich
Alyce Mikkonen
Andrea Miller
Anna Miller
Meridith Miller
Deborah Mills
Danielle Minor
Kellisa Mirabel
Ashley Mitchell
Trista Moffitt
Denise "Wingman"
    Molde
Wendy Molina
Katie Monaghan
Kate Moon
Julie Morales
Paige Moreland
Jami Morgan
Laurel Morgan
Katie Morris
Robin Morris
Michelle Morrisette
Tami Morton
Ginny Mosier
Kat Mudd
Kristy Muehlbauer
Jenni Mueller
Alice Munoz
Daniel F. Torres Muñoz
Rebecca Munro
Bethanne Murphy
Cassandra Murphy
Jennifer Murphy
Lacey Murphy

Michele Myran
Cheryl Myrum
Elizabeth Narolis
Kelly Nash
Antonia Nelson
Joan Nelson
Samantha Nelson
Shanna Nemitz
Christine Nichols
Kayla Niekrasz
Carrie Niezgocki
Jeanne Nihart
Courtney Nino
Dannah Niverson
Heather Noeker
Karen Noland
Taylor Noland
Tanya Nordin
Amy Norman
Jenifer Norville
Leigh Anne Novak
Amanda Nyenhuis
Kirstyn Oaks
Ashlyn Ocander
Sarah O'Connor
Liz O'Donnell
Jen O'Hair
Karen O'Leary
Jeni Oliver
Angela Baxter Olson
Corrinne Olson
Charlene O'Reilly
Joanne Ouellet
Kristyn Packard
Andrea Paguirigan
Tatjana Pantic

Ashley Parks
Crystal Paul
Jessica Pauly
Fiona Payne
Marisa Peck
Wendy Pederson
Colleen Peterson
Jasie Peterson
Sara Peterson
Tyra Peterson
Emily Petrich
Emily Pierson
Samantha Piette
Nicole Pilarski
Ashley Polomchak
Danielle Portillo
Marilyn Possin
Michelle Possin
Amy Powell
Heidi Powell
Jennifer Presley
Betsy Preston
Jodi Quinn
Masen Quist
Pam Quist
Keytelynne Radde
Fay Raisanen
Deanne Ramirez
Graciela Ramirez-Rivas
Dawn Rask
Samantha Ratka
Laura Rausch
Dawn Rehbein
Laura Reuter
Katie Ricca
Jenelle Ries

Sophie Riggsby
Amy Rinke
Sherry Ritter-Ramer
Abbe Roberts
Rachel Robertson
Sherri Robinson
Angie Robson
Erika Roche
Samira Rockler
Jenefer Rosado
Sarah Ross
Jessica Roza
Sabrina Ruberto
Jayna Rucks
Tasha Runyon
Mary Jane Rushford
Sarah Rushford
Elizabeth Rust
Dede Samford
Natalie Samples
Nancy Sanchez
Caitlin Sand
Barb Sanford
Jackie Saval
Kristin Schaefer
Ailiah Schafer
Briana Schalow
Tammy Schilling
Alisyn Schmelzer
Jodi Schulman
Sonja Schultz
Alethia Schwagel
Bailey Schwartz
Heidi Jo Schwartz
Tonya Schwartz
Caitlyn Schwarz

Pam Schwenn
Amanda Scott
Wendy Scott
Christine Sedam
Candace Seidl
Joy Sekera
Brianne Sellman
Elizabeth Shelton
Laura Shiff
Lisa Simms
Alaycia Sinclair
Rose Sisco
Jenn Skerbinc
Sarah Slusher
Ashley Small
Alicia Smith
Ashley Smith
Casey Smith
Charlotte Smith
Christy Smith
Devin Smith
Lisa Smith
Nan Smith
Olive Smith
Elisabeth Solchik
Laura Sonnee
Therese Sonnek
Areli Sotelo
Nicole Sousa
Vanessa Spencer
Sarah Spiczka
Laura Sprandel
Kristin Stai
Kate Stamm
Amy Steelman
Brittany Steffen

Patricia Steffen
Maile Steffy
Amy Steger
Melinda Stephan
Martha Stering
Tracy Stevens
Megan Stillwell
Shawna Stolp
Cammie Story-Green
Kari Stout
Stephanie Stowman
Nikki Strain
Mel Strathdee
Kris Strzalkowski
Mary Stuart
Amy Sullivan
Joanna Sullivan
Julia Sumrall
Cindi Tagg
Jessi Tarbet
Jennifer Tate
Casey Taylor
Jennifer Taylor
Danielle Tedrowe
Angie Thaxton
Annette Theel
Julie Thom
Teresa Thomas
Meggan Thompson
Elizabeth Thron
Crystal Thurow
Sara Thurston
Randi Tolonen
Jackie Torfin
Emily Torrance
Sara Towne

Kristin Treadway
Arleen Trevino
Bianca Trevino
Jennifer Turner
Kristi Morgan Turner
Rachel Turner
Kristin Uzzi
Bailey Valentine
Eileen Vazquez
Mercedes Veronica
Heather Vetsch
Danielle Via
Emily Viramontes
Amanda Vogel
Shannon Volker
Megan VonDeLinde
Michele Voss
Taylor Walkky-Byington
Fran Ward
Heather Warfield
Jenna Warner
Deena Warren
Nicole Wasieleski
Leah Weaver
Kimberly Webb
Miranda Webster
Marie Weisbrod
Jennifer Wendell
Andrea Westerfeld
Shawna Weston
Danielle Wettrick
Julie Whitcher
Tanja White
Danielle Whitmore
Ben Whittaker
Jenna Wild

Melinda Wilder
Jona Williams
Rhonda Williams
Cheryl Wilson
Jasmin Wilson
Ruth Wilson
Jennifer Witherspoon
Sara Witkowski
Kimberly Woelber
Julie Wood
Michelle Woodward

Amy Wroblewski
Lynda Wunder
Ashley Yakymi
Laura Yamin
Candice Zablan
Tracy Zachow
Stephanie Zanolini
Sara Zentic
Pamela Zimmer
Mara Zotz